THE TROUBLE WITH SECRETS

THE KILTEEGAN BRIDGE STORY - BOOK 1

JEAN GRAINGER

D1715408

GOLD HARP MEDIA

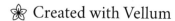 Created with Vellum

CHAPTER 1

KILTEEGAN BRIDGE, CO CORK, 1948

'Don't leave me, Paudie. Don't leave me. I'll die. I swear, I'll walk into the sea and I'll die.'

'Maria, why are you saying this?' Daddy's voice was strange – it was broken and sad. He was normally stronger sounding or something. 'Of course I'll never leave you.'

'I've seen the way Hannah Berger looks at you, Paudie. *Everyone* sees the way she looks at you, right there in the church in front of the whole parish, in front of her own husband. She wants you for herself. She's heart-set on having you.'

Lena kept very still in her special hiding place behind the carved and painted settle beside the fire. Her brother and sister were in bed, but she'd come down to fetch her doll. She was small for seven, and most days she liked it here behind this long wooden seat with the high back, which could fold down into a bed for visitors. You could hear things, and it was warm near the fire, and nobody gave you a job to do. But now she was listening to things she'd rather not hear, even if she didn't understand any of it. Mrs Berger couldn't have Daddy all to herself, even if she did find him useful around the estate. Daddy belonged to Mammy, and to her, and to Emily and Jack.

'This is all in your mind. I love you, Maria…'

'Then stop going to see her!'

'If we could afford for me to stop working up there, you know I would.'

A wild sob and a crash of crockery. Mammy had thrown something down from the dresser. Lena prayed it wasn't her favourite bowl, the one with the bluebells painted on it that Daddy had brought her from the fair in Bandon. He'd brought Emily a green velvet ribbon at the same time, to tie up her long blond hair. Emily was beautiful, tall like Mammy, and though she was only nine, people always thought she was much older. She could be bossy sometimes, but usually she was nice. Jack was small like Lena. He was only five. Daddy had brought him a small wooden donkey, just like Ned, their donkey that pulled the cart on the farm.

'Maria, Maria, stop now, love…' Daddy's voice was firmer. He was trying to calm Mammy, soothing her like he did with Mrs Berger's stallion up at Kilteegan House when it went wild in the spring. 'I can't stop going to the Bergers'. That's half our income, building stone walls, pruning the orchard, caring for the horses. Hannah Berger's not interested in me as a man. She just needs a strong pair of hands around the place. She's had nobody to do the heavy jobs since her father died.'

'Let her own husband do the work, now he's home from the war!'

'Ah, how can he do that, Maria, and him in a wheelchair?'

'There's that man of his, the Frenchman…'

'He's neither use nor ornament, that fella. All he does is wait on his master hand and foot, and he pays no attention whatsoever to anything that needs to be done around the grounds.'

'You're a fool. You can't see it – she's trying to seduce you, Paudie, with her red hair and her green eyes. I'm scared, Paudie, and if she gets you, then her husband will kill you. He's evil, Paudie. There's something terrifying about him.'

Lena felt a pain in her tummy when Mammy spoke like that, like she believed that evil spirits were in people. She was very superstitious. Sometimes it was fun when she told Lena and Emily and Jack about fairies and things like that, but mostly it was scary because it was a sign that things could be bad for days if Daddy didn't manage to coax her out of it. Lena wanted it not to be like that for Daddy, or for her and Jack and Emily, but when Mammy got into her imaginary world, she often stayed away a long time. It didn't happen often. She hadn't had a bad spell since last summer, when she'd screamed there was a demon on the stairs. Lena had wet her knickers, she got such a fright. Daddy had to tell Lena over and over that these things weren't true, that it was only in Mammy's mind, before she could get to sleep that night.

Daddy's voice was even firmer now, more like his normal self, like a big strong tree in a storm. 'Maria, my love, calm yourself. There's nothing to worry about, honestly. I go up there and do some work, and they pay me well. That's all. I love you.'

Mammy fell silent. She was still breathing harshly, but she let Daddy lead her over to the settle. Lena felt the wood creak as he sat beside her, and she heard the whisper of cloth on cloth as he put his arm around Mammy. He told her all about the wild flower meadow that would be growing between their farmhouse and the sea in the spring, in just a few weeks, and how they'd all take a picnic and go to the seaside. Lena could tell from the way his voice was gentle and low and rumbling that she was calming down.

Lena thought her tall, slim mother really was like a selkie, one of those magical tricky mermaids who look like seals in the water but who come to live with human men until they can't stand to be on land any longer and go back to the ocean. There was a picture of a selkie in a book at school, and she had long white hair, same as Mammy's, and it looked a bit like ropes coming down. Mammy tied her hair up most of the time, but sometimes it was loose and reached all the way down her back. She had eyes the same colour as the selkie too, pale as the sea on a summer's day, and her eyelashes and eyebrows were so light that it looked like she didn't have any.

Emily and Jack both looked like Mammy, pale-skinned and fair-haired, but everyone said Lena looked just like her father – dark silky hair, brown eyes and skin that only had to see the sun for a day before it went copper.

In the quiet, the fire crackled in the range and the night wind threw drops of rain against the window. The radio that had been on all this time in the background began playing the popular new song by Al Jolson, 'When You Were Sweet Sixteen'.

Lena's father started singing it softly under his breath. 'I loved you as I've never loved before, since first I saw you on the village green. Come to me, ere my dream of love is o'er. I love you as I loved you, when you were sweet...when you were sweet sixteen...'

And slowly her mother's breathing softened and the pain in Lena's stomach went away. Daddy swept up the bits of broken crockery in silence.

'Dance with me, Maria,' murmured her father.

Mammy still didn't answer, but she let Daddy pull her to her feet. And when Lena peeped out from behind the settle, her parents were swaying together around the kitchen table, her father's big strong farmer's arms around her tall, slim mother, Maria's head on Paudie's shoulder and both of them with their eyes closed. The broken crockery was in a pile in the corner, and it wasn't her favourite bowl – it was just that cracked yellow and green plate she'd never liked anyway.

Lena crept out of the kitchen, up the stairs of the two-story farmhouse and into the bedroom she shared with her sister. Emily was fast asleep, her long blond hair spread out across the pillow. Lena snuggled in beside her with her doll and lay on her back, gazing up at the sloped ceiling, the beams casting sharp black shadows in the moon-light. She was glad the storm had passed this time.

She hoped Mammy wouldn't spoil things be-tween Daddy and the Bergers, because she liked going up to Kilteegan House with him. He let her bring up a basket of their farm eggs, and Mrs Berger always gave her an extra penny to keep for herself. Sometimes Daddy kept Lena busy, weeding the vegetable garden or picking up the branches he pruned from the trees in the orchard. But other times she played with Malachy, the little boy who was there when he wasn't away at boarding school. He had dark-red hair like his mother, and the same grass-green eyes. They would play hide-and-seek around the garden if it was fine, and if it rained, they'd hide in the tack house, where the saddles and bridles lived, and lay out a clean horse blanket on the stone flags and sit and play cards or draughts.

CHAPTER 2

KILTEEGAN BRIDGE, 1955

*L*ena sat in the front pew, staring at her black shoes. Her black calico dress was too tight across her chest, threatening to pop a button. Mammy had made it for her for Hannah Berger's funeral six months before, but she was fourteen then and still growing; now that she was fifteen, it was already too tight. The priest was murmuring in Latin, swinging incense around the coffin that lay before the altar. On her left, Jack looked so pale, she thought he might faint. Lena tried to take hold of his hand, but he pulled it away. He was the man of the house now, Mammy had told him, so he thought he wasn't allowed to cry or show emotion any more. On her other side, Emily sat stiffly next to Maria; they looked like sisters, they were so alike. Both of them were in tears. Lena wished she could cry as well, but everything felt so unreal, she couldn't believe any of it was really happening.

Only three days ago, Daddy had been on his way out the door to check on the lambs and saw that the crafty old fox had stolen another one. Daddy and the fox had what he called a 'mutually respectful relationship'. The fox had a job to do, but so did he.

Daddy had trapped lots of foxes in his life. He tried not to kill things if he didn't have to, but this fox must have been especially clever if Daddy decided he needed to shoot it.

She wished he'd just trapped it.

'We're not the owners of this land, Lena,' he would say. 'Nor are we the masters of the animals and plants that live here. We're just minding it. It was minded by my father and his father before him, and now it's for us to care for, and in due time, Jack will take over.'

Daddy loved his farm.

She would never hear his voice again. Never.

Now her father was in that wooden box, and

the priest was telling everyone that Paudie O'Sullivan was happier now than he had ever been because he was at the right hand of the Lord. That was a load of rubbish. Daddy would never want to be anywhere except with his family.

It was Jack who had found him. Their father had been lying in his own blood in the top field with his shotgun, which he hadn't used for ages, beside him. Doc came from the village the minute he heard, but he hadn't been able to save his friend. It was a terrible accident, Doc told them. He must have fired at the fox, and his ancient shotgun had backfired, he was killed instantly. The doctor was nearly as broken by it as the rest of them. He had been Paudie O'Sullivan's best friend since they were children, and he was Lena's godfather, and he always came to see Maria when she was in one of her dangerously low moods.

The Mass was over now, and Doc, Jack and four other men from the village stepped forward to carry the coffin. Paudie O'Sullivan had been an only child, so there were no brothers to carry him, only his son and his best friend and his neighbours. Jack was barely tall enough for the task, but the undertaker put him in the middle and made sure the older men took most of the weight.

Lena's mother rose from the pew to follow the coffin, awkwardly, because she was very pregnant, her stomach huge under her loose black dress. Lena and Emily walked just behind her, holding hands. Emily squeezed Lena's fingers, and their eyes met briefly. Lena knew what her sister was thinking. Both of them had been dreading all morning that Maria would have one of her terrible breakdowns and scream the church down with fear, or else fall into one of her near-catatonic trances of melancholy. But so far, their mother had carried herself with great dignity. Maybe, like Lena, Maria didn't believe this was really happening.

The walk to the cemetery wasn't long, up a pale stony track fringed with wild monbretia under overhanging trees. The graveyard was on a hill overlooking the distant sea, and to Lena's surprise, the priest and coffin bearers headed towards the far corner, away from the O'Sullivan family plot where her father's parents and his two maiden aunts were buried. She touched her mother's arm. 'Is Daddy not going to be buried with Nana and Granda?' she whispered.

Maria said sharply, 'No. That grave is full.'

Lena fell instantly silent. There was an edge to her mother's voice that frightened her.

But then Maria softened and added, 'Anyway, girls, don't you think the plot I chose for him is much nicer?'

She was right. The plot over by the graveyard wall was lovely, shaded by a spreading chestnut tree and with a wide view of the distant bay. If it weren't for the stone weight of her grief, the beauty of the spot would have lifted Lena's heart.

After the graveside prayers and the sad, heavy rattle of earth and stones onto her father's coffin, Lena finally felt the tears come, and wanting to be alone in her grief, she walked a small distance away from the funeral crowd, muffling her sobs and wiping her nose with a scrap of hanky.

Blinded by grief, she nearly walked into Malachy Berger, who stood facing the Fitzgerald grave. She remembered him as the red-headed boy with bright-green eyes she used to play with as a little girl. She hadn't seen him in years except very briefly at his mother's funeral six months ago, and like her, he had grown since then – a couple of inches at least – and his hair was shorter.

The magnificent Fitzgerald family plot was right next to the more modest O'Sullivan family plot, where Lena's grandparents and grand-aunts were buried. Hannah's name and dates were the latest to be carved on the massive Fitzgerald headstone.

HANNAH BERGER née FITZGERALD
b.1919 – d.1955
Beloved wife and mother
Gone too soon

Only thirty-six when she died, five years younger than Lena's father.

Lena stopped. It felt rude to just walk on.

Malachy dug in his pocket and handed her a clean handkerchief. 'It's tough, losing a parent, isn't it?'

She nodded, wiping her tears with his handkerchief and handing it back.

'Keep it.' He said sincerely. 'I'm so sorry for your loss.'

Lena thought the words oddly formal for people their age, but she'd never been in this position before. Maybe the whole wretched business had its own language, where young people spoke so formally.

'Thanks,' she managed.

'I remember him kicking a football around with me, back when I was only six or seven years old. My father had only just come back from the war, and he was in a wheelchair, and my mother was lovely but useless at football. Your dad was one of the people I missed most when I went to boarding school.'

Lena smiled through her tears. It was nice to hear this boy remembering her father so fondly. 'I remember your mam as well. She was always smiling and singing. She was full of life, and she always gave me an extra penny for the eggs to keep for my own pocket.'

He looked sad at the memory. 'That's exactly how she was, full of life. She liked you too. She missed you when you and your father stopped coming, but I suppose you were busy on the farm.'

Lena sighed and nodded. 'I missed her as well.'

Still, it had been easier not to go up to the Bergers' big house these past few years. Maria had taken against any of her family having anything to do with them, forbidding her to go, something to do with not liking or trusting Hannah or her husband. Maria took sets against people for slights or insults, a few real but mostly imagined.

For a while, her father had continued going by himself – they needed the extra money. But then Emily, Jack and Lena had all got old enough to help on the farm, and Daddy bought a few more cows, and soon the O'Sullivan homestead was bringing in enough income from milk, eggs and vegetables for Paudie to stop working odd jobs at the big house altogether.

There was a sharp jerk at her elbow, and Emily hissed in her ear, 'Mammy says come back to Daddy's grave.' And Lena stuffed Malachy's hanky in her sleeve and went with her sister without a backwards glance.

The crowd was beginning to thin. Doc had arranged for tea and sandwiches at the Kilteegan Arms, and everyone was moving towards the cemetery gate. Lena and Emily linked Maria on either side, relieved the funeral had passed without their mother making any kind of scene. As they approached the gate, people maintained a respectful distance. Clearly Mrs O'Sullivan was in no fit state to make conversation. Then, Lena saw him. Auguste Berger sat in a wheelchair right beside the gate, and he appeared to be waiting for them. As they walked past, he put his hand out.

He spoke in a French accent. 'My sincere condolences. I know how difficult it is to lose your spouse, the sense of loss, of abandonment.'

Maria stiffened and glared at him, and Lena mentally braced herself. This could be the catalyst for hysterics; that tendency of her mother's was never far below the surface. The risk was made greater because she could no longer take the tablets she used to stabilise her mood for fear of damage to the babies. 'My husband did not "abandon" me,' she said stiffly. 'It was an accident. An accident.'

'Of course.' Auguste Berger tutted sympathetically as he gazed at her hugely swollen belly. 'So sad Monsieur O'Sullivan didn't live to see this child. Or I believe it is *children*? You're expecting twins, *non*? Two new lives to replace the two lives that were lost...' His voice was barely audible.

'Yes, thank you,' Lena responded, not sure what else to say. There was something unsettling about him. Everyone knew Maria was expecting twins because she had to see the doctor in Cork for her pregnancy, whereas everyone else who was expecting just went to Doc.

'Come on, Mammy.' Emily took their trembling mother by the arm and led her gently to the car the undertakers had supplied that was waiting in the autumn sunshine.

Lena glanced over her shoulder at the man in the wheelchair, who raised his hand to her with a charming smile. Auguste Berger, Malachy's father, was now the owner of Kilteegan House. His wife, Hannah, had been found dead of a heart attack in the orchard last spring. The house was her family place, not his. She'd been the Fitzgeralds' only surviving child, one brother dying as an infant and another in a horse-riding accident years ago. So Berger, as her husband, got it all: the big old house, the extensive grounds and a fine farm.

Behind him, holding the handles of the wheelchair, was that strange stocky Frenchman with his oily slicked-back hair. He'd arrived with Berger the day he came back from the war and had not left his side since.

Lena helped her mother into the car, and she could feel the pair's eyes on her and her family as they left Paudie in his final resting place.

CHAPTER 3

KILTEEGAN BRIDGE, 1958

*L*ena took off her shoes and crept up the moonlit path in her stockinged feet. It was nearly one o'clock in the morning. She'd never been this late home in her life and didn't want to wake anyone. Not her two-year-old twin sisters, Molly and May, who would never go back to sleep, and not Jack, who had to be up in a few hours for the milking, and especially not her mother, who might be in any sort of mood – madly happy or deep in despair or, worst of all, screaming obscenities at her for being up to no good with boys at the dance.

The front of the farmhouse was in darkness, but the moonlight was enough to help her find her way. She glanced up at the bedroom that had been her parents' and was now just her mother's. The light was off. Good – that meant Mammy was getting some sleep instead of wandering the house as she often did, talking to Dad like he was still alive.

It had been a hard few years in the O'Sullivan household since her father died. Lena and Jack had to leave school to run the farm, and it was so difficult – they had been only fifteen and twelve. Luckily, Jack had taken to farming like a duck to water and had learned a lot about old farming methods that were kind to the land. The neighbouring farmers were very good to them and looked out for them; everyone had been very fond of her father. Jack read voraciously about plants and animals and asked the advice of the old Traveller men and women who camped on their land each year about the various properties of flowers and grasses. He refused to use any of the new fertilisers on the farm, sticking to the old methods of cow shed muck, and sulphate of potash. Though it was more labour-intensive, their milk, beef and lamb were always in great demand. He'd told her about the discovery in

Switzerland and subsequent use all over the world of DDT – she'd forgotten the long name of it – and according to Jack, it was the worst thing ever dreamed up.

Emily would have helped more, but she had her hands full with the twins. Maria had fallen into such a deep depression after their birth that Doc sent her away to St Catherine's, a kind of nursing home up in Limerick, where she'd stayed for nearly a year. To be honest, it was easier at home without their mother, especially since Daddy wasn't there to ameliorate her moods. Even when Maria was in a happy frame of mind, it was difficult to deal with her. She might get a notion to redecorate the whole house, pushing all the furniture together in the middle of the rooms and painting all the walls lovely bright colours, until halfway through she got bored and started doing something else altogether, leaving them with half-painted walls. Another time Lena found her planting a rose garden at three o'clock in the morning, or she could decide she was going to make them all gorgeous clothes from bolt ends of cloth she'd picked up in town for next to nothing. Maria was a genius at making clothes; she'd made the dress Lena was wearing right now – a gorgeous fashionable tea dress of yellow silk, with covered buttons. She was so creative, but she hardly ever stuck to anything. Lena had finished off the dress herself because her mother had lost interest before it was complete. It was lovely, though.

That's likely why Malachy had noticed her in the Lilac Ballroom, among all the other girls.

'Malachy Berger.' She said his name in the cool night air. *Lena Berger.* It had a nice ring to it. *A ring.* She giggled. The two glasses of whiskey they'd had in his house after the dance had gone to her head. He was lovely, though. Most other fellas around here would take advantage of a girl who'd had a drink or two, but not Malachy; he was different to other lads. He'd offered her a lift home in his car – imagine, he had his own car, an amazing dark-green Volkswagen Beetle with cream leather interior and a Bosch radio – and on the way, he'd invited her into his house, where he'd introduced her to his father, who hadn't been shocked at his son bringing a girl home at that hour. Lena hadn't seen Auguste Berger since the day of her father's funeral, and though he'd unsettled her then, she decided it was probably that she'd been so upset, because tonight he was very welcoming and friendly.

Auguste Berger was obviously a sophisticated

man, and he had an exotic look about him – it was clear he'd spent his life somewhere other than Kilteegan Bridge. The way he sat in his big armchair by the fire, it wasn't obvious he had a disability. That strange manservant brought them whiskies on a silver tray and little sweet cakes called macaroons. It felt very sophisticated, drinking a whiskey and eating a French macaroon in the lovely sitting room, like something in a film. It was surely the best night of her life.

Malachy was as well-mannered as his father. She guessed it helped that he went to Larksbridge, a fancy boarding school up in Dublin, and not the tech in the next town like most of the boys from here did. He never once made any suggestive remarks or tried to grope her; he just spoke to her like she was a normal human being with her own opinions.

He was taller than when she'd last seen him, maybe five foot ten, with broad shoulders. His red hair had darkened to rich chestnut, and he wore it brushed back off his face in an actual style, on purpose, unlike most of the local lads, who looked like they were dragged backwards through a hedge. But it was his green eyes and long dark lashes that captivated her. His lashes would be the envy of any girl. He had white teeth

– Lena had a thing about teeth – and a square jaw. He looked like Cary Grant, she thought with a giggle.

When he asked her up to dance in the Lilac, she could hardly believe it. All the other girls were mad jealous, but she loved it. She knew she looked lovely in the yellow silk dress teamed up with her red high heels. She'd saved up for two months to pay for the shoes, but they were worth it even if they killed her feet. Doc had joked that he'd get her wages back from her when he was treating her corns and bunions from wearing shoes like that. She'd retorted that she had no notion of paying him a penny, that working for the local doctor, especially since he was her godfather and her dad's best friend, surely must have some advantages – free corn plasters and bunion paring maybe? She giggled again, feeling silly and carefree.

As she paused on the doorstep, a pang of familiar sadness threatened her happy mood. She glanced skywards, hoping Daddy could see her now. She was sure he would approve of Malachy; he'd always liked him as a little boy. She remembered them playing football together in the orchard of Kilteegan House.

She entered through the kitchen door and

hushed Thirteen, her father's beloved Border collie, before creeping up the stairs as quietly as a mouse. Jack was snoring, his bedroom door ajar. Molly and May in the next room had a little bed each but always slept together, and their door was open enough for Lena to see their tousled blonde heads and bare feet sticking out from under the blankets. Hopefully they were dreaming of puppies and kittens and ponies; at two years old they were obsessed with animals.

Lena was looking forward to bed herself. She normally shared the room with Emily, but her older sister was doing a course in bookkeeping in Cork and was in digs for the duration. She'd be home in about two months, and while Lena missed her, it was nice to have the bedroom to herself. She needed a few hours sound sleep before she had to get up and give Jack a hand with the milking and then go to her job at the surgery.

She pushed her bedroom door open, and her heart missed a beat, her mother was sitting on her bed.

'Where were you? Were you out dancing?' Her mother's pale eyes were anxious, as if dancing was a terrifying thing to do. Her long hair was loose and unkempt, and she wore her flowing sea-green dressing gown.

'Mammy, I was at the dance in the Lilac – I told you I was going,' Lena whispered, still anxious not to wake her siblings.

'There might have been bad spirits there, evil people, who would do you harm! You can't see them – you're like your father, too trusting. You haven't the ability to see them for what they are...'

'No evil spirits, just normal lads and girls like myself, Mam.' Lena kept her voice low and even; she would not react to this line of conversation. She placed her new shoes in the base of the wardrobe, then took the Pond's cold cream from her dresser and began to clean the make-up off her face.

Mammy had been good for quite a while now, cooking and taking care of them all. When she was happy and well, she was warm and kind and talented at everything she touched. Only yesterday Mammy had been encouraging her to go dancing in her new dress and saying how pretty she was. How Lena reminded her of Maria's own Aunty Betty, who went to America. How her lovely dark hair was so healthy and shiny, and it was because she rinsed it in lemon juice. And how her petite curvy figure was the envy of the parish.

But the downturn always came, and this was clearly it.

Lena knew she should be used to it by now, but it still shocked her every time, how sudden it could be. Poor Daddy put up with it for years. They'd gone to different doctors, and they'd even tried electric shock treatment, but that made Maria so bewildered and forgetful, it was even more terrifying. And in the end, they'd had to accept there was nothing to be done except send her to St Catherine's for periods of time when she was at her worst. They were kind there, and though Maria knew what it meant when she went there, she always spoke of their kindness when she came home. Sometimes it only took a few weeks, other times months and months, but when she came back, it was like the sun had come up again and their mother was back, all the mystery and demons and darkness forgotten.

Lena often wished she could just run away from the whole confusing thing. She was seventeen now, and Doc had given her a job on reception, so if she wanted, she could get a job in one of the nice clinics in Cork, or maybe even Dublin. But she worried about abandoning Molly and May, and Jack was still only fifteen and wouldn't be able to cope by himself – he was a sensitive boy, and Maria frightened him. Lena worried a lot about what their mother's illness had done to her little brother's sweet nature. He was a good-looking boy, fair-haired and tall, the image of his mother, and he had such a gentle disposition. But he had never got the guts up to even speak to a girl, let alone ask one out. He had no real friends – he'd left school early to run the farm, and farming was a solitary activity at the best of times.

Emily was two years older than Lena and had plans to marry Blackie Crean; the two of them planned to run his family's hardware shop in the village. It wasn't much of a dream, Lena thought, but Emily and Blackie had been together since they were in secondary school, and the prospect of a life together forever in Kilteegan Bridge seemed to make them both happy. Blackie's useless, idle, sticky-fingered father, Dick Crean, was gone, skipped to England, but he was no loss whatsoever. Mrs Crean ran the shop now, but she was crippled with arthritis so would be glad to hand it all over. Emily was sweet and would do what she could to help Jack and mind the twins, Lena knew that, but once Emily was married, she'd have the shop and then maybe her own children to look after.

'I'm tired, Mam, so I'll go to bed. Maybe you should too,' she said, trying to keep the sadness out of her voice.

'Not until you tell me who you were dancing with.' Her mother's voice rose a little – anxious, suspicious, angry.

Suddenly Lena felt so tired, bone-weary of it all. She pulled off her dress and slipped on her nightie. 'If you must know, I was dancing with Malachy Berger.'

Her mother paled and her jaw tightened. 'You are forbidden to be near that boy, do you hear me? Forbidden.'

Lena knew that crazed look but wasn't expecting the blow. It knocked her off her feet, and she landed painfully as she put her hand out to save herself.

The sound of her fall and the enraged scream of her mother brought Jack running, his fair hair standing on end as he gazed wild-eyed at them, wearing his pyjama bottoms and a vest. Behind came a confused and tousled May, a terrified Molly behind her.

'Lena, are you all right?' Jack ran to her and helped her up.

'I'm sorry, I'm sorry, I'm sorry...' The words came out in a sob as Maria rushed past her children, making for her own bedroom; she slammed the door so hard it shook the house.

'Awe you awright, Lena? Awe you hurted?' Molly, who couldn't pronounce her R's yet, asked fearfully, and Lena knew she needed to reassure them. Jack lifted her up and carried her to the bed. He was a gentle soul, always finding birds with broken wings or bottle-feeding calves and lambs that had been rejected by their mothers. He knew what that felt like.

'I'm fine, girls. I just had a tumble – it's my silly new shoes.' She tried to laugh through the pain and was rewarded by weak smiles from her little sisters. 'You too, Jack, don't worry. It was an accident. Just go back to bed.' Lena was exhausted and just needed them all to leave her alone.

CHAPTER 4

When Lena woke, her wrist was so swollen, she was unable to help Jack with the milking. She got the twins breakfast and then brought them across the fields to Deirdre Madden. Mrs Madden and her husband, Bill, had the neighbouring farm, and their daughter, Lucy, was the same age as the twins. Deirdre took care of Molly and May when Maria wasn't able to. Deirdre had always been helpful to the O'Sullivans; she knew the problem they lived with even though they never talked about it. And Bill gave Jack lots of advice about the farm.

Upon returning from the Maddens', Lena stuck her head around the milking parlour door. 'Run me down to the surgery, will you, Jack?'

He looked up from examining a cow whose udder had mastitis. He'd been up since six to get the herd in. 'You're not going to work with that wrist, are you? It's swelled up like a balloon.'

'I'll be grand. Sure, it's my left hand, and I'll get Doc to have a look at it when he gets a minute.'

'You need an X-ray in case it's broken. I could run you to the hospital in Bantry?'

'I'll see what Doc says – you know he's better than any hospital. Stop fussing.'

Doctor Emmet Dolan, whom everyone called Doc, was a big blocky man with brown curls and dark-green eyes. He lived alone over the surgery he'd inherited from his father, who'd been the doctor before him. He wore dark shapeless suits that seemed to be too big even for him, and his leather bag was so scuffed and worn, it was hard to tell what colour it had once been. But the sight of Doc was all the people of Kilteegan Bridge needed to feel safe and cared for. He possessed an innate sense of what might be wrong and was the most compassionate person Lena had ever met.

Doc had bounced her on his knee as a baby, patched up her and her siblings after childhood mishaps and had been a constant, solid presence in their lives. Even so, when he advertised in the post office window for a receptionist and she went for the interview, she told him that she only wanted the job if he thought she'd be good at it, not as a favour to her or her late father.

Doc had smiled at her. 'Trust me, Lena, you'll be good at it – you know how clever you are. My mother, God be good to her, did it for my father back in his day, but I've not had anyone. And honestly, with the health board breathing down my neck for records of patients and the taxman wanting to know more than I can ever tell him, I badly need someone to manage the paperwork and the appointments and that.'

Doc had been dead set against Lena leaving school at fifteen, although he understood that she had to because of the farm. Lena hated leaving school as well; she envied Emily, who was sixteen when Daddy died and so had got her final exams.

Jack looked doubtful at her suggestion. 'Well, I suppose if you have to go to work, a doctor's surgery is the best place. Is she up?' He glanced warily towards the house.

'No. I'd say she'll stay in her room all day. I've taken her up some bread and cheese and an apple and left it outside her door, in case she wants to eat.

'Get all the jobs done as best you can without

me, and meet me in the Copper Kettle at five – we'll have a mixed grill and you'll be back for the milking. Maybe Bill can spare one of his young lads to help you. I can collect the twins from Deirdre after tea. She says she doesn't mind having them all day – it keeps little Lucy out of her hair.'

'Righto. Come on so.'

They walked across the yard, and Jack opened the door of Daddy's old Morris Minor. Thirteen bounded out of the hay barn and jumped into the back seat – she loved a spin. She had been so sad when their father died, but Jack had filled Paudie's place in the dog's affections and now one was never seen without the other.

The car was immaculate and running as well as ever; Jack spent hours tinkering with it. They drove down the hill to the village in silence, both lost in their own thoughts, with Thirteen resting her chin on Lena's shoulder.

'Will we tell Emily?' Jack asked eventually.

Lena knew what he meant – that Maria was bad again, that the spell of happiness was over. Lena suddenly felt so weary of it all. Her wrist was really sore, and the chance of ever escaping this life seemed so unlikely. 'No.' She sighed. 'What's the point? She won't be back till next month anyway, and it will have blown over by then. No point in having her worry. There's nothing anyone can do to set it off or stop it – you know that, Jack. It just has to run its course.'

'I suppose you're right.' He turned into the square. 'Anyway, hopefully this one will be over quickly. Emily would only worry, and we can manage it, can't we? Were the girls all right this morning?'

Lena nodded. 'They seem to be able to block it out. They were on about Dinny O'Regan's dog having pups.'

Jack groaned. 'Oh God, don't let them persuade you to let them have one. We've enough to deal with besides adding a puppy to the chaos. Besides, I don't think Thirteen would take kindly to sharing her space with a puppy.'

The twins were always bringing injured or 'lost' animals home from the fields. Lena smiled. Jack hadn't a leg to stand on complaining about the twins adopting stray animals – he was just as bad – and she knew that he and the girls were too soft for this world.

He pulled up outside the surgery, and Lena leaned back and took her handbag from the back seat with her good hand. 'See you in the Copper Kettle. Thanks for the lift.' She gave Thirteen a pat on the head and the collie licked her hand, and then she left the boy and his dog to their day.

She let herself into the surgery awkwardly with one hand and switched the lights and heat on in the waiting room. The reception desk was neat and tidy, exactly as she'd left it the evening before.

In less than an hour, the waiting room would be full of people with their ailments, real and imagined, and Doc would treat each one as if they were his only patient that day.

The waiting room, surgery, small kitchen and her office were all on the ground floor of the big terraced house in the middle of the main street of Kilteegan Bridge, and apart from sleeping up-stairs, Doc spent almost every moment down-stairs. Last night, he would have sat in the kitchen at the back of the house behind the surgery, reading a medical paper, and nodded off in his chair over a glass or two – or three – of wine. He had no life really, apart from his patients. He had never married. His brother had emigrated to Australia years ago, and Doc and he had lost touch. He'd had a sister he loved, Annie, but she died of TB when she was sixteen. Lena knew sev-eral women had tried to turn his head over the years, but he was oblivious. It was sad, she always thought. He'd have been a lovely husband and father.

'That you, Lena?' he called down the stairs.

'And who else might it be?' she called up to him, chuckling.

He stood on the top step in his vest and trousers, face covered in shaving soap, his braces dangling down. 'Stick on the kettle there, love,' he said as he retreated to the bathroom on the landing.

Using just her right hand, she made tea for herself and poured it, then added another spoon of tea leaves because Doc liked his strong enough to trot a mouse on, as he said himself.

Moments later he arrived down. 'What happened to you?' he asked, immediately seeing her swollen wrist.

'I fell over last night, just as I was getting into bed.'

'Too much lemonade at the dance, was it?' He smiled, bending his curly head to examine it. He smelled of Imperial Leather soap.

'Something like that.' She winced as he pressed on the swelling. 'Is it broken?'

He shook his head. 'No, just a bad sprain, but you'll have to mind it for a few days. Why didn't you just ring and tell me? I can manage here on my own, you know. I did for years when you were a child.'

It was a running joke of his that Lena felt she was indispensable to him. The reality was that she didn't just do all the paperwork but also made sure he took care of himself and protected him from the worst of the local malingers.

'Go on out of that.' She grinned despite the pain in her wrist. 'You'd have keeled over of a heart attack if you'd kept going the way you were. I've taken years off you.'

He eased her sleeve up and sprayed her wrist with something pungent but instantly cooling before strapping it gently in a bandage and making her a sling, which he fixed with a safety pin.

'How's Maria?' he asked. Though he never would say as much, Lena immediately worried that he knew her mother was responsible for her sprained wrist.

She said defensively, 'She's been very happy recently, making lovely dresses and that sort of stuff.'

'But today?' He fixed her with his wise gaze.

She dropped her eyes. 'Well, today she's in bed. She is a bit low.'

'I might call out to her tomorrow.'

'OK.'

He touched her cheek. 'I know she can't help it, Lena. But that doesn't make it any easier to deal with, does it? If she's very low, I'll suggest she go to St Catherine's. She never wants to go, but she always feels better afterwards. Now, can Jack come in for you? Take you home?' He glanced at the clock; surgery would start soon.

'I'll do no such thing. I'll take an aspirin and sit here quietly, and I won't use my left hand at all, I promise. I can still answer the phone and deal with patients.'

'Ah, will you stop it, and have the whole place calling me an awful tyrant altogether?' Doc objected.

'Please, Doc, I'm better here.'

Something in the way she said it gave him pause. 'Is she that bad?' he asked gently.

She stayed silent, not wanting to betray her mother but not wanting to be sent home to her either.

Doc sighed. 'Right, stay. But if I think you're not up to it, I want you to lie on the sofa and rest – is that clear?' He was stern now, but she knew he was soft as butter really.

'Crystal.' She grinned.

She unlocked the door, and the day began

with coughs and colds and warts and aches and babies with rashes.

Old Seanie Hurley showed up with an infected cut, stinking of dung and with his filthy wellingtons leaving dirt all over the lino. After Doc had thoroughly washed and disinfected the cut, the old man insisted on paying his bill with duck eggs – 'for the baking', even though Doc had never baked in his life. Doc thanked him and told him the eggs were lovely. Sometimes she despaired of Doc's generosity, but he always said the point of being a doctor was to heal the people who needed healing, not to get rich.

The new curate came in, Father Otawe. He was the subject of great curiosity because he was a Black man from Uganda, the first ever seen in the town. The schoolchildren loved him because he told them stories about all the wild animals that were to be found around his village back home. They didn't seem to have any difficulty understanding his accent, even though Lena found it hard enough when he was trying to explain to her what was wrong with him – he had a grain of sand or a bit of something in his eye.

Doc had asked Chrissy, who owned the town's only café, the Copper Kettle, to deliver some sandwiches for lunch, which they both ate at their respective desks. Doreen Kiely from the chemist popped in to tell Doc that the new drugs he'd ordered had arrived, and when she saw Lena's wrist, she left and arrived back with two cups of tea and two slices of homemade sponge cake. Living in Kilteegan Bridge drove most young people daft, everyone knowing each other's business, but today Lena had to admit it had some advantages.

The rest of the day passed in the usual flood of ailments, and before she knew it, it was time to go home.

Jack was waiting for her outside the Copper Kettle when she arrived, carrying the box of Seanie Hurley's blue duck eggs, which Doc had insisted she bring home with her. Jack pushed the door of the busy café open and held it for her. 'How was your day?' he asked with a smile.

'Grand, busy, you know yourself.'

Lena smiled at the middle-aged woman with unusually brassy blond hair behind the counter. Chrissy refused to go to the hairdresser's, so her home dye jobs had varying degrees of success. This week she was almost luminous. 'Two mixed grills, please, Chrissy, with tea and bread and butter.'

They took a seat at the back in a booth like

they often did, and when their meals arrived, Jack tucked into the sausages, rashers, black pudding and fried potatoes hungrily. He swallowed, then asked, 'What did Doc say about your wrist?'

'It's only sprained. I'm to mind it for a few days, and it'll be grand.'

'So no more dancing for you.' He winked.

'Oh, I don't know – I don't dance on my hands.'

'How was the Lilac last night?'

'Ah, the usual crowd.' Lena shrugged. On the way there, she'd decided not to say anything at all about Malachy to her brother, or about drinking whiskey with Auguste Berger. But in the end, she couldn't help herself – she had to talk to someone, and there was nobody else. 'Do you know why Mammy dislikes the Bergers so much?' she asked, cutting up her bacon.

Jack shrugged. 'I don't know. She never liked Hannah Berger. Didn't she get some notion Hannah had an eye for Daddy or something? And she thought they were a bit high and mighty, looking down at the rest of us from their perch in the big house.'

'The poor man is perched in a wheelchair.'

'Sure he is, but even that fella that works for him, that Phillippe, when he goes shopping in the town, he acts like he's a cut above, always talking about how the milk and beef and lamb are so much better in France.' Jack sounded aggrieved, and Lena could see how he'd take it personally after all the hard work he did to make sure their meat and milk were pesticide-free.

'Well, I'm sure that's just Phillippe.' Lena knew she sounded ridiculously defensive, but she couldn't help it. 'I'm sure Auguste Berger is very nice and wouldn't say any such thing.'

Jack looked up in surprise from coating his sausages with mustard. 'Why are you so bothered about the Bergers all of a sudden?'

'No reason.'

'Hmm.' Jack raised a sceptical eyebrow.

'Oh, all right.' She felt herself go hot with embarrassment. 'I was dancing with Malachy Berger in the Lilac last night –'

'Ah, that explains it, all right.'

'Stop grinning like an eejit – it doesn't mean anything. But anyway, we went back to his house after the dance, and his father was there, and we drank whiskey and ate macaroons...'

'Ooh la la!' Jack teased. 'Macaroons no less? Did he make you do the washing up?'

'Stop it! He did no such thing. He treated me like a lady and said how much I look like my father, and then Malachy drove me home. He acted the total gentleman, and it was all lovely.'

Jack stuffed in a mouthful of toast, still grinning. 'Just so long as you remember you're my sister and not some posh lady from the big house, Lena O'Sullivan.'

'You don't think I'm a lady?' she teased.

'Of course you're a lady – you're a perfect lady. You're just not a snob, and I wouldn't want you turning into one, even if you do end up being called Lena Berger.'

'Some chance of that.' But even the sound of her name hitched to Malachy's gave her a hot little glow, and she had to hide her face behind her mug of tea. 'Do you want a dessert? My treat.' Anything to get off the subject.

'I certainly do,' he said enthusiastically, and Lena turned to smile and wave at the counter.

Chrissy was busy cooking, so it was Chrissy's fourteen-year-old daughter, Imelda, who sloped over, looking sullen. 'What do ye want?'

'Excuse me?' Lena smiled.

The girl had a full face of make-up and dark hair that could do with a wash. 'What?'

'Oh, I'm sorry. I thought you were speaking to us. Apologies.'

'I was,' Imelda answered, slightly on the back foot now.

'Oh, I must have misheard you. I thought you just said, "What do ye want." But clearly you didn't, because that would be such a strange, rude way to speak to a customer, especially considering your mother is always so friendly and helpful and has worked so hard to build up her business all on her own.'

Lena was very fond of Chrissy, who'd been widowed young, and knew from talking to her that Imelda was a scourge.

The girl coloured beneath the caked-on make-up and was about to say something when the look on Lena's face changed her mind.

'What would ye like to order?' she asked, if not with a smile, at least without the scowl.

'I'll have a piece of apple tart with ice cream, please, Imelda. Jack?'

'Sure, I'll have a bit of apple tart too. It sounds lovely.'

'With ice cream?'

'Cream only, please.'

'OK,' managed the teenager before slinking off back to the counter.

Jack grinned at his sister. 'So, Mrs Malachy

Berger, I'm glad you're around to put manners on us natives.'

Lena rolled her eyes at him. 'I wasn't being a snob. That one needs to wake up, or she'll ruin her mother's business. Look at us. We were fifteen and twelve when Daddy died, and we didn't go around looking like the world was against us – at least I hope we didn't – so there's no excuse for sour Imelda.'

Jack sighed. 'I hope not, but I'm not going to lie to you – sometimes I thought it was.'

Lena's heart broke for him, her sensitive little brother, and she reached over and squeezed his hand.

CHAPTER 5

When Maria O'Sullivan woke, it was dusk, the house was cold, and she knew she was alone. The framed photograph of her and Paudie was in the bed; she must have fallen asleep with it. She missed him with such intensity, it was hard to bear sometimes. She longed for his ever-constant, solid presence. He'd always assured her that the good days far outweighed the bad ones, and that he understood that she never meant to hurt him or the children and didn't blame her, but she knew what she'd put him through.

She dreaded the visit from Doc, which was sure to come once he saw Lena's wrist.

Lena was bound to have told him that she was

bad again, or he'd guess, and he'd arrive tomorrow, probably, and then it would be St Catherine's for a while. He wouldn't mention how she'd hurt her daughter, but he would know. Oh, poor Lena. A wave of sadness washed over her as she remembered the way she'd treated her. How could she do it? Why? Lena and the Berger boy were barely more than children, and they had a right to go dancing together. Her paranoid fears had nothing to do with them.

But Hannah, and the way she'd wanted Paudie, and that father of his... A wave of cold sweat prickled her skin.

Stop. Hannah was dead, and of course Auguste Berger wasn't evil. Why would she think that? She'd do anything, try anything, to make these mad thoughts go away.

She'd gone to a clinic in Dublin once, and had endured electric shock treatment. She was willing to do it, but it made her feel like she was under water, and Paudie said it wasn't worth it. It was no life. So now she went to St Catherine's, sometimes for months at a time – a whole year after Paudie died and she'd had the twins – and she dreaded the thought of that journey again, the sad feeling as she was driven through the gates and up the avenue. The nuns were kind. It was just that she left the convent with such hope each time, hope that this time it would be different, that she would be a better person. The arrival back there just signalled another failure.

Paudie was the only one who could really manage her when she was lost and drifting. He could talk to her in a way that made her feel less out of control. Where was he now? She needed him back so badly. But he was dead – she had to keep reminding herself. Had he died because of that red-haired, green-eyed witch?

No, that's ridiculous.

Doc told her that Paudie's death had been an accident, a terrible accident. And Paudie hadn't gone with Hannah Berger – it was all in her mind. A product of her illness, her paranoia. If he really had been with Hannah, she would have just walked into the sea.

Maybe she dreamed he was dead; maybe he was just outside milking the cows. Her mind made her believe awful things, so maybe Paudie wasn't really gone and he would come in and hold her in his arms and she'd feel safe again.

She thought she felt him beside her. Maybe it was his ghost, come to mind her. Maybe it was just in her head, like so many other things…

She remembered the night years and years

ago when she and her friend Bridget went to the dance in Bantry, before the Emergency. She'd lied to her parents and said she was going to a talk on art in the Crawford Gallery. She'd thought it was a terrible mistake at first, to go to the dance with Bridget. The loud music hurt her ears, and she found the lights too bright when they came on between the tunes. But then a big handsome lad, with brown hair that flopped over his forehead and huge hands, had asked her up. She felt light as a feather in his arms, and something about him, that night and every night afterwards till the day he died, made her feel safe and loved. Bridget had met a lad from Dublin, a right smooth-talker who turned out to be married with a baby on the way. But Paudie O'Sullivan was the real thing.

Later, after they'd met in secret a few more times, she had summoned up all her courage and sent a letter to Paudie, inviting him to tea at her home on Wellington Road in Cork. She prayed her parents wouldn't say anything horrible about her, that her father wouldn't tell Paudie that she was unfit for marriage, that she should be in an asylum by rights. That her mother wouldn't get that look, the one that said a small farmer from West Cork was not good enough.

When Paudie called to the house, he was put

in the dark parlour by Ethel the maid. The room smelled of mothballs and damp. She'd asked Ethel to bring tea. She was so nervous that when she poured it, there was more tea on the saucer than in the cup.

Her mother appeared then to meet him, cold and judgemental, and made pointed, brittle enquiries about his background. Her father came in from the gentleman's outfitters shop he owned, at 6:18 p.m. on the dot as he did every night of his life. George Hannigan looked like one of the mannequins in his window, stiff and perfect, entirely devoid of feeling. Maria still remembered the creases in his trousers, so sharp they could cut bread, and his black jacket, entirely free of lint or hair. He had alabaster skin and thinning hair combed across his shiny white head – even the comb marks were perfect.

Her mother, on the other hand, was rangy, large-boned, wide-faced, broad-hipped and narrow-minded. She and her husband cohabited in that house in complete isolation; Maria could hardly remember a conversation ever passing between them. But for the existence of her and her older brother, Ted, she would have sworn to it that they had never physically touched each other, let alone conceived two children.

Poor Paudie. He was the son of poor but loving parents, with not enough of anything. He'd been a real fish out of water that day, trying to be polite, twisting his cap in his hands. Her father had asked several staccato questions as to his station in life and his family's pedigree, and once he took over the interrogation, her mother had simply stared. It lasted a bare half hour but felt like a fortnight. But then Ted came home, and he saved the day as he always did, laughing and smiling, talking about football and the situation in Europe. She remembered seeing the visible relief on Paudie's face – a normal conversation at last.

Ted had told her afterwards that Paudie was a nice lad and she should grab the opportunity with both hands. That he'd met a girl himself, a German girl called Christiana, and he was crazy about her. He wanted to go back to Germany with her. She was in Ireland studying English, but her parents were expecting her back to Leipzig soon. He'd feel a whole lot better about going if his sister was settled down with a nice man.

She never again subjected Paudie to her parents. Once she had Ted's approval, they eloped, a very racy thing at the time, and got married in Gretna Green in Scotland with total strangers as witnesses and arrived back to Paudie's farm as man and wife. George and Irene Hannigan cut Maria off entirely after her elopement, and maybe it was better that way; she and her parents had always been a disappointment to each other.

Ted was gone to Germany, and soon after that the war – or the 'Emergency' – started. He'd never come home. She thought about Ted often, and wondered what had happened to him, which side he had got swept up on, German or British. Whichever it was, she hoped he'd survived. Maybe one day he'd get in touch. She'd written, of course, to his last known address – Cristiana's parents' house in Leipzig – but never heard anything back.

Paudie was his parents' only son and the farm was his, such as it was. Mr and Mrs O'Sullivan welcomed her, but soon both had passed away, he of cancer and she of the stroke she had at her husband's funeral. Maria was fond of them. They were the opposite of her parents, warm and loving and united in everything to the very end. Though Paudie was heartbroken at their loss, he was glad they went nearly together. They were so in love that for one to be left behind without the other would have been awful.

Maria's nerves were better in the early days on the farm. The hard work and fresh air did her good, and the times she was low were infrequent, and she managed to hide it when it happened. She had a bad episode after Emily was born; that was one of the worst ever. She'd broken so much crockery, and Paudie had been in shock, she remembered. It went on for months until eventually Paudie's childhood friend Doc intervened and got her into St Catherine's for a spell. She was calmer after that.

That was a very bad time in her marriage and she feared that Paudie would leave her, but they patched it up. Then Lena came along, and she struggled for a long time, but gradually recovered. But with Jack it changed again. He cried so much as a baby, she thought he might be a demon. She'd lash out in fear, and she couldn't bear to have her baby son near her. Either the sight of him repulsed her or else she would squeeze him with so much love that Paudie had to rescue him from her grasp.

In her last pregnancy, she remembered how proud he was. She was well again then. They'd go to Mass every Sunday with their little family. Her bump was much bigger – though she had no idea in the early months it was twins – and it was obvious to everyone that after the long gap, the O'-Sullivans were having another baby. She'd made herself a new maternity dress and coat and knew she looked blooming. She felt so proud of Emily, Lena, Jack and her handsome husband. Doc thought she was a bit big for the time, so he examined her and heard two distinct heartbeats. After that he insisted she go to Professor Wilkinson in Cork. Paudie would take her for her check-up every month, and they would have a cup of tea and a currant bun in Thompson's Bakery after each appointment. She'd been so happy.

But then Paudie died, and the rest of that pregnancy went by in a blur of agony. She gave birth to the twins without him there to see them and welcome them into the world, and after that she'd had to go to St Catherine's for a whole year. She never connected properly to Molly and May on her return, she knew. Emily was more like a mother to them. Maria wished she could get closer to her little girls, but they were entirely contained in their own world and didn't seem to need anyone else.

She got up and pulled on her dressing gown. Leaving her bedroom and coming out to the landing she called, 'Molly? May?'

The lights were off in the farmhouse, and all the bedrooms were empty. Where were her youngest children? They were only two years old. They must be with Lena or Jack, she supposed. Or Deirdre Madden from the neighbouring farm, who had a daughter the same age and was like an aunt to them. Her older children never consulted her as to what they were doing, or where they took the twins.

She wasn't a good mother. She knew that. She was better when Paudie was alive – he helped her – but now she just couldn't.

Her children. How different they all were. Emily, although she looked so like Maria, was earthbound like Paudie – solid and sensible, with her feet on the ground. Lena was like her father, with her dark-brown hair and eyes, but in her character, she was a mixture of both parents, headstrong and quirky but also with a strong streak of common sense that would hopefully see her through in the end. Jack – oh, Jack – so delicate, so sensitive. Like Emily, he was tall and slim and with Maria's fair hair and eyes. And the twins, blonde both, content in their own little world. Thank God none of her children had inherited her madness...

She bathed and washed her hair, then dressed in the silk blue-green dress Paudie had always liked and went downstairs. The range was lit, banked down and giving a warm ambient heat to the kitchen.

She held onto the porcelain of the Belfast sink. The net curtains on the window would not allow her to see her image in the dark. Paudie was dead. Of course he was. How could she have thought he wasn't. The pain of it crashed over her like it was yesterday.

It was half past six. Lena would be home from work soon, maybe, hopefully, bringing the twins, and Jack would be in from milking. She'd make their dinner, have it ready, and maybe she'd bake an apple crumble with custard too, try to make up for…well, everything.

The lights of the car made her blink as it appeared in the yard. Then she saw them, Lena with her arm in a sling, the twins climbing out of the car after her, and Jack and Thirteen heading for the cow shed, where their twelve cows would be waiting to be milked – they always came home by themselves when their udders were full.

Maria nearly ran back upstairs to get away from the evidence of what she'd done to her daughter, but she made herself stay where she was.

'Hi, Mam?' Lena said tentatively.

'Lena, my love, I'm so sorry. I never meant... Is it broken?'

'It's OK, Mam, just a sprain. I'll live,' said her daughter gently. 'Right o, Molly and May, let's run up and put on your nighties and brush your teeth.'

'No, sit down, sit down, Lena. I'll make the dinner for you...'

'Ah, it's fine, Mam. Jack and I ate at the Copper Kettle, and the twins got fed in Maddens', so we're fine.' Lena got the girls ready for bed and then allowed them a few minutes to play as she sank into the fireside chair, her father's favourite. It was always so strange to see her sitting in that chair, looking so like Paudie with her sun-kissed skin.

'But a cup of tea? I could make cocoa for the girls, and there's some currant bread in the tin?'

Lena smiled. 'Lovely.'

Delighted to be allowed to be useful, Maria busied herself. Behind her, downstairs now in their nighties and slippers and with Lena's en-couragement, Molly and May played with their dolls on the table.

She put the warm drinks in front of her daughters, and they took them gratefully, but in the case of the twins, warily. It was awful to see

Lena trying to manage with one hand, knowing it was her fault.

Jack arrived in from the milking, bringing the letters from their postbox at the end of the lane.

'Hi, Mam,' he said. He always had the same look of relief on his face when he realised the worst of the storm had passed. He turned to his sister. 'Bills,' he said, handing over the letters. 'I'm afraid you're the bookkeeper while Emily is away.'

* * *

LENA FLIPPED through the brown envelopes, dreading having to deal with figures. It was all right for Emily; she'd had a chance to learn this stuff. Maybe if Lena had been able to stay on in school, she'd be as good with numbers as her older sister. But there was no use complaining; they had to carry on.

Under the brown envelopes was a cream one with just Lena's name handwritten on it and no stamp. She glanced up at Jack, who winked at her. He must have noticed it but decided not to mention it in front of their mother.

Making sure Maria was busy at the sink washing the cocoa cups, she opened the envelope and extracted a small card with a cartoon drawing of a puppy with a lead in its mouth.

Dear Lena,

I was wondering if you'd like to go for a walk, or a drink, or to the pictures, or for a meal or a swim in the lake? Or anything, really? I'd love to see you again, whatever we're doing.

Malachy x

She smiled. Things were looking up.

'Who is that from?' her mother asked as she dried the cups with a tea cloth.

'Oh, just a patient. An old lady I helped to get her medical card sorted out sent me a thank-you card.'

'Wasn't that kind of her. But then you're such a helpful girl. I bet everyone who goes to Doc knows how lucky he is to have you.'

Her mother's gush of love almost brought Lena to tears. Sometimes she thought it might be easier if Maria was her worst self all the time – then maybe she could cut her poor mother out of her heart instead of loving her so much in this awkward, difficult way.

'I don't know about that,' she answered brightly. 'They're usually giving out yards because they can't see him the minute they call, and I'm the big bad wolf who says they have to wait for an appointment.'

'Well, Doc is such a busy man,' Maria said kindly. 'I know people come from all over the place to see him, people not from Kilteegan Bridge at all. The doctor in Kellstown is a right old dragon apparently, so people avoid him and come to Doc instead.'

'Don't I know it,' Lena agreed, standing up to move away the twins' colouring things. 'Right, you two, bedtime.'

'Is your arm very sore, love?' Maria asked, watching anxiously as Lena worked with one hand.

'It is a bit, but it will be all right.'

Maria's eyes filled with tears. 'If only your father were here…'

'I know you miss him, Mam, and that it's very hard for you.'

'It really is, Lena. He… Paudie knew how to manage me, when I was low, I mean.'

'I know.'

'Do I know who sent the card?' Maria asked.

Lena paused for a split second. She hated that disconcerting way her mother had of completely changing the subject without any warning.

'Mam, just a patient, I told you. It's Mrs Murphy, she's from out Dunmanway direction, I think.'

MARIA SAW the look that passed between Lena and Jack, unspoken volumes of shared understanding. *They don't love me at all.* She pushed down on the sudden surge of paranoid grief. She leaned down as her twin daughters kissed her goodnight and then watched Lena take them upstairs.

CHAPTER 6

Dear Malachy,
Wait for me at the gate Saturday, midday, down at the end of the lane that leads up to our farm.

Lena x

Meeting Malachy out of sight of the farmhouse wasn't anything to do with avoiding her mother. Maria had gone to St Catherine's 'for a rest' on Doc's orders. It was Jack she didn't want knowing. She didn't want him grinning and making stupid remarks about her getting notions of herself, the worst crime of all time in Ireland.

The phrase was 'notions of grandeur', but everyone just said 'such and such has notions', because to finish the phrase was to have, well, notions. Ireland was such a mad place, Lena often thought.

Now, as she made her way down the farm lane to the main road, avoiding the potholes, she was beginning to regret being so secretive. The heels of her new red shoes kept sinking into mud, and she had to hold up the legs of her trousers to keep them clean. They were white flared trousers that she'd bought second-hand in a shop in Cork last summer. She was wearing a striped polo neck jumper with loose sleeves to cover her wrist, which was still a bit swollen, but at least she'd been able to discard the sling. Her dark hair was tied up in a high ponytail, which she'd curled with pipe cleaners, and she hoped she looked nice.

When she got to the gate, it was ten to twelve and his car was already parked on the grass verge. Butterflies danced in her tummy. Malachy was gorgeous, but more than that, he was different, and here he was in his green Beetle at the bottom of their lane, waiting for her.

She went up to the passenger door, and he jumped out to open it for her. Then a shadow crossed his face. 'Oh, sorry, Audrey, I'm waiting for Lena O'Sullivan.'

'What?' She had no idea what he was going on about.

'You're Audrey Hepburn, aren't you? I'd say you're lost, Audrey – Hollywood is that way.' He pointed to the west. 'And I'd give you a spin, no bother normally, except I'm waiting for a cracking girl called Lena, so...' He shrugged apologetically.

'Go on, ya big eejit.' Lena giggled.

He grinned, and she noticed for the first time that he had a slightly crooked front tooth, but apart from that, he was a perfect dreamboat. He was a rugby player for his boarding school above in Dublin, and looked it. He was wearing a short-sleeved denim shirt and relaxed black canvas trousers. He took her breath away.

'Well, lovely Lena, where would you like to go?'

'I don't mind.' She settled herself into the car. It was a beauty and didn't smell of calf ration like Jack's immaculate but sometimes stinky Morris Minor.

'Well, we could go to the pictures if you want, or we could go to the pub, or for a swim... OK, maybe not a swim – the water is a bit cold.' He climbed back behind the wheel, then turned to face her. He smelled of a spicy lemon cologne, and she had to stop herself from reaching out to touch him.

'Let's go for a drink. We can't talk in the pictures,' she said.

'Righto. I presume we're avoiding the Donkey's Ears?'

'Most definitely.' The idea of her and Malachy Berger turning up in the busiest pub in Kilteegan Bridge would have tongues wagging for a week. By the time she got home, they'd have the banns read, the wedding arranged and the dress picked out for her. No thank you. Not to mention that while they were both young single people, Kilteegan Bridge had an unwritten code as to who fit where, and Jack's teasing would be nothing compared to the gossip that would follow her around if she and Malachy were seen together.

Lena always thought how hypocritical it was that people went on about the class system in England, with dukes and lords and all the rest of it, when it was just the same here – everyone had a place, and woe betide you if you had plans to elevate yourself above the station you'd been put in. Malachy Berger was socially above her, of that there was no doubt whatsoever, and she wouldn't risk drawing all manner of comment and snide remarks on something that might not last. It was 1958 not 1858, but still, in the cold light of day – instead of the warm glow of a dance in the Lilac Ballroom – Lena knew her place, and her place was most certainly not on the arm of Malachy Berger, that was for sure. He should be with one of Kieran Devlin's daughters – he was a solicitor – or maybe one of Professor Lamkin's horsey-faced girls. That was where he should be aiming, but he wasn't, and she was flattered and excited.

They drove through the next big town of Bandon and chatted easily as they went. She asked politely about the health of his father.

'He isn't great at the moment. His heart is weak since the accident, but he's getting worse lately, so I'm coming home from school to spend the weekend more often than usual.'

'I'm sorry to hear that. He's such a lovely man.' She felt guilty at how delighted she was that Malachy was obliged to come home for weekends. 'It must be hard for him, being confined to the chair. I'm assuming he was injured in the war?'

'He was, towards the end. At the beginning, he saw a lot of action in France, but he was captured in 1943 and spent the next year in a German POW camp. In 1944 he escaped, and that's when he was wounded. He spent the rest of the war in hospital.'

Lena could hear the pride in his voice, and a note of something else too, belligerence perhaps. Many people saw those who fought alongside the British against the Germans as traitors to Ireland, but she wasn't one of them. Watching the horrific Movietone clips of the refugees in Europe, emaciated, barely human creatures, she felt ashamed that her country did so little to help. She understood the argument: Ireland had been under British rule for eight centuries and was never going to ally with Britain in the infancy of her independence, but still, Hitler had to be stopped and Ireland hadn't done as much as it could.

'You must be very proud of him,' she said.

'I am, actually.' Malachy glanced at her as he drove, a smile of relief on his face that she wasn't going to say anything derogatory. 'I wish I knew more, but he doesn't tell me any of the details, not even what camp or hospital he was in. It was all very traumatic for him.'

Lena nodded. 'I know. Doc – Doctor Dolan, he's my godfather – he was over in England during the war. He was working in a Cardiff hospital, and he saw things there he never talks about either. So what happened to your father after that?'

'Nothing really. My mother never knew what became of him. His work was with the Resistance, so he couldn't make contact. As far as she was concerned, he went back to Alsace to check on his parents after the fall of France, and she never heard from him again. It wasn't until he got out of hospital in 1946 and came back to Ireland that she knew he'd even survived.'

Lena remembered something she'd learned in school about that part of France. 'Is that Alsace-Lorraine? Isn't that disputed territory or something?'

Malachy nodded. 'It was originally French, then the Germans annexed it in the 1870s. The French got it back after the Great War, then the Germans invaded in 1939 and took it back again, and with the fall of the Nazis, it became French again. My father's family are French, so are Phillippe Decker's, but it's a complicated place, it seems. I wasn't ever there, but I could imagine it would be a place with lots of bad feelings, given their history. Decker certainly embodies that anyway.'

Lena threw Malachy a glance, wondering why he said the name with a touch of venom.

Malachy was driving and seemingly didn't notice her unspoken question. He carried on. 'Anyway, my father was desperate to get back to her. They'd met in Dublin as art students. His parents were wine dealers on the French-German border, and he was supposed to be going into the family trade. He and Mam met and fell in love and got married, but then war broke out and he rushed back to France. I suppose he told her he wanted to check on my grandparents so she would let him go, but he joined up when he got there, and somehow they lost touch. I suppose it was chaotic over there or something – I don't know. As I say, he never talks about it. He looked everywhere in Dublin for her after the war, and then a friend of hers told him she'd moved back to Kilteegan Bridge to look after her widowed father. And when he finally got here, he found out that he had a five-year-old son.'

Lena's heart nearly burst with the romance of it all. 'Your mother must have been so happy when he appeared like that, out of the blue.'

'She was. She'd been sure he was dead when she didn't hear from him for all that time. They never worked out why all their letters had gone astray, but that's the way it was then.'

'What was that like, to meet the father you thought was dead?'

'It was strange at first, especially as he was in a wheelchair and his English wasn't good at all. He mostly spoke French and also the German he'd learned in the POW camp. He'd forgotten the English he learned when he came to Dublin. Phillippe was in the camp with him, and they speak both languages to each other. But my father's English is very good now, and he always speaks English to me.'

'So you get on with him well?'

He shrugged. 'He's a private man, and I've spent a lot of time away from home. I was sent to boarding school when I was seven, not long after he got back. But we've become closer in the last three years, I think. When my mother died, it was only him and me left.'

'I'm so sorry about your mam. Were you close to her?'

He nodded. 'Very.'

'Was she sick before she died?' she asked, then thought perhaps she was prying. 'I'm sorry if you think I'm being nosy.'

He smiled. 'No, it's all right. I know you're not. No, she seemed fine, taking care of my father and me – well, I was away at school, but in the holidays. I remember the last time I saw her was Christmas, a few months before she died. I went back a bit early to school because we were playing the Junior Challenge Cup Final. She drove me back, we had lunch in town, and she was happy. Happier than I'd ever seen her, to be honest. Then the next time I saw her, she was in her coffin.'

'Oh, Malachy.'

His knuckles were white on the steering wheel. 'That idiot Phillippe found her body in the orchard and carried her into the house and laid her on the sofa in the drawing room, right in front of my father, without any warning. My father had a fit of some kind, shock, I suppose, so Doctor Dolan was called.'

'Your poor father.'

Malachy braked suddenly to let a farmer take his herd of cattle across the road. He took a deep breath, then smiled at her ruefully. 'I'm so sorry. I can't believe I'm telling you all this. It's not something I usually tell anyone.'

'You can tell me anything you like, honestly. I'm happy to listen.'

He relaxed and smiled gratefully. 'I've never met a girl I can talk to like you. Most girls are terrifying, to be honest, and I'm a bit of an eejit. I go to an all-boys boarding school and haven't a clue what to say to women, but you're not like a woman...' He smacked his forehead with his palm. 'I don't mean you're not like a woman – you're gorgeous, like Audrey Hepburn. I mean you're not scary...'

'Well, I'm not exactly experienced myself in the fella department. The array of potential suitors on offer in Kilteegan Bridge isn't exactly enticing, and I never get to go anywhere else.'

'Well, it was my lucky night when you showed up in the Lilac. I never go there, but Donal Lamkin – you know, Professor Lamkin's son? A right clown, truth be told, but I have no other friends here and he goes to my school, so I know him. Anyway, Donal had his eye on a girl from Ballineen, so he convinced me to go with him to see if he could – his words, not mine – 'trap her'.

'And did he?' Lena grinned.

'He did, in his eye.' Malachy laughed at the idea. 'She has all her teeth and hair and looks nice and normal, and Donal looks like the love child of a hairy mammoth and a witch, so she took one look at him and bolted back for her friends. Honestly his teeth are like tombstones, and the fact that he had a dribble of egg down his tie didn't help. He decided to abandon me and drown his sorrows in the back of some old shebeen up the road. I was heading home when I saw you.'

Lena laughed. She knew the professor's son from dances past, and he was exactly as Malachy described. 'Well, I went with my friend Jenny, but she's going to Australia to work in nursing on Saturday – her aunt is matron of a big hospital there. So I'll be friendless in Kilteegan Bridge too.'

'Maybe we can be friendless together?' He winked.

'Maybe we can.' Lena felt a fizz of excitement.

He slapped the steering wheel cheerfully. 'It looks like we're hitting the bright lights of Cork City. Let's talk about what we want for lunch.'

She was almost disappointed. The drive had flown by. His car was so warm and comfortable; she felt like she would be happy to stay in it, driving and talking with Malachy, all day. 'I don't know Cork at all. You choose.'

'There's a gorgeous chipper up behind the college, Jackie Lennox's. How about we get some fish and chips and drive to the Lough? It's only a mile or two that way, and we can sit in the car and eat our chips and watch the swans and the ducks and keep on talking?'

She smiled and he instantly coloured.

'Or maybe you'd prefer a restaurant? Sorry, I

wasn't thinking. Of course, who'd want to eat chips in a car, for God's sake… Sorry…'

'I love chips, and I can't think of anything I'd rather do than watch ducks while eating chips in your gorgeous car,' she said reassuringly. 'It's the nicest car in Kilteegan Bridge, that's for sure.'

'My father bought it for me. He says Volkswagen are the best cars, and he even got them to put a Bosch radio in it. Even if he fought against them, he's a great admirer of German engineering.'

'Well, their technology certainly wreaked enough havoc, I suppose.'

'Are you sure you wouldn't rather something better? A nicer restaurant? I'm mortified…'

'Quite sure. And then we'll both stink of vinegar and chips and we'll be happy as Larry.'

He grinned at her. 'You're great, Lena, you know that? There's no one I'd rather have stinking of vinegar beside me.'

They drove up the narrow streets of the medieval city of Cork, squeezing around the corners. Whoever created the streets in the seventh century never imagined all the cars and buses, only horses and carts and carriages. The western area of the city around the university was full of student accommodation, cafés and corner shops.

It all felt so exotic and exciting, so different from the farm and Kilteegan Bridge.

Malachy pulled up outside the famous Lennox's and ordered her to stay where she was. 'You relax and I'll get whatever you want.'

'Fish and chips would be lovely.'

'Mushy peas?' he asked. 'Don't say I don't know how to show a girl a good time.'

She laughed. He was a lovely combination of cheeky and vulnerable, and she was loving it. 'All right, Romeo, I'll have mushy peas too, and a bottle of orange too please.' It was nice to be waited on.

'You're pushing your luck now, but I'm under your spell.' He leaned over, kissed her cheek and was gone.

She sat back in the warmth of his car and watched as he darted across the road and went into the chip shop. It was true what she'd said to him – she had no interest in the local boys. Daddy always said that she had ideas above Kilteegan Bridge, and he was right. Blackie Crean was all right, she supposed, but Emily could do much better; she was clever and beautiful and talented. Yet all Emily seemed to want was a nice, happy, peaceful life and a house full of babies in the same

76

village she'd lived in all of her life. Lena couldn't think of anything worse. She wanted to travel, to have experiences, to meet interesting people.

And Malachy Berger was certainly more interesting than the boys who hung around outside the garage every evening, or propped up the bar in the Donkey's Ears.

As he crossed back to the car carrying a steaming parcel wrapped in newspaper, she admired his athletic gait – he was muscular but lithe. He pulled the car door open and sat in. The aroma of salt and vinegar chips filled the car immediately.

'They use the best local spuds in there and cut them lovely and thick.' He plopped the steaming parcel on her lap. Under the outer packaging of newspaper, the fish and chips were wrapped in plain paper, which she thoroughly approved of. In the chipper in Bandon, they only used cheap newspaper, and the ink mixed in with the hot fat, making the chips look grey.

They drove for a few minutes until they came to the small lake in the centre of a suburban area just behind the college. Ducks, geese, swans and moorhens all waddled about in the spring sunshine. It was a warm evening, so there were lots of human families around as well, their little children throwing crusts to the birds.

They opened the chips and began their feast. It was delicious, and Lena sighed contentedly after taking a gulp of the fizzy orange to wash down the salty battered fish, then dug into her huge portion of golden fried potatoes. 'This is wonderful. Thanks.'

'My pleasure. So I've wittered on and on about me. What about you? What's your family like?'

Lena sighed inwardly. She didn't want to spoil the day by talking about how her mother was at St Catherine's, that Deirdre Madden on the next farm looked after the twins and that Jack was having to milk every cow himself because her left hand was too sore to use. Perhaps it was safer to talk about Emily.

'Well, my sister Emily is living here in Cork at the moment. She's doing a bookkeeping course to be ready for when she gets married.'

Malachy cast her a quizzical glance, and she laughed. 'Sorry, I know that sounds weird. It's just she's doing a line with Blackie Crean for years – you know, from the hardware shop? I'd say there'll be a ring there soon, and then they'll take over the shop from his mother. And while Blackie's great with the customers and knows everything about hardware and stuff, he's not the best with the sums.'

Malachy raised his eyebrows at her. 'Are you worried Blackie Crean isn't good enough for your sister?'

Lena hardly knew how to answer. In her opinion, Blackie Crean was nowhere near good enough for her sister, but that was a secret she kept deep in her own heart and had never shared with anyone. How did Malachy guess what she was thinking? 'That's a strange question,' she said evasively.

'Well, I just mean Emily is such a clever girl from what I remember from primary school. She sat in front of me in first class, before I was sent boarding, and I remember her as a very sweet soul. And the Creans are a bit, well, a bit rough around the edges.'

Lena relaxed and chuckled; she knew what he meant. Dick Crean was a devious snake of a man, but he took off for England about five years ago, allegedly to get work, though nobody had ever seen him lift a finger unless it was to lift a drink someone else paid for, and he hadn't been seen since, thank God. Before that, he would regularly go missing for months on end. Nobody had a clue where he went, but few cared. He was always on the lookout for a loan and wasn't above lifting another person's change off the bar counter. Lena remembered her father asking him once, most politely, to replace the ten-bob note he'd pocketed from the kitchen table on one of the few occasions he was in their house.

Blackie's older brother, Jingo, was cut from the same cloth. Black cat, black kitten, as her father used to say. He'd disappeared not long after his father; maybe they were together in England or somewhere. Poor Mrs Crean was devastated and mortified in equal measure by her husband and eldest son. She was decent and honest, and so, to be fair to him, was Blackie. They had a sister too, Joanne, but she married some fella from up the country and hadn't been seen for years either. Lena didn't blame her. If she'd had the misfortune to be born into the Crean family, she'd have hightailed it away as fast as lightning too.

'Ah, Blackie and his mother are nice. They're decent people. Jingo and the father are awful all right, but they're out of the picture. Mam went mad when she heard Emily and Blackie were close when they were about sixteen, but as I say, Blackie's nice.'

'What's his real name?'

'Would you believe I've no idea? Even the mother calls her sons Jingo and Blackie.'

'But why those names?'

'Well, Jingo... My Dad said it was because when he was born, Dick was in the Donkey's Ears of course, like always. He always put on a slightly British twang to his voice, and when he was told the news he had a son, he was leaning on the bar at the time, he just said, "By jingo!" and got the barman to give him a free drink on the strength of it. And Emily thinks Blackie is called Blackie because he was reared in the back of the hard-ware shop with all the coal, so he was always filthy.'

'And is he still black with dirt?' Malachy chuckled.

'Ah, Emily is after making a great job of him. In all fairness, he's clean as a whistle these days, but you know Kilteegan Bridge – once Blackie, always Blackie.'

Malachy licked chip fat from his fingers. 'I'm glad for her if she's happy. I always liked Emily.'

Lena nodded enthusiastically. 'She's honestly one of the nicest people I've ever met, and that's weird coming from a sister, I know, but she really cares for us, me and Jack and the twins. Especially the twins actually. She's kind of like a mother to them. She's always been that way, ever since she was little.'

'Well, she spared me getting slapped with the ruler by Sister Kevin more than once, so I'm forever in her debt. So are you close to your mother?'

The way he'd spoken so candidly to her about his own parents made her toy with the idea of telling him all about Maria, but something stopped her. Not that she didn't trust him, she did, but this precious time with him was for her and her alone. It was somewhere she didn't need to deal with her daily life, and she preferred to keep it that way.

'Yes. You know, all mothers drive you nuts, but generally yes.' Something about her tone must have shut him down, so they sat in silence for a few minutes watching a man push a child on the swing while his wife tried to ensure a toddler didn't fall into the lake while feeding the ducks.

Malachy took a sip of his milk; his upper lip had a white moustache. 'So tell me what it's like working for Doctor Dolan? Is he a terrible tyrant?'

She was grateful to him for changing the subject. 'He is not – he's lovely. But I thought you'd know that. Everyone loves Doc. Have you never been to him at all?'

'Not really. My boarding school has its own doctor, and I've never needed to go to one in this neck of the woods.'

'But your father must use him?' Then as soon as she said it, she realised she'd never noticed Auguste Berger on the list of Doc's patients, nor Phillippe Decker. 'Oh, does he go to someone else?'

'He does now. That one in Kellstown. I don't think much of him, to be honest, but Dad never wanted to use Doctor Dolan after Mam died and he had that turn. He seemed to set against him after that, I don't know why.'

Lena felt a rush of defensiveness on Doc's behalf. 'Well, Doc's great, and to tell the truth, a lot of the people from Kellstown come to Kilteegan Bridge to see him rather than their own doctor. He's my dad's best friend. I mean, they *were* friends since they were in baby infants together. Daddy was determined to go farming, though Doc says he had the brains to do whatever he wanted, and Doc came up here and went to college to become a doctor like his father before him. They stayed very close, so he's my boss but also he's my godfather...'

Malachy was looking at her with a worried expression. 'I'm sorry. I didn't mean to say anything bad about your godfather – I'm sure he's great.' He smiled ruefully. 'I love my dad, don't get me wrong, and he's been a great father, inasmuch as he could be, but…sometimes he's a bit…I don't know…prickly or something. He gets into dark moods, and then, well, it's best just to leave him. After my mother died, he didn't speak for months – he just couldn't. So I'm sorry. I don't know why he took against your godfather, but I'm sure it wasn't Doc's fault. I was just babbling on without thinking. Dad says I take after my mother like that.'

'It's OK. I like you babbling on,' she said, and he smiled at her, cautiously.

They finished the chips, and Malachy rolled up the paper and deposited it in a bin beside the little lake, then sat back in. Lena hoped the intimacy of the moment wasn't lost.

When he next spoke, his brow was furrowed, as if he was struggling to find the words. 'Look, I'm sorry how I keep on and on turning the conversation back to my mother. I mean, you lost your father only three years ago. What a terrible thing to happen.'

She sighed. 'Yeah, it really was. It was Jack that found him, because he heard Thirteen howling.'

'Thirteen?' Malachy asked, perplexed.

'My dad's dog. Well, Jack's dog now. Her full name is Thirteen of Diamonds – that's the horse that won the Irish Derby a few years ago. Dad won her as a puppy in a game of cards the day of the race, and so he called her after the winner. He hardly ever went to the pub, but he liked to have a flutter once a year or so and always bet a few bob on the Derby.' She smiled at the memory.

He nodded. 'Mam spoke a lot about your father actually, how kind and funny he was. Sometimes the loneliness got her down, you see. She was really lively, and I suppose life was a bit dull with my father's disability and Phillippe never bothering to talk to her except to give her instructions about what my father needed. She said to me how lucky she was to have someone reliable around the place like your dad, to keep her company and make her laugh.'

Lena felt a glow of pride for her father. Mrs Berger was right – Paudie O'Sullivan was kind, and he was one of those people who others relied on, went to for advice or help, and he did make people laugh with his dry wit. The whole village was devastated at his death. But as quick, another memory surfaced – one of her mother accusing Daddy of having something going on with Mrs Berger and Daddy telling her he was just working there, and then the two of them dancing in the kitchen.

Lena buried that memory and smiled. 'Your mother was fun too. She was always smiling or singing or making a joke. She often gave me and Jack toffees. Scots Clan, I always remember.'

He smiled. 'She used to order them by the box. I can't eat them any more – it makes me too sad.'

Lena understood perfectly. The pain of loss was sometimes still sharp, the small things, like the taste of a sweet or a smell, bringing much more poignant memories than the big things, like anniversaries or birthdays. 'I know what you mean. I can't smell a pipe without being trans-ported back to sitting on my dad's lap when I was small, him reading us a story by the fire, his pipe in his mouth. He stopped smoking years ago. Doc told him his chest was suffering, so he stopped, but he kept a pipe and used to clean it and fill it with new tobacco every so often – I think he missed the ritual as much as the actual smoking. So if I pass someone smoking a pipe, I get an al-most crushing wave of sadness.'

'I know, and it's nice to be with someone who

gets it.' Malachy placed his hand on hers, resting on her knee.

Lena nodded and willed back the tears. It was hard to imagine they were both gone now, Hannah Berger and Daddy. It was something deep she and Malachy had in common. He understood what it was like to lose a parent you loved, and to have your other parent driven half mad by the loss.

He touched her cheek, brushing away a single tear. 'OK, enough of the past. Let's cheer you up. What will we do now? A bit of trainspotting? Or I could take you to see the under eleven Cork Con rugby team playing Highfield? I mean, I'm pushing the boat out in the excitement stakes already, so...' He laughed. She found she liked the sound of it, and her heart lifted.

'I'm a cheap date.' She winked. 'A spin and a bag of chips and I'm happy.'

'Well, considering I'm skint most of the time, that's music to my ears,' Malachy replied as he reversed the car out of the space.

'Ah, but you won't be always, so maybe that's why I'm willing to slum it with chips and spins,' she teased.

'That's true. Stick with me, kid.' He did a terrible impression of Groucho Marx chewing his cigar.

She laughed. 'I hope you're planning to be an architect or an engineer or something, because if a career on the stage was your plan, you might need a rethink, and I might need to look again.'

He stopped to allow a group of elderly ladies cross the street and turned to her. 'Please don't look again.'

They navigated back through the narrow city streets, and he turned the car radio on. As the afternoon was giving way to dusk, he reached over and took her hand, leaving only one hand on the wheel. A song began, and as Al Jolson's voice filled the car, Malachy sang along in a rich baritone.

'I loved you as I've never loved before, since first I saw you on the village green. Come to me ere. My dream of love is o'er. I love you as I loved you, when you were sweet, when you were sweet sixteen...'

'My dad loved that song,' Lena said dreamily. 'He used to sing it while he was dancing with my mother around the kitchen. He loved Al Jolson anyway, but that was his favourite.'

'It's mine too,' Malachy said softly.

CHAPTER 7

*A*uguste Berger gazed out the window, though all he could see was the black night. He preferred to look out at night; during the day was too sad, too poignant a reminder of all he had lost. He didn't want to see his wife's garden, to remember her there, pruning her roses or playing with Malachy when he was a child.

He'd met her in Dublin in 1937. His parents had indulged his whim and allowed him to study at the Irish National College of Art. They were convinced another war was coming, and they advised him to emphasise his French rather than his German heritage when he travelled.

Hannah had been an art student too, a vibrant beauty with flying chestnut hair and the greenest eyes he'd ever seen, and she was delighted with him – a suave, elegant Frenchman with cosmopolitan tastes and a knowledge of wine.

One night, as he and Hannah lay in bed, the sheets tangled around their naked bodies, he listened as she expressed her horror at the news out of Germany, so he'd told her that before coming to Ireland, he'd had a fight with a man who had bad-mouthed the Jews and said Hitler should kill them all. She'd wrapped her arms and legs around him and said she was proud of him. She said she loved her brave Frenchman. And he simply adored her. He was intoxicated by her, insatiable, and the idea of another man ever looking at her, or touching her made the blood pound in his ears. Even now, all these years later, he tried and failed to block that image, his lovely Hannah, in the arms of another man.

Six months after they met, they were married. A rushed, romantic affair. Her mother was dead, her father too old to travel from Cork where she was from, so they married in the Catholic Church in Rather, near her digs in Dublin. The priest was given to understand, incorrectly of course, that a baby was on the way and, being a good French Catholic boy, Auguste was going to do the right thing. He didn't have his baptismal certificate on account of never having been baptised, but he forged a letter from 'Père Emmanuel' in Colmar, knowing the doddery old Irish cleric was never going to discover the whole thing was a work of fiction. Two years of married bliss was shattered by his decision to leave Hannah and return to Alsace-Lorraine, ostensibly to make sure his parents were safe, but in reality to fulfil his destiny as an officer of the Third Reich.

Hannah understood but was heartbroken. Leaving her was the hardest thing he'd ever done, and he promised to return as soon as he could, but his country needed him.

Maybe it would have been better if he's never gone back, things would have worked out better, but it was too late for all of that now.

He gazed into the clear night, barely able to make out the dark glints on the ocean in the distance.

Malachy was still out with that girl. The later they stayed out, the better. He was glad his boy was successful with the ladies. He was a fine-looking lad with a warm personality like his mother. *Let him sow his wild oats, and let him ruin Lena O'Sullivan in the process.*

It had been one of the strangest moments of his life when Malachy brought that girl home with him after the dance. There she sat, in her yellow silk dress and red shoes, grinning at his son like the cat that got the cream. Like she had every right to be there. What was that saying in English? A cat can look at a queen or something? Hannah used to read that book to Malachy, *Alice's Adventures in Wonderland*. They were in the middle of it when he came home from the war.

He tried to block out the image of his son looking back at Lena the same way. It had sent a shiver up his shattered spine. He'd seen that look before, between an O'Sullivan and a Berger. And the worst of it was how much the children looked like their dead parents – the O'Sullivan girl with her father's hair, the colour of chocolate, and bur-nished copper skin, so unusual in Ireland, and his son with Hannah's auburn locks and grass-green eyes.

That was what had given him the idea. Re-venge, as they said, was a dish best served cold. But now was the time to serve it. He might not have long to live. That quack from Kellstown had visited last week and told him that his heart was failing and there was nothing he could do about it. Auguste Berger didn't trust the Kellstown doc-tor; he'd rather have the local man's opinion. But he couldn't go to Dolan, not after the day Hannah

died and he'd had that turn. Auguste had no recollection of it, but Phillippe said Dolan had given
him an injection in the upper arm and had seen
the scar. Dolan had flinched before continuing
with his work, and Phillippe seemed sure that
he'd guessed the truth. How a rural Irish doctor
had recognised the significance of the burn mark,
he had no idea, but it was too much of a risk to
associate with him any more after that.

Afterwards, Auguste had waited for weeks for
a knock on the door, but it never came. He supposed he should be grateful to Emmet Dolan for
that, for respecting doctor-patient confidential-
ity. Or perhaps he had no idea. Either way, Auguste knew he had to keep his distance.

Still, the episode had left him stuck with this
quack from Kellstown, who said he couldn't do
anything about Auguste's heart. Though that was
a relief, really. This life would soon be over and
good riddance.

He wondered dispassionately about what happened next. He didn't much care about it either
way. If Père Joel from his school was right and
some kind of heaven was going to be waiting for
him, and Hannah would be there, and all those
who went before them too, that might be nice,
but he doubted if the rationale in which he was

raised was correct, that the good go to heaven and the rest don't. Well, in that case he wasn't going anywhere near heaven. So perhaps his natural tendency towards atheism was a better option. You died, your heart stopped, and that was that. Just like before birth – nothing.

Yes, the more he thought about it, the more he liked that idea. The alternative was not just unlikely but also rather frightening. *Yes, best leave it at nothing. Peaceful emptiness. No existence. Fine.*

He'd done what he needed to do on this earth, more than enough. He'd played his part. Malachy's education, that was paid for. And when his son had finished school and college, he would be wealthy, because the rare wines that Auguste's parents had stored in the hidden cellar would be worth a lot of money if sold through the right dealers. And this house, he'd promised that he would leave it to Phillippe, for saving his life and serving him faithfully all these years. Though some could argue Decker's action was simply a repayment of a debt from another time, another place. No matter now.

His mind wandered to their long friendship. Both Auguste and Phillippe had been born in the village of Éguisheim, just a few kilometres from the the beautiful historic town of Colmar in the

Alsace-Lorraine region, where the half-panelled medieval shops and houses were beautifully painted and the fountain in the town square was decorated with flowers. Yet as boys they were socially miles apart. Phillippe's parents were of modest means, his father the town *patissier*, whereas Auguste's were wealthy and well-regarded German wine dealers who had moved to the area before Auguste was born. There was in the 1920's a growing realisation that the Alsace Crément, a naturally sparkling wine, was equal to that from the Champagne region. They sourced that, as well as the delicious Pinot Gris, Muscats and Reislings for discerning clients all over Europe and even America. There was nothing they didn't know about wine. And he was their pride and joy.

He'd been August then, of course; the 'e' he added to recreate his French persona here after the war. Easy when you knew how.

Despite the disparity of class, he and Phillippe became friends at school. August's father was for sending his only son to an exclusive boarding school back in Germany, but his *mutti*, bless her heart, couldn't bear the thought, so he was sent to the village school with the winemaker's and shopkeepers' children. Even from that early age,

Phillippe was never seen without his friend August.

He was a handy friend to have on your side, built like a Breton – small and stocky, but he could bend a steel bar if he wanted to – coarse dark hair, olive skin, brown eyes, bulging muscles.

They had stuck together through thick and thin, and goodness knows there were some dangerous situations over the years.

Without his faithful Phillippe, he would have died that winter's night in the very end of 1944.

He was dining with fellow members of the Waffen SS in a splendid chateau high in the Vosges Mountains when the French Resistance burst in, no doubt emboldened by the advancing Allied armies who were encircling the rag-tag and exhausted remains of the army of the Third Reich. The officers, drunk on commandeered wine, and drinking like men with nothing left to lose, were too slow to react and were shot where they sat, but Phillippe, who rarely drank alcohol, killed every one of the attackers, three boys and one girl. Although not before the girl had fired her gun at Auguste, shattering his spine.

He'd been in such pain, he'd begged Phillippe to let him die, but instead the faithful man had carried him, slung across his shoulders, for miles and got him to a hospital in Strasbourg, where the German doctors saved his life. By then the Americans and French were driving the Germans back to the Rhine, the new world they had fought for was crumbling, and the Reich that should have stood for a thousand years was nothing but a broken dream.

Eastern France was in complete chaos by February of 1945, German soldiers on the run, many rounded up and placed in prisoner of war camps, refugees everywhere, the last stand of the Reich in Colmar, proved fruitless as the last German soldier was driven across the bridge over the Rhine on the 6th of March, but they went the other way. Against all the odds, Phillippe had got him to Brittany. They stole peasant clothes, stopped shaving and grew their hair. Their French was that of a native speaker, and they were able to disguise their Alsatian accents so they were accepted. Everyone was willing to give food and lifts to the two men from the Resistance, the brave fighter and his paralysed comrade.

A man with a branding iron and a bottle of whiskey, behind a brothel in Reims one wet night, made sure their blood group tattoos, sported by every member of the Waffen-SS, was obliterated from their arms.

It hadn't been very smart of Hitler's elite to mark themselves so indelibly. After the defeat, they all tried to get rid of it in many ways – cutting the skin, covering the mark with other tattoos. Phillippe had his tattooed over with an image of a woman. One man he knew had even shot himself in the arm. Auguste had been confident about the burn, so Phillippe saying Dolan recognised it for what it was made him uneasy.

That was the fate of his brothers in arms, to be looked at with disgust by unimportant little men like the Irish country doctor. But he had no regrets. There was no dispute in his mind that Hitler had the right idea, and as a young Alsatian back in 1939, he'd known where his loyalties lay. Time had dissolved his ardour; he couldn't care less now. Still, it was a pity the experiment hadn't worked. They'd come so close.

He glanced at the clock. 10 p.m. Phillippe would be up shortly to help get him to bed. The same rituals morning and evening, washing, changing clothes. If someone had told him years ago that a man would do the most intimate personal care tasks for him daily, he would have said he'd rather be dead, but actually it was all right.

Phillippe had a way of making him feel like it wasn't anything more than making a cup of tea or handing him the paper. He was strong as an ox, so lifting a paralysed man didn't strain him, which made Auguste feel less of a burden. It was routine and easy.

He entered the room quietly, as he always did. '*Bonsoir*. Are you ready?'

'Yes, thank you.'

With no fuss, Phillippe lifted Auguste and carried him to his bedroom on the ground floor. It had once been a drawing room, but it had been converted and adapted to Auguste's needs. They didn't converse as Phillippe undressed him and then put his pyjamas on. He needed to be brought to and from the bathroom, but thankful for small mercies, he could manage that alone at least.

After he was settled in for the night, Phillippe asked, 'Will you read or will I put the light out?'

There was a biography of Wagner on his bedside table.

'I'll read, I think. But, Phillippe...'

The man turned back to him. 'A glass of water?'

'No, no. I just wanted to let you know I've spoken to my solicitor and everything is in place. Malachy's education is taken care of, and this house is bequeathed to you. A copy of my will is in my desk, please take it for your own records.'

Phillippe nodded. '*Merci*.'

'You won't have long to wait.' Auguste settled back against his pillows.

'There is one thing you should know,' Phillippe said as he gathered some dirty cups.

Auguste raised his eyes. 'Yes?'

'Malachy has been maintaining contact with that girl.'

'He's a young man, Phillippe. He's allowed.'

'Her name is Lena O'Sullivan,' said the Frenchman, like he thought Auguste might have forgotten this vital piece of information.

Auguste smiled. 'I know, Phillippe. He brought her here one night after they met at a dance. I couldn't sleep so I got up.'

Phillippe looked at him quizzically.

'She is the daughter of the man with whom my wife was in love? The man she killed herself over? It's obvious – she looks every inch her father's child.'

Phillippe looked bemused. He knew how much Auguste despised Paudie O'Sullivan.

'You recall that night? The night I confronted her?' August asked his old friend.

Philippe nodded but already it was playing like a grotesque film in his mind. Never changing.

'Don't you love me?' Auguste had asked. 'Have you never loved me?'

She'd gazed at him in pity. Her pity was far worse than the disgust he'd seen days later in Doctor Dolan's eyes.

'I did love you, Auguste. You were everything to me when we were young and in Dublin, but I thought you were dead for years. I wrote and tried to contact you, but I never heard a thing. And then, when you came back...' She paused and hesitated to say it, but he urged her with his eyes. 'You were different.'

'In a wheelchair, you mean,' he said bitterly.

'Yes, but not just that. I could have coped with that. It's...the way you are *inside*. So dark and silent and sad and...and...*complicated*. I never know what you're thinking.'

'Unlike your simple Irishman?' he'd sneered sarcastically.

'Auguste, don't. I can't help loving Paudie, and he loves me, I'm sure he does. But he's so loyal to his family...'

'Or maybe he loves his wife?'

'She's not well, not right in the head. He feels responsible for her, but that's not love.'

'I suppose that's why she's pregnant again,' he'd jeered.

'Don't be ridiculous, of course she's not.' The certainty of Hannah's words were betrayed by the tremor in her voice. She knew he was telling the truth, that O'Sullivan's wife was pregnant.

He'd turned then to Phillippe, lurking in the shadows. 'It's true, is it not, Phillippe?'

'*Oui*, yes, it is true.'

She'd wailed with shock and ran from the room. He'd panicked and called her back, rolling himself in her wake, begging, grovelling for her love. If he'd not been a useless cripple in a wheelchair, he would have caught up to her and gone down on his knees to her. He cringed now at the thought of that pathetic display. And it was all pointless.

'I do remember August.' Phillippe said quietly.

It was Phillippe who cut Hannah down from the tree the following Sunday. She'd gone to Mass to see for herself if O'Sullivan's wife was indeed pregnant. Then, armed with the knowledge, his lovely Hannah had come home and tied a leather strap round her neck. Phillippe was in the yard so saw her first, and he ran and cut her down, but it was too late.

Now, back in the room, he quoted, '"You shall

not bow down to them or worship them; for I, the Lord your God, am a jealous God, punishing the children for the sin of the parents to the third and fourth generation of those who hate me." Exodus, I believe.'

'So you mean to exact revenge on his child for what he did?'

'Precisely.'

'And your son?' Phillippe was hard to read; he always was. Auguste couldn't tell if there was judgement there or not.

'He's a good boy. He's young and he'll get over it, but she won't. Exacting my revenge on the daughter for the sins of her father – there's a kind of cold comfort in it.'

'But what if Malachy finds out and blames you?'

Auguste dismissed that thought with a wave of his hand. 'My son is superior in every way to her. She's just a worthless drudge he can use for practice before he goes to university and meets someone who is worthy of him. In the meantime, Phillippe, as you're here, I have another request.'

Phillippe nodded again. 'Of course.'

'Follow the girl everywhere. She's like her father, I'm sure, so I doubt Malachy is the only boy she's giving her favours to. Gather the evidence. Watch her and report back to me.'

'Certainly.' Phillippe withdrew.

Auguste Berger lay alone in bed, fully awake, gazing at the ceiling, eyes wide open.

CHAPTER 8

*E*mily looked at her incredulously. 'Malachy Berger?'

Lena nodded sheepishly.

They sat facing each other on their twin beds. It was Saturday, and Emily had been home from her bookkeeping course since last night. Maria was back from St Catherine's, and due to their care, she was calm and content. She was baking with the twins downstairs; the mouth-watering aroma of buns from the oven wafted up the stairs. Molly's high-pitched voice could be heard issuing bossy instructions to her sister. Jack was out on the farm – Thirteen on his heels, no doubt – re-pairing ditches.

'And you never said a word?'

'I don't know… It's not like we're doing anything wrong. We're two young single people and we make each other happy, but for some reason, I just don't want to tell anyone. I suppose I'm afraid that someone would try to stop us, or think I was having notions above my station – you know what this place is like.'

'I do,' Emily said miserably. The whole of Kilteegan Bridge, including Emily, thought Blackie Crean would produce the ring any day, but there was still no sign of it and Emily had been getting looks of pity or smug satisfaction from some people in the village.

'How's Blackie?' Lena asked tentatively.

'He's fine, and he does want to get engaged but…' Lena could hear the defensive tone in her sister's voice.

'But what?' Lena asked gently.

'Ah, nothing. It's complicated.' Emily looked miserable.

'Tell me. I told you about Malachy.'

'OK.' She sighed. 'But keep it to yourself, for God's sake. There's a problem with the shop.'

'But what does that have to do with you two getting married?' Lena thought Blackie was as dull as dishwater, and his pitiful mother was what the nuns used to call a 'God help us', but he was the man Emily wanted and Lena hated to see her sweet-tempered sister made a public show of like this. And it seemed so unromantic, the shop having to come before marriage. Even their own parents had run away to Gretna Green – it was a famous story their dad had loved to tell.

'Well, he wants us to be set up, you know, with a business. And now there's some legal thing about the ownership, something to do with his father and Jingo being the oldest son. The two of them wrote from England, complaining to the mother and wanting her to sell the shop and send them the money.'

Lena gasped. 'Can they do that?'

'I don't know if they can exactly.' Emily sighed again. 'I mean, it was her shop left to her by her own father, but Blackie has to see a solicitor to make sure it's all OK before we can get engaged.'

'I can't believe they want a piece of it, when it's Blackie and Mrs Crean are running that place for years. And let's call a spade a spade – it's not exactly Cash's above in Cork now, is it?' Lena exploded; this was too much. 'That Jingo is some waste of space, the big thick head up on him, and he below in the Donkey's Ears drinking his dole every week, and everyone around him watching their purses because everyone knows he's sticky-fingered. The whole town was relieved when he followed his father to England. He's got some cheek. And as for slimy old Dick, gone like the snows of last winter, leaving his poor wife, though what class of an eejit was she to marry him in the first place, I don't know. And he thinks he has a claim? A boot where the sun don't shine is what him and Jingo should both get.'

Emily looked shocked at Lena's outrage. 'Lena, stop! That's Blackie's family you're talking about, you know, my future in-laws.'

Lena couldn't help herself; all the things she wanted to say over the years came bubbling to the surface. Was her lovely sister really going to shackle herself to that crowd? 'Ah, Em, I know Blackie is a nice lad, he's fine, but he's definitely not the best you can do. He's nice, but let's be honest, he's fierce boring. And I know poor old Mrs Crean tries her best, but she gave her life slaving away in that shop for nothing, and I just want better for you. Look, I just hate the idea of you hitching your wagon to that shower of eejits. You're gorgeous and lovely and clever. You could have anyone! But you and Blackie are only together because you always have been, so please won't you reconsider?'

For a split second, Lena thought she might have got through to her sister, but as the tears pooled on Emily's lower lids and then spilled over, she knew she'd hurt her deeply.

'I thought you really liked him...' Emily whispered.

'I do, honestly, Em, I do. I think he's...' She fought to find a fair word; she couldn't go back on what she said now, but she didn't want to be cruel. 'He's grand, really fine, for someone else, but I just think you're too good for –'

'And if someone told Malachy Berger that he was too good for you, too well got to be with someone like you, what would you think?'

'I don't mean that, it's just –'

'You think Blackie isn't good enough, you said.'

Lena thought for a second. 'I don't think he's good enough for you, and that's the truth. Not because of what he has or hasn't got, or who his family are, though God knows there's plenty to worry about between Dick and Jingo Crean. But I think he's not good enough because I know – you've even said it to me – you don't get butter-flies in your tummy when you see him. He doesn't make you feel like you'd want to walk off into the sunset with him and never see any of us again.'

'And Malachy Berger does that for you, does he?'

Lena coloured. 'Well, yes, he does actually.'

Emily stared hard at her, then bounced to her feet and dragged on a thick woollen cardigan over her dress. Her green eyes blazed in fury and hurt.

'Well, do you know what you need to do now, Lena O'Sullivan? You need to grow up and realise what life is like in the real world. Malachy Berger's above in that boarding school finishing his fine education, and then he'll go to college. And just you watch – he'll find someone else, someone from the same class as him, with a boarding school education behind her and some fancy family, not a girl without a shilling to her name, her father dead, her mother suffering with her nerves, coming from a bit of a wild old farm on the side of a hill and a menial job in a doctor's office.'

Lena was stung to the quick. Emily had never spoken to her, or anyone, like this. 'It's not a menial job! And I'm trying to better myself. I'm planning to do a course to try to get into nursing when I've saved up some money, you know I am...'

'Yes, well, whatever you're doing, it doesn't give you the right to pour cold water all over my plans, my dreams.'

'And Blackie Crean is your dream man, your ideal husband?' Lena knew she was pushing it, but she was also sure she was right. 'And is running a dirty old hardware shop your idea of a life?'

'Blackie's kind and he's honest and he'll look after me and treat me right, so yes, that's exactly what I'm looking for in a husband,' Emily said with certainty. 'And we have great plans for the shop if we can make it our own – you just watch us, Lena O'Sullivan, you just watch.'

'All right, it's your life,' Lena said wearily. She had tried.

'Exactly, it is. And I know you think you're too good for this, but for the record, if you think people might imagine that you're getting notions of yourself, they'd be right.'

Emily stormed out of the room, leaving Lena feeling very sorry she'd said anything at all. Emily was so kind, and she should probably have trusted her judgement, but honestly, Blackie Crean?

She'd planned on spending the day with her sister, but clearly that wasn't going to happen.

She gave Emily a few minutes to cool off, then followed her downstairs. There was a plateful of freshly baked buns on the table, and she grabbed two of them hungrily, much to the twins' delight.

'They baked them all by themselves,' said Maria, beaming. 'And as a reward, I'm taking the Morris Minor to Clonakilty and we'll all go grocery shopping and I'm going to buy them some sweets.'

'Come too, Lena! Come too!' begged the twins, all excited, but Lena didn't feel like it now. She had hoped Emily might still be around and they could patch it up, but she seemed to be gone already. Probably marching down the hill into the village, rushing into the arms of that great big lump Blackie.

'It's OK. I'll stay here and help Jack,' she said.

But when she found him, he was spreading seaweed on a field. Thirteen was sniffing the seaweed and taking pieces out of a bucket and carrying them in her mouth to where Jack stood.

'Is that supposed to do something?' she asked grumpily.

Jack turned and smiled. 'It does actually. As the seaweed breaks down, it leaves microorganisms that plants can use. Myself and my assistant here' – he rubbed Thirteen's head – 'are nourishing the soil. We used this field for beet last year, and that's very hard on soil and it takes ages to replenish, but this helps that process. It stimulates new growth.'

'Really.' She tried to infuse her voice with enthusiasm but failed.

'Want to help? There's a bucket over there.' He nodded at the tractor.

'No thanks, my wrist is still sore.' It was a lie, her wrist was fine, but she didn't want to listen to Jack going on about soil rotation.

'No problem.' He smiled and gave Thirteen a scratch behind her ears, which she loved, before going back to collect more seaweed from the large barrel beside the tractor.

At a loose end, Lena decided she might as well go into work and collect the book she'd recently ordered for herself. She planned to take some pre-nursing exams. Doc had been so encouraging, and she really felt she might get a place in a hospital to train as a nurse if she did well. Malachy was like her, dying to travel, to see some of the world. Imagine if she was a qualified nurse and he was an engineer after college and they just took off for an adventure somewhere? It would be amazing. She knew she was getting ahead of herself. They'd only seen each other four times; the last two were a trip to the cinema in Cork and a dinner in Bandon. They were careful not to be seen by anyone in Kilteegan Bridge. Surely she couldn't be imagining that they were so right for each other, could she?

CHAPTER 9

The village was busy that Saturday morning, with the weekly market in full swing in the square outside the church. Stalls with vegetables, eggs, baking, tools, shoes, all kinds of everything really, were laid out. The butcher was doing the usual roaring trade, his windows decorated in red and white, with metal dividers between the various cuts on display. Lena thought she'd pop in and get Thirteen a bone on the way home.

The doctor's surgery was closed on a Saturday, but Doc would be all day out on home visits. She had a key so she could call in for the book, but she'd decided there was another stop she wanted to make first. She crossed the street and spotted Nettie Collins, the local librarian, admiring her display of romantic fiction in the window of the library.

Lena didn't need to seek romance in the pages of a novel, she thought smugly. Since she'd met Malachy, her whole life was a love story.

Crean's hardware was doing a brisk trade, the farmers and local men choosing to browse the saws and wellington boots over the fare on sale at the market. She lingered around outside for a while, but there was no sign of Emily. She hated being at odds with her sister and longed to patch things up.

Disappointed, she stopped to look in the window of Maureen's Fashions in the slim hope there was something in there that wouldn't make her look like an off-duty nun or an old-age pensioner. As she suspected, there wasn't. It was all pastel cardigans and sensible skirts. Yuck.

Further on, the Donkey's Ears was open and busy as always. Corny Collins, Nettie's brother, was sitting outside on a bench, with his greyhound at his feet, and he and Lena exchanged thirty seconds of small talk about the weather. A few minutes later, she was out the other side of the village and crossing the bridge over the River Shanovee that meandered through the farmlands and villages of West Cork before flowing into the Atlantic.

Lucky river, she thought as she walked on, *off to see the big wide world.*

The graveyard up the next hill was bright with spring daffodils. She climbed over the little stone stile rather than opening the iron gates and walked up the long path to the corner where her father lay, with its view of the sea. Most of the plots between her father's grave and the Berger family plot had been filled in in the last three years. She knew who was in each grave. There were four old people who had lived good lives, but there was a twelve-year-old boy who had succumbed to the measles and a woman who had died in childbirth. She said a prayer for each, then stood before her father's grave under the long-fingered leaves of the horse chestnut tree.

She always smiled when she saw her father's headstone. Daddy's real name was Patrick, after his grandfather, but he was called the Irish version, Pádraig, and that was shortened to Paudie when he was small. The undertaker had suggested it would look more dignified to put Patrick or even Pádraig on the headstone, but Mammy told him that her husband was known to all who loved him as Paudie and that's what would be on his grave.

Lena's eyes read the words, but her heart didn't need to.

Paudie O'Sullivan
1914–1955
Beloved husband and father
Ar dheis Dé go raibh a h-anam dílis

His soul is at God's right hand. She hoped the inscription was right. If anyone deserved eternal happiness, it was her dad. The phrase was simple and strong and powerful, exactly what her father was.

There were some dead flowers there. She figured Mam must have come up last weekend and left them, so she took them and put them in the bin. She pulled a few stray weeds from around the kerbing, then sat on the narrow kerbstone that marked the only bit of land that anyone needs in the end.

'Hi, Dad. I thought I'd come up to say hello.' She swallowed a lump in her throat. She missed him so much, even now – especially now. She was fighting with Emily, Malachy was lovely but maybe Emily was right and she was foolish to set her cap at someone like him, and Mam was good at the moment but they were always just waiting for the next episode.

'I had a fight with Emily. I told her that Blackie Crean wasn't good enough for her, so she's really cross with me. And I've gone out a few times with Malachy Berger – remember him? Maria hit me when I told her I was dancing with him at the Lilac, and I remembered how she got it into her head that Hannah Berger was looking at you or something. It must have triggered that for her. And Em says I've notions of myself. I know it was just because she's upset, but maybe she's right – maybe I'm making a right eejit of myself. Jack's all right, but he hasn't a single friend except for Thirteen. He works and works, that's all, and falls asleep. Mam is worried about him, but you know how she goes about it all wrong. She tried to get him to go to the dance in the hall last week, but sure, Jack wouldn't go there in a fit. He got upset with her trying to force him. He came in from the yard, and she'd made him a new shirt and everything – you know how good she is at making clothes – but he wasn't having it. She looked heartbroken, and he just went off to his room like he always does. Molly and May are fine. I can't believe they never met you – it's so strange. But I'm sure you're looking down on them and you can see what great girls they are. May looks really like you, which means she looks like me, but they both have fair hair like Mam and Emily and Jack. The pair of them are obsessed with animals. We live in terror of them finding creatures to adopt. They had two field mice in a shoebox under the table the other night – one ran across my foot and I nearly had a heart attack.'

She looked up as a family came in the gate bearing flowers. She waited until they were gone further down the graveyard to resume talking.

'Em's really hoping Blackie will pop the question, but he can't because of Jingo and the father, it seems, though why she can't wait to tie herself for all eternity to that crowd of wasters, I'll never know. I couldn't think of anything worse, to be honest. Malachy is doing his Leaving in May, and I'm doing a pre-nursing course. If I get good enough marks, I could start nursing training, and Malachy's thinking of being an engineer. Maybe I'm jumping the gun – you know I always do – but it feels right, Dad. I can't explain it except that I feel like we fit together or something.' She sighed. It felt good to talk, and even if her father couldn't answer, she believed he was listening.

'I wonder what the future holds. Sometimes I just wish I could get away. Jack loves the farm, and Emily will be below in Crean's if that gom Blackie ever gets himself organised and puts a ring on her finger. But I have plans. I don't know what yet, but I want to see places, have experiences, you know? Not live and die in bloody Kilteegan Bridge.'

The creak of the gate caused her to look up again. The sun was on the horizon now so it was hard to see the man's face, but she instantly recognised the distinctive gait.

'Ah, 'tis yourself,' Doc said as he approached the grave.

'It is. I thought you were out with Mrs Doyle and JJ Barry all day?'

'I would have been, but I had to get an ambulance for JJ. He was savage with me, but he needs to be in hospital – that cut he got from the scythe is all infected and he needs intravenous antibiotics. He refused to go for poor old Margo, so she called me. She's a living saint, that woman, putting up with that cranky auld so-and-so.'

'And how's Mrs Doyle?' Lena knew the old lady had cancer and had been battling it for years.

Doc sighed. 'She's doing all right. We're managing the pain as best we can, but her heart is strong. To be honest, if she'd slip away now, t'would be for the best. Her poor daughter is run ragged, and that woman has no life now anyhow, but it's hard to die. People think they'll get a say in it, but we know not the day nor the hour.'

'Can she go to hospital?'

'She could, and they'd have her in the county home, no bother – I even checked and they have a bed – but Elsie promised her she'd die at home, and so that's what she wants to do. But people make all kinds of promises when things are all right that they can't fulfil afterwards when circumstances change, and they tie themselves in knots then trying to make the impossible happen.'

Lena felt a pang of sadness for her godfather. So much of what he did was kind of thankless, and he always tried his best, but people often didn't know what was best for them.

'Will I leave you to say a prayer?' she asked.

'Era, not at all. Myself and Paudie never did too much praying together over the years, so t'would be strange to start now. I just called in to say a quick hello to him – I always do when I'm passing.'

'I'm sure he's glad of it.' Lena smiled.

'I hope so,' said Doc sadly. 'It's hard to believe it's two years. Some days it feels like yesterday, and I think to myself, sure, I'll swing up to Paudie and we'll go for a pint or have a chat, and then other ways it feels like a lifetime since I saw him. Time is funny like that – it expands and contracts.'

They left the graveyard side by side. Doc's brown Ford Escort was parked at the gate. 'Can I give you a lift?'

'Have you eaten?' Lena asked, knowing the answer.

'Era, I had something this morning. I'm grand.'

'Come on then.' Lena climbed in the passenger door. 'I'm taking you to the Copper Kettle for lunch, no excuses.'

He looked amazed. 'Why would a gorgeous young woman like yourself be having lunch with this old codger on her day off instead of being off doing whatever it is gorgeous young ones do with themselves these days?'

'Because you know very well if I don't make you have lunch with me, you won't eat at all, and then you'll spend all evening poring over some dusty old medical journal while drinking a bottle of wine.'

He winced. 'You're a piece of work, Lena O'-Sullivan – your father always said it. I'm glad you're on my side and not against me.'

'Keep me sweet so, a pay rise wouldn't go astray.'

'Hm. We'll see about that.' He raised an eyebrow.

They took the last booth in the Copper Kettle, and Chrissy's daughter, Imelda, came over. When she saw it was Lena she had to deal with, she straightened her apron and smiled brightly. 'What would ye like to order?'

'I'll have the chicken salad sandwich, please, and a cup of tea and a piece of rhubarb crumble with cream. Doc?'

'I'll have a sausage roll and chips, please, and a coffee,' he said, handing Imelda back the menu. 'And sure, I'll have a bit of the crumble and cream for afters too. Thanks, Imelda.'

'You're welcome,' she said, with a glance at Lena for approval.

Lena winked at her. 'You're turning into a fine young waitress, Imelda. Well done.'

The fourteen-year-old flushed with pleasure as she scuttled away.

'Nice to see that young lady not scowling for once,' commented Doc, rolling up his cuffs. 'So what are your plans for the rest of the day, when you've finished forcing me to eat?'

'I was actually going to call in to the surgery for the book I ordered – I thought I might delight myself with the ups and downs of the lymphatic system – but it's after getting a bit late now. I'm going out later, to the pictures, so I'll be off home to get ready. Mam's made me another new dress, and I can't wait to give it an outing.'

'With Emily? I saw her this morning, washing the window of Crean's.'

'Was she?' Lena sighed. Maybe the reason she hadn't seen Emily outside the store earlier was that Emily had seen her coming and was hiding from her. 'Not with Emily, no. I've a date.'

'Well, well, well. Finally a fella good enough for you?'

'There are one or two in the world,' she replied archly. She remembered what Emily had said, about her acting aloof and a bit superior, but she wasn't. She just had bigger plans.

'And do I know this one?' Doc probed as their food arrived, delivered with another bright smile by Imelda. He ate slowly and sparingly. He never seemed hungry these days. Lena wondered if he had in fact had breakfast at all. Probably not.

'You do know him, I'm sure. It's Malachy Berger.'

Doc paused, and for a fleeting second a look passed his face, something she couldn't quite catch.

'What? What's wrong with him?' Lena was defensive now and regretting her confidence. Surely Doc wasn't like Emily. Surely he wasn't going to think Malachy was so far above her that she was wasting her time as well?

'Nothing, nothing at all...' Doc went back to his lunch, his head down.

'Well, clearly there's something wrong, so spit it out.'

He stopped and swallowed his food before looking at her. 'Is this your first date with him?'

'No. But he's not the King of Spain, you know. You'd swear he was Prince Charming and I was one of the ugly sisters, the way some people go on.'

'Some people?'

'Emily thinks he's too good for me, for one.'

'But you do like him?' Doc replied, and to Lena's shock, he didn't say anything about Emily being wrong.

'Yes. I'd hardly be going to the pictures with him if I didn't. Anyway, what's it to you?' Lena knew she had a tendency to belligerence, and that her jaw was set defiantly.

'Nothing, I just think...' Doc flushed; he actually looked upset. 'Look, I don't know, but Malachy Berger, I mean, he's hardly ever here, and once he goes to college...'

'He'll dump me for someone else, is it? He's just using me as a distraction while he's here? Thanks for the vote of confidence, Doc. Of course it's highly unlikely he actually likes me, I suppose?'

'Lena, Lena, that's not what I'm saying at all…'

'Then what are you saying exactly?'

'Oh, Lena, I don't know. His father is very strange. Unusual. Not the sort of man –'

She interrupted angrily. 'His father *likes* me actually. I suppose that's what makes him strange and unusual in Kilteegan Bridge, is it? That a rich man would like someone so far beneath him in station?'

'I don't think you're beneath him, Lena, quite the opposite. And I'm sure Malachy is a nice lad, I'm not saying he's not, but…'

'But what?' she demanded.

'I just don't think they're a good family for you to get involved with.'

'No wonder Auguste Berger doesn't like you or want you for his doctor,' she snapped. She pushed her untouched sandwich away and stood up, leaving Doc in the café alone.

CHAPTER 10

*L*ena fumed as she marched in a temper up the hill, sweat running down her back. First her mother, then Emily, then Doc. They were all just putting their own issues on her. Maria was insane, and she had a thing about the Bergers for some reason, totally unfounded of course. Emily was jealous, plain and simple, because Malachy was handsome and educated and going somewhere and Blackie had the personality of a dinner plate. And Doc, well, he was just like everyone else in Kilteegan Bridge, thinking everyone should keep to their own station in life and not get notions. Either that or he was in a huff because Malachy Berger's father chose the other doctor over him.

She was more shocked by her godfather's attitude than she was by Emily's, to be honest. She knew Doc had travelled the world as a young medic until he'd been forced to come home when old Doctor Dolan died. So it wasn't like he'd never set foot out of Kilteegan Bridge or never gone further than Cork for a couple of months, like Emily.

She stopped at the brow of the hill, where their farm began, and sat on a low wall looking down over their fields to the sea. If she tried hard, she could picture her father, with Thirteen at his heels, walking across this land. Her longing for him was like a physical pain, and unbidden, tears that had remained unshed until now flowed freely down her cheeks.

Dad would have understood. He would have liked Malachy and wished them well. He would never think Lena wasn't good enough for him.

She shivered; the sweat from the exertion of climbing the hill was now cooling on her skin. It was a bright clear day but a cold one. She should go home, get ready for seeing Malachy later; she'd already chosen her outfit. But all the good had been taken out of the evening now. She had nobody left to talk to.

She hated falling out with Emily. It was to

Emily she had gone when Bobby Langton was bullying her in primary school, or when she got her first period, or when she couldn't understand the Irish homework, or when she had not been asked to the dance in the town hall after the summer festival the year after she left school. Emily had always been there for her, in her corner, but now she wondered if that was all gone. She should never have said a word about Blackie – he was her sister's choice. She was filled with… not regret exactly, as her feelings on that match remained unchanged, but pain at hurting her sister. She should have kept her mouth shut. Her temper was too quick to erupt, she knew. On the other hand, she could never bear a grudge. She was always the one to seek the peace after a fight. Maybe if she found her sister and apologised, even if Emily was still angry with her, she'd feel better.

She should apologise to Doc too, she conceded, as her tears dried and the cold breeze cut through her coat. She shouldn't have walked out on him in the café. She didn't think Doc should have been so dismissive of her and Malachy, but she knew it came from a place of love. He was no replacement for her dad – nobody could ever be that – but he tried his best to be there for them all. He'd been a great godfather too, never forgetting her birthday or Christmas, and since they'd worked together, they'd developed an easy adult friendship.

She glanced at her watch. Almost three. She wasn't being collected by Malachy until six, so she had time to find them both, try to put it right. She would have a terrible night if she didn't. She heaved herself up and began the trek back down the hill.

She had to pass the surgery before she got to Blackie's shop. The light was on, so she let herself in. There was nobody downstairs, but Doc was obviously back – his coat was on the hallstand.

'Doc?' she called. There was silence, and for some reason she felt a stab of worry. The surgery, waiting room and old kitchen at the back were deserted, so she carried on up the stairs. In his bedroom, Doc sat with his head in his hands, looking very old and grey. 'Doc?'

He looked up with a start. 'Lena, you put the heart crossways in me. What are you doing here?'

'Doc, are you OK?'

'I am, of course.' He was smiling at her now. 'Have you come for your book? It's downstairs under the reception desk.'

'No, I didn't, I came back to apologise. I'm so

sorry for storming off – I shouldn't have done that. I was nearly home before I realised it, and I had to come and find you.'

'You came all the way back down the hill to say sorry to me?' He smiled again.

'Well, I hated that we fell out.'

He stood and put one arm around her shoulders, walking her back down the stairs to the reception. 'We'll never fall out, Lena, and for the record...'

'What?'

'Any man would be lucky to have you, so you must never imagine I'd think any boy was too good for you. I might think he's not good enough for my lovely goddaughter, but never the other way around. See, here's your book...'

She wasn't quite ready to let it go. 'Malachy's really nice to me, Doc, I promise.'

'I'm sure he is, and I've nothing against the lad, Lena. I'm sure he's a grand fella altogether. I'm just protective, I suppose. Your father isn't here to look out for you, and so I... I just want to do right by you, y'know?'

She reached up and kissed his cheek.

He blushed. 'What's that for?'

'Just to say thanks for looking out for me, and

even if it's not necessary for you to do it, it feels nice.'

She left him then, the book under her arm, and tripped up the street feeling lighter. The next moment, she saw her sister and Blackie walking hand in hand towards her, looking like they hadn't a care in the world, even though the precious hardware store that took all Blackie's time and energy was surely still open.

'Hi, Em,' she said sheepishly. 'Hi, Blackie.'

'Lena, how're things now?' he asked, a big beam on his face. Clearly Emily hadn't said anything.

'Grand. Yourself?'

'Grand altogether. Mam is doing a stock take, so she hunted us out of the shop, said we were in the middle of the way.'

'Ah great, where are you off to?' Lena was speaking to Blackie but made eye contact with her sister, who actually smiled at her – a bit awkwardly, but it was definitely a smile.

'We're treating ourselves to one of Chrissy's sticky buns and a cup of tea. Poor old Emily spent hours cleaning the windows, so she deserves it.'

'She certainly does,' Lena agreed, smiling back at her sister.

Moments later Blackie was accosted by a

farmer in such a disgustingly dung-encrusted jacket that the stink made Lena's eyes water, and with no preamble or small talk, he and Blackie fell deep in conversation about a treatment for sarcoptic mange mite.

'Emily, I'm so sorry. I spoke out of turn,' Lena said, pulling her sister aside.

To her horror, tears welled up in Emily's eyes. She said nothing but held out her hand to Lena. On her ring finger was an enormous diamond, the biggest Lena had ever seen, a deep cut set on a mount of tiny sapphires. It was beautiful.

'He hid it in a bag of feed,' Emily said, giggling though her tears.

'Oh, Em, congratulations,' Lena said, meaning it. 'If it's what you want, then I'm happy for you, so happy. I should have kept my big trap shut – I know nothing. You *are* happy, aren't you?' The tears rolling down her sister's peaches-and-cream complexion were a bit confusing.

'I am, so happy. I love him, Lee. I always have.' Emily drew her further away from Blackie and the conversation that had moved onto mastitis, hoose, roundworm and ringworm. 'I know you don't get it – I don't get it myself sometimes – but the idea of spending my life with anyone but him is horrible. I'm not settling for him – he's who I want. I know he's a bit of an eejit sometimes, and his family are a total disaster, but he's his own man. He proved it today, and when I said yes, do you know what he said?'

'No, tell me.' Lena's heart grew warm at her sister's delight.

'He said, "Emily, you and me are a family. Your dad is gone, your mam is a bit of a trial, my auld fella is a waste of oxygen, as is my brother, and my own mam is absolutely bate to the ropes from work, so it's you and me now, the two of us, on our own. Lena and Jack and the twins will move on from here, or do their own thing. And I can't promise you riches or a great lifestyle, but I can promise you love and loyalty, a home and a half-decent business and children if God blesses us."'

'That's lovely,' Lena said, once again meaning it. It might not have been Shakespeare, but it was from the heart.

'So you're happy for me, really?'

'Ah, Em, of course I am. I only ever wanted you to be happy. And I can see you are, so yes, I'm delighted for you both.'

'And you'll be my bridesmaid?'

'I will, of course.'

'And bring Malachy to the engagement party. I want to get to know him.'

Lena hugged her sister.

'So you told her, did you?' Blackie reappeared, the various parasitic infestations of cattle forgotten for a while.

'I did.' Emily beamed.

For a second Blackie looked sheepish, doubtful of his reception as a member of the family, but Lena gave him a hug. 'Welcome, Blackie. I'm delighted for you both. And that's an incredible ring – it's a rock.'

He relaxed, beaming again. 'It's the least my Emily deserves. She's one in a million, Lena, one in a million. I don't know what she sees in me, I swear I don't – any sane woman would run a mile at the name Crean – but I'm the luckiest man alive and that's the truth.' He was so honest and humble, he warmed Lena's heart.

'I'd have asked your father, God rest him, if he were alive, and I was going to go up to your mam, but now I suppose I'm asking you if it's OK?'

'Ah, Blackie, Emily loves you and you love her – what else is there? And I'm sure our dad would have given his blessing with a heart and a half.'

'Well, my crowd are not... Well, they're not the best, my father and that, and Jingo, well, he's a piece of work. But I'm not like them – I'm different.' He was at pains to point this out. Lena could have pretended not to know what he meant, but that would have been ludicrous; the goings-on of the Creans were common knowledge.

'I know you're different from them, Blackie. Welcome to the family.'

'Will you join us?' Emily asked as they approached the Copper Kettle.

'I'd love to, but I'm going out, so I've to go home and get ready.'

'On a date?' Emily asked, her expression unreadable.

'Yes,' said Lena firmly.

Emily held out her arms. 'All right. Have a great night, and I'll see you later.'

'Thank you, Em.'

For a long moment, they hugged, and then Lena turned to go home, feeling a lot happier than she had earlier.

Walking quickly, keen to be ready for Malachy in time, she almost bumped into a man who was coming around the corner. 'I'm sorry...'

It was that strange man who worked for Malachy's father. He nodded to her as he passed. 'Mademoiselle.' And was gone.

CHAPTER 11

Standing at her bedroom window, Maria smiled as she watched her daughter tripping across the yard, all dolled up in the new blue polka-dot dress she'd made for her, with the full skirt and narrow waist, a fashionable boat neck and three-quarter-length sleeves. She was such a pretty girl. She managed to make even the most casual outfits look good; her tiny but curvaceous figure made heads turn.

Maria wished she could ask Lena if it was the Berger boy she was seeing, but she knew Lena didn't want her to know. She didn't blame her, not after what happened the last time. It was fear that had made Maria lash out that night...fear of that man in the big house, the one who had killed Paudie…

No, it was all in her head. Paudie's death was an accident. Doc had said so.

She hated the idea of that woman's son having eyes for her Lena. That family brought nothing but trouble to their door.

She missed her darling husband so much. She longed to feel his strong arms around her, stopping her from disintegrating. She missed him in a way nobody could understand, but she missed him more for her children. He had been a rock of stability in their sea of uncertainty. Lena would have been able to talk to Paudie about Malachy.

She saw a flash of light in between the trees at the end of the lane. A car, the same as had come for Lena several times now. She prayed it wasn't him, but a strong sense of dread told her she was wishing in vain. Lena was never going to settle for someone she saw as ordinary. She was strong, like Paudie, but with a wilder heart. Lena longed to travel the world.

Paudie and the farm were all Maria had ever wanted. Her cold, loveless upbringing, the constant disapproval of her parents, meant the warm comfort of a permanent home filled with love was her dream come true. But Lena was different

– she was inquisitive, adventurous, bright. A live wire, bright as a button, but impetuous and stubborn too. Lena had big plans and none of them involved Kilteegan Bridge.

Emily, on the other hand, would settle down with Blackie Crean and be happy. Em was solid as a rock and wanted someone equally solid beside her; she would find the flightiness that inhabited her sister's soul too unsettling. Emily was like Paudie too in that way. Capable and happy with the hand life dealt her.

The thump of a car door, the sound of an engine, and her girl was gone.

The lights went off in the milking parlour; Jack would be finished. It was Saturday night. He should be rushing in to wash and change and go out with his friends to a dance or the pub, but he wouldn't do that. He didn't show any interest in girls, and he seemed to find the company of other boys awkward.

Of all her children, Jack was the one who worried her. He was so sensitive; he seemed to tremble sometimes. He reminded her of a dog Paudie had brought home from the mart one day when they were first married, a little lurcher. The poor thing had been wandering around the edge of the parade ring, cowering against the walls, thin as a rail and quivering, and Paudie failed to find her owner so took her home. After she got over her nerves – and it took weeks of gentle confidence building by Paudie – she was such a sweet, loyal dog, following him everywhere he went from dawn to dusk, and even sleeping in a basket beside their bed.

Maria smiled at the memory. Paudie had asked her what they should call the little dog the night he brought her home. With her pointed ears and almond-shaped dark eyes, she reminded Maria of a fairy, so they called her Puck after the character in *A Midsummer Night's Dream*.

Ten years later, Puck died peacefully in her sleep, having lived a lovely long life, and she was buried up the long field behind the milking parlour with all the other dogs and cats and loved family pets of the O'Sullivans for generations. Thirteen would be buried there one day, and whatever dog came after her. Paudie loved dogs. He'd said he didn't trust people who didn't like dogs but he always trusted a dog when they didn't like a person.

She didn't want Jack to be like those faithful pets, never leaving the farm until the day he died. Paudie had tried to reassure her that their only son was happy on the farm, that he loved nature and the land and was content. And it was true. The way Jack spoke about animals was different to other farmers – he had such deep respect for them. But that wasn't enough. She wanted him to have a life, see the world a bit, travel.

She closed the curtains and checked herself in the mirror. She was wearing a flowered skirt she'd made for herself only yesterday, and a pink cardigan that she'd embroidered with matching flowers. In another life, where she didn't have to spend half her time in St Catherine's 'resting', she would have loved to own a dress shop, sell gorgeous silks and cottons and fancy buttons and sewing machines, and advise her customers on how to follow simple patterns, or make up the clothes herself when they needed something special.

She probably inherited it from her father, who was an expert tailor and gentleman's outfitter. Not that he'd ever encouraged her in any way, but the natural ability had to have come from him.

She went out onto the landing and peeped into the twins' bedroom. They were playing with their dolls, talking to them in that funny little language they'd invented between them. She had no idea what the words meant, but they seemed to be able to communicate perfectly with each other. The twins were so united, so self-contained, sometimes it was as if they needed nobody but themselves. They looked alike, but they were a perfect blend of her and Paudie. It broke her heart to think he'd never met them; he would have adored them, and they him.

'Molly? May? Do you want to help me make some pretty clothes for your dolls?'

They jumped up, delighted. 'Marigold wants a pink dress!' shouted Molly, and May said, 'Alice wants overalls, like Jack!'

Downstairs, she set up her pedal-operated Singer sewing machine. The twins went through the odds and ends of material she had in her big box, and soon there were several items of tiny clothing pouring out from under her skilled fingers, elfin shirts and fairy dresses and vests for the teddy bears…

She loved these days when everything she touched turned to magic.

Later, while the twins introduced the dolls and teddies to their beautiful new wardrobe, she turned her mind to dinner. The range was hot; she'd been stewing the lamb for a shepherd's pie since early that morning. She'd used the stock from the bones of the joint they'd had during the week for flavour. The potatoes were their own and floury, mashed with their own butter and the top of the milk; they were delicious. She then buttered slices of stale bread, added sugar and raisins and made a creamy custard to pour over it all and popped it in the oven. It was Jack's favourite.

'Now, girls, let's set the table for our tea, then we'll out to the yard and call Jack? Tell him his dinner's ready, and tell him to wash the smelly cow poo off his boots before coming in.' She was rewarded with peals of laughter; the twins were of that age when just saying the word 'poo' was enough to set them off.

Emily arrived at the same time as Jack, and Maria hurried to set an extra place. 'I thought you'd be eating with Blackie and his mother,' she apologised.

'No, he's had to go to Cork to pick up supplies.' Emily sat herself at the table, then noticed the dolls, Marigold and Alice, sitting side by side on Lena's empty chair in their splendid new outfits. 'Mam, did you make these clothes?'

'We helped! We helped!' shouted the twins.

'Shh, you two. Mam, these are amazing. You know, when Blackie and me have the shop, we're thinking of expanding, getting in bolts of material and stuff for the farmers' wives and the other women of the town. I'd say they'd love it if you showed them how to make dolls' clothes and proper clothes for themselves and their children too? And maybe you could make some yourself to sell in the shop?'

It was uncanny; it was so like what she'd been thinking earlier, it was as if Emily could read her mind. Normally the thought that someone could see into her mind would have frightened her, but with Emily it felt natural and right, just like it had with Paudie when he knew what she was thinking. 'Oh, I'd love to, Em. If that's all right with Blackie and Mrs Crean.'

'Mam, they'd be only delighted.'

'Well, I'd love to do it. It would be great fun. And Molly and May can help me, can't you?'

The twins loudly agreed, and both Jack and Emily smiled at her. For the first time in a long time, a daring thought came into Maria's mind. *Maybe I'll be all right. Maybe I can survive without Paudie after all.*

As Emily examined the outfits on the dolls, Maria spotted the sparkling diamond. 'Is that...?'

Emily blushed. 'I was going to tell you straight away, but I was so impressed with the clothes. Yes, Blackie proposed today, and I've said yes.'

Maria blinked back tears. She longed for

Paudie so many times in the day, but this was a big moment. If he'd not been killed, Blackie would have come up and asked for Emily's hand, and that night, Paudie would have told her so her firstborn child appearing with a ring wouldn't be a complete surprise. But he was gone, and the loss of him took her breath away.

'I'm delighted for you, Emily. Blackie is a lucky man.' She hugged her daughter and wished for the millionth time she could have been the mother Emily needed all her life.

Jack washed his hands and took his place at the table. 'Will I get discounted feed now so?' He winked, and Emily punched him playfully.

'You will not! 'Tis that sort of carry-on, people thinking they shouldn't pay in time or at a discount or ever at all that had poor Mrs Crean nearly in the poorhouse. Crean's hardware is under new, much tougher management now.'

Jack chuckled, and Maria served the twins, and for the next few minutes, the five of them sat eating contentedly, the only sound being forks on plates, the clock ticking on the wall and Thirteen chasing rabbits in her dreams in the basket by the range.

Jack, clearly starving, was the first to finish, after forking the meal into his mouth at lightning speed. 'That was delicious, Mam. What's for dessert?'

'Bread-and-butter pudding, and that cream you brought up this morning.'

'Fantastic. Come on, you slow coaches, eat up.'

'When will the wedding be, Em?' Maria asked tentatively, fearful that she had no right to ask.

'We've nothing decided yet, Mam. There's some things to be sorted out legally with the shop first, but hopefully soon.'

'Can we be flower girls?' Molly asked.

'Well, have you a dress?' Emily asked seriously, glancing at her mother.

'Mammy can make us dresses,' May said with certainty.

'Well, if you can make flower girl dresses, then I'll have to have you two, won't I?'

'And Lena can be your bridesmaid.' Molly was getting excited.

'And me, can I be a bridesmaid?' Jack asked, and his little sisters giggled. 'I could put ribbons in my hair.'

Maria felt calm again. Her children were all right, in spite of everything. They'd survived her, and didn't hate her. Maybe it would be all right.

When everyone was finished with the pie, Maria cleared away the empty plates and set out bowls of bread-and-butter pudding and cream, even though Emily protested weakly that she was far too full to eat anything else.

Again, Jack was the first to finish, and at his hopeful look, Maria refilled his bowl and poured over more cream. 'How's the heifer that you had the vet up to look at?'

'She's good. I was afraid she'd picked up a parasite from the foxes and was going to miscarry, but she's grand.'

Molly and May scraped and nearly licked their bowls, then took them to the sink and washed them, setting them to drain. They were barely tall enough to reach the sink, but they did it. 'Thank you, Mammy, that was lovely,' they chorused, before taking their dolls and going back upstairs. They would play for a bit and then change into their nighties, brush their teeth and get into bed; then they'd shout down for a story and a goodnight kiss. They were such great girls.

Emily had stretched herself out on the settle. 'That bread-and-butter pudding finished me, Mam. I'm just going to lie here for a bit, and then I'll make us all a cup of tea.'

'It's no bother. Stay there – I'll make the tea.' She did, flying around the place. At the table, Jack pulled out his book on farming, the one he'd found in the second-hand bookshop in Clonakilty, and sat reading it. It reminded her of something.

'I saw a poster in the library the other day for a journal from America, for the new farming techniques. Nettie Collins said she could order it in for you, Jack, if you'd like.'

'Thanks, but most farming publications nowadays always seem to be selling all kinds of chemicals, pesticides and the like, thinking just because they're the new thing, they're better than the old ways that have worked for centuries,' he said, turning another page of his book. 'They might increase yield, but I don't think they're good for the land. They went into a frenzy of creating them during the war, to try to up food production, and it did work, but I suspect there might be a higher price than we realise for that. You can't interfere with nature like that and not expect consequences.'

Maria felt the old familiar sting of rejection, but she pressed on, her voice less strong now, she knew. 'But I read the poster, and this is different. It said the next edition was about a ranch and herbal nursery in Montana that doesn't use any chemicals.'

'Go on, Mam.' Jack looked up, suddenly interested, and she felt a surge of warmth at his approval.

'Well, they are experimenting on new ways of working the land without harming it or the animals and plants and rivers and all of that. Will I ask Nettie to order it in, do you think?'

'That would be great. Thanks.' He glanced at the clock on the wall. 'Cows will be waiting for me by now.' He pushed his chair back and took his plate to the sink, washed it and let it drain, then came back to kiss her on the cheek. 'And thanks for dinner, Mam. It was lovely.' The next moment, he was out the door. Thirteen saw him go and rose to follow him. On the settle, Emily was gently asleep, her diamond sparkling on her hand.

If only it could always be like this. If only Paudie wasn't dead. If only Lena would find someone else to turn her head than that Berger boy.

CHAPTER 12

A week later, Emily and Blackie had their engagement party at the back of the Donkey's Ears. Lena would have loved to take Malachy, but she was worried Maria would react badly to his presence despite the happy mood she'd been in for a while.

She'd had to explain to Malachy about her mother not wanting her to see him. She didn't tell him about how Maria had hit her, of course; she just blamed it on her mother thinking posh boarding-school boys like him only picked up local girls like her at weekends for a laugh and dumped them as soon as they went to college.

Malachy had winced and admitted he had a few friends like that at school, but he promised her mother would come round when she saw he was still with Lena years from now. It was the first time he'd said anything to Lena about the long-term, and she couldn't be sure whether he was joking or not, but she felt happy and light the whole day afterwards and was still floating on air when she went to Emily's and Blackie's party.

The Donkey's Ears was the sort of establishment that knew that the drinkers would come and empty their pockets regardless of the décor, so it was firmly stuck in the past but not in a charming way. The carpet, made of orange nylon and installed at cut-price rates during the Emergency, was sticky, and the fleur-de-lis wallpaper was flocked in red and gold and had, no doubt, fallen off the back of a lorry.

The publican, whose real name was Gerard Coughlan, was called Twinkle. He was a wrestler in a former life and was an enormous bruiser of a man with a mad head of red curly hair and a flaming red beard. The story goes that he knocked a customer out one night. The customer was warned repeatedly to behave himself but wouldn't listen and then decided to swing a punch at Gerard. When the man came round, he was clearly concussed and went on about seeing lovely twinkly stars. The name Twinkle stuck after that.

Twinkle had made an effort for the evening. He was dressed in a check suit with a yellow shirt and a red tie. Everything Twinkle wore seemed too small for him, and Lena thought he looked comical. He was a sweet man really, but he was just what was needed for the rougher clientele of the Donkey's Ears, as nobody would dare challenge him or laugh at him; he'd flatten them in one second.

Jingo and Dick were still on the missing list thankfully, so Emily and Blackie relaxed. Lena was happy to see Mrs Crean in a lovely pink dress with little blue flowers that she recognised as an old one of Mammy's that Emily must have got altered. Or maybe Mammy did it. Blackie's mother also had her hair in a nice set and even had applied a bit of powder and lipstick to her careworn face. It was lovely to see her in something other than the once-beige, now-grey housecoat she always wore. Again Lena saw the gentle, kind hand of her sister. The way Mrs Crean looked at Emily, with nothing short of devotion, made Lena smile. It wasn't a life she'd choose for her dear sister, but Blackie and his mother knew that landing Emily O'Sullivan was the best day's work either of them had ever done.

There was dancing from the local band, the Grafters, and cake, and Blackie made a lovely speech about how lucky he was that Emily agreed to marry him. Em beamed so brightly, she lit up the room.

Lena was friendly and polite to everyone. Jack would never come to anything social like the party, and Em wouldn't expect him to as he hated socialising, so Lena needed to keep an eye on her mother. The twins were staying the night with Deirdre.

Maria was chatting to this person and that, and Lena feared she seemed too high, too animated. This often happened before an outburst, then a low period. Everyone knew the situation, and Maria never drank alcohol so would probably be fine, but still Lena was on edge.

Derry Lehane, the local coalman who had bright-yellow teeth, was wearing a brown cardigan that hung from his bony frame. He was easily in his fifties, but he asked her to dance. Lena longed to refuse but could feel the presence of her dad, who would have been disappointed in her if she did. He always said it took so much courage for a man to ask a girl up to dance, that unless he was plastered or lecherous, the girl shouldn't embarrass him by refusing. One dance at arm's-length wasn't too much to ask to spare public humiliation.

'You'll be next,' he announced with glee, as Lena tried not to shudder. He had poor saliva control, and she could feel a spray of spit on her cheek as he spoke.

When older people said that to younger people whenever someone got married, she often thought she'd like to say the same to them at funerals, but she resisted the urge to give him a smart answer.

Thankfully the dance ended, and before he had time to suggest another, she thanked him and skipped away. She saw, out of the corner of her eye, Ollie Fenton, Kilteegan Bridge's only Teddy boy. He had a cousin in Chicago who sent him clothes and he'd spent one summer in London working in a pub, so he considered himself the height of sophisticated fashion. Lena took in tonight's extraordinary get-up. He wore an oversized drape jacket in black velvet, with satin lapels and pocket flaps, and high-waisted drainpipe trousers that made his already matchstick-thin legs look chicken-like and that came to an abrupt halt just above the ankles, under which were bright-green socks. He had a red silk shirt, and instead of a tie, he wore a leather cord clasped together by a metal thing bearing a native Indian design. His hair was greased back and teased into a quiff. And was he wearing mascara? Surely not. But his eyelashes were suspiciously dark. Lena thought she'd never seen a person who looked more ridiculous or who fancied themselves more.

Ollie had, on more than one occasion, tried his luck with Lena, but she always declined. She could never be with a fella who spent longer getting ready than she did.

Everyone watched as he crossed the dance floor in her direction.

'Will you drag me round the floor to save me from Miss Casey?' She heard Doc's voice in her ear. He must have come in the door behind her; he'd said he'd pop in. Eagerly she put her hand on his shoulder as the band struck up a waltz.

Doc was in fact a great dancer, and she felt relief and suppressed a giggle as Ollie stood, looking moody, on the edge. Miss Casey, the local primary school teacher, had great notions of Doc for the last three decades. Sentiments he didn't share, so he kindly and gently rebuffed her, but she was nothing if not persistent.

'Thanks for that. She was making a beeline for me,' he murmured.

'You saved me from Ollie the Octopus as well, so we're saving each other.'

Doc chuckled. Doc had never married, but it wasn't for want of interested women. He was married to his job. He'd confided to Lena last year that he couldn't give the kind of care he wanted to his patients if he had a wife and children at home, so he just never did. She knew he had a lady friend, someone who lived in Dublin. She never came to Kilteegan Bridge and Doc never mentioned her, but a few times a year he took a trip to Dublin and got a locum in to cover him. Any time Lena asked him anything about her, though, she was shut down immediately.

The night was a huge success, and everyone wished the couple well. The wedding would be next spring and though nobody said it, the best thing would be if all members of the Crean family with the exception of Blackie and his mother stayed on the missing list.

Lena drove herself and her mother home. Jack had taught her, and she loved driving. As they passed the entrance to Kilteegan House, Lena couldn't help but look up, and she saw that her mother did the same.

Lena waited. Maria was liable to do or say anything. But she didn't, and they drove home in silence.

* * *

THE FOLLOWING DAY, Malachy called before he headed back to Larksbridge for his last term and his Leaving Certificate exams.

As she sat into the car at the bottom of the lane as usual, he seemed preoccupied.

'What's up?' she asked.

'What?' He'd clearly been miles away. 'Oh, nothing. I'm fine…'

'Well, you might be fine, Mr Berger, but wherever you are, it's not here.' Lena laughed.

He looked at her, hesitated, then seemed to decide to tell her what was on his mind. 'It was just something happened in town, something someone said.'

'Someone? Come on.' She had a worried thought. 'Did you meet my mam?'

'Your godfather actually.' He put the car into gear and started driving.

'Doc?' She felt another stab of anxiety. She knew Doc still didn't like the Berger family. Only the other day he'd spotted Phillippe Decker standing on the pavement opposite the surgery and passed a very uncharacteristically sharp remark about 'that nasty Frenchman, always snooping around the place'. But when Lena had challenged him, he couldn't give a good reason for not liking the man.

'What did he say to you?'

'Nothing too terrible, don't worry. He just seemed disapproving and kind of warning me not to mess you around.'

She felt hot with embarrassment. 'Malachy, I'm so sorry. I told Doc about us, and he went really strange on me at first. He didn't say anything against you personally, but to be honest, he doesn't seem to like your father any more than your father likes him – I have no idea why. But he definitely acted like you and me weren't suited for each other or something. I suppose it's because, I don't know, you're richer, better educated or from a better-got family or something, and I'm from a small farm and left school at fifteen. We had such a row, and we've never ever had a cross word in our lives. I was really upset, but we patched it up, so I never said anything to you about it. Honestly, if your father wasn't so nice to me, I'd start to think everyone was on to something and give up on you altogether.'

But the thing was, Malachy's father *was* lovely to her, welcoming her often before or after their dates, and never passing a word about her poor background or her lack of education. In fact he'd offered her the use of the library if she wanted to borrow any books while Malachy was away at school during the week. So far, she'd only borrowed books when she went up there with him, but the way Mr Berger welcomed her, she didn't think it would feel odd to go there alone either. She'd borrowed *Wuthering Heights* and *Little Women,* and it was wonderful to realise there were whole worlds out there that she could enter at will.

Once, when she'd been going through the shelves waiting for Malachy to get changed, she'd found a small photo album containing black and white photos of Malachy as a boy, unmistakable even then. She wondered who the photographer was – perhaps his mother? To her amazement, one of the photos was of her own father, Paudie. In the picture, he was lifting young Malachy down from an apple tree. Paudie had a big smile on his face, and there in the background was Lena herself, maybe five years old at the time and clearly very anxious about her friend being stuck up in the tree.

As she was looking fondly at the picture of her father, the door opened suddenly, and Phillippe came into the library. For some reason she shoved the album back into the bookcase, feeling like she was doing something wrong by looking at it, maybe snooping into Hannah Berger's private thoughts and memories or something. Later, she told Malachy about the album. He didn't remember ever seeing it, but when they went to look for it, she couldn't find it again.

Now in the car, they drove in silence for a minute. Kilteegan House came into view.

'Do you want to come up to my place or will we go somewhere else?' Malachy asked.

'Let's go for a walk around the grounds. At least nobody will disturb us there,' Lena replied. Malachy would have to have dinner with his father before returning to school in the morning so staying close by was convenient, and she also didn't want anyone from the village seeing them together. She'd had enough of other people's opinions on her relationship.

He drove up the long avenue, parking by the orchard where once as a little boy he'd got stuck up a tree. Today all the apple trees were in blossom, pink and white, their long branches sweeping the uncut grass.

Before getting out, he took her hand. 'I don't care what anyone says, Lena, whatever mad notion they have that we shouldn't be together, because I love you.'

The words hung between them. He'd never said them before; neither of them had.

'I love you too,' she replied softly.

'Good. Great, I mean.' He grinned. 'Lena, you're the most amazing girl, beautiful and funny and whip-smart, and I can't imagine spending my life with anyone else. I hate the idea of anyone suggesting that this is just a fling for either of us. For me, this is the real thing – this is love.'

'For me too, Malachy, but are you really sure?'

'Am I sure of what?'

'Well, just maybe everyone is right, maybe I am getting ideas above my station. I know that's what everyone in Kilteegan Bridge will think if we start going around openly together. My father is gone, and we only have a small farm and no money really, and you're, well, a different class and maybe you'd want someone more like yourself eventually…'

'Lena O'Sullivan, you come out with some claptrap sometimes. I couldn't give a fiddler's about any of that. My father's told me I'm going to be rich when he dies. Apparently his parents have left me some sort of legacy – they were wine dealers before the war. So I'll have plenty enough for both of us, and I want to be with you. I want to marry you, Lena, if you'll have me?'

Lena felt the blood thundering in her ears. Was this happening? Was Malachy proposing?

He clearly mistook her silence for reticence. 'It doesn't have to be now. I know I'm still at school and we're young, but I just wanted you to know that I'm serious and that I –'

'I'd love to marry you, I really, really would!'

'I've no ring or anything, but we'll get one… Oh, Lena, this is great. I'm so happy.'

'Me too!' She wanted to jump out of the car and run around the orchard. All the blossoms looked brighter, whiter and pinker; the birds in the apple trees sounded like they were singing louder, and she felt as if her heart were singing along with them. 'But, Malachy, in a way you're right. I don't think we should tell anyone, at least till you've finished school.'

Malachy looked horrified. 'But I want to tell everyone now. I want to shout it from the rooftops before you have a chance to back out of the deal.'

'Don't worry, I won't be backing out. And it's not forever. But you need to focus on your exams without anyone giving out that I'm distracting you, and I won't be the reason you don't get the marks you deserve. You need to get into college, Mr Berger. Even if your grandparents have left you a legacy, you have to have a proper career or all that money spent on your education will just be one big waste.' She winked at him. 'So you get your head in the books, and after your exams, we'll tell everyone and have our own engagement party, and then we can get on with the rest of our lives. How does that sound?'

'It sounds to me that I am the luckiest man in the world to have such a woman willing to be my wife.'

'Doesn't a girl get a kiss to seal the deal?' She smiled.

He took her in his arms, kissing her passionately. They had been growing more and more frustrated with just kissing, but Lena knew how easily a girl could get a reputation and so she always stopped anything before they got too carried away. But as Malachy kissed her, she felt her body respond to him with increasing urgency.

She slid her hands inside his shirt; the skin of his chest was warm and inviting. He groaned against her mouth. 'Oh, Lena...'

She'd never gone this far with a boy. In fact

she'd never kissed any boys before Malachy – she was not going to go around kissing people she wasn't serious about.

She caressed his skin, kissing him hungrily as she tentatively allowed his hands to explore her body. He'd always respected her and had never pushed things this far before, but her reaction was encouraging rather than stopping him.

Without saying a word, Lena opened her car door and walked around to his side. He looked perplexed and so handsome, his neat hair standing on end, his shirt pulled out of the waistband of his trousers.

She opened his door then and held out her hand.

'What?' he asked, confused.

'Come with me.' She smiled, and he did as she asked. She pushed open the little side gate to the orchard, and they ducked through the trees that had grown so wild since her father had stopped pruning them years ago. Beyond were the stables where Hannah's horses, including the wild stallion, had been kept, but all the stalls were empty now that their mistress was dead.

The tack room smelled of leather and dust, but it was private, with no windows. The horse blankets were clean, in a neatly folded pile, and there were two bales of hay. On the cobwebbed shelves, next to a can of linseed oil, was a set of draughts and a pack of cards, the same ones she and Malachy had played with when they were children.

She bolted the door from the inside and gave Malachy a knowing look, and then pulled the bales apart, making a bed. She laid a blanket over the hay and took his hand. 'Remember us playing cards in here when we were little?' she asked.

He nodded, his Adam's apple moving as he swallowed nervously. 'Are you sure this is...'

'Safe? We'll be careful.'

'No, I meant, is it what you want?'

She didn't answer but kissed him again, sliding her hands up his back this time, feeling shivers of delight. He responded, and soon they were a tangle of bodies in the sweet-smelling hay. Lena didn't need to tell him it was her first time, and she knew it was his – he'd confided to her a few weeks ago that he'd never gone all the way with anyone – and while it was uncomfortable, it was also glorious. Afterwards, she snuggled in his arms, the blanket wrapped around them both.

'Oh, Lena, I...I don't know what to say. I feel like I should say thank you. Is that the right thing?' He chuckled.

'I love you, Malachy Berger.'

'And I love you. And someday, hopefully not too far away, you'll be Mrs Lena Berger and I'll be the proudest man in Ireland.'

They chatted in the shared intimacy for a while, planning their future together as the sunlight faded between the top of the tack room door and the roof.

Then Lena kissed him again. 'You'd better get back to your father, have your last dinner with him before you go back to school.'

Malachy groaned. 'I'd rather stay here with you in my arms forever, but I suppose you're right.'

'And will you come to see me in the morning to say goodbye before you get on the road to Dublin?'

'I certainly will. What time will you be up? I'm supposed to be back in school by midday, but I don't mind being late.'

'You don't need to be late. You're talking to a farmer's daughter. I'm always up at six to help Jack with the milking. I'll try and leave him for five minutes between six and six fifteen to run down the lane and see you. Don't go until I'm there.'

Malachy was on his feet, buttoning his shirt. 'I

will, and I'll wait for you all day if necessary. I won't go without seeing you.'

She stood on tiptoe and kissed his lips. 'It's all right. I'll understand if you're in too much of a hurry.'

'I won't be, though. I love you, Lena. I'd rather not be leaving you at all.' He kissed her once more. 'I can't imagine how I'm supposed to just go back to school, knowing you're my wife-to-be but pretending you're not. You're so beautiful.'

'You're fairly beautiful yourself.' She giggled, and he ran his finger down her face.

'I'll get some, well, you know, so you don't get pregnant…if we can do this again? There's a fella at school whose father is in London, so he goes over fairly often and can bring…' – he coloured – 'them back.' He looked so nervous and hopeful, she felt a wave of love for him.

She knew what he meant, but she'd never actually seen one. They were completely banned by the Church and therefore could not be bought in Ireland. 'That would be a good idea, but after the exams.' She smiled. 'I know God wouldn't let us get caught out the first time, I'm sure of that much, but we'll be careful from now on. People will have plenty to say about us in time, so let's not give them any more gossip.'

'How on earth am I supposed to keep my mind on exams when all I'll be able to think about is how soon before I can have you in my arms again?'

'Well, you'd better, young Berger, because I want a big fancy house and a flash car, so I'll thank you to keep the head in the books.' She grinned.

'Yes, ma'am.' He saluted her jokily. They replaced everything as it was before and pulled the hay out of each other's hair, and left the tack room.

CHAPTER 13

*A*uguste Berger sat in his armchair by the fire, his useless legs resting on a low padded footstool. He was listening to the sound of his son's car driving furiously away down the avenue. Malachy wasn't supposed to go back until tomorrow, but he needed to get away now. Auguste remembered with a sigh the passion of youth.

'You told him?' Phillippe asked in German as he set a glass of brandy down next to his employer. He then poked the fire, stirring up a thin flame.

Auguste nodded, cradling the brandy glass in his bony fingers. 'Indeed. I got through to him in the end. He knows now what she is, and why she won't do for him.'

'Did you tell him everything I'd reported to you?'

'I did, but not all at once. I wanted it to seem like I was reluctant to hurt him or sully the girl's name. So at the beginning of dinner, over the soup, I just suggested it was better he break it off. I said he didn't need to know why, but he should be a good son and do as I asked. I said there are lots of girls in Dublin or further afield better than Lena O'Sullivan.'

Phillippe stood looking at him, the poker still in his hand.

Auguste smiled. 'As you'd imagine, he was very indignant. He said he didn't understand, that I'd encouraged the relationship, that he thought I liked her a great deal. He even told me they'd been planning on getting married.'

'We didn't expect anything else...'

'Indeed. She had her hooks into him deeper than I'd imagined. So I trod carefully. I said I had liked her...at first. I'd thought she was charming and wholesome, and I'd been sad to find out that wasn't the case. Naturally he protested her innocence, saying she was a pure, simple country girl from a good, honest family. He even quoted that man at me, how everyone, including his own mother, had loved Paudie O'Sullivan. You can imagine how hard I found it to restrain myself.'

'But you did, August.' The Frenchman addressed him with the German pronunciation of his name. He replaced the poker and stood with his arm resting on the mantelpiece.

'Of course. We ate our roast beef in silence, but I could see him thinking and wondering what it was I hadn't told him. In the end, I sighed, and asked if he wanted to know what I had heard. Of course he wanted to know – no human being could resist – although he said he knew it was going to be lies and false rumours.'

'Did you mention St Catherine's?'

'That's where I started. I told him she was a liar and could not be trusted and that he was naïve to believe anything she said. I asked him what his precious Lena had told him about her mother. It was clear he knew nothing. So then I told him that Maria O'Sullivan spends half her time in the mental hospital, that she was inclined to be violent. And when he found an excuse for her lying to him about that, I told him how her brother was always consorting with the Travellers, the ones that stole the copper tank from the top field two years ago. And then I mentioned how the sister is marrying into a criminal family, the biggest thieves in Kilteegan Bridge, and that her family is delighted with the match.

'And when he kept making excuses for her, I reminded him that all the evidence shows that madness and perversion and a propensity to crime run in families – it's *in them* – and that if he and that tramp were married and had children, then those children would have that underclass blood.' He winced as a familiar spasm of pain gripped him. 'My pills, Phillippe.'

Phillippe handed him the little silver box of tablets, and Auguste took three with a gulp of brandy. He doubted the pills given to him by the quack from Kellstown did him much good, but the mere act of taking one calmed him, or maybe it was the brandy.

'And was that enough to convince him?' asked Phillippe, replacing the silver box in the writing desk, then returning to his position by the fire with his elbow on the mantelpiece.

'Naturally he said it was all lies and exaggerations, but I knew I'd rattled him, and I let it sink in while we ate our dessert. The lemon meringue was delicious, Phillippe, by the way. Almost as good as your father's.'

The Frenchman inclined his head. Baking was

a man's activity where they came from, whereas here it was the domain of women only. Hannah hadn't enjoyed allowing Phillippe into her kitchen, and it had been one of many bones of contention between her and his assistant. On one occasion she'd asked Auguste to remove kitchen duties from Phillippe completely, but if he would have agreed, he would have been subjected to stodgy Irish food, not the feather-light delights Phillippe could conjure up. He'd suggested to Hannah that she be the one to leave the kitchen, let Phillippe cater for everyone, but she'd refused that outright.

'When we were drinking our port, I returned to the subject, quite casually. I said I hoped he hadn't got himself into a situation he felt he couldn't get out of, that I hoped she hadn't brought him to the tack room like she did with the other boys...'

Phillippe's dark eyes locked with his. 'And he believed it?'

'Of course. Why would his papa lie to him? The poor boy went bright red and started sweating, and I just sighed and shook my head and said gently, "Oh, Malachy, do you really imagine you were the first boy she brought to that tack room? Why do you think she knows it so well? There's no harm in sowing your wild oats, lad, I'm not criticising you at all, but I'm afraid that little slut isn't for you. She's only making a fool out of you."'

'Did he ask how you knew?'

'I said Hannah had complained to me before she died how Lena O'Sullivan, who used to come here and play as a child, was now taking advantage – at her young age, only fourteen – of the property for fooling around with local boys. She worried it was a sign the girl had inherited her mother's madness, because madness and loose ways often go together.'

'Didn't he ask why you didn't mention it when he started seeing her?'

'I said it was because I thought perhaps she'd mended her ways, and I didn't want to be unfair to the girl. But then one night last week, I was sitting at my bedroom window with my night-vision binoculars, watching for owls. And then I told him I stayed on watch for several nights, just to be sure of what I'd seen. And, oh dear, there was that married farmer from next to the O'Sullivans – I forget his name – and then Blackie Crean from the village, her own sister's fiancé, and then there was Professor Lamkin's boy...'

Phillippe was shaking his head. 'It worked

then. He passed me on the stairs, barrelled past me. He packed his clothes so fast, his bedroom looks like a hurricane hit it. He's upset, of course, but as you say, he'll recover soon enough.'

'He'll be fine. He's a strong, healthy specimen. He has his exams to distract him, and he'll go to college and make a good match. In the meantime, Phillippe, pour me another brandy and one for yourself, and get out the backgammon board.'

THE NEXT MORNING Lena helped Jack bring in the cows. It took longer than usual. Mostly they arrived in by themselves when they were ready to be milked, but a couple of the young ones were new to the business and galloped to the wrong end of the field. As soon as she could, she made an excuse and ran off down the lane, sure that Malachy would be waiting for her.

It was 6:20 a.m., but there was no Volkswagen Beetle. There were no fresh tyre tracks in the mud, either, and anyway, if he'd arrived in her absence, he surely wouldn't have driven off without seeing her?

She stepped out into the road, looking in the direction of the big house. No car. She waited a full ten minutes before running back up to the farm, milking two of the cows, then rushing back down again to the gate. Still no Malachy.

She started to worry. Was he ill? Had something happened? No, probably he'd just overslept.

All morning, in between milking and helping her mother make breakfast, she ran up and down the lane until it was time to go to work in the surgery. She walked fast all the way, so she had time to take a detour past the gates of the big house, where she paused to look up the drive. No car. In the drawing room, she could see a man standing at the window. He wasn't tall enough to be Malachy. *It must be Phillippe Decker,* she thought. She hurried on, confused about why Malachy had broken his promise to her. It must have been something very important to get in the way of his seeing her, and she was sure he'd write to her as soon as he could to explain.

At work, Doc seemed tired and looked pale. 'Are you all right?' she asked, checking the appointment book for the day.

'Grand. I was up with poor old Eileen Doyle last night. She finally passed away around six this morning.' He ran his hand over the shadow of stubble on his jaw.

'God rest her. It will have been an ease to her,' Lena said. 'Have you been to bed yet?'

'No, not yet. And I've a full day today, so I'd better get a clean-up and a shave and get cracking.'

Lena noticed the first two patients on the book were local people who were not too demanding. 'I'll pop over to Nettie and to Blackie's mother then and ask if they wouldn't mind coming this evening instead. At least you'll get an hour for a nap, and then I'll make you a breakfast to keep you going. They won't mind.'

Doc exhaled, the exhaustion catching up to him. 'What would I do without you, Lena? Never leave, will you?' He sighed.

'Well, I've not been doing as much studying as I should and I'm hardly ready for my pre-nursing exams, so I suppose I'll be here for the foreseeable anyway.'

'Really?' She could see something like relief flood his face. 'Ah well, you're sure of a job here as long as you want it.'

The rest of the day flew by. Lena managed to put some people off altogether and arrange the other appointments so that Doc was finished by five. She dealt with the blood reports back from the lab, did the prescription orders and arranged specialist appointments in Cork for four patients.

'I've to call to that clown JJ Barry this evening,' Doc said as she closed the door on the last patient. 'Apparently he doesn't like the tablets, says they don't agree with him, and is insisting he get different ones…'

'You'll do no such thing, Doc.' Lena was firm. 'You'll eat this dinner I've had delivered from Chrissy – it's roast chicken, spuds and carrots – and then you'll get into bed and have a full night's sleep for once. That cantankerous old pest can wait for his new tablets. They don't agree with him? That fella'd fight with his fingernails – the Blessed Virgin herself couldn't agree with him. So don't mind him now, and it's dinner and bed for you.'

'Well, I told him I'd call…'

'And I told his wife you wouldn't. She agreed with me – no harm to him to wait. She came in earlier, so that's that.'

'An early night does sound nice.' Doc yawned.

'Well, off you go. Your dinner is warming in the oven. I put it in when Chrissy dropped it over. Be sure to eat it now.' She took her coat from the hook and let herself out.

Molly and May ran down to meet her as she walked up the hill home.

'Hello, you two.' She laughed as they ran into her arms. 'Everything all right?'

'Mammy is crying over Daddy, and she says he's not dead at all,' May said, and Lena's heart sank.

'Poor Mammy. Don't mind her – you know how she is sometimes. She believes things that aren't true and needs a good rest. Have you had any tea?' she asked, trying to keep her voice light and cheerful.

They shook their heads.

'All right, let's see what's there. Is Jack in the yard?'

'No. The Travellers are down by the riverbank, and he's down there with Paddy,' May reminded her.

'All right, what would you like for tea?'

'Beans on toast!' they chorused. It was their favourite.

'Consider it done, princesses.' Lena bowed low, and the girls giggled, then took a hand of hers each as they walked home. It was at times like this that Lena feared she would never be able to leave Kilteegan Bridge. Jack was good to the twins as a big brother, but he was out on the farm all day, and Emily would soon be living down in the hardware shop. If she was gone, who would mind these little girls when Maria was ill?

She made the beans on toast and then went to check on her mother. Maria looked hunted, haunted, as she sat up in bed, her hair down, the photo of Paudie cradled in her arms.

'Mam?' Lena asked gently. 'Are you all right?'

Maria shook her head. 'I'm so sorry, Lena...'

'I know, Mam, I know,' Lena soothed. Maria had been getting gradually more manic since the engagement party, so it wasn't a surprise.

'I think I need to go to St Catherine's again.'

'That's fine. Don't worry – I'll get Doc to arrange it tomorrow...'

'Is Paudie really dead, Lena?' Maria asked, her eyes deep pools of grief.

'He is, Mam.'

'I can't bear it, I just can't...'

With tears in her own eyes, Lena sat on her mother's bed and held Maria in her arms, stroking her long pale hair as she sobbed help-lessly on Lena's shoulder.

* * *

No letter came from Malachy.

Lena wrote twice a week to his school, but nothing came back to her, so she had no way of knowing if he'd even received her letters. Perhaps they were very strict in an exam term – maybe they weren't allowed to write or receive any letters when they were supposed to be focusing on their studies? Having left school so young herself, she had no idea how it worked. She thought about asking Emily, but she was afraid her older sister would give her a look that meant 'I told you so.' The same with Doc.

And there was something else that didn't come.

At first she chose to ignore it. Everyone had always told her it couldn't happen the first time, so in the beginning she found it impossible to believe. Six weeks after Malachy left without saying goodbye, she sat at the breakfast table, barely able to focus with the nausea.

'I could make you some nice warm porridge if your tummy is bad?' Emily offered. Emily had been around at home more than usual because Maria was in St Catherine's and might not be back for another month or so. Molly and May were playing under the table, waiting for Emily to bring them across to Deirdre Madden at the farm next door.

'No thanks. I'll just get to work.' Lena stood up and bolted out, and it took every ounce of strength she had to wait until she was out of the yard to vomit in the ditch.

She wiped her mouth and her eyes. Whether the tears were from the vomiting or from fear, she had no idea. Her period was always like clockwork, but she was four weeks late. Between that and the daily nausea, it was getting harder and harder to pretend everything was OK.

She knew Malachy was sitting his exams next week and then he'd be home. He would marry her in a heartbeat, she was sure of that, but this wasn't what she wanted. She would have liked to wait until at least a year after Emily and Blackie, and enjoy the whole experience, but now, well, now she'd have the busybodies looking up at the calendar as they always did at a quick wedding, their knowing nods and pursed lips speaking the volumes they longed to say.

She was so disappointed. She didn't want a baby, not yet at least. Sometime in the future, of course, but after she'd lived a bit. She was only seventeen and had such plans…

But this changed everything.

She walked down the hill, feeling marginally better after throwing up, and arrived at the clinic.

Doc was already in his surgery, checking the results of blood tests that had come in the post.

'Morning,' she called to him, taking off her coat and sitting at her desk, preparing for the day.

To her surprise he came out and stood before her, gesturing with his thumb that she should go into the consulting room.

'What? I've to get the physiotherapy referrals done this morning...'

'In you go now.' His tone was gentle but brooked no argument. Not saying another word, he shooed her into his office and got her to lie on the examination table, where he lifted her jumper and gently palpated her abdomen through her blouse, then pulled her jumper back down and stood looking at her solemnly over his glasses. 'Well, I expect you know what I'm going to tell you?' he said.

She wanted to say no. But she knew. Of course she did. She sat up on the edge of the examination table, her legs dangling down, her cheeks burning. 'I'm so sorry.'

'Don't apologise to me. I take it Malachy Berger is the father?'

She felt a spurt of angry defiance. 'Who else would it be, Doc? I'm not going around making babies with all and sundry now, am I?'

Doc sighed and ran his hands through his unkempt curls. 'Do you know how far along you are?'

'Six weeks and one day. But it's all right. You don't have to think I was carrying on with a boy without even an understanding, as they say around here. We're going to get married.'

He looked directly at her, his face filled with something. Concern certainly, and compassion too, but also something else. He said nothing for a long moment, just looked at her, his features inscrutable. Eventually he sighed. 'Oh, Lena. Whatever it is, my darling girl, it most certainly is not all right.'

He turned with his back to her and then went out to the waiting room, where no patients had been admitted yet. She heard him go outside and put the closed sign on the door, something he'd never done, then he came back.

'Look, Doc, I'm upset and worried obviously, but Malachy and I will be all right. We love each other. He'd already asked me to marry him before any of this happened, but we didn't want to say anything until Emily and Blackie got married. And we thought he should take his exams first, but they'll be over by next week and then...'

She was still sitting on the examination table.

He pulled over his chair from his desk, sat in front of her and took her hands in his.

'I know it's a bit of a shock but –'

'Lena, love, listen to me.' His eyes were dark with worry.

'What? You're always the one telling young ones it's not the end of the world, that they're not the first and they won't be the last, it's the 1950s, this scandal will wrap tomorrow's chips – you always say that. You've always been very kind to girls who find themselves in trouble, often when their families or Father Dineen are going mad, so why are you looking so sorrowful at me? I've told you, me and Malachy are getting married.'

'If that was the case –'

'What do you mean, "if"? I'm telling you!'

'Oh, Lena. You know before when I said I didn't think you and him were a good idea?'

'But you said it was nothing to do with him, that you thought he was a fine lad. It's just his father you don't like. Honestly, we'll be fine. I know you probably think we're too young, but it's too late now. He'll be home once he's finished his exams, and we'll –'

'That's not it.'

'What?'

'Oh Lord, Lena, I wish I didn't have to say this...'

'Say what?'

'Darling Lena, I heard something... I mean, I was told... I should have said. I thought you already knew. I thought he must have written to you as well. I didn't realise you still imagined...'

'Doc, for God's sake...'

He held her hands tighter. 'There's no easy way to say this, so I'll just say it. Malachy isn't coming home after his exams. He's going travelling with some friends, Lena. He wrote to me to say you and him were finished and he wanted me to make sure you were all right. He said he knows I'm the nearest thing to a father that you have now, and he said he was sorry he had to break his promise to me about taking care of you, but that he was sure I'd understand, that you were both so young and had your whole lives ahead of you, and he knew you'd find a local boy who suited you better.'

'Stop it. Stop talking. I don't believe you.' Lena pulled her hands out of his. She felt the room spin and gripped the side of the table. The churning in her guts erupted into a spew of vomit, all over the floor and Doc's jacket. 'Oh... Oh...'

'It's all right, don't worry, love.' He pulled his suit jacket off and got a towel to wipe the floor.

Lena was shivering uncontrollably now.

'Come up, come upstairs. You've had a shock.'

In a daze, she allowed herself to be led up to the spare room at the front of the house, never used. He helped her off with her shoes and her jumper and skirt and socks, also covered in vomit, and he pulled back the bedclothes. In her blouse and slip, she climbed between the sheets. Then he tucked her in.

'I'm going to get you a cup of tea, and I'm going to call Emily to bring you fresh clothes.' He crossed over to the side table and returned with a porcelain bowl decorated in flowers. 'In case you get sick again.'

She turned her face to the wall, ignoring him. It was all she could do not to retch again. Her mind was in a whirl. Malachy would never do this to her. Doc must be lying. But why would he lie to her? He never would – he loved her like he was her father – so it must be true… Was the letter he'd been sent a forgery? A joke, a prank played by one of Malachy's schoolmates who Malachy had told about Lena?

When Doc arrived back moments later with a hot cup of tea, she was sitting up, ready for him.

'Show me the letter.' Her voice sounded dull to her own ears.

'Ah, Lena, don't be upsetting yourself. I've told you what it said. Emily will be here soon. I said you weren't well, not anything critical, but you were in need of some care and clean clothes –'

'Show me the letter.'

'All right.' He sighed, went to the bookshelf on the landing, took out an envelope from between two books and handed it to her. With trembling hands, she pulled out the letter and unfolded it. Her stomach turned over again when she saw it was written in Malachy's educated handwriting, the same hand in which he'd written her all those love notes, slipping them into her pocket for her to find when she got home.

Dear Doctor Dolan,

I'm sorry to have to write you this letter, and I'm very sorry to have to break my promise to you to take care of Lena. As you are the nearest thing to a father she's got, I feel like I should explain myself to you. I'm sorry to do this, but Lena and I are not suited, and knowing Lena as you do, I'm sure you understand why. Lena is a lovely girl, but she's not who I thought she was. I was young and foolish and thought I was in love. I will not be returning to Kilteegan Bridge once I have finished my examinations; instead my father has suggested I go travelling with some friends, so that is what I will do.

Please tell Lena I am sorry, but I'm sure she will get over it quickly.

Yours faithfully,

Malachy Berger

She was sick again, into the lovely old bowl, as Doc held her hair back.

CHAPTER 14

$\mathcal{A}$ day later, Lena sat miserably in Doc's kitchen. The surgery was closed for the evening, but being May, it was still bright outside.

'You seriously want me to give this baby away to some stranger and then come back here and pretend everything is fine?'

He patted her hand. 'I know this isn't easy for you, and I wish I didn't have to ever have this conversation, but if you do as I suggest, then at least when this is over, you'll be able to get on with your life as if it had never happened.'

'But it's my baby…' Her voice was hoarse from the rawness of the emotions churning inside her. It felt unbearable. She was pregnant; a person was growing inside her body. She was this baby's mother and Malachy his or her father. It was the only evidence of what had been their love – what was *still* her love. Was she supposed to let their child be reared by strangers, in a different country?

'I know it's hard, but 1950s or not, it's for the best. And it will be better for you over there than here. The mother-and-baby homes in this country are terrible places – I couldn't let you go to any of them.'

'I wouldn't be in one for long...'

Doc placed his hand on Lena's. 'Listen, love. A girl in Kellstown found herself in the same position as you. Her mother and I were in school together and I hadn't seen her for years, but I bumped into her one day and she told me the story. Her husband is a harsh man and threw the poor girl out. The doctor there is a fool and the priest is worse, so between them they cooked up that she would go to one of those places up the country somewhere. I knew nothing about it until recently. It happened a few years ago, otherwise I would have tried to do something. Anyway, she was allowed one telephone call to her mother, but the mother learned afterwards that the nun was standing beside her the whole time so she was forced to say everything was fine.

'My friend's daughter described being made to do hard manual work in the laundry, washing sheets for the whole town. She described girls as young as thirteen in those places, no comfort, no care, just harsh judgement. My friend's grand-daughter was born after days of labour, a breech birth with no pain relief or support, and the poor girl nearly died. The baby was immediately whisked away, probably adopted in America for a fine big fee, and the girl was kept in the laundry for years "paying off her debt". At one point she managed to write a letter to her mother telling her everything – the laundryman took it and posted it for her – but even then her mother couldn't get her out.'

'That's horrible.' Lena had heard of girls being sent to the nuns in disgrace. Everyone guessed it wasn't a pleasant experience, but nobody ever talked about it.

Doc nodded. 'It is. The poor mother was heartbroken and wracked with guilt that she stood by and allowed her husband and doctor and priest to behave as they did. But she didn't have the power to stand up to them, and so she lost her daughter. The young woman took her own life.'

'That's awful.' Lena's eyes filled with tears.

'So you see why I can't let you go to one of those places?' Doc was gentle but insistent.

'But if I went to England, where would I stay even?' She had never gone anywhere before, no further than Cork with Malachy. 'I can't get a job, I'll be showing soon, and who'd employ an unmarried pregnant girl...'

'I've found you somewhere nice, and it's not in England – it's in Wales. I have a good friend there, another doctor. We worked in a military hospital together during the war, in Cardiff. He was a Jewish refugee from Germany. He escaped with his widowed sister and her son, and we all shared a flat in '43 and '44. He stayed, and his sister, Sarah, lives nearby. She's married to a Welshman now, with a few more children, and she's a very sympathetic person – she's happy to let you have a room in her house in exchange for helping with the children and occasionally sitting behind the counter in her clothes shop. I've told her how good you are with people and how all my patients love you and that I'm sure it will be the same with her customers. She knows your situation, but I've agreed we'll get you a ring and say your husband was killed in a farming accident.'

'You have it all planned out, don't you?' In a fit

of defiance, she glared angrily at the man she had seen as a surrogate father all these years. 'But what if I won't give up this child? If I go ahead and keep the baby for myself, what then?'

He looked at her pityingly. 'You would ruin your life, Lena. You'd have to give up your dreams of being a nurse, and I don't need to tell you that life can be very cruel to children born out of wedlock.' His words fell like stones, each a dull thud.

'You sound like all the rest of the curtain-twitchers in this place.'

He sighed. 'Maybe so, but I'm telling you the honest facts, Lena. God knows I wish it wasn't the truth, that society was more forgiving of women and that all children were seen as a blessing and joy. But it isn't so, and I'd be doing a very bad job of looking after you if I pretended otherwise. I can't bear to watch you do something that would destroy the rest of your life. I believe in God and in heaven, and that one day we'll see those we loved who have gone before us. I imagine meeting Paudie, and I want to face him with a clear conscience. I vowed to look after you when I held you in my arms that day in the church, and you small enough for your feet to fit into my hand and your head in the crook of my arm, and now it's time to make good on that promise. This is the best way I can do that.'

'I'm scared, Doc.'

He took her hand; even his touch was more gentle than normal, as if she were a piece of fragile glass that might shatter at any moment. In reality she did feel like she was glass, but already shattered, with sharp, pointed edges doing damage in every direction.

'I know you are, love, but I think you should go to my friend's sister in Wales. We'll tell everyone here that I've found you a good nursing course to do over there for a few months. You've been saying you were interested in nursing, so it's not too much of a leap.'

'I haven't any money.'

'Don't worry about that. I'll pay for your train and ferry tickets. I was going to give you a raise anyway, so I'll count that towards it, and as I say, Sarah will pay you so that will provide for extra pocket money.'

A long second passed as Lena considered the plan. He was right. She had no options. She had fleetingly thought she might go to Auguste Berger, tell him everything, but the letter said it was he who was encouraging Malachy to stay away, and it was presumably Lena he wanted Malachy to stay away from.

Why, though? The question played over and over in her head all night. Was Malachy just one of those boys out for what he could get? Was everyone right when they said boys like him don't really want girls like her as girlfriends and wives? That he only said all that stuff to get her to sleep with him? And now she was left, like so many before her, high and dry? There was no other explanation.

'All right, I'll go.' She sighed, suddenly so weary and depressed. She had no more fight in her.

'Good. I'll book the boat from Cork for next week. I'll drive you myself. We'll say there was a last-minute place available on the course. Saul's sister, Sarah, will meet you in Swansea.'

'OK, Doc,' she said sadly, and he drew her into a hug. She inhaled the soapy-clean smell of him, heard the beating of his heart, and she felt safe, at least for now.

'Everything will be all right, Lena.' He kissed the top of her head. 'You'll survive, I promise.'

* * *

SHE PACKED A SMALL BAG – some clothes, a photo of her father. She considered bringing a picture of her and Malachy taken in one of those photo booths. But she had too much Cork pride in her soul. Malachy didn't want her, and she would not pine after him like a fool.

His Leaving exams would be over by now, but true to his word, he never came back. Her heart breaking, she sat at the small dressing table and took out a sheet of paper and a pen.

Dear Malachy,

I don't understand why you don't love me any more. You were the only boy I've ever loved or been with, and my heart is broken forever. I know I'll never be properly happy again, not like I was with you, but I'm going to try to get on with my life because the twins need me, and Mammy – she needs me too. Emily is great, and Jack is too, but I think I remind Mam the most of Daddy, and she talks to me more than the others, so I suppose maybe my role in life is to stay with her as she gets older and look after her. I'm having to go away for a bit because I'm carrying our child. Doc says I have to give it up, for everyone's good. I can only dream how if we'd got married and raised our child together, how happy I would have been...

With tears running down her face, Lena folded the unfinished letter and tore it up into a million pieces so they could never be pieced to-gether and read, and let the tiny scraps fall into the wastepaper basket.

Then she wrote another letter for her family, explaining that Doc had got an early morning telephone call, that there was a cancellation on a nursing course in England and he wanted her to do it, so it was all a big rush, and that she'd write properly next week. She just didn't feel able for prolonged goodbyes.

Emily was sleeping peacefully in the other bed. Lena dressed and picked up her bag and crept out of the room.

Out on the landing, she peeped into the twins' room. They'd just started Irish dancing in the vil-lage hall – in Kilteegan Bridge kids started almost as soon as they could walk – and two little green dresses with gold trim were hanging on the wardrobe door. Emily was very excited when their mother made the dresses for the twins; she thought they'd be another great thing to sell in the shop. She was rapidly changing it from a hardware shop to a general drapers as well.

The twins were snuggled with their arms and legs around each other as they'd done since birth.

Lena looked in on her mother, who was also deep in sleep. She'd returned from St Catherine's two days ago and seemed calm and happy and well able for life. Doc had promised to keep an eye on the situation and make sure everyone was looked after properly.

Creeping into the room, she kissed her mother on the cheek. 'Goodbye, Mam.'

Her mother stirred and muttered, 'Goodbye, love,' but then settled back into even deeper sleep.

At the bottom of the lane, a car was waiting for her, and her heart ached. It was Doc's Ford Escort, not Malachy's Volkswagen Beetle.

* * *

As she waited to board the ferry, a huge white ship called the *Innisfallen*, Doc reached into his inside pocket and extracted a thick envelope. Handing it to her, he said, 'There's the tickets, and my mother's wedding ring to wear, and the address and number of my friend, Saul Hoffman, just in case anything happens and you miss Sarah in Swansea. There's some English money in there too, and some Irish. Call me if you need more.'

'You don't have to give me money as well, Doc...'

'I'm your godfather, so I do. And anyway, I want to. Lena, I love all of you, as you know,

though I don't often say it. But you and I have always had a special bond. I don't have any children
of my own, but I see you as a daughter and I want
to look out for you.'

'What am I going to do without you?' she
asked sadly.

'I'll be here, love, at the end of the phone,
whenever you need me.' He hugged her again,
and she walked up the passenger ramp onto the
ship.

CHAPTER 15

Two days later, Lena sat at the dinner table of an unfamiliar house in a leafy suburb of Cardiff. The Evans family couldn't be kinder. Sarah was German and Jewish, but her husband, Charlie Evans, was from Cardiff. He worked in the bank and was a real character. They had four little ones, two boys and two girls, all under ten, and Sarah's son Eli, whose Jewish father had been murdered by the Nazis in Germany, lived with them too. He was twenty-two now and studying to be a doctor like his Uncle Saul at Cardiff University. He wasn't there the night she arrived; he had late tutorials, his mother said.

Sarah was dark-featured and small – her husband towered over her – and her wavy black hair had streaks of grey. She had a cupid's bow mouth, red without lipstick, and a scar above her left eye, which she told Lena she got when a Brownshirt hit her with the butt of his gun one night, for no reason other than that she was a Jew. He'd come into the bookshop where she worked and demanded all books by 'Jews or Jew-lovers' be removed and destroyed. She protested, and he'd hit her with the rifle. Her brother, Saul, had stitched it up, but the scar was clearly visible. She spoke softly and was gentle in her movements. Lena instantly liked her.

The house was large and detached, with plenty of room, and Lena was given her own bedroom the day she arrived. Sarah told her that she knew why she was there and that she was so sorry for her being in such a tragic situation, but that she and her family would do anything they could to make it a bit more bearable. Lena had sat on the bed, overlooking a lovely park where children played on swings, and suddenly out of nowhere, the enormity of it all threatened to overpower her. She cried then, the first time since saying goodbye to Doc in Cork.

Sarah came in with a clean bath towel to give her and found her, and she'd hugged her and soothed her. 'It feels like the end of the world now, *liebling*, I know it does, but you'll be fine.'

Lena had lain awake all that night, listening to the strange noises of a different house, old wood creaking and pipes knocking, sounding cacophonous. She tried to imagine what her baby was like. She'd found a book about pregnancy in the library. Of course she hadn't taken it out – that would have given Nettie Collins a conniption – but she'd peeked into it when she knew no one was looking. It was amazing just how tiny her baby was. It didn't look like a baby at all at this stage, more like the embryo one of their sheep had miscarried when it got a fright from a loose dog.

Lena had never thought much about religious things, but she went to Mass like everyone, and now all the fears of her childhood bubbled to the surface. Was she doing a terrible thing, giving away her child? She'd been intimate with a man before marriage – that was another sin – and God was punishing her with a baby. But could an innocent child be a punishment? And if God was supposed to love everyone, what was He thinking, allowing her to get pregnant? Or did God care about that? Had God sent her a baby on purpose, and she was callously deciding it didn't suit her to be a mother?

Eventually the dawn streaked across the sky and the day came. Sarah explained that she would get the children off to school and then she could take Lena to see the agency that would arrange the adoption. Apparently it wasn't a straightforward process. There were lots of papers she had to sign so she couldn't go back on her word, and then after she gave birth, the baby would be cared for in a foster home until the social worker assigned to it was sure there was nothing wrong with its health, and then proper adoptive parents would be found.

Lena waited until the voices of the children getting ready for school and their mother calling them to brush their teeth and find their shoes ended with a slam of the front door. She needed the bathroom but didn't want anyone to hear her retching, so she lay still until she was alone. Then she crept out onto the landing and barely managed to reach the bathroom before throwing up violently. She clung to the porcelain toilet, sweat beading on her brow as her insides lurched over and over. Eventually, when there was nothing left, she dragged herself upright. She caught her face in the mirror and was shocked. She was deathly white, her dark hair hanging limply around her face.

'Oh, Dad,' she whispered, 'I need you so much now, I really, really do. Send me something, some way to get through this, some sign that I'm not all on my own. I'm so scared, so ashamed. I feel awful and I'm terrified.'

She washed at the sink and tried to tidy herself up a bit, then sat on the toilet, her head in her hands. The tears flowed in earnest then, hot and bitter.

Afterwards, crossing the landing, she physically bumped into a young man she assumed was Eli. He was tall and rake-thin, with sandy hair and freckles. He had a kind smile that crinkled his brown eyes.

'Oh!' She was mortified. She hadn't realised anyone was in the house. He would have heard the vomiting, the crying, and she knew she looked horrendous. 'I'm so sorry, I-I thought... I didn't know that you...' She tried to push past him, her cheeks flaming.

'Hello.' Eli smiled again, and his kind face

made her feel worse. She couldn't cope with sympathy now. 'You must be Lena. It's all right.'

His accent was sing-song, not in the way a Cork one was; it was very distinctly Welsh but melodious. For some reason she'd expected him to sound a little bit German, like the way Sarah pronounced certain words, but then she remembered he was only a child when he came to Wales. He was completely Welsh. She remembered her father saying all Welsh people could sing, and she could imagine why. Their accent was almost a song itself.

'I'm sorry, I just need to go and get dressed.' She pushed past him and went into her room, leaning on the door.

After she recovered, she dressed in what she normally wore for work. She thought it might make her look more serious to the staff at the adoption agency, not like a flighty young foolish girl who got up to all sorts with men. She realised that was probably stupid, that the adoption agency did what it did whoever you were, and Sarah had promised her that passing judgement wasn't part of their remit, but still.

She waited in the room for Sarah to come back from dropping the children. She sat on the bed in her navy skirt, white blouse and pink cardigan, her hair tied up in a ponytail, her face washed. She wore Doc's mother's wedding ring.

There was a gentle knock on the door and Eli's voice called, 'Lena?'

Oh God.

'I just made you a cup of tea and some toast. You probably don't feel like it, but it might be good to try to eat something?'

Her manners won over her reluctance, so she got up and opened the door. He held a tray of tea and toast, with marmalade and butter in little pats.

'Thank you, Mr...' Sarah was Evans and she knew Saul was Hoffman, but she didn't know what she should call him.

'Oh, call me Eli, everyone does. I tried to change it to something more British when I was about twelve, but trying to get my family to do anything is like trying to herd cats, so Eli I was born and Eli I'll stay. My surname is Kogan – that was my father's name. Mum's family were Hoffmans.'

She smiled at him, weak and wan, but at least it was a smile.

'There we go, that's better.' He grinned and handed her the tray. 'You can come down, join me if you like, or stay up here, whichever you prefer?'

She glanced around the room then, the place where her thoughts had given her not one moment of respite, and suddenly some company from a cheerful, kind person felt very inviting. 'I'll come down so.'

'Tidy,' he said, taking back the tray. She had no idea what he meant by 'tidy', but it didn't seem to require a response, and she followed him down the stairs.

They sat at the mahogany table with a lace tablecloth, and she nibbled at the toast. Though the idea of any food entering her system caused her stomach to contract painfully, she tried to swallow something.

'I've got the morning off today,' Eli explained. 'Usually we have lectures at nine, but today's professor is off on some business, so we're off the hook. I always thought grown men at university wouldn't be whooping for joy at a half-day the way we did in school, but it's no different.'

'Do you enjoy your studies?' she asked.

'I do. Well, I don't mind it. I'm looking forward to being qualified.' He winked. 'I don't know how good I'll be at it, but at least I'm chatty, see? People are nervous usually when they visit the doctor, so I think having someone prattling away about this and that and not making a big deal of it is probably good for patients not to feel so terrified.' He took a bite of toast. 'Or maybe it's very annoying, I don't know. We'll soon see, I suppose?'

'How long before you qualify?' She didn't mind him prattling on; she liked his Welsh accent.

'Two months. I'm almost there.'

'And will you practice here in Wales?'

He leaned over conspiratorially. 'I'm not sure. Everyone assumes I will, but I think I want to go somewhere new, somewhere exciting, maybe Kuala Lumpur or Timbuktu or even New York, something like that.'

Lena laughed. His enthusiasm for life was infectious, and once she'd thrown up, she actually felt all right.

'Or maybe Ireland. What's Ireland like?' he asked.

'Not as exciting as New York, I can assure you of that,' she answered ruefully. 'Well, maybe Dublin or Cork might be OK, but where I'm from, Kilteegan Bridge, well, whatever word could be used, exciting is definitely not it.'

'Ah, everyone thinks where they come from is

boring – they know it too well. But if you're away for a while and you look at it with fresh eyes, it might surprise you.'

'I suppose you're right. And it is beautiful, even I can tell that, even though I've been looking at the same view every day of my life. We live near the sea, in West Cork, and the rolling green fields, the old bridge over the river and the ruined Norman Tower on the edge of the town are all very picturesque, I suppose. My brother, Jack, and my sister Emily wouldn't be anywhere else. Jack loves the farm, and Emily is marrying the man who owns the local hardware store. But I don't know. I'd like to do something different, go somewhere, but we'll see.' She was surprised at how easy it was to talk to him. If he knew the reason for her being there, not a widow but a foolish pregnant girl come to give up her baby because she wasn't married, he clearly wasn't unkind enough to bring it up.

In fact, he seemed to know she didn't want to talk about why she was there, because he instantly changed the subject to a very funny story about a trainee doctor leaning over a volunteer patient while being observed by the professor and the entire class; he was so nervous the poor student doctor broke wind. The way Eli had of telling the story, describing the faces of everyone there, caused Lena to laugh for the first time in what felt like months. Eli was definitely working hard to cheer her up, and strangely she was starting to feel better.

Sarah arrived back, and it was time to go. Lena fetched her coat and followed her out the front door. Eli waved after her from the doorstep. 'Good luck, Lena. I hope everything goes well.'

'Thanks, Eli.' She waved back as she got into Sarah's car.

Once they reached the adoption agency, Sarah insisted on parking and going in with her to get her settled. Despite Lena's assertions that she was all right and could manage alone, she found herself glad of the older woman's company.

'I know what it's like to be a young woman in a strange place. When I came here, my brother was working all the time as a doctor, and Eli and I had to make our own way. I hardly spoke English and had just been widowed, and we'd escaped from the Nazis who wanted to kill me and my boy like they had my Elijah, so I know what it is to feel alone and vulnerable.' She patted Lena's hand and smiled kindly. The traces of her German accent were softened now, but it was still there on some sounds.

Lena wondered how hard it was to be German in England in the years since the war. She'd never met a Jew before; there were not very many in Ireland, and all she'd ever heard from the priest was that Herod was King of the Jews and ordered the killing of Jesus. Lena tended to tune out at Mass, so apart from that nugget, she hadn't much more knowledge. But Eli and Sarah could not have been kinder.

They waited a while in reception, then a young man appeared, who asked Sarah to wait downstairs. He led Lena upstairs and down a corridor before presenting her at a desk where a middle-aged woman sat typing.

'Marjorie, this is Miss O'Sullivan. Can you get her details, please? She'll be seen by Mrs Singh afterwards.' And he was gone.

The receptionist was efficient but gave no indication she was remotely interested in Lena apart from her date of birth and medical history. Once Lena had filled out the necessary paperwork, the receptionist sent her to wait in a private room. There was a sofa with a pale green throw and one chair. The glass was opaque, so she couldn't see out.

After what seemed like an hour, another person appeared. She was beautiful, with dark-brown skin, almost-black eyes and the darkest hair Lena had ever seen. Lena thought she was only a few years older than herself.

'Good morning, Miss O'Sullivan.' She smiled. 'My name is Mrs Singh, and I am a social worker.' She spoke in an accent Lena had never heard before, enunciating each word perfectly.

'Hello, Mrs Singh.'

The beautiful woman sat in the chair opposite the sofa. 'I understand you want to have your baby adopted because you're not married to the father?' Her words cut like knives, but her face was kind.

Lena swallowed. 'Well, I didn't know... I mean, this baby, the baby's father said he was going to marry me.' She felt her face get hot with the shame of the admission.

'I'm sorry, Miss O'Sullivan. I'm afraid that happens a lot.' She spoke quietly and slowly.

Lena wanted to explain to this woman that she wasn't an idiot, that she hadn't been foolish. 'I really thought he loved me...'

'I understand,' the social worker said calmly.

'And I'd have the baby if I could. But my godfather – he's a doctor in Ireland – he doesn't think I should try to raise this baby myself. He thinks I should give it up for adoption...'

'Your godfather is very sensible. So what we need to do first is get some consent forms filled in.'

'I don't know if I… I mean…'

'Please, be assured nothing will happen without your consent. This is a frightening time, I know. I won't try to convince you in either direction, but if I can help you with any questions you might have, feel free to ask.' She was gentle and gave Lena the impression that she'd seen this before, a young woman hesitating and worrying about whether she could go through with giving a baby away.

'Look, Lena.' She put down her pen. 'Can I call you Lena?'

Lena nodded.

'All right. I'm Nyra. And even though we look different, we come from similar backgrounds, very family-oriented, sometimes judgemental, right?'

Lena nodded again.

'I think if you give this baby up, Lena, you'll be doing exactly the right thing for yourself and your family, but most importantly for your child. As the child of an unmarried mother, he or she would face a great deal of stigma, here or in Ireland. But if you allow him or her to be adopted, this baby will be brought up by two loving parents who have the income to support a child, and who have been waiting for a long time for their own baby. A baby is the most beautiful gift you can give to anyone, Lena, and you have no need to be ashamed. In fact, you should be proud of yourself for making a decision that brings happiness to so many people – the child, his or her future parents and, in the end, even yourself.'

Lena's mind was in a whirl. 'I still need to think. I need some time.'

'Of course.' Nyra stood up. 'This is not something to be done lightly. Go away and think about it. Be sure what you are doing is what you want, because there's no going back. When you've made up your mind, you know where to find me.'

'Thank you, Nyra, thank you very much.' Lena meant it from the bottom of her heart.

'You're welcome, Lena, and good luck.' The woman left, her unsigned forms in her arms.

Lena picked up her bag and walked past the woman on the reception desk, who looked up from her telephone call, down the stairs and into reception, where Sarah sat waiting for her.

Sarah sighed sympathetically when Lena told her she hadn't felt able to sign her child away without thinking some more about it. 'I know you're worried and doubtful, Lena, and I wish I could say to you it would be fine if you chose to keep him or her, but that just would not be true. You must make up your own mind. But please, at least know you can stay with us for as long as you need to,' she said kindly as they drove back to the house.

CHAPTER 16

*L*ena walked for hours and hours over the next week, past Llandaff Cathedral and into the gardens of Victoria Park. There was a playground in the park, and often she sat on a bench watching the little children climbing and jumping and laughing. Would her child be like them? Would he or she grow up with a Welsh accent, having no idea they were in fact an Irish child?

She pictured the baby as a little boy for some reason. One who looked just like Malachy, a handsome red-haired, green-eyed boy; that's the way he was in her mind every time she closed her eyes. She wanted him for herself so much... But Doc was right – it would be no life for either her or her child in Kilteegan Bridge. She could not consign her son to a lifetime of being looked down on.

Sometimes she imagined just running away, having her baby and never going home to her family... But how could she bear never to see the twins or Jack or Emily again? And her mother would need her more and more as she got older.

She realised one of the big reasons she'd been putting off her decision was this baby was the last thing she had of Malachy, and she wanted to cling to it. He'd been her first love and maybe her last. She wasn't a silly romantic who would kill herself for love, but at the same time, she wasn't the sort of girl who could just switch off her emotions and move on without a backwards glance. If only she knew why Malachy had changed his mind. She could never accept he'd just used her, however much it looked that way.

But she also had Paudie's common sense. Her feet were on the ground, and she knew that as much as she secretly hoped Malachy would magically change his mind, it wasn't going to happen. In the world as it was, it would be impossible to give her baby a good life, raising him on her own. So whatever her future held, she had to give him away. It would be her first and last gift to him, a happy well-kept life with two doting parents.

After she'd made her final decision, she felt lighter than she had for days, and while whatever awaited her was a heartbreaking prospect and she had no idea how on earth she was going to do it, she knew she was going to go through with it. And in the meantime, she had to earn her keep and start working in Sarah's shop.

She caught the bus to Pontcanna, where the Evans family lived, and got off at the top of their road at the corner shop called Ali's Bazaar, which had struck her as so exotic when she first saw it. Cardiff was an eye-opening experience. People were there from the four corners of the world, and she had to work hard not to stare at all the different faces she encountered.

She knocked on the red front door of the large semi-detached house with the well-clipped garden out front. Sarah opened it. 'Oh, Lena, there you are...'

'Sarah, I'm so sorry for being away with the fairies the last few days. I just needed to clear my head, and I'm sorry it's taken me so long.'

'Not at all, *liebling*. Come in, come in off the step and tell me all about it in the sitting room.' She ushered Lena into the house.

Passing through the hall, Lena saw the small children were eating their tea at the kitchen table. 'I'm disturbing your meal. I'm sorry…'

'Please, stop. I kept a plate for myself and Charlie for when he gets home from work, and for you as well in case you were hungry, so we can all have ours together in a while,' Sarah said kindly. 'Now, sit down and let's talk.'

They sat on the striped sofa together, and Sarah turned to face her. 'Tell me your decision.'

'I've decided everyone's right about the adoption. I obviously can't raise a child alone with no support, and Malachy will never change his mind and come back to me – he's obviously not the person I thought he was – so it would be no life for me or for my child. The circumstances of my baby's birth are not of the child's doing, and they deserve a lovely life with parents who love them.'

Sarah took her hand. 'For what it's worth, I think you're doing a brave, wonderful, generous thing.'

'Well, I never should have got myself into this mess in the first place, but anyway, my decision is made. And I'm ready to work now. I know you were only offering to put me up out of kindness, and I'm so grateful. I'll help you in the shop however you like, and I'll babysit so you and Charlie can get out once in a while, and I'll do bits around the house. I can clean and cook and do everything – I'm not normally as useless as I've been the last week, I promise.'

Sarah squeezed her fingers. 'Nobody thinks you're useless. You're a lovely young girl who's been treated very badly and had her heart broken by a silly boy but who is now picking herself up again and looking forward in the best way she can. And good for you, Lena. Emmet spoke about you with such affection. He loves you and he's so proud of you – we all are.'

Lena blinked back tears. Nobody called Doc 'Emmet' except these people, who obviously held him in high regard. She longed for one of his hugs.

After Charlie came home, Lena ate dinner with him and Sarah, a delicious *cholent*, a Jewish beef dish. Charlie launched into a funny story about a man who was ordered by the courts to pay a debt. He didn't want to pay but was being compelled to, so he came into the bank and ordered the amount, which was over a hundred pounds, in pennies. Apparently the complainant had bought a greyhound from the man, the bank's customer, and the greyhound was as slow as molasses. The dog was sold on its pedigree, and sure enough, both mother and father were champion racers, but this dog was bone-idle lazy, it would seem. The bank staff tried to talk him out of paying in pennies, but he wasn't for changing. He said he'd pay the debt if he had to, and a penny was a legal form of currency, so the other man couldn't refuse it but it would be extremely inconvenient for him.

Eli was out at a late lecture, but the smaller children had come into the kitchen for a glass of milk, hearing their father's voice. They listened in giggles to the story of the pennies as the youngest, Alys, who was only four, claimed a place on Charlie's knee and the other three clustered around his chair.

'But, Daddy, wouldn't the other man just bring the pennies to the bank and change them into notes?' one of the boys, eight-year-old Rhys, asked.

'Indeed he will, Rhys, and that leaves your poor old chump of a dad trying to get it all sent back to the treasury.'

Rhys and his brother Bryn, a year his junior, laughed at this, but Gwen, who was between Bryn and Alys in age, looked worried. 'Will you have to count it all, Daddy?' she asked.

Charlie put on a martyred face, but then it

transformed into a wide grin. 'No, I'll get Miss Jones to do it.' And he winked theatrically.

This caused the children to laugh for some reason, and Sarah explained to Lena. 'Miss Jones is Charlie's secretary, and she decided he was getting too fat so has banned all pasties and sausage rolls and buns and cakes from him during the working week.'

'She's a tyrant, I tell you, Lena. The woman has no heart. Nothing nice for poor old me who works so hard. She even checks my lunch to make sure my lovely wife hasn't smuggled something delicious in my lunchbox.'

'Gwyneth Jones has the right idea. You would eat your own body weight in pasties if someone didn't stop you.'

Charlie was definitely inclined to be portly, but he didn't seem to care. 'See what I've to put up with, Lena? Tyrants, all of them. But not my darling children – they are beautiful and feel sorry for their dear old dad.' He whispered something in Alys's ear; she giggled and slipped off his knee and ran to the pantry, returning moments later with an iced bun.

Sarah looked mock disapproving as Charlie bit into the cake, much to his children's delight.

'Right, you naughty lot, bedtime,' Sarah announced, clapping her hands. 'If I don't get an early night myself, I'll be found fast asleep on the kitchen table in the morning. Charlie, will you clear away while I put them to bed?'

'I'll clear away.' Lena jumped up.

'No, no, love, you've had a long day…' Sarah protested.

'No, honestly, you sort the children out and I'll tidy up. Please.' Lena wanted to be useful.

'Can you read us a story then, Daddy?' Gwen asked.

Charlie stood up and yawned dramatically. 'You know the trouble when I tell you bedtime stories, don't you?'

'You fall asleep before us,' the four little ones chorused.

'Yes indeed.' He held up his hands like claws and spoke in a spooky voice, causing the children to scatter, screaming. 'So I'll have to tell you a very scary story tonight so I'll be too terrified to fall asleep.'

'Honestly' – Sarah rolled her eyes at Lena – 'sometimes I think I have six children and he's the biggest of the lot.'

Charlie scampered up the stairs after the children, who were laughing and giggling at his antics.

Lena's arms were up to her elbows in sudsy water when Eli appeared through the back door.

'Lena, how nice to see you again.' He grinned. He switched on the big wireless as he passed it, tuning it to a popular music station. Immediately the room was filled with the sounds of Cliff Richard and the Shadows.

'Hello, Eli. Sarah's left your tea under the grill there.' She nodded at the covered plate being kept warm.

'Great, I'm famished.' He took the plate and sat at the table, wolfing the beef casserole with gusto.

'How was your day?' she asked.

'Abscesses.'

'What?'

'Abscesses in the ear, causes of, treatment for, what to do, what not to do,' he said through a mouthful of potato. Then he did an impression of someone with a deep, sonorous and somewhat tedious voice. 'One slip of the hand and draining a simple abscess in the ear becomes brain surgery, and while I think in time some of you lot may become reasonably competent GPs, brain surgery is certainly beyond you, so concentrate.'

Lena laughed.

'That's our prof. He's a wit but never smiles – no matter what, he can't crack even a tiny upward movement of lips. We try to make him laugh, but he's legendarily droll.'

'So you're an abscess expert now, are you?'

'Abscessman!' He chuckled. 'Like Batman, but in a white coat and can't do any interesting stunts.'

'But if you had an abscess in your ear, then you wouldn't give a monkey's about Gotham City and you'd badly need someone who could make the pain stop,' Lena replied as she took a tea towel to dry the dishes.

'A lady who has her priorities straight – I like that.' He winked as he washed his own plate and took another tea towel to dry it.

She tried to replace the dish for the casserole on top of the cupboard, but it was too high. Eli took it from her, as he could reach it easily. His hand brushed off hers as he took it, and he flushed pink.

Before she could say anything, Sarah appeared back downstairs. 'All in our double bed in their pyjamas, while Charlie scares the living wits out of them with monsters from the deep.'

'Hello, Mum.' Eli kissed her cheek, and she patted his face affectionately.

'Shalom, *leibling*.'

'Sit down, let me make you both a cup of tea,' Lena offered.

Sarah sank gratefully into a chair. 'That would be lovely, thank you, Lena.'

Eli lingered around the kitchen, watching as Lena heaped tea leaves into the scalded pot.

'Should you not have your head in the books?' Sarah asked her son with a raised eyebrow. 'Your exams are only a few weeks away, and I can't face Bessie Evans sneering at me because my own son clearly wasn't good enough to be a doctor.'

'Mum, you know the B-word frightens me,' he said jokingly.

'Well, it frightens me more, so back to the books with you.' She shooed Eli out.

'My mother-in-law has never forgiven me for what she calls "saddling her son with another man's child and a Jew to boot", so nothing Eli ever does is good enough for her.'

Lena placed a cup of tea in front of her, and when Sarah asked her to join her, she made a second cup and sat down at the table. It was incredible how quiet the house was now. Sarah had turned the volume down on the wireless but hadn't switched it off. Some presenter read the news as they sat companionably together.

'Charlie will fall asleep, and all four of them

will still be in our bed, and I'll have to move them. Same every night.' Sarah grinned ruefully.

'He's a lovely father. They adore him, you can see.'

'He is. They're lucky to have him. Eli too. When my first husband was murdered by Nazi thugs, Eli was only six. After that, my brother, Saul, and I escaped to England, so Eli only remembers bits of his father. Charlie has been a wonderful substitute to him all these years. I've got Emmet to thank for meeting my darling husband, by the way.'

Lena paused in surprise, with her cup halfway to her mouth. 'Really?'

'Oh yes. When we were all living together, me with Eli and Saul and Emmet, all of us crushed into that little flat beside the hospital, this boy I met in the bank asked me out to a dance, but I said I couldn't, that I had my son to look after. I had very little English then, but he persisted, and one day when we were walking down the street, Emmet, Eli and I, we bumped into Charlie. He was as incorrigible then as he is now, so he asked me out again, and before I could refuse, Emmet said he would mind Eli and immediately took him off to the park to kick a football. Charlie and I went for a cup of tea. Then one thing led to another...'

'That's a lovely story,' said Lena, delighted.

'It was. And our story wasn't so different from yours – it just had a happier ending. But there were lots of people who thought he was mad, his mother leading the charge. A widow, a German and a Jew, and another man's child into the bargain. But Charlie didn't care about any of that. We married in secret. Well...' She coloured.

Lena looked at her quizzically, and Sarah blushed deeper. 'Let's just say Rhys was a little premature?'

Lena knew what she meant and immediately felt better. If anyone understood the terror of an unplanned pregnancy, Sarah did.

'Charlie and I got married the moment we found out. He's a good man, and he wasn't going to leave me to cope alone, and luckily it turned out to be the right thing for both of us. We've been very happy and went on to have the other three, so things fell the right way for me. So you see, Lena, you're not alone. There but for the grace of God go I. I was lucky, I got away with it, and now I'd like to pay that luck back and help you.'

'Did your family ever meet Charlie?' asked

Lena, before realising it was a stupid question – Sarah's face looked suddenly so incredibly desolate. 'I'm so sorry – I didn't think.'

Sarah sighed. 'It's all right. No, they never did. I never heard from them after the war. They lived in Leipzig, where I'm from, but Elijah and I moved to Berlin in 1930 so I didn't get to see them once he died. I had to get Eli away. I tried after the war, but there was nothing. The authorities are still going through the records even now, but it is not likely that my parents survived.'

Lena eyes flooded with tears. 'It was the same with my uncle, my mother's brother, Ted. He was living in Germany with a German wife, and we don't know what happened to him even now, but we think he must be dead.'

For nearly a minute, the two women sat in silence, remembering the dead and missing them, and then Lena said, 'I'm so glad you found happiness again with Charlie. I'm sure it's what Elijah and your parents would want for you.'

'I think they would. But Charlie's mother, Bessie Evans, was none too pleased. She's a right snob and hates the Jews, so she was disgusted with me and Eli, and his father is too henpecked to open his mouth to her. She's a difficult woman, angry and strange, but not every mother is an angel, I suppose.'

'Mine is difficult too.' Lena surprised herself. She never spoke about Maria, but Sarah had been so honest with her, and made her feel so much better about herself, that she felt like being honest in return. The other woman let her talk, never interrupting, until Lena had revealed the whole big mess about Maria's mental health struggles, and how she had to go to St Catherine's so often, and how she'd been so angry about Lena seeing Malachy, something to do with thinking the Bergers were a terrible family even though Auguste Berger was in a wheelchair and couldn't hurt anyone if he tried.

'You poor girl. What misfortune to have to endure, and so much responsibility on such young shoulders.' Sarah's sympathy started off Lena's tears again. Sarah didn't try to stop her but just let her cry, for herself, for her father, for Malachy, for her mother.

After a while, Lena took a deep breath, wiped her nose with the handkerchief Sarah had handed her and smiled weakly. 'You don't know how grateful I am for you taking me in, and I promise to be as helpful as I can be.'

'I know you will, and you won't be bored.'

Sarah laughed. 'Although you are expecting a baby, so you'll have to take care of yourself. And we need to agree on the exact same story for the neighbours to avoid the tongues wagging. Emmet told me to say you're the niece of a family friend who was born and brought up in Ireland, and that your husband was killed in a farming accident. What name will we give him?'

'Maybe Pádraig. My dad was Pádraig, but everyone called him Paudie – it's even on his gravestone.'

'Well, that's settled then. Pádraig O'Sullivan was your husband, and you have a baby on the way and needed some help, so you came to stay with us for a while. We needn't get into the details too much, but despite the blessed mercy that British people aren't as curious as others might be – back in Leipzig everyone knew everyone's business – there are some who love an old nose around other people's business.'

'You have to give me plenty of work to do. I can get the children ready in the mornings, walk them to school, cook and clean the house, that sort of thing...'

'That's lovely, and I won't always say no to that, but the place where I really need help is in the dress shop. It's only a tiny place, and I had a lovely woman working there for me, but the poor thing has cancer and I'm desperate to keep the shop going so I can continue to pay her – she needs the financial support because she has no other family. Do you know anything about dressmaking and things like that?'

Lena nodded eagerly. 'I do actually. I was telling you the difficult side of my mother earlier, but when she's having her good times, she's very talented with clothes, and she taught me lots of tricks and tips about patterns and the right materials to use. I wouldn't be any way as useful as her, but I wouldn't be afraid to talk to the customers about it.'

'That's wonderful.' Sarah beamed. 'That's perfect for me, and when the time comes to have your baby, we'll make sure you're taken care of, and you can decide then what you'll do next.'

CHAPTER 17

*L*ena's days from then on transformed into a pleasant routine. Once she was past the first twelve weeks of her pregnancy, she began to feel better, and working in the shop every day was great fun. Sarah was amazed how many more women started coming in now that Lena was there to advise them on fashion and what might suit them best. The shop also sold patterns and fabric, so she was called on regularly for advice on how to do dressmaking. Instead of this side of the business negatively impacting the boutique side, it actually helped it. Women would always buy ready-made things for themselves, but they would often pick up a pattern and some material at the same time to run up something for their children. This was the generation that grew up in wartime, so making do and mending were built into them. It didn't always go according to plan of course, and Lena was even willing to dig customers out of a hole when they came in with a dress gone wrong; she would fix the worst of it and cover up any lesser mistakes with lace and buttons.

The shop didn't even feel like work, just fun. Lena loved fashion, so it was bliss to spend ages trawling through wholesale catalogues looking for the next big trend. Sarah said she had a knack for it, and Lena thought maybe she was right. Lena had a good eye for what worked on people maybe. Sarah said she should consider it as a career once this was all over. It was surprising to Lena how impressed everyone was with her small bit of knowledge; her mother had been doing far more complicated stuff for as long as she could remember.

She wrote to Maria, saying how she was working in a dress shop at weekends to pay her bed and board and asking her for any advice. She also enthused about her 'nursing course', and it wasn't such a terrible lie because Eli was lending her lots of medical books and she really was studying for her pre-nursing exams in the evening, after everyone else had gone to bed. By the time she was six months gone, she had fierce indigestion and the baby was kicking a lot; it kept her awake, so she made the best of it by reading the books.

She also wrote to Emily and Jack, and enjoyed getting their letters in the post. Jack was devouring the farming journals that Maria had ordered for him from Nettie Collins in the library, and he was full of information about the ranch in Montana. And Emily was deep in wedding preparations. Luckily the happy couple had set a date for early March – Blackie not one to rush into anything still, it would seem – so Lena wouldn't miss the big day. She promised Em she would be there and be her bridesmaid. Emily wrote back suggesting a shopping trip in Cardiff, but Lena said how she was so busy, that she had her exams coming and had to work in the shop at weekends, so it would be better to wait and see each other in Ireland.

The twins drew pictures on cards for her of different animals they had 'rescued' – a baby bird, a rabbit, several cats (one of which ate the bird) – and either Jack or Emily posted them, and they made her smile.

Doc wrote every week and promised to visit

as soon as he could get away, but she knew his patients wouldn't let him, so she wasn't holding her breath. Someone was always in need of him in Kilteegan Bridge, but she missed him.

In one letter, he told her that he'd answered Malachy's letter as she'd asked him to, telling him that Lena was in great spirits, that she was getting on with her life and had no need for anyone to look after her, that she was a wonderful girl with a great future, and it was a pity some people couldn't see that, but she was much better off without a man who didn't respect her. Malachy hadn't answered, but Doc heard he got a scholarship to study in America. He seemed to have had some dreadful falling out with his father and had not been back to Kilteegan Bridge since he left, but no one knew why. At least Phillippe Decker had stopped hanging around the town so much.

Lena had cried for a while after reading that letter. Malachy gone to America... It seemed so final. She realised a part of her still hoped somehow he'd reappear and announce he was going to marry her and take care of her and their baby. But it was a stupid pipe dream, and she scolded herself for being a fool.

Sometimes she wrote letters to Malachy, like she'd done that last night in Ireland, telling him that she still loved him, that she was carrying their child. And then of course she tore the letters up again and burned them in the fire. He was gone and free, and she was too proud to force him home to marry her, if he even would, which seemed unlikely.

Eli finished his medical exams and went to work with his Uncle Saul in Cardiff Royal Infirmary as a junior doctor, and he got his own digs right next to the hospital so he was near to work when he was on call. Lena found she missed his good-humoured presence around the house. He made her laugh and never asked about her so-called late husband or commented on her ever-expanding girth, for which she was grateful.

He wrote to her regularly, which surprised her; they became kind of pen pals. They didn't discuss anything too heavy or serious; he told her funny stories about hospital life, and she told him about his little brothers and sisters and the dress shop. She wondered why he bothered really, as her life was fairly humdrum. Not that she was complaining. He was still talking about going to New York or Timbuktu, but he didn't seem to be doing anything about it. And he sometimes mentioned the daughter of the landlady, Janice Stiller, a nice Jewish girl. He said she was a quiet, gentle person and made a fine shepherd's pie, almost as good as his mother's. Lena suspected he would settle down with this Janice Stiller and give up his dreams of travel. She hoped he would be happy either way; he was such a nice lad.

She'd become so fond of the younger Evans children and felt very much like their big sister. It took the edge off the loneliness for her own siblings. Rhys and Bryn were so funny, a right little pair of ruffians. No matter how neat and tidy she had them going out to school in the mornings, they managed to come home looking like the wreck of the Hesperus. Alys and Gwen were adorable, and when they discovered she could make dollies' clothes, they kept her very busy with requests for so many different outfits. She didn't mind; it gave her something to do when the shop was quiet and reminded her of Molly and May.

One day Charlie came home in a rage from visiting his mother, the fearsome Bessie Evans, always called by her full name, with the news that she wasn't at all pleased about Eli being a doctor now. She supposed Jewish refugees were all right, but felt they shouldn't be taking up professions that should be filled by British people. Every time Bessie Evans said something like that, Charlie would fall out with her for months on end, but then his father, Owen, would beg him to make contact again. Owen said it was too hard for him having to put up with Bessie Evans by himself, and Charlie would relent and unwillingly go visit. Sarah confided in Lena that she lived for the periods of what Charlie called 'picture no sound' from his mother; she was an absolute weapon by all accounts.

It made Lena realise that however difficult her own mother was, with her visions and demons, at least Maria had a good heart and would never put someone down for what they were...except Auguste Berger, perhaps. Although after what Malachy had done to her, Lena thought maybe Maria had been right about the Bergers after all; maybe both the Berger men were all charm and no heart.

So she settled down and passed the months in the house and shop, seeking out ways to be useful. A life of work on the farm and at home when her mother was ill, and also in Doc's surgery, proved very useful to her. The Evans house was a place of love and laughter but also of chaos and disorder, and soon she had it transformed. The linen cupboard was full of clean, folded sheets and pillowcases, Lena changed all the beds once a week, and the children's clothes and shoes were mended, polished and replaced in their individual wardrobes. She'd made little bags for each of the little ones for their socks and underwear, so there was no more screaming and looking for socks in the morning. She dropped Charlie's suits, shirts and ties to the dry cleaners each Friday and collected them on Tuesdays, so he always had a fresh supply. He had been offered a promotion, and his new boss had commented on how he'd really smartened himself up – they all said they had Lena to thank for it. They insisted on paying her wages on top of her bed and board to share in their good fortune.

The baby was due the first or second week of January, and she was scared but not terrified. Something told her everything would be all right. She'd spoken again to Nyra Singh at the adoption agency, and the social worker had been very helpful, firm but kind. She said it was best to take the baby right away; prolonging things only made it harder. She explained that once they took the child, there would be no way of finding them again, and to leave the baby with her for any length of time would only cause further heartbreak. She assured Lena that the families chosen as adopters were all vetted well and regular checks were made as to the welfare of the child, so she need have no concerns in that regard.

She'd also explained that once the baby was born, the case would transfer to another branch of the service, so Lena would be assigned a new social worker. That made Lena sad, as she'd built up a rapport with Nyra, but she supposed she wouldn't have any relationship at all with the new one. The person would take the baby and that would be that.

Lena knew she would be sad, but a part of her, if she was honest, was looking forward to having her life back, to pursuing her own plans and ambitions. Now that she'd been gone from Kilteegan Bridge for so long, and everyone was managing fine without her, perhaps she didn't need to go back for a while. She had entered for the pre-nursing exams in Cardiff. The next round was in May, and she thought if she passed them, she might begin her nursing training here, live in a nurses' residence and begin her new life. The thought made her giddy with excitement.

Eli came to stay for a few days over the Christmas holidays, and they slipped easily into their old ways of banter and fun. He'd not seen her in a while, and while he was too polite to comment, she knew her new huge self must have been a shock. She got a fright herself when she looked in the mirror.

One evening, he suggested he take Lena out to dinner.

'Are you mad?' Lena laughed. 'And me like a beached whale?'

He grinned. 'Why not? Even whales have to eat.'

'Go on out of that. Why don't you go back to your Janice Stiller and take her out wining and dining instead.'

She was only teasing him, but a shadow crossed his normally cheerful face. 'Why do you say that?'

Lena could have kicked herself; he looked so hurt. 'I'm so sorry. It's just you mentioned her in your letters so often...'

Eli exhaled. 'Only because she's one of the few human beings I see that aren't doctors or nurses or bleeding like stuck pigs or wrapped up in bandages in the emergency ward. She and I are not an item, never were and never will be. She's as quiet as a mouse and actually besotted with the other lodger, a chap called Shiply, who has no visible source of income but is renowned for the power of his persuasion with the ladies. I don't know why she bothers with him, but she does.'

'I'm sorry,' Lena said again. Obviously Eli had some feelings for this girl and she'd rejected him.

'Don't be,' he said. 'So, dinner?'

And this time, she hadn't the heart to refuse him. 'Well, if you insist, but we probably won't find anywhere with it being Christmas.'

He laughed, cheerful again. 'Don't worry, I'll sort it out. Now go and make yourself even more beautiful.'

Compliments slipped easily off his lips. He wasn't lecherous or sleazy, but she saw the way people just seemed to warm to him, and the flattery, whether it was directed at an old lady in a tea shop or the man in the grocer's, felt good-natured and genuine.

She trudged slowly upstairs, easier said than done, to make herself halfway presentable. She hadn't anything nice to wear, as nothing fit her any more, but Sarah had given her a navy maternity dress of hers, so she put her pink cardigan over it and teamed it with a pair of boots she'd treated herself to last week. She put a little make-up on and pulled the new boots over her slightly swollen ankles.

She came back downstairs, having tied her hair up in a high ponytail and used Sarah's curling iron on the ends to create her signature

Audrey Hepburn look, the one Malachy had loved, and Eli watched her as she descended.

'Will I do?' she asked.

'Just about,' Eli replied, his voice husky for some reason.

'Careful I don't fall on you – you'd never recover,' she joked as he helped her on with her coat. It was freezing outside, and the garden was white with snow.

'What are you saying? That I'm a weakling?' he teased as he helped her into the front seat of his new Aston Martin.

'No. And wow, this is a nice car! You've been riding around on that ratty old bike for so long, it's hard to imagine you in a grown-up car.'

'Oh yes, all grown up, I am. Eli Kogan is a man, and he's got a big-man car. It's a DB4 two-door, four seats, convertible British Racing Green, Italian design, British engineering, star of the London Motor Show of 1958, first car capable of zero to one hundred miles per hour in twenty-one seconds,' he proclaimed loudly, much to the amusement of his younger siblings, who were building a snowman in the front garden.

'How much was it?' she asked, aghast.

'The bishop wouldn't ask you that, as you're

so fond of saying.' He winked; he loved all of her Irishisms.

'Four thousand pounds – I heard him telling Daddy,' Bryn revealed, his eyes like saucers.

'They're paying you too much.' Lena grinned as he settled her in. The car smelled of leather, and Eli had kept the engine running so it was lovely and warm inside.

He jumped into the driver's seat and tooted the horn at the children, who waved them off.

They drove, chatting amiably, until he turned into a car park.

Lena gasped. 'You're not serious.'

'What?' Eli looked innocent.

'Tell me you didn't book dinner in the Royal Hotel.' She hoped he was joking.

'Well, it *is* Christmas, and while I might be Jewish, I *do* know the story. So just like poor old Mary, traipsing around Bethlehem looking for a bite to eat and a place to rest her weary head, Joseph – that's me in this scenario – finds her a comfortable spot. Now I couldn't get a donkey or a load of sheep, though a chap I know from out Barry way did offer me a few geese, but I thought they'd be more trouble than they're worth, and besides, I don't think there were any geese in the Bethlehem story...'

Lena pealed with laughter. 'You're bonkers. You know that, don't you?'

'Absolutely,' he said as he helped her out.

Lena felt self-conscious as the exquisitely dressed waiter led them to a table, but he didn't bat an eyelid and obviously thought they were husband and wife, a mistake that Eli didn't bother to correct. They had the set Christmas menu, and they even had a glass of wine. Lena wasn't much of a drinker, and she'd not had any at all since leaving Ireland, so she felt it go right to her head.

'I think I'll just pop to the ladies,' she said, standing dizzily, and to her horror she felt a gush, then the sickening sound of liquid pouring onto carpet. She panicked. Doc had warned her in his letters that the moment her waters broke, she was to go directly to hospital.

'Lena? What is it?' Eli asked, but before she had time to reply, he saw the puddle on the carpet between her feet and sprang into action, leaping up to take her arm.

A waiter arrived at a smart trot, looking appalled, but Eli waved him away. 'Sorry about the carpet, mate, but it seems babies care nothing for Axminster. Here's my card – send us the cleaning bill. We need to get going, I'm afraid.'

The waiter glanced at the business card and

visibly relaxed as he read 'doctor' beside Eli's name; at least he'd be good for it.

The next minutes were a blur as Eli half carried her to the car and drove at speed to the hospital. 'Wait, Eli, this isn't the hospital I'm booked into…' she began, but gasped as another contraction forced her to stop talking.

'I know, but that one is on the other side of town, and I don't want to risk you destroying my leather upholstery giving birth in my splendid new car.' He winked.

A porter was outside with a wheelchair, having just delivered another patient to their waiting family. 'Oi, sir, we'll be needing that!' Eli shouted to his retreating back.

The porter turned and assessed the situation. 'Righto, love, in you get.' He helped Lena to sit. By now the pains were coming. Not unmanageable, but regular.

They were wheeled in, and soon she was whisked away by a team of orderlies and nurses, her clothes removed and a gown put on. She was examined, and the doctor determined that she was almost there. The pains were coming more rapidly by then, and growing in intensity, but she was focused. She would do this.

CHAPTER 18

The woman from the agency wasn't notified, as would have been the case in the hospital where Lena planned to give birth, and so nobody at the hospital was aware that she planned to have the child adopted.

She was handed her son, a lovely, perfect little boy with a cap of dark-red hair and blue eyes with just a hint of green, just like his father.

As she gazed in awe at him, Eli appeared with a flustered-looking matron. 'Your husband was most insistent we let him in, even though visiting hours are over,' she said with a disapproving glance at Eli, who looked suitably humble. 'So five minutes, no more. New mothers need their sleep.'

'I'll be gone before you know it, Matron,' Eli promised.

'My what?' Lena giggled as the nurse shut the door behind her.

'Well, she wasn't going to let me see you otherwise, and those chairs outside in the corridor are very uncomfortable. I think she only relented because I'm a doctor. Anyway, let's see the little mite.'

Lena held the baby out so Eli could look at him.

'May I?' he asked, holding out his arms.

'Of course.'

She handed him her son, and Eli cooed into the little wrapped bundle, then said sternly to the baby, 'You owe me for a carpet and a dinner, mate, so don't you forget it.' He turned to Lena then. 'Was it awful?'

'No picnic, but I'm all right.' She took the baby back and gazed at him once more. 'He's beautiful, isn't he?'

The infant wrapped his baby fist around her little finger and held tight.

'He is. He looks just like you.'

'He looks like his daddy, actually,' she murmured, mostly to the child.

'Then he's a fool not to be here to see his son,'

Eli said, and it was the first time she realised he knew her baby's father was still alive and not dead in a farming accident. She flushed, but at the same time she was grateful to Sarah, because of course Eli knowing the truth was the reason he'd never asked her any awkward questions that would have forced her to lie.

They heard footsteps in the corridor. Eli ducked down on the window side of her bed, with his finger to his lips.

The matron opened the door. 'Ah, he's gone, good. It's past midnight, and I'm going off shift now – I should have been gone hours ago. But if you need anything, ring the bell and the night nurse will come to you. We have four mothers in labour at the moment and two more due in, so manage yourself as best you can, dear. They'll be very busy.' She shut the door.

Eli popped back up.

'She'll murder both of us if she finds out,' Lena warned.

'She's gone home to her bed. She cares not a jot for you or me. So what's his name?'

Lena gazed into her baby's green eyes. 'Well, Nyra Singh from the adoption agency told me not to name him, although all the time he was inside me, I was sure he was a boy and I've been calling him Emmet, after Doc, so it's hard not to think of him that way…'

Eli said gently, 'I meant his father's name.'

'Oh.' She flushed again. 'Malachy, Malachy Berger. I suppose you know the story?'

Eli nodded. 'Mum told me before you arrived. Not gossiping, but she thought I might say something hurtful by accident if I didn't know. I do have a habit of putting my foot in it, as you well know.'

'He doesn't know about Emmet.' It was important to Lena that Eli understand that.

'You never told him?'

'He left me before I had the chance. And he's gone to America now.'

'Do you still love him?'

Lena gazed down at Malachy's son and nodded sadly. 'I don't think I'll ever stop.'

Eli stroked the baby's head with his forefinger. The child gave a soft whimper.

'Do you think he's hungry?' asked Lena. 'Matron said for me to feed him if he was, but I don't know how?'

'Well, it's not my greatest area of expertise, but paediatrics was part of my studies. I think maybe if you unwrap him so he's not so restricted in his movements and put him to your breast, he'll know what to do? I can leave if you'd rather…'

'Stay, please,' she heard herself say.

Lena unwrapped her son so he could move, and just as Eli suggested, put him to her breast. He latched on instantly and began to feed. 'He's doing it,' she said in amazement.

'Clever chap.' Eli grinned.

She fed him, and Eli got his wind up and changed his nappy, dressing him in the vest and smock the hospital provided. Lena used the time to have a wash, change her nightie and brush her hair.

As dawn tried to break through the dark Welsh clouds, Lena slept and Eli dozed off in the chair beside her bed, Emmet on his chest.

The morning sounds of the hospital woke them both.

'I'd better go back to Pontcanna and tell the folks,' Eli said, looking out the window at the cold January morning with its gunmetal-grey sky.

Lena smiled at him, snuggling down with her baby against the pillows. 'Thank you, Eli. Thank you so much for everything. I don't know what I would have done without you.'

'That's no problem, glad to be of assistance.'

He paused. 'Will you still want to see the adoption people?'

She looked down at her son, contentedly asleep in her arms again, and realised just how naïve she'd been, thinking she could just hand him over and move on with her life.

'I suppose so. They said it's best to take them right away, and now I see why...' Lena's eyes filled with tears.

Eli nodded sadly. 'My mother will bring your bag in for you, I'd imagine. She'll be keen to visit.'

'Thanks again, Eli. You're a great friend.'

He nodded, then placed his hand on the baby's head and said, 'You take care now, little man, and have a good life.' He leaned down and kissed the infant's head and then Lena's cheek. 'Bye, Lena. I'll be seeing you.'

CHAPTER 19

For the rest of the morning, Lena sat on the bed, propped by pillows, and held her son. He opened his eyes and they locked with hers, and she felt something she'd never experienced before. She loved her family, and Malachy, but not like this. This was as if a compartment in her heart that she never knew was there suddenly opened and he filled it completely. No matter what happened now, she knew she would never be the same again. She was a mother, and she had a son.

She wondered if maybe she could tell the agency that his name was Emmet. It had a nice sound to it; it was an interesting name, a name that could take him interesting places.

'Where will you go, little man? What will you see and do?'

She cuddled him and smelled his head, the sweet baby aroma of his neck, trying to consign it to memory forever. She sang the songs her father used to sing to her, and told him stories of Malachy and his mother and father. She told him about Kilteegan Bridge and Doc and everyone who lived there.

'I'd love to keep you, darling boy, more than anything in this whole world, I would. I love you so much, more than I ever imagined I could actually, but some nice couple will take you who have a fancy house and a nice car. They'll bring you on holiday to the sea and send you to a posh school, and you'll be someone in this world. It's too complicated to explain to you, but I would have loved you, I swear I would.' She was sobbing into his little head now. 'But I can't. The world won't let me keep you, so I have to let you go.'

Sarah came to visit, bringing Lena's bag with clothes for herself and the baby, and a blanket Lena had knitted for him specially. After admiring Emmet, Sarah asked gently about her adoption plans, and offered to speak to the matron on her behalf. The matron tutted and sighed and looked very disapproving once she was told, and said she should have been informed before, that it was all very irregular.

A woman from the adoption agency appeared later that day, also complaining that she should have been informed earlier, and that it was most unfair on the birth mother to have had to spend all this time with the child. The woman didn't look at all like Nyra Singh; she looked to be any age between forty and seventy, wearing a beige and brown checked skirt, sensible flat shoes and a beige jumper. Instantly forgettable, Lena realised. Maybe the ones who took your baby away looked like that on purpose, so you wouldn't remember.

'I'm sorry, my dear. We try to make this as painless as possible.' The woman took the baby from Lena's arms and dressed him in clothes she'd brought, a white sleepsuit and vest.

'I have some clothes and a blanket I knitted for him,' Lena said, but the woman shook her head.

'We use our own, dear, don't worry.'

Another woman appeared then, a young blond, blue-eyed girl, clearly the assistant to this nondescript woman, and the baby was thrust in her arms. And before Lena could say or do any-thing, she was gone.

'Hold on, I just want to –' she began.

'Please, dear.' The older woman turned and smiled, not unsympathetically. 'Trust me on this – a long teary goodbye won't help. He'll be fine, well-loved and taken care of. That's all you need to know.'

'But I…I…I wasn't ready,' she managed.

'Nobody ever is, dear, even if they've only just given birth.' The nondescript woman patted her hand and then extracted a sheaf of paper from her handbag. She produced a pen and flicked through the pages to the last page, where a black line and an X indicated where Lena should sign.

'I'm not sure –' Lena began again.

'Look, can you raise him? A single girl with no means of support, financial or emotional? Can you offer him a comfortable home? Nutritious food? Warm clothes? A quality education?'

'Well, not really, but –'

'No. That's the answer. It's hard, but the truth. I've seen this a hundred times. Nature is strong, and the urge to keep your baby is a powerful one, but you must do what is best for him, and for you, and this is it. Society is not kind to women like you, or their babies, so this is the biggest act of love you can give him.'

'But can I see him, or even know how he's getting on?'

'How would that help?'

'I'd know he was all right,' Lena said through her tears.

'I'm telling you he will be all right, and so will you. Now, sign the paper and set about rebuilding your life. You're a young woman, and I'm sure marriage and children are on the horizon for you. The little chap will spend three months in top-quality foster care while we make sure he's healthy and developing well, and then we'll find him a loving home, and I can promise you he will be adored.'

'Can you tell his new parents that his name is Emmet?'

'But it isn't.' The woman's compassionate look belied the harshness of her words. 'His name will be whatever they give to him. Now sign these papers, and I'll be gone, and that will be the end of it.'

Lena thought she might be sick. Their son. Emmet was hers, hers and Malachy's. Already she felt his loss like a gaping open wound.

She robotically signed the page. The woman whipped it away and folded it quickly, placing it in her handbag.

'Take good care of yourself now, dear. It will

be lonely for a time, but remember you did the right thing.' She turned to go.

As she opened the door, Lena called after her. 'Please, at least tell them his name was Emmet. They might decide to...'

But the woman either didn't hear her or chose not to. She left, closing the door behind her, and Lena was left alone.

* * *

THE HOSPITAL WAS against discharging her the next day, claiming she needed longer to recover, but she couldn't bear to stay. Memories of him were everywhere. The hospital took his crib, but she hid the little vests and smocks she'd dressed him in and held them to her nose, desperate to get even a faint memory of his baby smell. She kept the blanket she knitted as well; it was green like his eyes and the grass of home. She folded everything neatly in the bottom of her bag, ready for when Sarah came to collect her.

They drove home in silence to Pontcanna, Sarah clearly knowing she didn't want to talk. Back at the house, Lena went up to her room and got into bed and cried herself to sleep. She had barely woken when Sarah arrived at the door with a tray of tea and toast.

'I'm not hungry, Sarah, thanks,' she managed. The last thing on earth she wanted was company. She needed to be alone in her grief, just her and the memory of her son.

'I know, but you have to eat something. So sit up, just for me.' The older woman was kind but insistent, and rather than be rude, Lena reluctantly sat up.

Sarah placed the tray on her lap and sat on the end of the bed. 'It must have been so hard, Lena. I can't imagine.'

'I…I loved him, Sarah. He was perfect, so perfect…' Her voice was raspy, and talking hurt her throat.

'I know he was. He was a smashing little lad, and why wouldn't he be? His mammy is beautiful, and I'm sure his daddy was gorgeous too.'

'He was.' Lena smiled at the memory of her first true love.

'I know today is the worst day, and I'm not saying you'll get over it in weeks or even months, but in the end, you will be all right.'

Lena dropped her eyes, the toast dry in her mouth. She knew Sarah was trying to be kind, to make her feel less hollow, but she was wrong. Her body would recover, she hoped, though right then she felt like she'd been hit by a bus, but her heart would never heal. She would never get over the loss of her son, never.

'Doc rang. I told him the news. He said to phone him when you were up and about.'

'I will but not yet.' A sudden thought occurred to her – maybe this was Sarah's subtle way of telling her that her time with them was up. It had to end sometime. They'd been more than kind, and she wouldn't be able to do much for a couple of weeks, not until she'd recovered from the birth. 'I'll be out of your way as soon as I'm able.'

Sarah looked shocked. 'Lena, you are part of the family now, and you can stay here for as long as you like. To be honest, I think we'll all be heartbroken if you leave us. But I understand you need to get on with your life, and we won't stand in your way. But there's no rush whatsoever – take all the time you need.'

THE DAYS PASSED QUICKLY and simultaneously so sluggishly that Lena thought she might be going mad. Emmet was there with her in her dreams, the sturdy weight of him in her arms, his dark-red hair, his green eyes, the way his little fingers curled around hers, his rosebud mouth on her breast. She hated to wake, that gradual coming to the real world, where Emmet belonged to someone else and she just had a battered and bruised body and sore, tender breasts full of milk for a baby long gone.

She managed after a few days to get up. Sarah gave her some cabbage leaves and cold flannels to help with drying up her milk, and despite the older woman's protestations, she started helping around the house again, a little at first and soon back the way she had been. Another week, and she was serving in the shop.

Charlie never mentioned anything to do with the baby, and she didn't blame him. He clearly didn't know what to say, but each Friday on the way home from work, he bought the children a toffee lollipop each and never forgot a magazine and a Fry's Chocolate Cream bar for her. It was hit and miss with the magazines; sometimes it was interior design, once it was crochet, about which she knew nothing, but often it was fashion or films. And anyway, it was the thought that counted.

Once, as she folded laundry in the kitchen, little Alys asked where the baby that was in her tummy had gone, and she couldn't help crying. Charlie overheard his little daughter's innocent question, and he appeared, distracted Alys with a dolly, sent her to play with her sister and came back in. Without saying a word, he held Lena in his arms and let her cry, rubbing her back and making soothing sounds. She relaxed in the comfort of the big man's fatherly embrace and sobbed until she had no more tears. Then she wiped her eyes with the handkerchief he handed her. 'I'm sorry.'

'Nothing to be sorry for, love. Look, I don't know much about it, Lena, but I do know this. If someone took one of mine at any moment from the second I laid eyes on them, I could not cope with it, so I think you're being very brave, and Sarah and I are very proud of you.'

'Thank you.' His kindness brought on a whole new wave of tears.

Eli came to see her at the weekend and tried his best to cheer her up. He took her to the pictures to see a silly comedy based on double entendres and slapstick, and while she wasn't in the mood to be cheered up, she did find herself giggling occasionally. They went for curry afterwards, a food she'd never tasted till she came to Wales but found she loved.

'I hear Bessie Evans finally came visiting. The war is on hiatus again until the next time,' Eli said. 'How did you find the old dragon?'

'She didn't think much of me, I'm afraid.' Lena grinned. Charlie's mother had dropped by unannounced two weeks ago and had spoken to Lena like she was gentry and Lena an under housemaid. 'I'm not sure what she didn't like about me. Everything, by the looks of it, and being Irish was definitely a black mark.'

Charlie had pulled Bessie Evans up sharply and told her that Lena was a cousin of Sarah's from Ireland who was helping out with the shop and the children, and Bessie Evans had just sniffed.

'She doesn't think much of most people, so I wouldn't worry about it. She thinks I should be cowering, cap in hand, in gratitude for the bountiful generosity of her country in taking me in. And if you think she doesn't like the Irish, you should hear her on the subject of Jews. She's had to tone it down because Charlie would cut her off permanently if she said what she really thought, but that woman can convey disapproval percutaneously.' Eli smiled. 'That's a medical term for "through the skin". I'm such a show-off, aren't I?'

'You really are.' She grinned.

He looked different these days, she thought, less carefree and student-like. Now he was every inch the professional doctor, with his nice car and subtle cologne. Gone were the ratty old pullovers and trousers that had seen many better days, always cinched around the ankle with a bicycle clip when a bicycle was his only mode of transportation. He'd cut his sandy hair, which had always been nice but wild and unkempt, and now he looked so neat and tidy that she was surprised he wasn't making better headway with his landlady's daughter. Surely he was a catch? Still, it wasn't her business.

'So,' he asked over dinner, 'I know we never talk about Emmet, and we don't have to if you don't want to of course, but since I'm one of the only ones who ever met him, I want you to know you can talk to me about him any time you want.'

She smiled. 'Thanks, Eli, you're so kind.' She paused, trying to put her feelings into words, and was surprised she felt she could with him. She found even thinking about Emmet in her waking hours almost unbearably painful. 'It is very hard. I don't sleep much. I see his little face every time I close my eyes. I can smell him, and I dream of him every night. Sometimes I wake in a sweat, thinking of him crying and nobody coming to him. He's in a dark room, in a cot with bars, crying and crying and nobody comes… And he just wants me, and I want him and…' Her voice cracked on the last words.

He reached over and held her hand on the table. 'I know you're lonely and worried about him. It's normal, and you wouldn't be human if you didn't feel that way. I'm sure he's being very well looked after, but I can't imagine what it must be like for you. I think of him often too. And for what it's worth, I'm glad you got to spend some time with him. I don't think if they'd whipped him away immediately, this would be any easier.'

'I believe that too. My body thinks I'm a mother, and it's behaving like I am one. But I'm not,' Lena said sadly. It felt nice to have someone who had met him, and who thought he was perfect too.

'Lena, *you're* that wee lad's mother, and you always will be. And maybe your lives will join again at some point – you hear of it, don't you? So don't give up hope. All of my family, apart from my mother, my uncle and me, were murdered by the Nazis. Aunts, uncles, cousins, grandparents, neighbours, friends, my father, all of them. So I know I will never see them again, in this life anyway, but you know that saying, "where there's life, there's hope"?'

Lena nodded.

'You gave Emmet life, Lena. Allow yourself a little hope.'

'I'm almost afraid to,' she admitted.

'Hope is free, Lena. Nobody can take that from you, not while you and your baby live and breathe. There is always hope. Cling on to it. It might be years, and yes, it might be never, but without hope, there is nothing.'

'Do you really think of him?' she asked.

Eli nodded. 'A lot, to be honest. He was such a perfect little person, so pure, no hatred or preju-dice in him, just a little boy. And he was yours, so, you know, he was lovely.' He coloured then, his pale skin flushing pink. 'So what's next for you? Back to Ireland, do you think, to the bright lights of Kilteegan Bridge?' He clearly wanted to change the subject.

She considered it. 'Sarah and Charlie have said there's no rush for me to move on, although I know I have to soon, but I do need to figure some things out. I might take my exams and then apply for nursing training in Cardiff, I don't know.'

He beamed. 'That's wonderful news.'

'Although my sister Emily is getting married

in March, and I definitely have to be home for that. And then we'll see.'

'So life goes on?' asked Eli gently.

She paused and gazed into his eyes. 'Nothing will ever again be like it was before, but I have to let him go. It's excruciating, but we have to let go of what we can't have no matter how much we want it, don't we?'

'We do, Lena. I suppose we do.'

LEAVING Wales was much harder than Lena had anticipated. She'd grown so fond of the Evans family. Eli was working and so hadn't been able to come to Swansea to see her off, but Rhys, Bryn, Gwen and Alys clung to her in tears at the quayside.

'You'll come back soon, won't you?' Charlie asked, as Sarah dabbed her eyes, every bit as sad as her children.

'I will, Charlie, I promise,' Lena said, hugging the big Welshman who'd been so kind. 'Very soon. I have my exams, which I can't miss – not after telling everyone back in Ireland that's what I've been up to.'

'Well, plenty of studying then, and no gallivanting around the pubs, getting up to all sorts of mischief.' He waggled his finger at her, mock stern.

Sarah giggled through her tears. 'Don't mind Charlie. He's only interested in your cooking. He said just before he fell asleep last night, "I hope you got her to teach you how she makes those scones." The only good thing about you being gone for a while is we won't eat so much.'

Lena gave little Alys one last hug, and the child clung to her. Eventually Charlie had to peel his little daughter out of Lena's arms, and Lena fought the tears as she walked up the gangway, passing her ticket to the purser. She climbed the stairs inside and went out onto the deck. As she stood at the railing of the ship, it blew its loud horn and pulled away from the quay, the Evans family waving at her from below. She continued to stand there as the land became less and less distinct and eventually disappeared. The land that was now home to her son, who would grow up never knowing that he was Irish.

CHAPTER 20

The weeks that followed were a flurry of activity. The wedding was planned, and Dick Crean was securely in Scotland the last time anyone checked so wouldn't show up to ruin anything. Jingo had turned up but had been warned by a very determined and serious Blackie that if he put so much as a toe astray, not to mind a foot, he would live to regret it every day of the rest of his life.

Emily was so thrilled to have her sister back, it felt good. Jack was just the same, working and spending all his time with four-legged creatures and avoiding two-legged ones inasmuch as was possible, unless they were the Travellers in their caravans who came and went, halting for a week

272

at a time on the O'Sullivan land. Jack liked the Travellers, though many people were wary of them. One of them, a boy around Jack's age called Paddy, was the only friend Jack ever seemed to have. They stayed for a few weeks in spring and again in autumn, and the two boys were insep`-`rable for that time.

Lena was back working for Doc, trying to sort out the mess he'd made of her neatly arranged files while she'd been gone.

Maria seemed well, and the twins were happy. They'd grown in the months since Lena had seen them and seemed equally at home in their own house or running across the fields to the Mad`-`dens' farm next door to see their friend Lucy and be fed by Deirdre if 'Mammy was tired' that day. After the wedding, the three little girls were going to the seaside to stay in a caravan with Deirdre and Bill for two weeks, and they were so excited. Lena took the twins and Lucy to Cork on the bus and bought them swimming costumes and rubber rings. They had their tea in the city, and Lena was delighted to see the sparkle of fun and contentment in her little sisters' eyes, and it was nice to see them welcome Lucy into what had been their closed little world.

* * *

Dear Lena,

Greetings from Wales!

I can't believe it's been two weeks since you left. I know I've written three times already, and the exciting life of a Cardiff doctor must surely keep you on the edge of your seat, but I'll try to keep the medical horrors to a minimum this time, although what you could have against leg ulcers and goitres, I've no idea. It's taking all of my strength not to tell you about a pus-filled abscess I had to lance yesterday, the contents of which sprayed the nurse's uniform. To say she was not best pleased is to understate the case.

I was at home yesterday and took Bryn and Rhys to a football match. They were talking about you a lot and wondering when you were coming back. I told them you were only barely home, but I must confess to sharing my little brothers' impatience.

It was hard to go there and not hear you singing your sad Irish songs. Haha!

Lena smiled. Eli used to always ask her if there were any happy Irish songs.

I can barely think of what to write because that's all my news since I last wrote, but I'll try. Oh yes, I went to hear a band on Sunday – you would have loved it. I went with a bunch of people from here, and we had fun, though the car we were travelling in broke down on the way home and we had to hitch a lift. Much to my annoyance, our saviour was an old farmer who had – yes, you guessed it – an evil-looking bunion, so of course I had to pare it for him, for free. You know how I hate being charitable – ha!

They'd been to a restaurant a few days before she left, and he'd been in the middle of telling her a story and had left the waitress a tip of a shilling instead of the half-crown he'd intended to leave. The same waitress wasn't backwards in coming forward and called him a skinflint. He'd been mortified and went to great lengths to explain it was a genuine error, and Lena had teased him about being stingy ever since, when in fact the complete opposite was true.

Mum is really missing you too. I hate to say, their lovely comfortable home has descended into P-L (pre-Lena) levels of chaos, and Charlie longs for the days when matching socks were not just a lucky coincidence.

Mum made scones, allegedly following your recipe to the letter, but, well, all I can say is yours never tasted like that. Charlie suggested we could use them as weights or maybe as stones to throw at the crows that steal the blackcurrants off the bushes.

She smiled again. He really was a ticket. It was

an unusual sensation, smiling. She realised she didn't do much of it these days.

Anyway, my dear Lena, please come back. We need you. Socks, scones and tidiness notwithstanding, we all miss you so much, and me a bit more than everyone.

Your friendliest friend,

Eli

PS Did you like the story about the cheese-rolling competition?

PPS I'm so stupid I forgot to ask – how was the wedding?

Doc was in with a patient, so Lena took some notepaper from the drawer of the reception desk and started her reply. She tried to sound much more cheerful than she felt.

Dear Eli,

I see you couldn't resist going on about skin eruptions in the end, so try this for size. I've been in Doc's surgery all afternoon. I just popped in to sort out his files, which are a complete shambles, and a mother brought in her toddler, who immediately had a very dramatic projectile vomit all over the floor, herself, her mother and some on my shoes. I'd only cleaned up when Mick Cronin, who works in the butcher's, came bursting in the door having cut through the tendon of his thumb while getting Father Sheehan's chops, and he was spurting blood everywhere. He opened the door with his bloody hand, and Sister Assumpta (who's a complete tyrant, so good enough for her) didn't realise the door handle was covered in blood so got herself and her habit smudged with the platelets and plasma of Mick, much to her horror. Just when I thought that was all I could cope with, a big hairy man came in, bellowing that Doc had no right to be giving his wife 'a rubber yoke that is flying in the face of God'.

I know that sounds like a peculiar accusation, so I'd better explain. Doc will prescribe a contraceptive device to women who've had so many kids one more might actually kill them, but it's in contravention of canon law to interfere with the 'natural reproduction process', and Doc has had many a run-in with the clergy on the subject. His response is always the same, that they should look after their parishioners' souls up in the church and he'll mind their bodies in his surgery. Anyway, in the midst of the chaos, shuddering nuns, spurting butchers and vomiting kids, Doc gave the husband a very short answer, something along the lines of a man who has eleven children and spends all of his money in the Donkey's Ears had no business lecturing anyone about what God would or wouldn't approve of.

Finally, Geraldine Cronin appeared from the post

office, lugging a heavy parcel of books for Doc that Fergus the postman was refusing to carry up on account of his bad back. Fergus and his back means anything more than a postcard has to be collected from the post office. He's bone idle and nothing else wrong with him, but also I think Geraldine likes coming to see Doc. She and him go way back. They were friends all their lives, and sometimes I wonder if there's ever been a spark of romance there...

I wish she'd move in and take care of him if that's the case. He's gone very thin in the last few months, even more so than normal, but I'm not surprised. If I'm not here to mind him, he just drinks and smokes and hardly eats at all.

Yes, thanks for the story about the cheese-rolling competition. I read it out to the twins, and it made them laugh so much that Molly, who had a pain in her tummy, forgot all about her ailment, so you truly have healing powers.

The wedding thankfully went off without a hitch. Mainly because Deirdre's husband, Bill, and his brother, Hugh, stood either side of Jingo for the entire duration to ensure he behaved himself.

Doc appeared out of the surgery, ushering his last patient out the door, shutting it after them and turning the lock. 'Well, that was some day, wasn't it?' he said.

'It was indeed.' She replaced Eli's letter in the envelope and folded her own into the same envelope as well; she'd finish it later at home.

'What's that you have there?'

'A letter from Wales.' She looked up with a smile.

Doc beamed back at her. 'It's nice to see you smile. It feels like a long time since I saw it.'

'I'm fine, Doc, I really am. Just thinking about these exams, I suppose. I need to get back to my books.'

'I'll drop you home, will I?'

'I'm all right, thanks. I'll walk. I need the exercise.' She put her coat on and was about to leave when he spoke again.

'You can talk to me about it if you want to, you know. You don't have to pretend it didn't happen.'

She was going to say no, she was fine, but then the words wouldn't come out. The truth was, she was far from fine. Each day her longing for her baby got worse. Watching mothers with their infants waiting to see Doc gave her a physical pain. She often clung to the blanket she'd made for him. His smell was long gone from the wool, but she willed herself to remember. He would be almost four months old now. Far from feeling better, Lena was sinking deeper and deeper into despair. Some days she feared she was becoming like her mother, obsessing, retreating from the world.

'I could heat us up some soup that Chrissy from the café brought over? She's as bad as you, always on at me to eat. And we could have a chat, if it would help?' His gentle voice offered balm to her broken heart.

'Thanks.' She took her coat off again and followed him into the big sunny kitchen at the back of the house. Doc's mother was a wonderful cook – her skills and generosity were legendary – and it was many a poor mouth was fed from that kitchen. Lena doubted if Doc had bought so much as a saucepan since she died years ago, so there was an air of bygone days about it, but still it was homely.

They ate Chrissy's homemade vegetable soup, accompanied by soda bread and followed by a queen of puddings and custard, and all washed down with pots of tea.

'Tell me about him,' Doc said gently. It was the first time she'd been able to mention her child since coming home, and the floodgates opened.

Lena blinked back the tears, swallowed and

tried to speak. The words at first sounded raspy. 'He was beautiful, Doc, so perfect, and I called him Emmet after you. The woman from the adoption agency said he'd be given a new name, but he'll always be Emmet to me.'

His eyes, suspiciously bright too, locked with hers. 'I never knew that. Thank you. That's a great honour.'

She poured out all her misery, and when she'd finished, he spoke.

'Lena, my darling girl, I can see that your heart is broken. What you did was so hard, so brave. You carried him, gave birth to him, and now, please God, he has a wonderful life ahead, cared for by people who'll love him. Emmet won't know the difference, but you'll carry the scars of this all your life. I've seen it so often. So I'm not saying you'll forget him, or you'll get over it. You won't. But you will smile and live and hopefully love again.'

She sighed deeply. 'I can't see it, Doc, I really can't.'

He reached for her hand across the table. 'Then trust me, Lena. It's true.'

'Would Daddy be disappointed in me?' She asked the question that had been on her mind since she came home. She hadn't even been to his grave yet; she couldn't face it.

Doc smiled slowly. 'You could never disappoint him, Lena, no matter what. He adored you from the day you were born, and nothing you could ever do or say would change that.'

CHAPTER 21

*J*ack came into the farmhouse kitchen rather abruptly as Lena was at the table, finishing her letter to Eli. The rest of the household was in bed, but he'd been out lambing with Bill Madden, and he went straight to the sink to wash his hands.

'Do you want a cup of tea?' she offered.

He shook his head and instead went to the sideboard and took a bottle of whiskey and two glasses. The bottle was from before the time of her father's death.

'What's going on?' she asked, bemused, as he opened it and poured them each a glass.

He pulled a chair over and sat opposite her. 'I'm going away for a while, Lena.'

Lena was astounded; Jack never went anywhere. 'Where?' she asked.

'America.' He raised the whiskey to his lips.

'What? Why?' In her shock, she took a big mouthful of the whiskey, and it burned all the way down. 'I don't understand, I didn't know you were even thinking of…'

'It's been on my mind for a while now, but I wanted to wait till you came back to say anything.'

'What about the farm?'

'Bill Madden is going to mind it for me. It adjoins his land anyway, and he's taking it all on, the milking, the sheep, everything. He'll have the profit of it until I come back, but he's going to make sure there'll be enough money for Mam and you and the twins now that Emily is married.'

'But, Jack, you're only sixteen –'

'I need to see the world, Lena,' he said, more confident than she'd ever seen him. 'I need to find out things, the sort of things no one would have taught me at school even if I'd been able to stay.'

'What sort of things, Jack?' Lena asked gently.

He smiled, that slow, shy smile rarely seen but so worth it when it made an appearance. 'That's what I'm going to Montana to find out.'

'Montana!'

'Remember those magazines Mam ordered for me? Well, there was an article in there that led me to other reading, some things by a woman called Rachel Carson. She's talking about the conservation of the earth, how using the new artificial pesticides is so bad, the damage it's doing to plants and animals, getting into the food chain. She's talking about different methods, some ancient, some new. And that ranch in Montana I'm on about, they're trying out her theories.'

'And you want to see how it all works, with your own eyes?' Lena had never seen her brother so animated.

'I really, really do. And I wrote and told them how interested I was in what they were at. There's a man who owns it called Chuck Frawley – he's part Chippewa, that's a Native American tribe – and I told him what I'd been doing here with the Traveller cures, the treatment of mastitis using thyme oil on the udders and increasing the number of milkings, and how lemons were also helpful. Some of the methods he was familiar with, but he didn't know for example that Epsom salts and treacle is a great cure all, or using bluestone for scour and fluke. He thought I was joking when I told him that as well as milk and eggs we'd give a drop of whiskey to an ailing animal to pep him up. And anyway, we've been corresponding, and he's really interested in some of the old cures and ways we manage the land. He gave me some great advice about using sandalwood bark to heal eye infections in lambs, and last week Chuck told me I had to come out and show him what I know, and he'll show me what he knows of the Native American cures. He explained there are lots of people working there, from all over the world, all with the same idea in mind. So I thought I'd give it a go.'

'Wow!' Lena sat back and took another sip of her whiskey; she needed it.

'Do you think I'm mad?' Jack asked, suddenly not the bold adventurer but just her insecure brother again.

'Not a bit. I'll miss you so much, but I think it's brilliant, Jack, I really do. And Mam will too – she's always been pushing you to get out and about. Dad and Bill Madden were friends for years, and Molly and May practically live on that farm now anyway. Bill is an honest man – he won't cheat you, so I think you're dead right.'

'It might not work out, but...'

'It might not, but you'll have had an experience, and that's worth something. Go for it, Jack, and Bill will make a fine job of this place.' Lena raised her glass and clinked it off her brother's. 'Let's both go forward, Jack.'

She stayed up after he went to bed and went back to her letter.

Emily looked radiant in the wedding dress our mother made for her. It was the most beautiful ever seen in Kilteegan Bridge – everyone said so.

The strange thing is Emily told me secretly she thinks she is already expecting her first baby. That means she and Blackie might have got a bit ahead of themselves, which I must say I never thought they'd do; they're so keen to do everything right. But I suppose as the wedding was only just around the corner, it didn't make much odds, especially as Blackie is a real rock and hardly about to leave her at the altar, unlike what happened to yours truly. I wasn't keen on Blackie to begin with, but he's turned out to be a proper man, and they are really united and face the world as a team. Sometimes I envy her, but if anyone deserves a bit of happiness, it's Em. I'd love you to meet her sometime; she's lovely, much nicer than me, haha!

I'm delighted for her and Blackie, of course, about the baby. Emmet takes up so much of my mind, waking and sleeping, wondering if he's all right, worrying if they are taking proper care of him, trying to imagine what he looks like now. It never ends.

Doc has been asking me what I will do after my

exams, will I train as a nurse in Cork, but I don't know. Somehow I feel I want to train in Cardiff, maybe because I'll feel closer to Emmet that way. I know I should try to move on from thinking about him. It's not doing either of us any good. But I don't know how to do that, Eli, I swear I don't.

She paused. She was so grateful to have his friendship. He and Doc were the only people she could be truly honest with about her son, and Eli especially because she knew he thought about the little boy too.

I told Doc about Emmet recently. He was very touched that I named him for him, though I doubt one single person in Kilteegan Bridge could tell you Doc's real name. It felt nice to talk about him a little, but it's not the same as telling you, because you were there. I'm sorry if I'm so dreary. Sometimes I think you must dread seeing a letter from me on the mat, another tale of woe from across the Irish sea. But know this – I would go insane without you to talk to, so thank you, Eli, from the bottom of my heart. I don't say it enough, I think.

Anyway, I'm coming back to Wales next week to take the exams in May, and perhaps we can spend some time together. I'm worried just stepping on Welsh soil will make me feel even worse. Sometimes I feel like I'm playing a game of snakes and ladders. I keep trying to climb the ladders and think everything is going to be all right and I did the right thing giving Emmet away, and then just as I feel a small bit OK, I slide right back down the snake.

So if you are not very busy with work or anything else –

In his previous letter, Eli had made a wry joke about Janice Stiller being dumped by the other lodger, Shiply, who had skipped owing three months' rent. So maybe it was back on between Janice and Eli. She hoped it would go smoother this time; he was lovely, and any girl would be lucky to have him. But she wouldn't pry; it wasn't her business.

– perhaps you could pick me up from the ferry? I know Sarah would be happy to do it, but it would be so lovely to spend a bit of time with you. I think you're the only person who can make me laugh these days.

Your moaniest friend,

Lena

She licked and sealed the envelope.

CHAPTER 22

*L*ena stood at the railing watching the land come into focus as the ship sailed into Swansea harbour. She'd spent an uneventful voyage chatting to an old man – at least he looked very old to Lena – who had a German accent. He introduced himself as Klaus Rizzenburg. He was friendly and seemed nice enough, and he told her that he'd come to visit Ireland after being finally released by the Russians from a prisoner-of-war camp.

'I saw a postcard, and it looked so calm and peaceful, I was drawn to the place. I came for a few weeks in 1950 and never returned to Baden-Baden.' Now he was on his way to Swansea to see his cousin.

'My friend Eli and his mother are Jews – they had to get away,' she'd said early in the conversation. If this man was a devoted Nazi, he was not someone she would like to speak to. A sadness crossed his old, wrinkled face.

'Bad, bad times. I can't believe what we did. All of us. It was like we were crazy, under a spell. We can never make amends, or try to apologise. Words, actions...nothing is enough. Nothing. I was only a boy, seventeen when the war broke out, but I will not tell you I had to join, I had to participate – that is not an excuse. I did it. I was in the Wehrmacht in France, and I saw terrible things, carried out terrible orders. I won't ever forgive myself. I never should.'

Lena did a quick calculation. If he was only seventeen in 1939, he was only in his late thirties. He looked decades older.

She told him about her Uncle Ted never having come home, and he asked which city Ted had lived in before the war. When she told him it was Leipzig, the man pointed out that Leipzig was in East Germany, which was now behind the Iron Curtain, and maybe that was what stopped her uncle from getting in touch.

'I am now a historian at the university in Cork. If you need help trying to find your uncle maybe, or family, please, do get in touch.' He handed her his card. 'Also your friends – if I can help in any way, please just ask.'

Something about him made her sure that he was telling her the truth about being filled with shame and remorse.

He left her then, to gather his things, and she stayed up on deck, watching the land become bigger.

As they approached the busy port of Swansea, she felt a panic in the pit of her stomach. She'd been so broken leaving here, so utterly depleted, and now just the thought of being back in the same country as Emmet but unable to see and hold him... She wanted it and simultaneously dreaded it.

A steward appeared and asked her to go below deck and gather her things, as disembarkation would be shortly. Lena fetched her small bag and queued up at the gangway as the ship was docked at the quay. Her hand was sweaty as she gripped the handle of her case, and the perspiration prickled her neck and down her spine as she waited for the door to open.

Eventually it did, and then she saw him, Eli, his face in a wide beam of welcome, and her heart flooded with relief. He'd come to meet her, and suddenly she felt like whatever happened, she would be able to cope. He grabbed her bag and gave her a one-armed hug. 'Jump in the car. We won't hang around in Swansea. I'm taking you for lunch in a fancy pub I passed on my way into the town,' he announced cheerfully. 'It has some proper ale on tap, and roast dinners.'

Only fifteen minutes later, after a whirlwind drive in Eli's plush car, they were sitting in a quaint Victorian pub, Eli enjoying a pint of warm flat beer in a short stubby mug with a handle. He'd bought a half of beer for Lena as well, but after one sip, she proclaimed it so awful she wouldn't use it to dip sheep. He'd laughed and then gone back to the bar to buy her an orange juice with lemonade.

'Now,' he said, putting down his beer and wiping his mouth on the back of his hand, 'there's two fine plates of roast beef and Yorkshire pudding on the way, and in the meantime, why don't you tell me how you've been.'

Reluctant to bore him with her troubles like she did in her letters, she forced herself not to talk about Emmet, even though he was always uppermost in her mind. Instead, she told him all about Jack's sudden lust for adventure, which Eli said made him envious; he said he'd love to just drop everything and go see the world himself.

'Not when I've only just found you again. You'll have to stay around until I'm sick of you.'

'I'm sure that won't take long. Now tell me how you really are.' The roast beef had arrived, and he picked up his knife and fork.

Again, she didn't want to spoil things, so instead of saying what was in her heart, she talked about the wedding and Emily's coming baby and life in Kilteegan Bridge, until eventually he stopped her, his hand on hers.

'Lena, you know what I'm asking. Of course, don't tell me if you don't want to talk about it, but what I'm really asking is how are *you*, not how is every other person in Ireland.'

She dropped her eyes and sighed. 'Oh, Eli… Really? You must be so sick of my miserable goings-on.'

'I'm not at all. I want to hear about everything you think, everything you feel. I'm here for you, Lena. Just tell me.'

'OK.' She raised her eyes to his. 'I'm grateful to you for listening, and I do want to tell you, I really do – you're my best friend – but after I've told you, please talk to me right away about something else or I won't be able to stand it.'

He nodded and sat facing her, listening.

She said in a rush, 'I thought I'd get over Emmet, but I just can't. I think of him day and night. I'm no more free than I would have been if I'd kept him. I should never have given him up. I thought I had no way of keeping him, but I should have found a way. I should have. And I felt pressured to sign the paper, and then it was all too late. People meant well, Doc, Sarah, the adoption people, I know they did, but it wasn't the right thing for me, it just wasn't. I know it's hard to be an unwed mother, and an illegitimate child, and people discriminate and all of that, but none of that matters now. I just want my boy. And now it's too late. And I'm going to be unhappy for the rest of my life. If I could even just hold him in my arms once more, be sure he's happy and looked after...' She stopped, clenched her fists on the table, then said hoarsely, 'It's too late.'

She paused for a long while. 'So that's it. Now let's talk about something else before they ask us to leave for putting people off their lunch with our long faces.' She smiled weakly.

His eyes were deep pools of compassion, but he said instantly, 'OK, how about this. I thought we might take a few days, go up the coast a bit, maybe to Blackpool even, and we could see the lights.'

'Just the two of us?' she asked, surprised.

He coloured. 'Well, if you don't want to...'

'No, it's not that. I'd love it, but it wouldn't look very seemly, would it? And I know you say it's nothing, but surely Janice wouldn't...' She smiled.

He groaned theatrically. 'How many more times must I say it? Janice is a nice girl, but we're not an item, never were, never will be, Lena.'

'I'm so sorry...'

'Why?' He gazed at her directly now, suddenly not in a jokey way.

'Why am I sorry?'

'Yes, why?'

'Well, because I know you had a thing for her, I suppose, and I don't want you to be hurt – you're my friend.'

'Oh, Lena.' He sighed and put his head in his hands.

'Oh, Lena, what?' She was getting frustrated now.

'Nothing. Don't worry, Janice Stiller couldn't and wouldn't hurt me.'

* * *

BACK IN PONTCANNA, Eli carried her bag to the door but then kissed her on the cheek and ran back to the car, saying he had to go or he'd be late for his evening shift. With her bag at her feet, she knocked on the familiar red front door and was promptly enveloped in hugs and kisses by the Evans children, who led her up to her old room, announcing proudly that they'd been cleaning it for days. Sarah called hello from the kitchen, but the children wouldn't share Lena just yet. The room had been tidied in a rather haphazard fashion, but the children had properly aired and dusted, and there were creased but clean sheets and pillowcases on the bed. She assured them she was very impressed.

They told her excitedly about the plans they had made to bring her to Tenby and to walk the path from Haverfordwest all along the coast to Solva and St Davids, and how they'd been promised a trip to Chester Zoo.

'Every treat we asked for was put off until you came, Lena,' Rhys said with a gap-toothed grin, 'so we get to go everywhere now. And we're all going to Uncle Saul's birthday party tomorrow. He's very old, so he has to make a special birthday out of every one he has because he might die.'

Lena went back downstairs and was hugged tightly by Sarah.

'Saul is all right, isn't he?' she asked.

'Oh, he's fine. He was joking with the children that he was so old, and they took it to heart. I think he's regretting it now.'

Lena breathed again. Saul was no more than fifty-five.

Later that evening, with the children in bed and Charlie at a work meeting, Sarah and Lena settled down in the kitchen together as they'd done hundreds of times before, drinking tea.

'Will you come to the birthday party tomorrow?' Sarah asked her, and Lena was pleased to be invited.

'I will, of course.' She hadn't met Saul and Ann Hoffman often; they were busy people, what with him being a consultant and Ann a social worker. But what she'd seen of them, she'd loved, and she had a message for Saul from Doc, asking him to visit Ireland if he ever had a moment to spare from work.

Lena sat and chatted with Sarah for a while, telling her all about her mother and Emily, and Jack's new adventure and the twins' holiday. She felt warm and relaxed; it was lovely being back with this kind family.

Sarah beamed at her as she poured a fresh cup. 'You seem so much better than when I last saw you, love. I was so worried putting you on the boat home, so afraid you wouldn't be able to cope, but you did, it seems. And that's the hand of your dad – I believe it – helping everything settle into place like that.'

Lena smiled back. It didn't really feel like everything had settled into place, but maybe it was true; maybe her father's hand was the reason she was feeling a bit better since she'd come back to Wales, instead of feeling worse like she'd thought she would.

That night she lay in the familiar bed, the creaky sounds of the Evans' Victorian house welcoming her. She remembered her first night there, pregnant, terrified, lonely, heartbroken. What did she feel now? No longer terrified, and she could never feel lonely around these people, but heartbroken? She touched that place in her heart where her son remained, like a tongue testing a sore tooth, and yes, it was still raw and painful.

THE NEXT DAY, the sun was strong, and she wore the yellow silk tea dress she'd not worn since she'd danced with Malachy at the Lilac Ballroom all that time ago. She was such a different person to the girl who left Kilteegan Bridge last year, and she would never again be her. But as she pinned her dark curls in an up style she'd seen in a magazine and ringed her eyes with kohl, she recognised, just for a second, the girl she once was, the one Malachy said was like Audrey Hepburn. She slipped into red strappy sandals and realised her daily walks in Ireland had tanned her skin a little and she looked, if not a carefree young woman, then certainly a more optimistic version of herself than she'd been for a long time.

Charlie Evans whistled when she came downstairs, and the children giggled.

'Oh, Lena, you look gorgeous!' Sarah gushed. 'So pretty.'

'You look lovely yourself,' Lena complimented her. Sarah had a great eye and chose well for the shop as well as herself; today she was beautifully dressed in a tailored powder-blue trouser suit with matching shoes.

'Come on, lads,' Charlie said to his little sons. 'Look at the bevvy of beauties we'll have on our arms today. We're lucky men.'

He insisted that Bryn give Lena his arm, and Rhys escorted Gwen and Alys, while he led his wife to the car amid much giggling and joking around.

Saul's birthday party was held in the Hoffmans' garden, a picture-perfect setting in suburban Cardiff with a pond and lots of flower beds. A string quartet played softly in the corner, and uniformed waiters circulated with drinks and hors d'oeuvres. It was the poshest event Lena had ever been to.

Saul welcomed her warmly, as did his wife, Ann, who was gently but efficiently managing the entire show. They had no children of their own, and Lena could see from the way the Evans kids were welcomed that they were the light of the Hoffman couple's lives.

Lena was sitting on a stone bench, enjoying a glass of real French champagne and letting the sun shine on her face, when she felt someone's shadow cross her. She opened her eyes and saw Eli. He had a pretty woman on his arm. She was older than Lena, with blond hair and blue eyes. She wore a cerise-pink frock with a baby-pink coat over it and had a matching handbag and shoes.

'Lena, this is Clare Winton,' Eli said. 'I believe you've met before.'

'No, I don't think...' But then, to her shock, she knew, despite the very different clothes. It was the woman from the agency who had taken Emmet, not the nondescript one who had made her sign the forms, but her much younger blond assistant. *Of course. The girl must be a social worker, so she is a friend of Saul's wife.*

'I asked my aunt especially to invite Clare,' said Eli. 'I thought she needed a break from her work.'

'Oh...' Lena put the glass of champagne down and promptly spilled it all over the ground. 'I'm sorry, so clumsy...'

'Don't worry, I'll get you another one.' Eli smiled and picked up the empty glass. 'Clare, why don't you sit here with Lena. I'll get you both a drink.' And he headed away to the drinks table.

'So,' said Clare as she settled down beside Lena, 'it's nice to meet you properly, Lena. Eli has told me a great deal about you.'

'It's nice to meet you too...' She was doing her best to be polite, but she could hardly get the words out. So Eli did have a girlfriend – not the mousy Janice but this hateful glamorous blond who had taken away her son. Oh God, it was unbearable, in so many ways. Of course, Eli would have had no way of knowing; he hadn't been there... But then what had he meant when he said he believed they'd met before?

Clare continued calmly. 'Look, I know this must seem bizarre, me turning up like this, but it's not a coincidence – you're not going mad. Eli asked his aunt to invite me – I know her through work – because he wanted me to talk to you.'

Lena stared at her, her head spinning. 'I'm sorry?'

Clare looked kindly at her. 'Eli saw how worried you were about your son, and he thought I might be able to reassure you.'

And then Lena couldn't talk at all. She felt faint; her heart was racing. How was this possible? How had Eli managed this, to get the very social worker who had taken her child away to come to this party and talk to her?

'But why would he do that? I don't understand...'

Again, Clare helped her out. 'Eli, as I hope you realise, is a very persuasive chap. There's not a nurse at the Royal Infirmary who doesn't complain about the fact his heart is already bestowed elsewhere. So he convinced me to come to talk to you, and here I am. Now, what would you like to know?'

Finally, Lena found her voice, though it was very croaky. 'How is my baby?'

'He's very well. I saw him just the other day, and he is in excellent health and a very cheery little chap. He's hitting all his developmental milestones, and we're very happy with him.'

'Oh...' Lena burst into tears.

The social worker shifted towards her along the bench and turned to face her, shielding her from the view of other guests. 'I'm sorry. Eli thought you'd want to know he was well and happy. Maybe you'd rather be left to forget...'

'It's not that. Thank you for coming. I'm so relieved he's well, but I'm just so sad I can't see him for myself. I made such a terrible mistake in giving him up, I know that now, and if there was any way to undo it, I would.'

Clare looked sympathetic. 'I understand it is hard, extremely so. But however much you might wish it, the world has not changed enough to make a comfortable life for you both. I work with a lot of impoverished families, and so I have some knowledge of how rigid society can be when it comes to illegitimate children.'

'But he's my son. *My* son.'

A long second passed. Clare seemed to be contemplating something. 'Might we talk? In private?'

Lena felt her mouth go dry. 'Of course... I...' But it wasn't her house, so she had no idea where to go.

'Follow me. I've actually been here before.' Clare walked in through large French doors to a sitting room and out into a hallway, then she turned right, and Lena found herself in what was clearly Saul's study.

Clare closed the door. 'That's better.' She gestured that Lena should sit. 'As I said, Emmet is fine.'

Lena's tears flowed again. 'You call him Emmet?' she asked incredulously.

'Yes. I was told what you'd said, and it rather suits the little chap actually.'

Lena's heart flooded with gratitude. She remembered how the older woman hadn't even acknowledged her request on that horrific day, but clearly she'd heard her and told her assistant.

'I shouldn't be doing this, I suppose, but...' Clare opened her pink handbag and extracted a photograph of a solid little baby with a mop of red hair and big green eyes. He was grinning and had a little soft toy in his hand.

Lena gazed and gazed, feeling she would never be able to get enough of him.

'He's a sweet little boy, always chuckling,' said Clare.

'I... He's so beautiful...' Lena's voice sounded strange to her own ears.

'We'd found him some perfect adoptive parents – the wife had red hair and green eyes, because most people like the child to look like them – but then she got pregnant naturally all of a sudden after trying for years.'

'Oh, that's wonderful for her.' Lena genuinely meant it.

'It is, truly. But it means they didn't want to adopt any more.'

'So where is Emmet now?' Lena asked cautiously, her heart racing again.

'He's still in the foster home, being cared for very well. And in due course, we will look to have him adopted by another couple.'

Lena could not take her eyes off the photo.

'You may keep it if you wish,' said Clare kindly.

Lena looked up at her. 'Thank you. You're so kind.' She paused and then asked, 'Could I see him?'

'Oh, Lena...' Clare sighed.

'Please, just for a few moments. It would mean so much to me. I...' The tears flowed down her cheeks again. 'I don't sleep. I think about him all day, every day. If I could just see him for myself, just hold him in my arms for a moment. Please.'

Clare looked away momentarily, deep in thought. 'Very well. And this is as much for Eli as you. He's been pestering me for news of the little lad since he tracked down who his social worker was. I've been promoted since that day in the hospital, so I do have the authority, though it's very irregular. You may visit him at the foster home, but only once, and just a short visit. And then you must leave him to his life, Lena, for both your sakes. Do I have your word?'

Lena nodded, stifling a sob. 'Thank you, Miss Winton, thank you so much.'

'Call me Clare.'

Clare gave Lena a card with the name and address of a home called the St Christopher Residence, in Duffryn, on the road to Newport. 'I'll tell them to expect you on Tuesday at ten?'

'I'll be there.' Lena swallowed. Was this really happening?

'Very well, and please, do not tell anyone that you're doing this. I would get into all manner of hot water for allowing it. If he were with his adoptive parents, which normally he would be by now, then there would be no way I would countenance it, but under the circumstances, I hope it can give you some peace of mind.'

'Thank you again. This means more, well, more than anything.'

Clare nodded. 'I suspect Eli will want to come with you, the way he's been going on, and that is also something that shouldn't be allowed...' Her voice softened. She clearly had a soft spot for the handsome young doctor.

'Oh, please, yes. I don't have a car. I could ask him to take me?'

'Just Eli, Lena, no one else.'

'I promise.'

'And there it ends?'

Lena nodded firmly. She'd have done a deal with the devil if it meant seeing her child again.

CHAPTER 23

$\mathcal{L}$ena watched as the Welsh countryside slid by the window.

'You all right?' Eli asked.

Lena nodded. It wasn't true. She was sick with nerves.

In her eagerness to get there, they were much too early. The home was only ten minutes away from where they were now, and there was still an hour to go before the meeting with her son.

Eli pulled into a woodland park where picnic benches were dotted around, but as yet, no families had come to spend the day.

'Shall we go for a walk? Kill a bit of time?' he asked.

'All right. I'm sorry for making you leave so early, I just...'

'Didn't want to be late. I understand.' He smiled and got out, going around to her side to open the door as he always did for her.

They walked along a path that was bounded by a still stream, covered in lily pads. Willows hung almost to the water level, and the morning sun was warm. A profusion of wild spring flowers, buttercups and bluebells, grew in the grass on the other side of the path, and Lena thought it might have been one of the most beautiful places she'd ever been.

Being a weekday morning, it was deserted.

'I never even thought to ask if you had to work today?'

Eli shook his head. 'No, they can cover for me. This was more important.'

'Thank you, Eli. I don't know how I would do this, or any of it, without you. I can't believe you tracked Clare down and persuaded her to do this.'

'You're welcome. It wasn't difficult to find her once my mother told me the name of the agency. Clare was a bit sticky about it at first, but I turned up the charm to max...'

Lena laughed. 'You certainly did. She was all melty about you, as apparently are all the nurses at the Royal Infirmary. Oh, Eli, you are such a good friend. I don't know how I got so lucky to have you, but I think my dad sent you to me. The first morning I was in Sarah and Charlie's house, I asked him to send me something, some way to get through this, some sign that I wasn't all on my own. And then when I came out of the bathroom, you were there.'

He led her to a bench, where she sat down, closed her eyes and turned her face to the sun. She slowly inhaled and exhaled, trying to slow her racing heartbeat. She would see her boy soon. Would he know who she was? He couldn't recognise her obviously, but would he know somewhere inside his little self that she was his mother?

Eli didn't sit, and when she opened her eyes, he was standing before her, just looking at her.

'What?' she asked, shielding her eyes with her hand from the strong sun glinting through the trees.

He swallowed.

'What?' she asked again.

Eli inhaled, and she noticed it was ragged, like there was something he needed to get off his chest.

Lena smiled. 'Spit it out. It can't be that bad.'

He didn't return her smile; instead he looked more serious than she'd ever seen him. He looked different to when she first met him, but there was still a roguishness to him, like he was only seconds from having his shirt hanging out and his hair an untidy tangle.

'I want to say something to you, but I'm scared that if I do, it will ruin everything between us.'

'You're worrying me now.' Lena laughed. 'Ah, Eli, nothing you could say to me would ruin anything. Just say it, whatever it is.'

'OK, here we go.' He exhaled. 'I love you, Lena O'Sullivan, and I would give anything to marry you. I know your heart is with Malachy, and he is the great love of your life, and that if he wasn't such an idiot – sorry, I had to say that – you two would be together. But – and maybe it's the daftest idea you ever heard – but if you can't have him, maybe you'd consider me? Because I swear to you there isn't a man alive who loves you as much as I do.'

Lena was lost for words. Eli Kogan, the man she thought of as her best friend, was proposing to her? What? Surely not?

'Just hear me out, Lena, before you say no.' He sat beside her and took her hand in his. 'I've been thinking this through for a while.'

THE TROUBLE WITH SECRETS

Lena was trying to process what he was saying.

'Well, just that it seems like an act of God, or maybe the hand of your father or something like that – my mother thinks the dead help us – but Emmet is still not adopted, and they will have to find him new parents. If we got married, we might be able to apply, and we could raise him together...'

'But how would we explain that to everyone?' Lena's mind was racing.

'Everyone like who?' he asked. 'My mum and Charlie would be only delighted.'

'Well, your grandmother, for example, she doesn't like –'

'Firstly, she's my stepfather's mother so no re-lation of mine. Secondly, she doesn't like anyone, so Bessie Evans can like it or lump it, I don't care. And anyway, if you want, we'd leave here, go somewhere else, America maybe, then go back to Ireland after a couple of years. A couple of months either way in Emmet's age won't matter at that point. We might even have one of our own by then, a little brother or sister for him?'

Blood thundered in Lena's ears. Was she imagining this? She forced herself to focus. 'You can't marry me just so I can have Emmet. I can't let you throw your life away because of me, even if they would allow us to have him.'

He looked at her in astonishment. 'Are you mad? Throwing my life away? Lena, I want you to *be* my life. I want to marry you, baby or no baby, that's the first thing. Since I met you, I… Look, you're beautiful and funny and so clever, and you make me laugh like nobody can, and I would love to be your husband. It's you that would be putting up with me, for the sake of Emmet, but I promise I'll be the best second-best husband there's ever been…'

'You could never be a second-best anything, Eli Kogan,' she said sincerely. 'But this is all so un-expected, I just don't know what to think… And Clare told me I was only being allowed to see him once, and for a short time, and normally even that would never be possible.'

She knew she sounded ungrateful when Eli was offering her the moon and stars, but she mustn't get her hopes up, she just mustn't. To have them dashed would break her heart all over again.

'Lena, whose child is he?' Eli asked.

'What do you mean?'

'Whose is he?'

'Well, he's mine, or he *was*…'

'He's *your* boy. You gave life to him, he came from you, and no bit of paper signed the day after giving birth by a scared, vulnerable young woman can change that.'

'But they won't ever –'

'If they say no, we'll fight it in court. He's your child, not theirs.'

'But even if that were true, I just can't allow you to give up your life, though your generosity –'

'Argh!' He ran his hands through his hair in frustration now. 'You're not hearing me, woman! I love you regardless of Emmet. I want to marry you if you'll have me, and I want to have other children with you, but if we could start with Emmet, wouldn't that be something?'

'I...I... Are you sure? It's just I had no idea, Eli...none... I really thought Janice Stiller...'

'Short of writing it on my forehead, I don't know what else to say to you about that. I have never had any interest in Janice. It was her that was after me. Though it's ungentlemanly to say it, I don't want her, or any other girl for that matter, because I fell for you that first day when you'd been vomiting and crying and looked terrible...'

She laughed. 'Thanks very much.'

'You know what I mean,' he said quietly.

She glanced at her watch. It was nine thirty. 'Oh, we have to go.' The meeting with Emmet was in less than half an hour.

He stood up and held out his hand to her. 'Look, we don't need to talk about it any more now. We can discuss it another time, or never again if that's what you want. I only asked you now because…well…if we told the agency we're engaged, they might take the idea of us wanting him back more seriously.'

Lena thought for a moment. As the time had worn on, the months of her pregnancy and the months since, the pain of losing Malachy had subsided, but she still loved him; she couldn't turn off that emotion like a tap.

Standing before her now was a different man, and that was it, she realised. It wasn't just that Eli was physically different to Malachy, tall, sandy-haired and freckled while Malachy had alabaster skin, deep-red hair and green eyes. Eli was completely different in another way. She was a girl when she was with Malachy, and Malachy was a boy. She was a woman now, a mother, and Eli, for all his joking about, was a man. It was like comparing apples with oranges. And she found that the contrast was good.

Did she love Eli? Yes, of course she did. She

felt a deep connection with him, friendship, trust and, yes, love. The passion she had for Malachy, that burning, was not there, but maybe that's not what marriage was about. And maybe it would be there if she allowed herself to think of him that way; she had never considered him like that before. Maybe she would have, if she'd not been so crushed under a weight of grief and loss since she met him. Blackie didn't give Emily butterflies, but she knew now that her sister loved him dearly despite all that, and she was right to. And Eli would make a wonderful father for Emmet...if that dream came true.

'You're sure it's what you want? It's not out of pity? Because God knows I *am* a pity.' She smiled ruefully.

'I'm completely, totally, not one shred of doubt sure,' he confirmed, and a glimmer of hope shone in his eyes. He was telling the truth, she knew.

'Then yes, I would love to marry you, Eli Kogan.'

He swallowed. 'You would?'

She nodded and laughed. 'Very much so.'

He held her in his arms and kissed her for the first time, and for Lena it was as if all the pieces of the puzzle suddenly started to form a picture.

* * *

LENA FELT Eli's hand in the small of her back, nudging her forward into the room that looked like a suburban sitting room. She'd been expecting an institution of some kind, a large, imposing grey building, but this place was smaller and looked more like a private home. There were toys in the garden, and in the hallway parked neatly were several well-used tricycles and scooters. The house smelled clean, and the décor was pastel and bright prints. The front door was open, and a smiling young lady in an overall with a sweet little toddler held by the hand directed them to the sitting room to wait.

In that room there were two sofas facing each other and a coffee table with a dried flower arrangement, and the walls were wallpapered with tiny pink flowers. The curtains were lace, and she could see out to the side gardens beyond, where a nurse had several babies on a rug.

Clare Winton appeared within seconds, and behind her, carrying Emmet, was another nurse, a middle-aged woman with very yellow teeth who looked like she was chewing on a wasp, she was so annoyed by the situation. It was as if all of a sudden Lena were rooted to the spot. She ignored everyone else, her gaze fixed on her son, who seemed oblivious to his nurse's displeasure and was happily sucking on his teething ring. His cheeks were a little red and clearly his teeth were coming, but it did nothing to take from his good humour. He looked well cared for. His hair was as it was in the photograph, slightly longer perhaps, and curly. He was dressed in a blue outfit, little trousers with feet and a matching jumper, and Lena thought he was the most adorable child she'd ever seen in her life. It took every ounce of her strength not to grab him and run.

'Please, Miss O'Sullivan, Dr Kogan, have a seat,' Clare offered, more formal now than when they'd met at the birthday party.

'Thank you,' Lena said, but she remained standing, never taking her eyes off her son. 'We've just got engaged,' she blurted out. Realising it sounded strange then, she blushed.

Clare beamed, and the nurse looked a little surprised but said nothing. Clare took Emmet from the nurse. 'Thank you, Sister. We'll manage from here.'

The woman looked as if she was going to say something, but Clare's slightly raised eyebrow and determined smile made her rethink, and so she handed the baby over and left.

'Well, congratulations,' Clare said. 'And please, spare a thought for all the nurses from the Royal Infirmary who will be sobbing into their hankies tonight.'

'Ah now, that's not true,' Eli protested.

'Ah now, it is,' said Clare with a wink at Lena. 'But now to business. This is Emmet.' She changed her tone to one that made the baby giggle. 'And he's a very handsome chap indeed, aren't you, Emmet? Would you like to meet someone nice, little man?' She walked towards Lena with Emmet in her arms. 'Lena, would you like to hold him?'

For a long, long moment, Lena just stood there, frozen. She was overwhelmed by fear that if she took him, he would scream and cry like she was a scary stranger and hold out his chubby arms to Clare, demanding to be brought back to safety.

But then her arms lifted as if they had a mind of their own, and to her astonishment, the baby allowed her to take him without complaint.

'Hello, Emmet,' she managed, inhaling the baby scent of him. 'I've missed you so, so much.'

'Hello, young man. You've grown a bit since I saw you last.' Eli smiled at him over Lena's shoulder, and Emmet giggled and reached up to grab his tie. 'Ah, a bit of a snappy dresser as well, are you? Don't blame you, mate. A good-looking boy like you needs some fancy gear, doesn't he?' Eli made Emmet laugh fully now, a deep rolling chuckle, and then he said, 'Why don't we sit down and talk to Clare, Lena, about my plan?'

'Oh yes? What's this then?' Clare asked, smiling at the scene of mother and baby reunited. Clare, Lena and Emmet sat on one sofa and Eli opposite, where he started playing peek-a-boo with a giggling Emmet across the coffee table, ducking down behind the dried flower arrangement then popping up again.

'Hopefully nothing that will invoke further ire from Nurse Jennings. She's horrified that I'm allowing this. I wouldn't be surprised if she wanted me dismissed. She's been running this place alone for the last year, so my interfering ways are not welcome.'

Lena gasped, horrified. 'Are you at risk of dismissal?'

'Well, I sincerely hope not. Ann Hoffman has promised to stick up for me. She's on the top rung of our profession, so hopefully that will provide enough cover. Now then, talk.'

Lena took a deep breath. 'I... We... Well, now we're getting married, Eli and me, we'd love to have Emmet back. I know I signed him over, but I didn't want to, it was just everyone told me it was the best thing for him. But now things are different. Eli and I, well, we're getting married, and we can provide for him. Eli is a doctor, as you know, and we could give him a good life, brothers and sisters hopefully, and a loving home –'

'Lena.' Clare's friendliness had suddenly turned to professionalism.

'Please don't say no, please...' Lena felt her baby slipping away again, and she held him and kissed him and inhaled his sweet baby smell in case it was their last time together in this world.

'Lena, Eli, listen to me.' Clare carried on calmly as Eli sat back and folded his arms, alert. 'I'm not going to say no. I'm not going to say yes either, but I will tell you that I will have a meeting with the board and we will discuss it.'

'She's his mother,' Eli said firmly.

'Indeed, his biological mother, but what is right must be taken into consideration.'

'Returning him to his mother is the right thing,' Eli said, sitting forward now, his big brown eyes fixed on the social worker. 'Look at the way they are together. Have you ever seen anything more natural and perfect –'

'She signed the papers, Eli,' said Clare. 'She gave him up for adoption.'

'Fine, then my wife and I want to adopt him. I'm a respectable doctor and a married man, or I will be soon, and as icing on the cake, it just so happens by a fortunate coincidence that I'm marrying his biological mother.'

'And how do I know you're going to stay married to her?' asked Clare. 'I know Lena is heartbroken, and I sympathise, I really do, but if you two are getting married just to have him back...'

Eli glanced at Lena and smiled adoringly. 'Clare, I want to assure you, our engagement is not a stunt to get him back. I love Lena, I always have. And I know I'm not his biological father, but I so much want to be his dad, and he will have a wonderful life with us, I promise you. I'll love him and care for him and do the best I can for him. My mother and stepfather adore Lena, so do my little brothers and sisters – Emmet would be coming home to such a loving family. And as a child who lost everyone except my mother and uncle, I can't tell you how important it is to grow up with your people around you who love you. Not just me and Lena, but everyone. Lena's family in Ireland, her brother and sisters, her mother, her godfather, we'd all adore him.'

'And you, Lena?' asked Clare, clearly trying not to smile. 'Do you want to stay married to this man for your whole life and take the consequences?'

'Of course.' She locked gazes with the young social worker. 'I do, and I want him to be Emmet's father. And I know I gave Emmet up, but it was because I was a single girl with no support, and as you pointed out before, the world is cruel to people like us. Look, I know it won't be plain sailing, I'm not stupid, but families deal with all sorts of things, don't they? Emmet was born before we married, and yes, people will gossip, I suppose, if they find out, but let them.'

'But as you say, Eli isn't Emmet's father, and is your plan to lie to Emmet about that?' Clare asked pointedly.

'Eli *will* be his father,' Lena said with conviction. 'Not biologically, that's true, but in every way that's important. If he asks us when he's older, I suppose we'll tell him the truth, but I don't know. It's down the road anyway, but we'd do what was best for him, I promise you that. If he was adopted, he'd be raised by two people to whom he had no connection biologically, and it would be up to them whether or not they told him the truth, so at least this way, one of his parents is a blood relation.'

Clare sighed. 'Well, I believe you are both sincere. This is the most unusual case I've ever worked on, I don't mind telling you, but I will try my best. It's not up to me exclusively, and I might as well tell you, there will be opposition.'

'Will it help if we marry as soon as we can?' Eli asked eagerly.

'It certainly can't do any harm. So I'll take Emmet now – it's almost time for his morning nap before lunch – and I'll be in touch.'

'Please, one more minute,' Lena begged in alarm.

Clare hesitated, then melted. 'Very well. I'll leave him with you two for a moment, but just a moment.' She stood up and left the room, and Eli came to take her place beside Lena on the sofa, putting his arms around both her and the baby.

Lena leaned against him and gazed down into Emmet's soft green eyes. 'Emmet, my darling boy,' she began, her voice quivering with emotion. 'We'll do all we can to take you home, your dad and me...' She glanced at Eli, and he smiled, a tear forming in his eye. 'But, darling baby, if I don't ever see you again, I want you to know how much I love you, and maybe when you are grown up, you can come and find me.'

'So long, little man,' Eli whispered, kissing him on the forehead. 'I don't care what we have to do, we'll get you back. Just hold tight.'

Clare appeared again; it was like she'd only been gone for a second. 'I'm so sorry, but Nurse Jennings is having a fit. I really must take him now.' She gathered Emmet in her arms, and he whimpered, holding out his little hands to Lena.

'There now, Emmet, everything is all right,' Clare soothed him, crossing the room to another internal door. 'I'll take him this way, so if you two could see yourselves out. I'll be in touch.'

'When?' Lena couldn't help herself calling after the young woman as she stepped out of sight.

'As soon as I know,' Clare called back, and she was gone.

CHAPTER 24

*N*either of them spoke until they were on the main road again. Lena sat with her face pressed to the passenger window, staring blindly at the woods, the fields, the hills. Her heart was full of love but also fear. Would she ever see Emmet again? She was sure Clare Winton would try her best, but what about the faceless board of officials, the ones who were sure to raise objections? It seemed so cruel that her whole life was in the hands of strangers who had never met her.

It was Eli who broke the silence. 'Will we go back via the registry office?'

She turned to him in amazement. 'You mean, get married now?'

He rolled his eyes humorously. 'OK, OK, no need to look so horrified. No, not married, but we have to give notice, and the sooner we give it, the sooner we can get hitched. And Clare said –'

'How much notice?'

'Twenty-eight days, as far as I know.'

'So that's...' – Lena did the calculation in her head – 'the tenth of June? Two weeks after my exams?'

'I guess. Will your family mind if it's a registry office? It's just, it can't be a church wedding because I'm Jewish, and it can't be a synagogue because you're Catholic. But we can still buy you a beautiful dress and have flowers and throw rice and all of that...'

She reached over and took his hand and held it. It was the first time she'd ever done something so intimate, and he looked both surprised and pleased. 'Eli, I couldn't give a hoot about any of that,' she said. 'I just want you.'

'You want me?' His brown eyes sparkled. 'It's not only...?'

'I want to be married to you, Eli. The more I think about it, the more I love the idea. And I couldn't care less about the fuss. Emily won't be able to come to the wedding anyway, being pregnant, and Jack is in America, and Mammy wouldn't be able to travel. The only person I'd really like to invite is Doc, and your parents of course, and Saul and Ann, because those are the people who know about Emmet and who have stood by me and helped me. Doc wants to visit his old friend Saul – he's been threatening to do that for ages.'

Eli nodded, navigating around a lorry spewing fumes. 'All right. Although I do want you to have flowers and a dress and –'

'Honestly, I'm happy with a nice simple trip to the registry office, with those closest to us. Maybe not your step-grandparents, though...'

Eli laughed out loud. 'A Jew marrying an Irishwoman? That's Bessie Evans's worst nightmare. She wouldn't come if we paid her a million pounds.'

'Just as well.' Lena caught her breath. 'Though if we get Emmet back, I'm sure she'll have plenty to say about that.'

It was the first time she had dared to mention Emmet's name since leaving the foster home. She said in a low voice, 'Do you think it will happen, Eli?'

He squeezed her hand warmly, and she realised she was still holding his. 'Do you know, Lena? I really do think it will.'

'Are you just saying that because it's what I want to hear or because you really believe it?'

'He's your son, your boy. Who else should have him? Clare is on our side. She'll persuade the board.'

'Maybe...' But she didn't dare to hope.

They drove back to the city, still holding hands in the car, and as they drove down past the gothic Cardiff castle, he suddenly pulled into a vacant car space.

'What are we doing?' she asked, puzzled.

'Come on.' He ran around and opened the door for her, and as she got out, he took her in his arms and kissed her. Behind them some builders demolishing an old shop started whistling and catcalling, but Eli just turned and shouted, 'She's a cracker, isn't she? We're getting married!'

There was a loud cheer from the builders and some smiles from passers-by as Eli led her, laughing, by the hand along the street.

They stopped outside Jonathan David Jewellers in the Royal Arcade. 'Right, soon-to-be Mrs Kogan, let's get this official, shall we?'

Lena allowed herself to be led into the sumptuous shop. The cabinets were glistening with diamonds and jewels, watches and pieces of fine jewellery.

A heavyset lady in her sixties with the whitest hair in the most extravagant beehive hairdo Lena had ever seen appeared. 'May I help you?' she asked.

'I hope so. We're looking for a ring,' Eli announced with pride.

'Certainly, sir. What kind of a ring are you interested in?' She glanced at Lena's hand, and Lena was glad she'd removed Doc's mother's ring that morning

'We want an engagement ring,' replied Eli, gazing adoringly at Lena.

'Well, you've come to the right place.' The woman smiled and pulled out a tray of simple gold rings with tiny diamonds. 'How about you take a look at these, madam?' Then she drew Eli to one side for a discreet word. Lena suppressed a smile. She'd heard of this – the woman was asking him the budget, and she would show more trays accordingly.

'Whichever one she wants,' he said, loud enough for Lena to hear.

Endless trays were brought out; the array was staggering. Some of the rings were so huge and heavy, Lena joked she'd need a wheelbarrow to carry them around. In the end, she chose an exquisite teal sapphire in a cushion cut surrounded by quarter-carat diamonds. The band was a combination of white and yellow gold, and it was the most beautiful ring she'd ever seen.

'An excellent choice, madam. It's elegant, unusual and understated.'

'Just like you,' Eli whispered in Lena's ear.

When the woman murmured the price, Lena overheard and almost took the ring off, protesting it was far too much, but Eli hushed her. 'It's not too much. Nothing could ever be too much for you, my darling.'

He kissed her while the woman went to the back and made out the receipt. Eli wrote a cheque, and Lena felt a pang.

'Are you sure? It seems –'

'I *am* a doctor, you know? And I've had bugger all to spend any money on in the last while, since my favourite person on the planet insisted on living across the Irish Sea. So please, don't worry, it's all fine.'

They walked hand in hand back to the car, strolling along in the spring sunshine as the builders stopped again to give them a round of applause.

'Let's go straight to Pontcanna after the registry office,' suggested Eli. 'I can't wait to tell

Mum and Charlie, and the kids will go crazy with excitement...'

Lena found she got a warm feeling when Eli said things like that. Had she never really thought of him as a boyfriend? She tried to think back. She'd been so distraught about Malachy, then having to leave her baby, that there had been no room in her head or heart for anything or anyone else. 'I wonder when Clare will tell us what the board decided?'

'Soon, I hope.' He opened the passenger door for her.

'We should tell them straight away, Sarah and Charlie, I mean.'

'About Emmet or about us?'

'Both.'

'Righto. But first, the registry office.'

The process was straightforward, because that morning Eli had insisted they both bring their passports and birth certificates to the foster home as a form of identification, 'just in case Clare isn't there to meet us', although of course it turned out to be 'just in case Lena agrees to marry me'. So all that was required at the registry office was for Eli David Kogan, bachelor, to declare his intention to marry Lena Maria O'Sullivan, spinster. They signed some forms, a copy was made of their documents, and that was it. The wedding was set for the tenth of June.

'Where will we live?' Eli asked, the question clearly occurring to him for the first time.

She thought about it as they walked to the car. 'I don't know. I suppose it depends on whether or not we get Emmet back.'

She sat in and Eli got in beside her. 'Supposing we do?' he asked. 'Where would you like us to bring him up?'

'I don't know, Eli. I mean, if we do by a miracle win him back, then we can't return to Ireland for a while, not until a reasonable length of time has passed and we can pass him off as ours. But – and I never thought I'd hear myself say it – I'd like for him to grow up in Kilteegan Bridge. It's a lovely place for a child. Everyone knows everyone, and I want him around Mam, and Doc, and Em and Blackie, and the twins and Jack. We'll let it be known that we got married, and so long as we leave it a good long time before going back, who will question Emmet's age? We can say I met you through Doc and left Ireland to marry you. What do you think?'

'I think it sounds marvellous, so let's just keep our fingers crossed. I'll need to finish the contract

I'm in here anyway, so maybe we can rent a house near the hospital for the time being?'

She crossed her fingers and held them up, trying hard to smile.

'We've not really talked about the visit, have we?' he said gently. 'How do you feel now you've seen him?'

'Oh, Eli...' She gulped, finding it suddenly hard to speak. 'I just love him so much, and I can't imagine not having him back. I just can't. And I'm trying to remain calm, trying to see if I can just stay patient and pray and hope that they find in our favour, but the alternative, Eli, I don't know...' She turned and faced him. Because they'd never been courting, she never flirted or showed her best side; he saw her warts and all from the start. 'I might not be able to bear it if she says no.'

He looked her in the eyes. 'Let's figure that out when we know. For now let's just hope and look forward to our wedding, because whatever we face, we'll face it together from now on.'

'You're a marvel, Eli Kogan, you know that?' She leaned over and kissed his cheek.

'I do.' He winked at her, then pulled out into the line of traffic.

As he drove, she looked down at her ring. It

was the most beautiful thing she'd ever owned, and she moved her hand this way and that, watching it sparkle. 'Eli, please don't think this is all about Emmet. I'm delighted about you and me, really thrilled. Thank you for asking me to marry you.'

'The pleasure was all mine.' He suddenly grew serious again. 'I know I'm not your first love, and I know you'd rather be with Malachy if things hadn't turned out –'

'Stop right there. Now listen carefully. I want you, not as a consolation prize or as second best, or as a way to present myself as a more fitting mother for my son. I want to be married to you because I realise now that I love you. I can't believe it never occurred to me before, but I was such a mess since I met you. But, Eli, you are perfect for me. You're funny and so kind and very handsome, and I'm going to be so proud to say I'm your wife. I mean it, so no more of this stuff about the past. I did love Malachy too, but it feels like a lifetime ago and I was a different person then. I was hurt and heartbroken that he abandoned me, but he did, and that's how it goes, so please don't think I'm still holding a torch for him, because I'm not.'

'Do you really mean that?' he asked, staring

ahead as they stopped at a pedestrian light to allow an old woman with no less than six tiny yappy dogs to cross the road.

Once again, she took his hand. Of course she loved him. He was her best friend, her wonderful, kind, reliable Eli. She said, 'I really, really do.'

CHAPTER 25

*D*oc gazed down at Lena as they stood together on the steps of the civic hall a month later. He looked thinner than ever, and tired, but he was elegantly dressed, and his eyes were full of love for her.

'It should be Paudie here today, not me,' he said.

'I don't agree.' Lena smiled up at him. 'I'll miss Dad all of my life, but this bit, the whole thing with Malachy and Emmet and all of it, that's been with your support, and so it's right that you're the one by my side today. I'm going in there to marry a man I love, and maybe if my prayers are answered, we'll make a family with Emmet and return to Kilteegan Bridge together sometime. I know I said I wanted to travel the world and get away from there, but I feel differently now. I want Emmet to grow up around you and Mam and my sisters and Jack. I had a great childhood there, though it drove me mad at times, but it's such a beautiful place to raise a family. So I'm ready to do this, and there's nobody in the world I'd rather have beside me today than you.'

'And Malachy Berger?' he probed gently.

She stuck out her chin, her old defiant gesture. 'I loved Malachy and I would have married him, but he abandoned me, and that's something Eli will never do. And now he's in America, making his fortune or whatever, so that's that. We were children, Doc, and that's the truth. It felt so real, so intense, but they say first love does, don't they? But that wasn't real, not like Eli and me.'

'I must say, I like this fella a whole lot better,' he said. Eli, Saul and Charlie had taken Doc to a rugby match three days ago, and they'd not appeared home until the small hours, a bit the worse for wear.

'I like him too.' Lena winked.

'And his parents are good people,' said Doc pointedly. Lena knew he'd never liked Malachy's father. 'And they're delighted with you.'

'Thanks, Doc.'

Although it was quite true, Sarah's delight was tempered with something else. When Eli had first announced the engagement, his parents had been thrilled. But when Lena and Eli had explained why they were getting married as soon as possible, Lena had seen the shadow of doubt in Sarah's eyes, so she wasn't surprised when Eli's mother came up to her room later and sat on the edge of her bed, looking worried.

'Do you love my son?' Sarah had asked her, without any introduction.

Lena looked her full in the face. 'I do.'

'And what about Emmet's father?'

'He's in the past. I won't see him again.'

Sarah continued to gaze at her. 'I'm so very fond of you, Lena. So are Charlie and the little ones, and Eli is wild about you. I couldn't talk him out of this even if I wanted to, but as fond as I am of you, I must be honest. I think you're still in love with that boy in Ireland. My son deserves better than to be someone's consolation prize.'

Lena took a deep breath and reached inside herself for the honest truth. 'Sarah, I love your son. As I told him, Malachy and I were kids, and yes, if he'd stuck by me, we would have married. But it was another lifetime ago. Malachy is my past, but Eli is my future, forever hopefully. I'll be a good wife and mother to his children. Your whole family have been so kind to me, and I promise you that I never, ever want to do anything to hurt him.'

Sarah stared at her so closely, it was as if she were trying to see into her soul. Then she sighed and said, 'I believe you, Lena. I believe you don't ever want to hurt him. And if that's good enough for Eli, then that's good enough for me. That man downstairs would follow you to the moon if it was what you wanted. And I love him and you, and I wish you both all the very best.'

'Thank you, Sarah. I mean it, thank you so much. Does it matter that I'm not Jewish?'

Sarah smiled. 'Elijah, Eli's father, was more devout than me. I grew up in the Jewish faith, but his family was definitely more observant. But he loved his son as I do, and he would want first and foremost for him to be happy. As for me, after what I saw, what was done to our people in Germany and elsewhere, well, for me there is no God – how could there be?' The sadness and depth of her loss were there to see on Sarah's face.

'I can't imagine,' Lena replied. Sarah and Eli rarely mentioned all they endured in Germany before escaping, but it had affected them both deeply, she knew. 'I hope the dead can see us, my father, Eli's, and that they know we found each other and we're happy.'

'I hope so too.' Sarah nodded sadly.

Now, on the steps of the registry office, Doc took her arm. 'So will we go in and do it? You look beautiful, Lena, really beautiful,' he said sincerely.

'Thanks, Doc.' She grinned.

She had bought her wedding dress on a shopping trip with Sarah; Sarah got her a great discount, being in the business. The dress was made of ivory shot silk, and outrageously, it was short to the knee, with cap sleeves and a sweetheart neckline. It cinched in on her tiny waist, and the skirt was tulip shaped. She carried a simple bouquet of white roses and had a short veil on her head, and on her feet she wore the most beautiful cream sandals, perilously high, but since Eli was six feet three, she could wear heels as high as she liked. As she'd dressed, she'd felt a pang for Malachy. He used to hate when she wore heels as he was under six foot and didn't like it if she looked nearly as tall as him. That all felt like something that had happened to someone else.

The smallish room was full enough not to be a sad occasion. Sarah and Charlie and the four children, all looking cute and spotless due to dire warnings from their mother that they were not to move a muscle since breakfast, and behind them, Saul and Ann Hoffman. Two of Eli's friends, Dai and Ewan, also came with their girl-friends. Lena had been introduced to them in recent weeks and really enjoyed their company. Dai was a dentist and Ewan was a sheep farmer, another friend who endured the disapproval of Bessie Evans. Dai was engaged to Sally, a bubbly primary school teacher with long chestnut hair, and Ewan brought a girl called Doris, who Lena and Eli had only met once; she was from Birmingham and seemed very friendly. Eli's friends were charming Welsh men who loved rugby and who could sing in rich baritone at the drop of a hat.

True to Eli's prediction, Bessie Evans had blown a gasket when Charlie informed her that Eli was marrying Lena. She'd told him that if he imagined she'd be coming to the wedding, then he had another think coming, and Lena felt sure she said lots of other things too that Charlie didn't tell her. She'd vowed to never speak to Eli again, and that suited everyone perfectly.

'I know I shouldn't say it,' Sarah confided after the big showdown, 'but Charlie envies Eli. He had me in stitches in bed last night trying to come up with ways to get himself excommunicated too, as life would be so much easier.'

Lena walked on Doc's arm up the short path between the seats, with Alys and Gwen throwing rose petals before them, to where Eli stood. He looked handsome in a charcoal suit, white shirt and gold tie. His eyes glinted with delight and mischief when he saw her, and as he shook hands with Doc and Doc put Lena's hand in Eli's, he bent and kissed her.

'Oi, not yet! You're jumping the gun there, son,' Charlie, best man and witness, joked, despite Sarah's nudging him to behave. Everyone laughed and the ceremony began.

The registrar, a pale, bald man in his fifties who looked like he hadn't smiled in decades, was efficient but not animated, and the ceremony was over within minutes. The small party found themselves outside on the street, confetti being thrown.

'One for the *Examiner?*' a man asked as he stepped out of the registry office; he had a professional-looking camera.

'Ooh, you're really Cardiff royalty if your wedding makes the *Examiner.*' Charlie laughed as the entire group stood together and let the photographer take the shot.

'Go on out of that. He hangs around here all the time. I've seen him loads of times in the last month. They use the wedding picture on a slow day.' Eli grinned.

Doc insisted on taking everyone to lunch at the Criterion, a beautiful restaurant a few miles out in the country with views over the Brecon Beacons. They wined and dined, and everyone was in wonderful spirits.

As best man, Charlie gave a long, humorous speech in his lovely lilting Welsh accent. 'Ladies and gentlemen, boys and girls, firstly let me welcome Lena officially to the family. She arrived into our house last year, and we've never looked back. She is hilarious, and can sing like a nightingale, and our children adore her. I recently got promoted, and I'm convinced it's because my socks always matched under the stewardship of Miss O'Sullivan.'

There were ripples of laughter.

'She makes us realise every day how wonderful our lives are by singing Irish songs of misery and misfortune.'

The group laughed again.

'And it is her fault, and hers alone, that for most of last year, my socks matched but none of my trousers fit because of her baking. Eli fell in love the first day he saw Lena, and I know that for a fact because I felt the exact same way the day I met my Sarah.' He looked at his wife sitting beside him and smiled. 'Seriously, though, Eli, Saul and Sarah endured so much, and I thank God every day he brought them safely to us. And now, to see the boy I consider my son married to the love of his life, well, that's just perfect. I hope and pray that his father, Elijah, and all of the Kogan and Hoffman families, and Lena's dad, Paudie, can see him now. I know he would be as proud of these magnificent young people as we are. So, ladies and gentlemen, I invite you to raise your glasses in a toast to Eli and Lena.'

'To Eli and Lena,' everyone chorused.

'And now I'd like to invite Doc to say a few words.'

And after the laughter and applause, Doc also rose to his feet. He spoke without notes, looking at his goddaughter the whole time. 'I met Lena the day she was born – the minute she was born in actual fact, because I delivered her. I didn't mention to my best friend, Paudie, her father, that it was the first baby I'd ever delivered. He was nervous enough because there was no time to get Maria, Lena's mother, to the hospital. So you could say I learned on the job as it were.

Lena surprised us all, coming two weeks early, and has continued to keep us on our toes ever since. She soon proved to us all that she was infinitely smarter, funnier, kinder and more beautiful than we even imagined, and as Eli will no doubt know, she's a determined young lady, so I'd choose my battles wisely.' He winked at Eli, who laughed. 'Of course, it should be Paudie standing here before you today, but he was taken from us, so I've been standing in as best I can.'

'And doing a brilliant job,' Lena added.

'I don't know about that, but I do know he would be, as Charlie said, so, so proud today. If it was possible, Lena's mother, Maria, and her sisters and brother would have been here, but I assure you I bring with me their very best wishes. Eli, she's a marvellous girl, as you know, and you seem to be a perfect match for her. The exact right mixture of intelligence enough to challenge her, funny enough to entertain her, handsome enough to keep her, and you clearly love her as much as she loves you. So once again, to the girl I've always seen as the daughter I never had, the beautiful bride, Lena, and her new husband, Eli, I wish you both a lifetime of love and all the happiness you both deserve.'

Lena wiped a tear from her eye as Doc finished, and Eli squeezed her hand under the table.

Before she knew what was happening, Eli, Saul, Charlie, Ewan and Dai got to their feet and Eli spoke. 'Lena, we have done a very, *very* little bit of practice' – he gave a sheepish grin – 'but we wanted to sing something for you. You sing all the time, going about the place, those beautiful, sad Irish songs, so I thought it might be nice to share one of our Welsh ones with you today. It's called "Tra Bo Dau", and it's a traditional Welsh love song. The words say that no matter that treasures come and go, so do many things with time, but that when two people have loving hearts, then that lasts forever. And following that, we'll try "When You Were Sweet Sixteen". I'm sure it's with a Welsh accent, but that's the song that Paudie used to sing to Maria, Lena's parents, so we thought it might be nice to have it today.'

The small room was filled with rich male voices, singing in an enchanting four-part harmony. Lena glanced at Doc, who smiled and gave her a nod.

They did a marvellous job of both songs, and the men sat down to enthusiastic applause.

Then Saul rose to his feet and, with much ceremony, handed the happy couple the keys to the

Hoffmans' holiday cottage in the Cotswolds, complete with housekeeper, to use for their honeymoon. Ann assured Lena the larder was stuffed and it was all ready; they could go that evening and stay as long as they liked.

Later, Lena went to find Eli, who was deep in some sort of serious conversation with her godfather. She beckoned him away and whispered, 'What will we do if they call about Emmet while we're away on honeymoon? I gave them Sarah and Charlie's number, and if we're not there, they might think we're not interested...'

'Darling, I knew about this in advance. There's a phone in the cottage, and I've told Clare exactly where to find us, so please don't worry.' He held her tight and kissed her. 'Let's enjoy this time to ourselves. I have a feeling we're going to be parents soon enough, and then we'll have a lot less time just for each other.'

She relaxed in his embrace. 'Thank you for singing that song. It brought back so many memories. You are all amazing singers.'

'Thank you, Mrs Kogan, for the compliment. All Welsh people can sing, and my father was a wonderful tenor. He used to sing in the shower, and I remember hearing him when I would sit on the landing of our house in Berlin to play with my toy cars.'

'I wish I'd met him,' she said quietly.

'I wish that too.' She could hear the loss there. It was hard to have such a big day without someone so integral; she understood it. But Eli had Charlie and she had Doc, and if anyone knew that fathers came in all forms, not just biological, they did.

CHAPTER 26

They set off for the Cotswolds in the mid-afternoon and arrived in the early evening, with the sky still bright and sunny. As Eli drove carefully through the narrow lanes, Lena admired the rolling grass hills, the neat stone walls and honey-coloured villages that were all in perfect condition, very different from the wildness of Ireland's west coast. The Hoffmans' stone cottage in the village of Stanton had a thatched roof, dark timbers and windows made of tiny diamond-shaped panes of glass.

Eli parked in the cobbled street, then insisted on carrying Lena over the threshold, where they were greeted with giggles by the housekeeper, a plump, friendly woman with a broad country accent. Even though Eli had been there several times before, she insisted on showing Lena around the house, teaching her to tread carefully on the uneven polished stairs and bringing her into one of the two tiny bedrooms tucked under the eaves, which had sprigged curtains, a huge wooden bed and a feather mattress. The bathroom next door was ancient, with a claw-footed bath, and she cautioned Lena that when the stove was lit, the water got very hot and not to burn herself.

Downstairs was a tiny drawing room and a big stone-flagged kitchen, with a table where they could eat; it was already set with heavy silver cutlery and serving spoons and blue dinner plates. True to Ann's promise, the Hoffmans' larder was stocked with local cheese and wine and fresh potatoes and other vegetables, and in the fridge were lamb chops, a whole chicken and a joint of beef from the local butcher. The housekeeper, Annie Fowler, explained that fresh-baked bread and creamy cow's milk would be delivered every morning, and that they weren't to worry about a thing – she would pop in every day to tidy and dust and leave a dinner ready for them while the young couple relaxed and explored the local countryside.

Then Annie proudly opened the back door to reveal a typical English country garden, full of hollyhocks and snapdragons and alive with tiny birds and colourful butterflies. Lena and Eli wandered out happily hand in hand and walked down a gravelled path. At the end of the garden ran a bubbling stream, and Lena was delighted by the family of moorhens paddling up and down, the chicks bobbing along behind their mother in single file.

For a moment she was reminded of the lake in Cork, where she'd watched the ducks with Malachy... Then she pushed his memory away and held Eli's hand tighter.

Back in the house, they found that Mrs Fowler had already gone, but she had left a chicken pie on the table, with a bowl of buttered tiny new potatoes sprinkled with chopped fresh mint. There was also an open bottle of French red wine with two crystal glasses, and she'd left a note to say there was a trifle in the fridge for dessert. So there was nothing for them to do but sit down, and for Lena to serve the pie.

The strange thing was, even though usually he talked non-stop to her, it suddenly seemed like Eli had nothing to say. And as hard as Lena tried to come up with a subject of conversation, she couldn't get him to do more than grunt.

By the time they'd nearly cleared their plates, Lena had drunk half a glass of wine and decided this was ridiculous. 'Cat got your tongue?' she asked crossly.

He smiled weakly, then ate another potato. 'You're not talking much yourself.'

'Yes, but that's because *you're* not talking.'

'Which came first, the chicken or the egg?'

'OK, clever clogs. I'll try again. Isn't this a lovely house?'

'It is.'

'Do you know it was built when Shakespeare was alive? That's over five hundred years ago.'

'Amazing.'

She waited a moment, then sighed. 'Oh, come on, is that all you're going to say?'

He looked at her, and for the first time, she realised how pale he was, and the hand that held his fork was shaking.

'Eli, what is it?'

'I...'

A terrible thought came to her. 'You haven't changed your mind, have you?'

'Changed my mind about what?' He looked confused.

'About...us, Eli. You know. Me and you. You've been so kind and generous, maybe you've not been thinking properly about what you want...'

'Lena, stop.' He had gone even paler under his freckles. 'Please. You know it's not that, it's...'

'What?' She was getting exasperated.

He burst out, 'It's that I don't know what... I mean... It's that I don't know what *you* want, Lena. And I want to do what you want. I don't want to push you faster than you want to go. I mean, I rushed you into this – well, I suppose life rushed you into this, and I'm so happy to rush into it myself – but maybe you –'

'Darling Eli.' She reached across the table for his hand.

'Lena, there are two bedrooms and plenty of bedding, so you see, you don't have to, not if you're not ready...'

Lena's heart swelled with love for this tall, gorgeous, sandy-haired, brown-eyed man who adored her so much. She pushed her plate aside and stood up, holding out her hand. 'Come on, Eli. I think we should leave the trifle until later, don't you?'

She led him up the narrow staircase, taking care as Annie said on the uneven surface, and went into the room with the big double bed. She had no idea how experienced Eli was – they had never discussed it – but he had lots of girls interested in him, so presumably he wasn't a complete novice. Her one encounter with Malachy in the hay barn was the sum total of hers.

She took both his hands in hers and looked up into his eyes. 'Malachy and I only did it once, and before him I'd never even kissed a boy, so if you're thinking I'm some kind of expert in these matters, then you're wrong. But I'm ready, and very willing and excited, to begin our lives as husband and wife, in every way.'

He sighed as if the weight of the world were released from him. He bent his head and kissed her, gently at first but later with more urgency and passion. She found her hands caressing him, her fingers thrilling to the hard masculine curves of his back as they pulled at each other's clothing. He unzipped her going-away dress, a green and gold figure-hugging one Sarah had ordered as a gift, and she felt no embarrassment or awkwardness as it slid from her shoulders. Eli was her man, her husband, and she was his; she was ready.

* * *

IN THE MORNING, they feasted on fresh crusty bread with local farm butter and slathered with Annie's homemade blackberry jam and drank pots of tea. They were still not talking much, but this was a happy silence, not like the awkward speechlessness of last night.

After breakfast, they decided to explore the village and its surroundings. They looked into old churches with musty tapestries and ancient tombs, stone knights with stone dogs at their feet and medieval ladies with cherubs clustered around them, representing all the lost babies because so many died very young in those times. Lena stroked the cherubs' little stone curls and thought of Emmet.

They had lunch in the Mount public house and drank the local cider, which Lena liked because it was sweeter and fizzier than the awful English ale, and after lunch they took a walk down to the river. Eli kissed her a lot in between pointing out two salmon in the river and one bright flash of blue that he thought was probably a kingfisher. In Lena's tummy, something fluttered a little... But then everything was so new and different at the moment, and her mind was still in a whirl over Emmet. It was hard to say what was causing her excitement, although she did think Eli looked very handsome in his open-necked green shirt and loose cream trousers.

Back at the house, another car was parked behind Eli's, a plain white Ford. As they approached, laughing together at one of Eli's silly jokes, a woman stepped out of the driving seat.

'Hello, you two.' It was Clare Winton, dressed in her neat black working clothes and looking very professional.

Lena's laughter dried on her lips. 'Hello...' she breathed, her heart racing. Clare looked so serious, and there were she and Eli laughing like they hadn't a care in the world when maybe they should have been looking all serious and sad to show how they missed Emmet all the time – she knew Clare Winton took her job very seriously.

'So you seem very happy on your honeymoon,' said the social worker calmly.

'Yes, yes, but we only got married yesterday. Oh dear, maybe we should have invited you...' Lena knew she was gushing stupidly, but she couldn't help it. Her knuckles were white, she was clutching Eli's hand so tightly.

'Well, I assume you know the reason I'm here. The board met this morning, and the most irregular case of Emmet came up for discussion. After much debate, and after my faithful promise that you and Dr Kogan were now properly married and your union wasn't just a matter of convenience, which I am happy to see it is not –'

'No one has ever been more properly married,' said Eli, 'and less conveniently.'

Clare's mouth twitched. 'Indeed. And as I was saying, after I gave them my assurance that you will live in a situation suitable for a child, then they are willing to allow you to adopt Emmet.'

Lena opened her mouth to speak but no sound came out.

Clare was looking at her. 'I take it that is still what you want?'

'I...' she managed. 'I...' The tears flowed then, and she felt her legs crumble beneath her. Eli caught her as she wept against his chest.

'Clare,' he said, with laughter in his voice as he spoke over Lena's head, 'I'm afraid my wife's a little overwhelmed with this information, but despite her tears, I can assure you, she is delighted.'

Clare smiled. 'I understand. It is a very emotional time for her. Perhaps you should bring her into the house and give her a cup of hot sweet tea, or even a splash of something stronger. When she's recovered, there are some legal formalities for us to go through, but they shouldn't take long.

I'll wait here until you call me.' And she got back into the car.

Inside the house, drinking the sweet tea with a splash of brandy Eli had made for her, Lena was incredulous. 'They're giving him back to me?'

'It certainly looks that way.' He grinned. 'But there's forms we need to sign, so get that into you and best foot first and all that. Now I'll go and call Clare in.'

Lena sat there, shaking. She couldn't get out of her mind that this was all a dream, and that not only Clare but Eli and everything around her would suddenly melt away and she would be back in the hospital after having had Emmet, being forced to sign a very different set of forms...

When Eli and Clare reappeared, the sense of being in a dream grew even stronger, because there in Clare's arms was a sturdy little baby, drowsy looking, with red hair and green eyes and reaching out his arms to Lena as soon as he saw her. He must have been sleeping in the car.

'Oh, oh, oh...' In a moment, she was on her feet. She took him from Clare, and he snuggled his face into her neck. She held his wriggling body to hers and breathed in the beautiful baby scent of him. The three of them and the baby stood together as the sun streamed in the kitchen window, and Eli told her later that nobody watching could have been under any doubt that Emmet knew exactly who his mother was.

'I don't know how to thank either of you,' Lena choked out. 'I never dared think this day could come, and none of this would have been possible, oh, Eli, if you never proposed to me, and, Clare, if you'd not bent the rules to let me see him. I can't tell you... I feel so blessed that I...' Her voice cracked.

'No thanks necessary. It's been perfectly obvious to me from the start that this little boy is exactly where he should be.' Clare smiled. She pulled a sheaf of papers from her bag, and when everything was signed – Lena did so in a trance, but Eli made sure everything was correct – she put them back in her bag and reached over and smoothed Emmet's curls. 'You have a lovely life with your mummy and daddy now, Emmet, and may God bless you.'

Emmet beamed back at her, his face covered with Annie's chocolate pudding that she'd left in the fridge for their dessert that evening, and which Eli had been surreptitiously feeding him.

'Oh, I'm sorry! You had him so spotless...'

Lena said, hastily trying to wipe his chocolatey face. 'I promise we'll take such good care of him.'

'I know you will.' Clare smiled again. 'Every baby gets messy when their dad feeds them chocolate. Now, I'll be off...'

'Can't we get you some lunch after driving all this way? There's this lovely lady called Annie, and she's left us a wonderful stew?'

Clare Winton wouldn't hear of it; she said she had to get on and that besides, they needed time as a family now.

After they'd waved her off, Eli phoned his parents, and Lena could hear Sarah crying with joy. And then it was her turn to call Doc, who also shed tears, although he fiercely denied it. 'I've just got a bit of a cold. So when are you coming to see me with my precious little namesake?'

'We'll give it a year or so, and then we'll come to Ireland. We can be a bit vague about dates and births and weddings and all of that. I'll tell Em and Jack the truth of course, I should have told them when I came back for the wedding but everything was so up in the air then, but as far as everyone else is concerned, Eli and I got married ages ago and Emmet was a honeymoon baby.'

'Well, he wouldn't be the first one of those, I suppose,' Doc said, and she could sense his concern. 'But there will be talk, Lena. You know how this place is.'

'Doc, I know you think lies and secrets are a terrible idea, but this one really isn't. I don't want the poor child to have the stigma of being born out of wedlock. Nobody there knew I was going out with Malachy – well, except you and my family and Malachy's father. But it's not public knowledge, so there's no reason they'd suspect he wasn't Eli's. It's best this way. I've thought it out, and I don't want to be shaming Emily when she has to look respectable running a shop, or to have people saying nasty things about me to Mam – she's not able for it.'

'I agree, Lena, but why does a lie have to be told at all? Do you plan on coming back for long? I know you'll visit but...'

'Oh no, we won't be just visiting, Doc. Eli is going to finish his contract here and then hopefully we're going to live in Kilteegan Bridge. He loves the idea, and I'm sure he'd get a job in the hospital in Bantry or even Cork. And I never told a living soul there about the pregnancy or anything except you, so if you'll keep our secret, everything should be fine.'

His voice softened. 'I thought getting away from here was your goal?'

'It was my goal, but I want Emmet to grow up where he has roots and family, and besides, you'd fall apart completely if I left you forever.'

He chuckled. 'I'm not denying that one bit – you should see the state of my files already. It's just...' He sounded worried again. 'Well, the truth has a way of getting out. There's Eli's family and friends in Wales?'

'I know, but we trust the small number of people who know the truth not to say anything, and we'll just have to leave the rest to fate. I know you're always saying that secrets are never a good idea, but I can't come up with anything else.'

There was a long pause while he thought about it. Then he said, 'Lena, I can't imagine anything more lovely than to have you home. And you're right, Emmet deserves to be protected from silly gossip.'

'Could you put a word in with someone at the hospital? I know you know the head of the Bon Secours Order. Eli will need a job, and he's a great doctor.'

'Oh, I don't think we're going to have to banish Eli to the nuns,' said Doc. 'I think he'll be able to work right here in Kilteegan Bridge if he wants to.'

'What?'

'Well, I'm not getting any younger, Lena, and it's time to wind down, I think, or at least go part time, and so I couldn't think of a safer pair of hands to share my practice with than Eli. I told him at the wedding that if he ever wanted to think about it, the offer was on the table.'

After the phone call, she flew into the garden, where Eli was walking Emmet around in his arms, showing him the butterflies and stopping him from grabbing a bee. 'You never told me that Doc offered you a partnership in the surgery?' she said happily. 'It will be wonderful. We can go back, in due time of course, and you can work with Doc and I can run the practice...'

Eli looked at her a little oddly. 'I think it's going to be a bit more than that, Lena. That night he and I and Dad went out to the rugby together...well, we had a good chat. Doc's not well.'

A cold shiver ran down her spine, but hastily, she pushed away the thought of anything being wrong with Doc. 'Oh, he only needs some proper looking after, Eli, to make sure he doesn't stay up reading all night, just drinking and smoking and not eating. As I told Doc, we'll let some time go by. Emmet is a little like me. I asked Clare, and she said that while he was developing fine, he is small, so we'll get away with it, I think. Even if people suspect, what will they say? We're married, nobody back there knew about Malachy and me, so it's all going to be fine. The sooner I'm back there, the better.'

In fact, caring for Doc was another good reason to go back to Kilteegan Bridge. She took her son from Eli and held him close, hardly daring to believe this was happening.

IN THE END, they stayed for nearly another nine months in Cardiff. As adoptive parents, they had to face regular checks from social workers for the first few months, although Lena didn't mind; she was proud how Emmet was thriving. Eli had a year's contract at the hospital to work out, and while Lena had passed her pre-nursing exams in May with top marks, she was now just enjoying time with her baby.

The letters from Ireland came regularly. She'd told Jack and Emily the truth, and they were as she predicted – a bit shocked of course, but supportive. Em had a baby girl called Nellie, and Lena daydreamed of her and Emmet growing up as friends and cousins. Lena wrote to her mother, apologising for getting married behind her back but saying she didn't think anyone would approve and that she and Eli had become close as pen pals through Doc and he'd invited her over and she went. Her mother wasn't to be trusted with the truth because Lena couldn't be sure it wouldn't get blurted out in a rage sometime. Her letters suggested she and Eli were together and married for much longer than they were. She mentioned how much she was looking forward to introducing Maria to her grandson, but that Eli was very busy with work and as soon as he could get away, they would. She hated lying, but it was the only way.

The twins had started in junior infants, where they were learning to write their letters, and they sent her cards saying things like, 'CAT DIDE PLIZ COM' and 'NUW CAT STRIPPY'.

Her mother was very happy making Irish dancing dresses for Emily and Blackie's shop, which were flying out the door, and she made a beautiful outfit for Emmet, which thankfully just about fit him. Lena got Charlie to take a snap of him in the outfit and posted it home to her mother. Maria wrote to Lena that she felt better than she had since Paudie died.

Jack wrote from Montana saying how the ranch was all he imagined and more. He'd made a lot of good friends in America, including a young ranch hand called, inexplicably, Skipper, who Jack planned to bring back to Ireland to show him the farm. Bill Madden was keeping everything shipshape in Jack's absence, and not a single calf or lamb had been lost, though the fox had got in and devoured a chicken.

Doc wrote that it was a quiet year, no flu epidemic thankfully, and everyone's health was so much better since the new TB vaccine. Without her, his filing system was in disarray and his appointments written on backs of envelopes, but people made allowances and he managed, just about. He could have found a replacement – she told him to do so – but he didn't. He said he was waiting for her, and no one could take her place in the surgery or in his heart.

In the end, it was spring of the following year before Lena found herself once more on the quay in Swansea, surrounded by the Evans children and being hugged by Sarah and Charlie. But this time it was all so different. She had tall, handsome Eli at her side, and Emmet was strapped into a big Silver Cross pushchair.

'Take care of my son,' whispered Sarah, giving Lena one last hug before releasing her. 'He's my firstborn and all I have left of his father.'

'I will,' promised Lena. She knew how Sarah felt.

'Come on, come on,' Eli called as he pushed Emmet's pram up the ramp onto the ferry. 'No point saying all these goodbyes if we don't get to actually leave.'

Lena showered the little children in one last flurry of kisses and hurried after her husband. 'You're all coming on holidays to Kilteegan Bridge once we're settled, so it's not for long.'

The voyage was peaceful, and Emmet didn't get seasick at all. He loved watching the splashing of the waves and waving his hands at the seagulls that followed them, and by the time they arrived in Cork, several of the ferry crew knew him by name.

Eli had booked them into the Imperial Hotel in Cork, a magnificent suite with two bedrooms, because the boat docked late and they'd had enough travelling. Emily drove a large Morris Traveller now, and the following morning she and Nellie brought Maria to Cork to meet Lena, Eli and Emmet and take them back to Kilteegan Bridge. Eli would need a car, but they would attend to all of that in good time. Of course her husband and son charmed them, and they were soon deep in friendly chat with Eli and oohing over baby Emmet. Maria asked Eli about his family and said sincerely how sorry she was about his family while also telling him about her brother, Ted, who'd been an officer in Hitler's army. It might have been awkward, but Maria had an innocence to her, a kind of childlike honesty that made it hard to resent anything she said. She admitted that she was surprised when she heard of their romance, but if they were happy, then she wished them all the best. Another mother might have gone more mad, demanded more details, so Lena was glad of her mother's ethereal nature for once, and was happy to see her calm and reasonable. Emmet was transfixed by his granny's long, almost-white hair and smiled happily in her arms. They fit all of their cases and Emmet's baby things in Emily's car for the trip back to West Cork.

When they arrived back in the village, Maria insisted they stay at the farmhouse until they found a place of their own. Lena unpacked and, as soon as she could, took Emmet and Eli out to show them around the farm. The would visit Doc later.

She was surprised to see that they'd installed an electric milking machine, which allowed them to expand the herd. Jack had returned from Montana with his friend Skipper in tow, and the two of them, with Thirteen on their heels were inseparable.

She smiled, remembering how Mammy used to say that the arrival of electricity had banished the ghosts and the fairies and how Daddy said all it did was show up the dirt; people thought their houses were clean enough until the harsh judgemental gleam of the electric light showed them otherwise.

The farm was clearly more profitable now with the bigger payment from the creamery, so Jack and Skipper, who showed no signs of returning to Montana, had replaced Susie, their ageing dray horse, with a red little Massey Ferguson tractor. Susie hadn't gone to the glue factory – Jack was far too fond of his animals for that – so she was out grazing with the sheep, eating far too much grass and very happy not to have to pull anything heavy any more.

Nobody batted an eyelid at the arrival of Skipper Malone. His family were Irish, he proudly proclaimed, his great-grandfather having left from somewhere in Galway during the Potato Famine of the mid-1800s. He was a gregarious lad, who despite his Americanness blended right in, and he thought everything about Ireland was amazing. Emily said that Maria loved him, and he complimented her cooking and even flirted with her a little bit, and the twins followed him and Jack around like little ducklings. It was a peculiar set-up, Lena supposed, but it worked.

Jack had written when she was still in Wales and told her the whole story. Skipper's mama, as he called her, was dead, and his daddy took off with a showgirl when Skipper and his brother, Wyatt, were in their early teens, leaving them to fend for themselves. His brother married a saloon owner's only child, Laurie-Lee, and together they now ran the Bucket of Guts Saloon and Grill in Bozeman, Montana. So his older brother had made something of himself, against all the odds. When Jack met Skipper, he was a casual labourer on the farm in the Yellowstone River Valley, and so coming to Ireland with Jack seemed like as good an idea as anything else.

Maria had been telling her how Skipper was a genius with horses and was rapidly gaining a reputation all over the place as someone who could bring even the most terrifying of animals to calm. He never used a stick or a whip but seemed to almost communicate with the horse. Even Bill's bucking black stallion that nobody could tame was, within an hour or so, following Skipper around the barn, docile as anything. He said he learned it watching the wild mustangs on the Pryor Mountains, how they interacted with each other, and according to him anyway, once you spoke their language, it was easy.

* * *

THEY WALKED DOWN THE HILL, the place feeling instantly familiar, as if no time at all had passed but she was a different person now, not just married with a baby, but she was an adult. Doc opened the door, looking so pale and frail that it was as if a stiff breeze could blow him away. It gave Lena quite a shock, and she began to wonder about his poor health Eli had mentioned. But when she asked Doc about it, he just brushed her off and told her not to worry. 'As soon as you're back at work, you can fatten me up like a Christmas goose, and with Eli helping me, I'll get all the rest I need.'

They had tea and fruit cake with him and Lena tried to hide her distress at her godfather's condition. Eli chatted easily though, he had a gift for that, making people relaxed.

After Doc's they walked around the town, everyone anxious to meet Lena's new surprise husband. There were a few raised eyebrows, but by and large the pen pal, whirlwind romance, honeymoon baby story was believed. They blessed the baby and one or two people hanselled him, a tradition of putting a silver coin in his hand and then placing it under the mattress of his pram as a talisman against poverty.

Then she led Eli up to the graveyard, pushing the heavy pram against the steep hill.

'I need you both to meet my dad,' she said as they carried Emmet's pram over the rough ground of the cemetery.

Lena lifted Emmet out of the pram and took him to the headstone. 'Now then, Emmet Kogan, this is your grandad's place. His name was Paudie O'Sullivan, but you would have called him Granda, and he would have been mad about you.'

Eli placed his hand on her shoulder. 'Hello, Paudie. It's nice to finally be here. Lena's done a good job telling me about this place, but it's more beautiful than I could have imagined. I wish I'd met you, but rest assured I'll take good care of your daughter and the rest of the family now inasmuch as I can.'

Lena turned and kissed his cheek. 'I love you,' she whispered.

They walked back, chatting easily. It was

springtime, so the fuchsia and montbrecia grew in wild profusion in the hedgerows, and the azure Atlantic glistened on the horizon. Jack's lambs frolicked and played in the field, and Eli stopped to show Emmet. She'd long ago told him about her mother and her illness, so she wasn't worried; besides, Maria seemed good at the moment. They entered the house to the aroma of baking and saw her mother take an apple tart from the big Stanley oven. Eli helped her by finding a board to place the hot dish on, and it felt like he'd always been there.

She and Eli would share the bedroom that once belonged to her and Emily, the beds pushed together, and Emmet would share with the twins.

It had been such a strange, long journey from that room to Wales and back again.

CHAPTER 27

There was no getting away from the fact that she felt a pang of sadness as she stood outside Kilteegan House. Eli had Emmet; she would never risk coming this close to the house with him.

Lena had taken a deliberate detour on her way back to the village, after collecting her mother's fresh soda bread, butter churned by Jack and a pot of homemade blackberry jam. The twins loved collecting blackberries every year, and Lena was convinced they ate as many as they picked.

She hoped the treat would help fatten Doc up. He was so thin, even still with her efforts to feed him several times a day. He hadn't much appetite, and she was making the portions she gave him smaller, but he didn't even eat much of those.

They had moved to Doc's large double-fronted terraced house in the centre of town, so there was plenty of room, and Eli said he preferred to be there in the event of a night call or an emergency. Doc had done enough of them in his time; he deserved a full night's sleep by now.

Doc's patients were mad about Eli, and Doc was beginning to complain that they preferred the chatty Welsh doctor to himself, but Lena knew Doc really liked Eli too. It was wonderful how the two men she was closest to admired each other, and Doc seemed less stressed now that Eli was part of the furniture of Kilteegan Bridge. Everyone cooed at Emmet when she took him out in his pram, and she was non-committal at comments that he was big for his age.

She was so thankful that nobody ever knew about her and Malachy, because the reality was Emmet was the spitting image of his father. She dreaded ever running into that odd Phillippe Decker. Auguste Berger had not come outside his front door in years, but Decker would surely see the likeness. She knew the chances were tiny – Doc said he'd not seen either of them in ages – but she was still vigilant. They were the only other people outside of her family who knew she and Malachy had been together, so she felt relatively safe. Undoubtedly, people had opinions, but since nothing could be proved or disproved, she got away with it. The fact that everyone loved Doc and now Eli so much definitely helped still the wagging tongues.

Eli had forced Doc to go for tests in the hospital, but they had yet to hear the results, so she hoped her policy of feeding Doc all his favourite foods and stopping him drinking and smoking too much was paying off. No news was usually good news when it came to that kind of thing.

She looked up at Malachy's home. The trees in the orchard of Kilteegan House were heavy with fruit, just as they had been two years ago when she had led Malachy through it by the hand, towards the tack room where they'd played as children. It was frustrating how her mind kept going back to Malachy, again and again. How could he have been so loving and passionate, and then walked out on her without a word, without any explanation except to tell Doc in the letter that she'd 'understand'. It seemed crazy that he could hate her for what happened between them that day. It went against everything she thought she knew about him, but maybe she really was just a naïve girl who saw what she wanted to see and not the truth.

She had to get Malachy out of her head. It was Eli she loved, and she'd promised Sarah never to break Eli's heart.

The curtains were drawn across the drawing room windows, but suddenly one of them stirred. She put her head down and hurried on home, to Emmet, Eli and Doc, as a light rain started to fall.

* * *

'IT'S THAT GIRL,' said Phillippe, looking through a gap in the heavy drapes. They kept the curtains mostly drawn in the big house now because Auguste Berger hated the view of the garden.

'What girl?'

'Lena O'Sullivan. She was standing there in the lane, looking up at the house.'

'She's back, is she?' Auguste tried to think.

'I heard she's married now, to a Jewish doctor.'

'Jewish?' In disgust, Berger looked up from the backgammon board. 'How could her church allow it? The Catholics hated them as much as we did. Look at how their pope, Pius the Twelfth, helped us. He knew what our plan was, and he was glad. He could never say that outright, but he

379

might as well have done. They deny it now, bleating about him saving so many of them, but I know the truth. My God, after all our efforts to clean the world. Ugh, they get everywhere, like cockroaches. However many you exterminate, somehow they pop up again.' He sighed. 'We could have solved it had we been allowed to.'

His manservant looked at him, never commenting either way. They didn't need words of explanation, not after all these years.

Auguste winced. The pain came in waves, sometimes leaving him breathless. Phillippe handed him the pills without being asked. He swallowed down a handful with a mouthful of whiskey. He was supposed to take two at a time, but he might as well be eating bonbons for all the good two did.

The days of Phillippe pushing him around the grounds in his chair, admiring the flowers and trees in bloom, or sometimes even going shooting rabbits, were long gone. Those were better days, but Auguste had not left the house in months.

'Have you written to Malachy?' His voice was a rasp now, he knew.

'I have. He wrote back saying he would come as soon as he could get away.'

'Good, good. Six months the hospital gave me, but some days...'

After a while, as the chemicals eased the pain, a grim smile began to form on his lips and his blue eyes brightened. 'Perhaps when Malachy arrives, we should invite the girl.'

The Frenchman recoiled. 'Really? Why?'

Auguste Berger shrugged. 'One last pleasure for my final moments.'

DOC WAS RESTING upstairs as Eli wolfed down the lunch Lena had made for him between morning and afternoon surgery.

'How was your morning?' Lena asked, bouncing Emmet on her knee.

'Fine. No major dramatics. Actually, a rep called to tell me about a new drug for the treatment of conditions such as the one your mother has. We might give it a try if she's interested. He's saying it's having good response so far.'

'I'm sure she'd try it if you thought it was a good idea.' Maria trusted Eli every bit as much as she had trusted Doc.

'And then,' he said through a mouthful of ham and cheese sandwich, 'there was that peculiar chap, a Frenchman apparently. He was across the road from the surgery today, just watching. When Doc came in to say hello to old Mrs Canty, she mentioned he was there, and I got the distinct impression Doc didn't like him much. It struck me as peculiar, because I don't think I've ever heard Doc say a bad word about anyone.'

'Phillippe Decker. He works up at Kilteegan House as a kind of assistant to Auguste Berger.'

'Malachy's father?' Eli looked up.

'Yes, him.' Lena stood, Emmet perched on her hip. 'Hmm. I wonder why he's around. He almost never comes to town. Doc never liked him, or Auguste Berger for that matter. It was strange. I often meant to ask him why, but I don't like to bother him when he's a bit under the weather.'

Eli put down his spoon and reached for her hand. 'Look, I know you don't like to think about it, but Doc's health –'

'Doc will last forever,' she said fiercely. She knew Eli was trying to tell her something, but it was not anything she wanted to hear.

'Lena…we have to –'

'It's time you were back in the surgery, and I promised Mam I'd bring Emmet up today. She wants to show him the kittens that were born last week.'

Eli sighed and stood up. 'See you later then, love.' He kissed her.

Lena popped Emmet in his pram and walked up to her old home. Electricity poles now lined the road, and she tried to remember what it was like before all the public streetlights. Ireland felt like it was moving on at such a pace. Eli was even talking about getting a television, though she wasn't sure they needed one.

He'd installed a wet battery radio in the waiting room, and now it was commonplace to find patients waiting after their appointments and hanging around afterwards for the news or the farming bulletin. She smiled. Eli loved gadgets, and he loved making people happy.

She stopped to admire the view, showing her son their farm and the emerald-green fields, full of fat happy cows chomping away. Her dad would be so proud of Jack; he'd made such a good job of it all. And Mam was well enough. She'd been low for a few weeks back in the spring, but she was all right these days. Having Emmet was like a new chance for her, someone who loved her and had no history.

Maria was inside, leafing through a catalogue of patterns. Emily had asked her to select a few more easy ones to sell in the shop, and it was proving a great draw. She even worked one day a week there now and spent her day giving advice about how to run up lovely things for all the family. Lena was glad she was so well, but there was that old familiar dread that the spell of good humour was going to end; it always did.

'Lena and Emmet, I'm delighted to see you. Hello, little man.' Maria lifted him out of the pram, and he giggled and babbled delightedly.

'Shall we go to see the little kittens? They're above in the barn. Your aunties are taking great care of them.' Maria cooed, and Emmet gazed in solemn adoration. Together they crossed the yard.

Skipper was on the idling tractor, lazily smoking a cigarette and gazing peacefully over the fields all the way to the sea, the dog curled up beside him. Jack was loading bales of hay onto the back of it.

'Hello, Skipper.' Maria waved Emmet's little hand.

'Hey, li'l dude,' Skipper called, jumping down. 'Y'all comin' to see the new kittens?'

'We are,' Lena answered.

'They're jus' startin' to open their eyes, but y'all be careful, 'cause Sooty's mighty protective of her little ones, just like a mama should be.'

'Don't worry, we'll admire them from a distance.'

'One minute, I got somethin' for li'l Emmet.' He walked with them to the barn. On a shelf was a little boat, twigs all lashed together to make the body, and with tiny fabric sails.

'Oh, Emmet, look!' Lena handed him the boat, which he examined curiously. 'Thank you, Skipper, that's so kind.'

He blushed. 'I made some for the twins. They were racin' them with Lucy in the stream yonder.' He gestured with his thumb to the small tributary that ran through their land. 'So I said I'd make one for Emmet too.'

Skipper was dressed in a plaid shirt and heavy canvas trousers held up with a belt bearing a huge brass buckle. He was exotic enough without the hat he always wore, but with it he looked like something from a film. When she'd complimented it on the first day she met him, he informed her it was called a Stetson and that he'd won it in a game of poker from a guy in Salt Lake City, Utah.

'Well, we love it, don't we, Emmet?' Lena grinned, and Emmet chewed the twig holding up the sail.

'My pleasure, ma'am.' He grinned and tipped his hat.

They admired the kittens, some tortoiseshell, others black and white, all guarded diligently by Sooty the farm cat, while Skipper and Jack went back to work. The farm was running like a mouses's heart as her Dad used to say and Lena was glad to see it. Jack was in his element.

Before she left, she had a cup of tea with her mother, who insisted on packaging up some lamb stew and potatoes for their tea and placing it in the bottom of the pram.

Reflecting on how peaceful Maria was these days, and giving a prayer of gratitude for it, she pushed the pram down the hill once more.

As she turned onto the main street, she saw him, that Decker again, just watching. It was unnerving. He looked at her, his gaze never dropping, and it made her very uncomfortable. She was tempted to confront him, ask him what he wanted, but something stopped her. She held his gaze, and he eventually nodded and turned to go.

She shuddered involuntarily. Did he know about Emmet? Was that why he was there? Did Malachy know she'd had a child, or did Auguste know? She was probably imagining it, but she had to ask Doc what he knew.

The surgery was busy, but she had the key and let herself in the back. In the big warm kitchen, she found Doc asleep in his chair, the plate of bread and jam she'd made him for lunch pushed to one side. His head was tilted back against the chair, and his face looked yellow and drawn, the skin stretched over his bones. Gently, she kissed his forehead.

His eyes flickered open and he smiled. 'Not asleep. Just resting my eyes. What's that wonderful smell?'

'Maria's lamb stew. Will I give you out some now?'

'Oh, yes please, I can never resist Maria's stew.' But she noticed that when she placed the bowl in front of him, he only dipped the spoon in the gravy and licked it.

She sat at the table. The presence of the Frenchman had unsettled her. Doc knew something, she was sure of it.

'Doc, you've always said that if being a country doctor teaches you anything, it's that there are no big secrets that can be kept without causing disruption and pain. Honesty is always best, not only in and of itself, but because a lie only festers with time and the truth always comes out in the end.'

'And I still think that, in most circumstances,' he said, dipping his spoon again and licking it. She wished he'd scoop up a chunk of meat or potato or even just a carrot.

She took a deep breath. 'Do you remember when I was...with Malachy...you told me you didn't like his father or that French man that worked for him. You always said he was sneaky or something.'

He fixed her with a gaze that spoke volumes. 'I do

'Then you need to tell me why you think that, Doc. I know there's something about the Bergers that you don't like, more than just how Malachy treated me. That Decker, he's been hanging around, and I can't say why but something feels strange. If there was something I should know, you would tell me, wouldn't you? I'm nervous they know about Emmet.'

Doc pushed the uneaten bowl of stew away and rested his head in his hands. 'Oh, Lena.' The words sounded like they were such a huge effort to say. 'Berger couldn't know about Emmet, but there is something. I promised Paudie not to say anything about any of this, and then he died and...'

'Whatever it is, Doc, Dad would want you to

tell me now if he thought Emmet was at risk. Doc, you have to tell me what's happening.'

Doc reached for his glass of wine, and although she was tempted to take it away, she didn't. 'All right, Lena, I'm going to break the vow I made to my best and oldest friend. You need to know. I should have told you before, I know, but anyway, here it is. But before I do, you have to remember, he was only a man, a good man going through such a difficult time. Your mother was in St Catherine's for months at a time after each child was born, and each time he wasn't sure if she was going to come home. And young Hannah Berger was up at the big house, thinking she was widowed with a little boy to care for and nobody to help her. Her father was dead, and she had that big old place growing wild around her...'

'Doc, what are you trying to say? Do you mean...'

'Your mother was in St Catherine's most of that year. Things were very bad for her after you were born, and your father was terrified she'd hurt herself or, worse, hurt you. He never intended it, or set out for anything to happen, but Hannah offered him comfort, love, peace, something he'd not had for so long. He regretted it, he really did, but they were two lonely, battered souls and they got together.'

Lena tried very hard to focus, but Doc's words were hard to process, like she was hearing them under water. Her stomach lurched again and she was afraid she'd throw up, but she swallowed and managed to croak, 'Go on.'

Doc looked pained. She knew he would rather never tell her this but felt he had no choice. 'Hannah hoped he'd leave Maria, but he couldn't. He tried to explain to her that it wasn't an option, that he'd made a vow to his wife. He'd loved Maria from the day he met her and would love her to the day he died. But Hannah was heartbroken and he was distraught. He never set out to hurt anyone, Lena, you must believe it.'

'But how could he do it to Mam, to us?' She was trying to picture her lovely dad as a man like that, a man who goes with other women behind his wife's back. It just didn't seem possible that he would be part of a sordid love triangle.

'It didn't go on for long, a few weeks. The guilt of it nearly killed him. Hannah said that if he wasn't willing to tell Maria everything and leave her, then he was to go and never contact her again. I suppose she hoped the threat would force his hand. But he left and didn't go back, and

Hannah stayed above in the big house, alone, and Maria came home from St Catherine's. Her assessment said she was agitated in the hospital, and it was felt it was best to get her back to her husband and baby. She clung to Paudie like a limpet, one minute afraid to let him out of her sight, the next screaming at him to leave her...'

'Did you know about the affair?' Lena felt the tears before she realised she was crying.

Doc looked at her sadly. 'Not until it was over and he came to me. There were so many nights we spent at that time, just talking. He was so broken then. He wanted to do the right thing, but what that was, he'd no idea. Mostly he wanted to know, should he tell Maria.'

'What did you tell him to do, Doc?' Anger replaced her sadness. So many lies. 'Did you tell *him* it was wrong to keep secrets?'

He looked her straight in the eyes. 'No. I told him he couldn't tell her, that it was too cruel. Speaking as Maria's doctor more than Paudie's friend, I urged him to say nothing. I said she was fragile enough and something like this would send her over the edge. In those days she was often threatening to walk into the sea.'

Dimly, from somewhere remote in her childhood, Lena remembered her mother weeping...

'Don't leave me, Paudie. Don't leave me. I'll die. I'll swear, I'll walk into the sea and I'll die. I've seen the way Hannah looks at you, Paudie.' And her father saying, 'Of course I'll never leave you.'

She burst into tears again, and this time, Doc drew her into a hug. She clung to him, her tears soaking into his soft checked shirt. She tried to imagine her father, longed for his solid presence, but then her father wasn't the man she'd thought he was. She wanted to hate him, to rage at him, but she couldn't. He was gone, and Hannah Berger was gone. 'I'm so angry at him. I feel so let down that he would do that, be unfaithful, but he had such a hard life with our mother. It's not her fault, I know… He must have been lonely…' Her voice was barely audible now, the pain of recall filling every word. 'So maybe if he got a bit of love, a bit of a break from it all, who am I to judge?'

Doc rubbed her back and let her cry for all that had happened, then wiped her eyes with his handkerchief when the sobs subsided. 'I'm sorry, love, I'm so sorry,' he whispered. 'I should have told you before maybe, but I didn't want to spoil your memory of him. He was such a good man, such a wonderful father, and even after all I've said, a true and loving husband.'

'And that was the end of the affair?'

'On your father's side, yes. But Auguste Berger came back in a wheelchair from the war, with a manservant who was as dark and cold as himself, and they frightened Hannah so much that she asked Paudie to come and work up at the house again and make sure she was protected.'

'And did he?'

'It was good money – he couldn't turn it down. He assured me they were over each other.'

'And were they? Did this...their affair...begin again?' Lena's mouth was dry; her head was reeling.

'They were friendly, that's the way he saw it, but...'

'But what?'

'I wonder if she ever let go of her longing for him. Maybe she didn't. Maybe that's why she went to Mass one day and, on the way home, fetched a halter from the tack room and went back to the orchard and hung herself.'

Lena put her hands to her cheeks, her head spinning as she tried to hear what Doc was saying. 'No, it was a heart attack...'

'It wasn't, Lena. I was called to the house. By the time I got there, Hannah Berger was on the sofa in the drawing room where that French manservant had laid her, and her husband having a seizure, and the rope mark was as clear as day around her neck.'

'You wrote heart attack on the death certificate.'

'Lena, I was never going to mark her death down as a suicide. I never do that if I can help it – families have enough hardship without me doing that. It was illegal then, and it's still against the teachings of the Church. She wouldn't have been buried in consecrated ground, and her poor little son, Malachy, would have to grow up with the stigma.'

'Another secret,' she said a little bitterly.

'Yes.' Doc nodded slowly. 'And I don't regret it. What I do regret is not doing more about something else I discovered that day, when I opened Auguste Berger's shirt to give him an injection. His muscles were in spasm, and it was to relax them. I don't know who I could have told about it – it's not like we were ever at war with Germany.'

'What do you mean? He's French. He fought with the Resistance there during the war…'

Doc shook his head. 'Lies.'

Lena struggled to make sense of what he was saying. 'Auguste Berger…Malachy's father…he was a *German* officer?'

'Yes. Not just that, he was a true Nazi. The Waffen-SS, they reported directly to Himmler during the war and were the worst of the worst.'

'But how did you know that?'

'They used to tattoo their blood group on the inside of their upper arms, thinking they would stand a better chance of survival if they were injured – that way they would get the correct blood type. But what it did in actual fact was help to identify them after the war, even though many of them, like Malachy's father and presumably that Decker too, maimed themselves to get rid of the mark. When I worked in the hospital in Cardiff with Saul, we were told to look out for the tattoo or the scar it left behind. And there, on Berger's inner arm, was a deliberate burn mark. Maybe Decker noticed that I saw it and told him or something – After that, he stopped using my services and I didn't see either of them again for ages, until that nasty piece of work Decker started following you around like a bad smell. I don't know what he wanted, but I knew he was up to no good, just as I know that now.'

'So why is he hanging around now, after all this time?'

'I don't know, Lena. Maybe it's all coincidence and imagination and I'm a stupid old man. All I know is that Auguste Berger hated Paudie and blamed him for Hannah's suicide. Your dad told me himself the way Berger looked at him gave him chills. He hated going up there by then, but Hannah was so scared, he felt like he was abandoning her if he didn't go. Maybe Hannah told Auguste about the affair before she hung herself. Maybe a part of her hoped her husband would take his revenge on Paudie for breaking her heart.' He looked at her sadly. 'Maybe he did take revenge.'

She stared at him, her heart pounding. 'What do you mean?'

'The gun that backfired? I never understood that, the way the bullet went in, the type of injury. It didn't sit right with me, and so soon after Hannah...'

She gasped. 'You think my father killed himself too?'

'No. Of course not. He wouldn't do that. No, I mean it's unlikely a backfire would have caused the injury he had, but there was no other explanation, nobody else there.' But he shook his head, his old forehead deeply wrinkled. 'It troubled me then and it troubles me still. I thought of saying it to the guards, but I had absolutely no proof of any foul play, and unless I told them about

Hannah and your father, there was no motive for it to be anything but as it seemed. And you were all so young, and Maria pregnant with the twins by then and everything, I just thought it might be better if I focused on helping you all rather than going off making wild accusations against a man in a wheelchair, accusations I could never back up.'

Lena concentrated on what Doc had told her. Was her father's death not an accident? Hannah Berger's wasn't, she took her own life, but her father would not have done something like that. So that left another, scarcely comprehensible, possibility.

'Doc, do you think Malachy's father might have killed Dad? Or told Phillippe to do it?'

'Lena, my love, like I say, I have absolutely no evidence.'

'So what happens now?' Lena's voice sounded strange to her own ears, like a child's. 'Am I in danger from Berger, or Decker? Is Emmet?'

'I can't see why. His hatred was for Paudie. As you say, he was always nice to you. But I think we just have to be careful, pet. He's an odd one – they both are.'

'If you're paranoid, so am I.'

'Sensible girl,' said Doc. 'Leopards don't

change their spots, and that Auguste Berger is bad news.' He pulled the bowl of stew towards him. There was more colour in his cheeks now, as if a weight had been lifted off him, and this time he ate several pieces of lamb, a potato and two carrots.

CHAPTER 28

*L*ena told Eli what Doc had said. He took her seriously but agreed they couldn't go making wild accusations with no proof. Eli said he noticed Decker walking past the surgery nearly every day, but that could just have been because the chemist was nearby; rumour had it that Auguste Berger's health was failing, and the doctor from Kellstown was coming and going at least twice a week.

Auguste Berger wasn't the only old man who was dying. Even Lena had to admit that Doc was now very sick. By the time September came around, he was forced to take to his bed. Lena nursed him while her mother minded Emmet and Eli took over the whole practice. Doc finally admitted to her it was cancer. She was furious at first with Eli for not telling her, though later she had to admit he did try several times and she refused to listen. But in the end, she accepted it was Doc's right to choose to tell her when and why he was dying.

The last weeks of Doc's life slipped by in a haze. He asked her to write to his friend in Dublin, the woman he visited a few times a year, and she'd had a letter back from her, a Dr Anthea O'Halloran, in beautiful copperplate writing. She expressed her sadness and asked Lena to pass on her love to Emmet. Lena never knew what the nature of their relationship was, but she was glad he had some comfort or friendship anyway. There was an endless stream of well-wishers leaving casseroles and cakes, and the twins made cards saying 'GET WELL SON DOC' and covered them in pink hearts. Geraldine Cronin from the post office visited for an hour at a time, although in the end, Doc preferred only Lena.

They sat and talked, and sometimes she read to him, and then as time went on, she just held his hand. Eli made sure Doc was in no pain, even if it meant a level of sedation that lost him to her for hours on end. She and Eli took turns sleeping in the room; they didn't want him to be alone.

When he woke, in brief moments of lucidity, he said he hated being a nuisance and offered to go to the county home.

'You'll be going nowhere, Doc,' Lena soothed. 'Eli and I can take care of you.'

'You're so good to me, Lena,' he whispered, a tear sliding out the side of his eye.

'You're my other daddy, Doc. Of course I'm going to mind you,' she said, tears flowing down her own cheeks.

It was a mild morning in October when Lena climbed the stairs to the bedroom with a tray of tea and a small bowl of goat's milk yoghurt, which Skipper made for Doc every day; it was one of the few things Doc would agree to eat because it was so delicious and smooth.

She'd slept in the room on a camp bed, and Doc had slept all night, restful and in no pain, and when she woke, she crept over and kissed him gently on the forehead. His breath was steady and even, and he opened his eyes for a moment and smiled at her.

'I'll just give Emmet his breakfast and get myself ready for the day, and I'll be back then. You just rest on there.'

He nodded. 'You're so good to me, Lena.'

'Sure, I love you,' she'd replied simply, and went to get her son.

An hour later she entered the room once more. Her old friend was lying back on his pillows, a quilt embroidered beautifully for him by Maria and the twins over him, a contented look on his thin face. The window was slightly open, and the curtains were billowing slightly. Lena set down the tray on the chest of drawers and moved around the bed to close the window and open the curtains. 'I've brought you Skipper's special yoghurt, Doc. He dropped it down first thing. He said to tell you that old billy goat gave him a right puck when he was milking the nanny, so you better enjoy it.' She turned to him. 'Doc?'

But Doc, a faint smile on his old beloved face, was gone.

* * *

LENA'S GODFATHER was laid to rest in the graveyard next to his best friend, Paudie O'Sullivan, under the horse chestnut tree overlooking the sea. It was the largest funeral the town had ever seen, and everyone for miles around – man, woman and child – felt personally the loss of Doc Dolan.

Saul, Sarah and Ann came from Wales – Charlie stayed at home to care for the children – which was so touching, and it was nice to have them there, reminiscing and remembering the man she saw as her other father.

A week later, the town solicitor, Kieran Devlin, asked Lena and Eli to attend the reading of the will, and they discovered that Doc had left them everything, the surgery and the house, his old Ford Escort car, endless medical books and a few pounds in the bank. It came as no surprise to Lena that Doc wasn't a wealthy man; he hardly charged for his services, and many people never paid at all. He could never see a child go hungry or be sick for the want of medicine, so often he paid for things for his patients from his own pocket. For Doc, it was never about the money.

She was so touched at the appearance at the funeral of Dr Noël Browne, a doctor who had gained notoriety because of his war with the Irish Medical Council, the government and the Church in his efforts to have his mother-and-child scheme passed into law. The bill would have given free medical care to all expectant mothers and their babies, but the powers of Church and state resisted it, citing it as communist and paving the way for gynaecological care not in

keeping with Catholic principles. Doc had sup-
ported Dr Browne vocally and in the press by
writing many letters to national newspapers, de-
nouncing the shunning of the forward-thinking
doctor.

The house was so empty and sad without Doc.
It was his place; every corner, every book, every
picture on the wall was his. The grief at his loss
brought back all the memories she had of when
her father died, and so many nights Eli just held
her in his arms as she cried. She'd taken his
clothes and sent them to St Vincent de Paul, but
the one in Cork; she couldn't bear to see someone
in his clothes around the town.

Doc's house also had no garden, and she and
Eli had decided they would like one for Emmet
and any future babies they might have. So the
night after the reading of the will, they made
plans to rent rooms at Doc's to a dentist, a chi-
ropodist, a physiotherapist and an optician, as
well as to provide space for the health board to
install the district nurses in the house eventually
and make it a medical centre, saving people long
and expensive trips to Bandon or even Cork.
They felt Doc would approve.

A few weeks after the funeral, Lena went to
lunch in the Copper Kettle with Emily. Emmet

and Nellie sat beside each other babbling away and seemingly understanding every word the other said, and Emily told her at length about her latest plans for the shop.

'Mam is so amazing. When she's on form, she works so fast. I need a whole extra section to sell the clothes she makes, the patterns and the material – not just the Irish dancing dresses but baby frocks and doll's clothes and dresses for the Communion. We're hoping to buy the house next door and expand into it, and one day maybe we'll even have a second shop in Bandon.'

'Why stop at Bandon? Why not Cork?' suggested Lena.

'Blackie says Cork is hard to break into and the rents are very high.'

'Well, I'm not going to second-guess Blackie, but all I'm saying is maybe a way down the line, when you've got a better relationship with the bank because you can say Dick Crean and Jingo are history, then I can't see anything stopping you, Em. If anyone in the world can make a go of it in Cork, it's my big sister. You've really turned the shop around – it's nothing like the dark smelly place it used to be. It's really lovely now, bright and clean, with something for everyone.

Eli's Uncle Saul bought a lovely leather bag there when he came for the funeral.'

Emily blushed with pleasure. 'You should have said – I'd have given him a discount.'

Lena laughed. 'He's got no need of it, Em, he's loaded. But lovely. I just meant it's a place anyone would like to shop now, fair play to you.'

'Thanks, Lena. I told you, didn't I, Blackie and I had plans? While you were going to go off and never darken our doors in Kilteegan Bridge again.' Lena knew her sister was only teasing her for fun. 'But the magnetic draw of Ireland's most exciting village was irresistible.'

'And you're dead right, I couldn't stay away.' Lena smiled. 'I didn't realise I'd ever think Kilteegan Bridge was the perfect place to live, but once I had Emmet, I knew it was where I wanted him to grow up.'

'It is lovely. And I know everyone is stuck in your business, but usually it's out of kindness. I mean, look at the crowd that turned up for Doc? Sergeant Keane said he never saw the like.' Nellie started squawking, Emmet had taken her toy, so Emily lifted her up. 'How do people have more than one? She's lovely but exhausting. And Blackie wants at least four. How about Eli?'

'He says it's up to me, but he says he loves

being a father and can't wait for Emmet to have a little brother or sister.'

'Eli's a lovely man and a great doctor, and I'm so glad you make each other happy. Here's to our husbands and children, and to Kilteegan Bridge.' Emily lifted her glass of orange juice and tipped it off Lena's, and they both laughed with pleasure.

CHAPTER 29

*T*hat afternoon, leaving Emmet having his afternoon nap upstairs and Eli seeing patients in the surgery, she walked up to the farm with a thirteen-pound salmon for her mother, which needed to be baked in the range. The patients were always paying Eli with rabbits and bags of spuds and other produce, and he was as bad as Doc for agreeing to it – neither of them were doctors for the money – and the oven in their kitchen just wasn't big enough to cope.

She found Jack and Skipper playing snap on the kitchen table with the twins and Thirteen lazing in her basket beside the range. Maria instantly took the salmon from her, gutted it and popped it into the range with parsley, lemon and butter. It was amazing how well her mother was these days; maybe it was just that she was getting older and the years of childbearing over. Lena often felt guilt about never telling Maria the truth about Hannah, that she'd been right to be suspicious, but what was the point of upsetting her picture of Paudie O'Sullivan as a loving father and husband? It was a true picture, just cracked in one corner, and maybe that flaw didn't matter, not now.

Although if the affair had caused Hannah's suicide, and possibly led to Paudie's murder, maybe that would be a different matter. It was too horrible to even consider, and while she believed Doc, she also knew that he had seen so much suffering during the war that he would be naturally predisposed to assume the worst of a Waffen-SS officer.

Despite her disquiet, life rumbled along peacefully in Kilteegan Bridge. She found that the calm predictability of life there, that had once so irritated her, now was oddly soothing.

Molly and May were blossoming into the sweetest pair. Like Jack, they hadn't much interest in the books – their spelling and writing were dreadful, even for their age – but they loved animals and the farm and Jack and Skipper, and they were so happy, Lena never said anything about homework that was done sporadically at best.

Skipper took her out to see a medicinal herb garden he and Jack had built, Thirteen faithfully trotting behind them, and with great pride, he told her that farmers in the mart were asking them for some of the remedies they made for cattle. Knowledge Nolan, a local farmer, so nicknamed because he knew everything, or at least thought he did, told Skipper that their mastitis balm was the best he'd ever used.

On the way back down the hill, with a third of the warm cooked salmon wrapped up in her basket and three stray cats at her heels, she deliberately kept walking, never looking up at Kilteegan House as she passed.

The knock at the door of the surgery came just after they'd closed the door on the last patient, at half past eight, as she was about to serve up the fish with mashed potato to her starving husband. 'You stay here out of sight. I'll get rid of whoever it is unless it's a complete emergency. It was the same with Doc – they've no regard for your private time. Do not come out,' she warned him as she placed salmon, carrots and potatoes on his plate, then she wiped her hands on her apron and went to unlock the front door. It was dark outside, and for a moment she couldn't make out who had come for the doctor at this hour.

The stocky, black-haired Frenchman stood there.

'Oh...' Lena hadn't seen him in a long time and was slightly taken aback. 'If you are looking for Dr Kogan, I'm afraid he's –'

'It's not him I'm looking for, Madame, it is you.' He was calm, his English still heavily accented.

'What on earth would you want me for?'

Eli must have been listening because he appeared within seconds. 'What's going on? Lena?'

The Frenchman looked at Lena's husband with ill-concealed disgust. 'I just need a private moment with Mademoiselle O'Sullivan.'

'Why?' Eli asked coldly. 'And she is Mrs Kogan now.'

Phillippe ignored him and addressed Lena. 'Mademois – Madame, pardon. Monsieur Auguste Berger desires you to attend his bedside immediately, as he wishes to speak to you before he dies.'

Lena stared at him in shock, shrinking back

towards Eli. 'What do you mean? What does he want to speak to me for?'

'That's not for me to say. He just said he needed to explain something to you, about the past,' Decker said. 'But this is wasting time, Madame. My employer is dying as we speak. Please, we must hurry.'

She made a split-second decision and took her coat from the hook by the door. 'Eli, look after Emmet.'

'No, wait, I'll call Emily to mind Emmett,' said Eli. 'You're not going up there without me.'

'*Non*, Madame, now...'

Eli was already dialling. 'I'll tell her to come as fast as she can.'

'There's no point,' Decker said to Lena. 'My employer won't let your husband into the house, Madame. This conversation is for your ears alone.'

'I'm not letting her go anywhere without me.' Eli was insistent.

The Frenchman locked eyes with Lena. 'Surely Madame has no fear of a dying man? One who always made you feel welcome? You are in no danger, I assure you. Please, we must hurry. You alone, not him.' Decker threw Eli a disparaging look.

'Eli, I have to go,' she begged. The question that had tormented her since that day Malachy dumped her was possibly going to be answered; she couldn't let it go. 'Follow me to the house if Emily comes, and wait at the gates. Don't come in. I'll be fine, please...' Pulling on her new red coat, she ran out the door after the stocky man, who ushered her into the car that was waiting in the cobbled street.

It wasn't until they were driving through the drizzly dark that she realised she knew this car, that she'd been in it many times during a long-ago summer. It was Malachy's Volkswagen, with the faint scent of cologne – Malachy's scent. Her heart turned over.

Why was Decker driving Malachy's car? Had Malachy come home because his father was dying? No, he'd gone to America; he must have left the car behind for his father's manservant to make use of. Though she'd never seen Decker driving it before; he always walked to and from the village like she did herself.

They swept in through the high iron gates and up the gravelled drive, pulling to a halt in front of the main steps. Leaving Lena to open her own door, he went bounding up the steps two at a time, paused impatiently while she followed him, then showed her across the hall and through high double doors into the library. He didn't come in himself but retreated, closing the doors, leaving her alone with the dying man.

Auguste Berger lay propped up by cushions on the long sofa by the window, a tartan blanket over his wasted legs and a small round table beside him, on top of which were a decanter of brandy and three glasses. His eyes were closed.

Holding her breath, she crossed the room softly to the sofa, her eyes on his face all the way. He looked so grey and wasted; his face was as thin as Doc's when he breathed his last. But when Auguste suddenly opened his eyes, the resemblance ended. Unlike Doc's brown eyes, which were warm and kind even when he was in pain, Auguste Berger's ice-blue gaze was cruel and hard. With a shudder, she retreated a step.

He seemed amused by her revulsion. 'So you came. Welcome back, Lena,' he whispered, and his lips stretched across his teeth until it was like being grinned at by a skull. 'Not a pretty sight, am I?'

'I...'

'There's a prettier sight in that chair by the fire.'

She spun around, her heart missing a beat.

Malachy was sitting in the Queen Anne wing-back, leaning forward, clearly as amazed and shaken to see her as she was to see him. He stood, moving towards her. 'Lena, what are you doing here?'

The drawing room swam around her, and Malachy rushed, steadying her by her arms. 'I'm so sorry to frighten you. I had no idea you were coming.'

'You need not worry about her, Malachy. She is quite capable of taking care of herself.' Auguste Berger pointed with his cane at a striped over-stuffed sofa. 'Please, Lena, have a seat.' Malachy guided her to it and sat her down.

As soon as she recovered, she snapped, 'You don't know me, or anything about me, Mr Berger. So whatever it is you or your son have to say to me, I can assure you it's not remotely necessary.'

'Then why did I see you standing outside my house, gazing so sadly at the orchard?'

'That was months ago, and I was just out walking, for God's sake. And I was upset you'd let the orchard get so overgrown, after my father worked so hard to make it nice.' She was furious with herself. Why had she let her feet draw her to this house, even for that one single time?

Malachy was on his hunkers beside the sofa, his cream trousers stretched tight over his thighs, looking up at her, his green gaze roaming across her face. He looked like he had when she last saw him. Less boyish, more grown up, but he was the same Malachy she remembered. The kind green eyes, the dark-red curls. It was like looking into her son's little face. Suddenly her two lives were converging, and she panicked. She didn't want this, whatever it was. She wanted to get away, from both of them. She tore her eyes away from Malachy's and glared at his father, standing up. 'I've no idea why I am here, Mr Berger, and I don't care. I'm going now.'

'Oh, call me August, please.' The way he pronounced it was different to the way he'd introduced himself when she first met him. The rolling 'Auguste' sounded so French, but the more guttural, sharp 'T' at the end of his name sounded much more German.

'You're here, Lena, because I thought you might like to know how my wife died.'

'I know how she died,' she said quickly, with a worried glance at Malachy. Why ruin the memory of his mother for him? 'It was a heart attack.'

'Wrong. It was suicide.'

'Look, this has nothing to do with me. I don't want to be here. Malachy, I'm sorry about your mother, truly, but...'

But Malachy only shrugged, looking sad and drained. 'I already know, Lena. Dad told me yesterday. And if your godfather was still alive, I'd thank him for keeping it a secret all these years. I don't know why my father is insisting on telling *you* now, though.'

Berger shrugged. 'Because your mother's suicide is only a small part of the greater truth, Malachy, and I thought the two of you should hear the rest together. Also, I wanted Phillippe to have time to leave the country. That's him driving away now, I believe...'

He leaned over and, using his cane, pulled the heavy drapes aside. There was the sound of tyres on the gravel, tail lights the only brightness in the dark night, driving fast away.

'Oh, don't look so anxious, Malachy. He'll leave your car in Cobh before he takes the boat. Pour me a brandy please, one each for you and her as well. Please, Lena, allow me this brief indulgence, and then I promise you can go on your way. A dying man's wish – it's not too much to ask?'

Malachy, who had stood to look out the window, did as he'd been asked, and then, as his father swallowed and coughed, he poured a brandy for himself and one for Lena, which she refused with a shake of her head. He went to sit at the end of the sofa, his eyes fixed on Lena's face.

Again, she turned away from him, towards Auguste Berger. As soon as she looked at him, he began speaking again, his papery voice cracking on every word.

'The greater truth is that while I was away, fighting for a new world, your father' – he nodded at Lena – 'seduced my helpless lonely Hannah, and after I returned, a soldier with a disability, who had served with honour, he mocked me and said I'd never be man enough for my wife –'

'My father would never say a thing like that!'

Berger looked at her smugly. 'So I see you knew about their sordid affair.'

She glanced at Malachy, who had his head in his hands. 'My godfather told me, and he also told me it happened while Hannah thought you had died in the war, and my own mother was in –'

'The lunatic asylum,' Auguste finished.

'A rest home for her illness, and maybe not expected to come home. My father and Hannah were wrong and foolish, but it was forgivable –'

'Was it forgivable for your father to drive my wife to suicide by breaking her heart?'

'That's not true. The affair was long over when she died.'

'Over for whom? You've seen this photo Hannah took of him, haven't you, Lena?'

He handed her a small black and white photograph, and she realised she had seen it before. 'No, I...' It was the photo of her father helping Malachy, aged only five or six, down from a tree, watched by her anxious childhood self. 'My father was playing with me and Malachy. I even tried to show it to Malachy, but someone had removed it when I went back to look for it.'

Auguste sighed as if exasperated by her stupidity. 'Couldn't you tell, little Lena, that the photographer was in love with her subject, then and every moment until she died by her own hand?'

'That's not true –'

'That was the tree she hung herself from when I told her your mother was pregnant again.'

'No...' Lena's head was spinning. What was happening here?

'For a long time, my wife believed your father's lies, that it was her and only her he loved. She was convinced he was going to take her away with him. But your mother's pregnancy was proof he had lied to her. He was never going to leave his mentally inferior wife. In fact he was going to continue to have her in any manner he wished. That was the man your father was, my dear. A big brute of a man, led only by the basest of instincts, to copulate with any female that would have him. No more than a beast of the field. But my wife, *my beautiful wife*, was too gentle and precious for such a person. She was foolish, thinking she meant something more to him than just another cheap conquest. Seeing your mother's pregnancy forced her to realise what he was, and she couldn't bear it. She tied a halter around that very tree, climbed the stepladder used to pick the high fruit, placed the leather strap around her neck and kicked the ladder from beneath herself.'

Still with his face in his hands, Malachy sobbed.

'Malachy, please don't believe this nonsense. I don't know why your father's lying like this, but my dad was honest with Hannah. They were both lonely and sad and they found comfort in each other, but in the end, they were only friends. I don't know why she did what she did –'

'Your father led her to believe he was her future. He lied to her. He might as well have killed her himself with his own hands.'

'Liar!' In a rage, she stood up and marched to the door. The gilt handle turned, but the door didn't budge. When Phillippe had left the room, he had locked it from the outside.

'Please don't go, Lena.' Her tormentor laughed, a horrible wheezing sound. 'Don't you want to know the rest of the story?'

She whirled around, glaring at him, pressing her back hard against the locked door, her heart pounding. 'What do you mean?'

'Dad, I don't know why you're –' Malachy began.

Berger held his hand up to quieten his son. 'You're sometimes weak and foolish, just as your mother was.'

'Tell me what you mean by "the rest of the story".' Lena's voice was low. Doc's suspicions suddenly made more sense now.

'Well, there's just that part about the gun that backfired on your father?' His ice-cold eyes were dead, his face giving nothing away. 'It was made to fire that way.'

'No, it wasn't. Doc said it was old and broken.'

'It was indeed, which was why Paudie O'Sullivan hadn't used it in years. Some rubbish about not killing things unless he had to. I hear your limp-wristed brother is following in those particular footsteps. You see what I mean?' He turned to Malachy. 'Weak.' He rested his head on the chaise and closed his eyes, as if reminiscing.

'It was simple. Phillippe stole the gun from your father's shed – O'Sullivan was careless – and Phillippe engineered it such that it could backfire. We just watched him as he set a trap for the fox. Then using his own gun, Phillippe shot him. He carefully fired the old shotgun, which of course backfired as we intended, and placed it beside your father. Phillippe had the best firearms training in the world, the Wehrmacht saw to that. The flat-footed buffoons you call the police here assumed that it was a backfire, and they were happy to call it a terrible accident.'

Lena wanted to be sick. 'You murdered my dad in cold blood.'

Auguste smiled, and she wanted to scratch his blue eyes from his emaciated face. 'But it wasn't murder, it was a terrible accident. At least that's what your Doctor Dolan wrote on the death certificate. He was another moron, and he was your father's best friend. So although Phillippe is taking the precaution of leaving the country, that's only in case you decide to take personal revenge, not because he fears the Irish police.' He chuckled.

'Oh my God...'

'Sit down and take a sip of brandy to calm your nerves.'

Shaking, she took a step back into the room. 'Is this what you've brought me here for? To tell me you murdered my father? I hope you burn in hell.' Her voice cracked.

'Thankfully that will not happen, as there is no God. However, in reply to your question, no, I am not asking forgiveness for your father's murder. It was a justifiable homicide, a crime of passion as we call it in France.'

Again, Lena glanced at Malachy, who still had his head buried in his hands, his shoulders shaking with grief. Did he know all of this? His father wasn't a brave Resistance fighter but a Nazi? A murderer? She looked back at Auguste Berger, who had opened his eyes again, his hideous death smile curling around his thin lips.

'But I do seek forgiveness, Lena, from both of you, for how I used my son as a weapon to break your heart.'

'What?'

'My son was happy to forgive your mad mother, your degenerate, unnatural brother, your sister for marrying into a family of thieves...'

'How dare you talk about my family like that!'

He sighed. 'Do you want to hear the truth or not?'

Shivering, she fell silent.

He nodded. 'Good. Now, I warned Malachy how any child of yours and his would be genetically inferior, a madman, a thief and pervert. Again, he dismissed the truth. The odd thing was, it was the lies he believed.'

'Lies?' Malachy jerked up his head, the tears still streaming down his face. 'More lies?'

'What did you tell him?' Lena asked.

'I told him how you brought so many men and boys to the tack room – Bill Madden, Blackie Crean, Donal Lamkin...'

She pressed her hands to her ears. 'You're insane! Doc was right – he never trusted you and he was right not to. You talk about my mother. She's fine, but you? You twisted, evil man.'

'That was all lies?' repeated Malachy, on his feet. 'How could you... You saw what it did to me. To think I ever loved you, you bastard. You broke my heart too. She was the only girl I've ever loved, the only girl I will ever love...'

'Do you hear that, Lena? And now you're married to someone else, a Jew no less. Isn't that heartbreaking? Your one true love really still loves you, and now, my dear, like my wife, you find yourself married to someone you wish you could be rid of – but you can't, can you?'

Malachy launched himself on the frail body, his fist smashing into the hideous old face. The old man's hands clawed at the air as if he would strangle his own son.

'Malachy! No!' Lena pulled him off. 'He's not worth going to prison for.'

'You, you...' Berger hissed, frothing at the mouth, his face rapidly swelling from the blow Malachy had landed. He was writhing from the waist up like a hideous puppet, before he clutched at his heart and fell back, choking incoherently. 'My pills... I need my pills... Get Phillippe... Call Phillippe...'

'Phillippe's gone! Where are your pills?' screamed Lena, searching along the mantelpiece, pulling books out of the bookcase, while Malachy stood frozen in helpless shock. 'You have to tell me where they are!' She rifled the drawers of the writing desk by the window. But Auguste Berger, now choking to death, his son standing rigidly over him, not moving, was no longer able to speak.

She wanted him to live so he could face justice for his crimes. Thinking quickly, Lena climbed out the window, landing in the flower bed, now overgrown with thorny old roses, not pruned for years. They pulled at her skin and clothes, but she didn't feel it. She saw him then, his car coming up the drive, and ran to him, meeting him outside the old house.

'Come quick, Eli! Auguste Berger is dying!'

Grabbing his black doctor's bag, Eli sprang from the car. 'Show me where he is.'

Together they raced up the steps. The front door of the house was standing open, and Phillippe had left the key in the library doors. She unlocked them and threw them open. Malachy was still standing motionless, staring at his father writhing in pain.

Eli ran to the dying man. 'Emmet's asleep in the car, Lena,' he called over his shoulder as he went. 'I couldn't find Emily. Can you bring him home, please? I'll deal with this…'

CHAPTER 30

*L*ena turned the big vehicle carefully in the narrow lane and drove back to the village, where she parked outside the surgery in the cobbled street. Emmet didn't even wake when she lifted him out of the back seat and carried him up to bed, placing him lovingly in his cot in the room beside hers and Eli's.

Then she went downstairs and sat at the kitchen table and wept, with her head on her arms.

Maybe an hour later, there was a knock at the front door. She glanced bleary-eyed at the clock. Half past ten. Eli must have left his house key on the ring with the car key. She hurried to let him in.

But it wasn't her husband.

It was Malachy, pale and wild-eyed. 'Let me in...'

'Where's Eli? What are you doing here? Malachy, it's too late...'

'Your husband and I talked, while we were waiting for the undertaker. Then, when the undertaker arrived, I said I had to get out for some fresh air. I couldn't bear to discuss coffins, so Eli said he'd take care of it for me. Please, Lena, let me in.'

She stood aside, and he brushed against her in the narrow hall. 'Where can we...?'

'In the kitchen.' She pointed with a shaking hand towards the door at the end of the hallway.

He went ahead, and she followed him after locking the door again.

'Did you know?' she asked. 'Any of it?'

Malachy shook his head. 'No, nothing. God, Lena.' He ran his hands through his hair, clearly distraught. 'May he rot in his grave for his terrible lies and for keeping us apart.'

'Do you really think your father got Phillippe to murder my father, or was he just saying that to hurt me as much as he could?'

'I've no idea. If you'd asked me that an hour ago, I'd have said of course not, but now... I suppose that secret died with him, or it's with Phillippe, wherever he is now. On the road to Cobh, I imagine, unless that's another lie. Lena...' He took a step towards her, but she moved back. Her heart was beating like a bird going wild in a cage. He held out his hands to her, his green eyes bright. 'Lena, I can't believe I trusted him. When he said I wasn't the first with you, that there were so many others, I was wild with jealousy. And then when I came back at the end of the summer to ask you myself, he told me you'd gone away to Wales with another man. Oh God, I was beside myself. I fled to America. Can you ever forgive me for believing him?'

Lena thought for a moment, testing her feelings for this boy, now a man, before her. 'Malachy, listen to me now. I was so confused and hurt when you left, and now I know why you did that, even if I don't understand it. But please, for the rest of your life, have a bit more sense, will you? Learn from this, and before you just blindly believe everything you hear, maybe hear it from the person involved rather than a third party. You should have spoken to me. And I know he was your father and all the rest of it, but I can tell you for a fact that no matter who told me something like that about you – Doc, family, friends – it wouldn't matter. I'd have given you a chance to explain. You should have given me that opportunity. It was the least I deserved.'

'But you forgive me?'

Lena sighed. 'Yes, I already have, because not to would hurt *me* more.'

'Oh, thank God...' His eyes, so vulnerable and scared, suddenly shone with happiness. 'Then we have a chance? We can start again?'

The idea of Malachy coming and begging forgiveness had played over and over in her mind since he left her, but now that the moment was here, she found it had no impact on her whatsoever. Was he seriously suggesting they get back together after everything?

'No, of course not, Malachy. I'm married.'

'But nobody in America will know that. You're meant for me, not him. A week today, I'm sailing back to New York. I'll buy you a ticket and come to fetch you. Or just come with me now...'

'Malachy, you're not listening to me. I can't. I won't. I don't want to.'

'You can, Lena! We're right for each other, we always were! If it wasn't for my father's lies... Please, I'm begging, just give me another chance.'

Emmet's cry cut through Malachy's speech. Lena hesitated for a moment and then went upstairs and picked him up. His entire bedtime routine was disrupted, and he didn't know what was happening.

'It's OK, darling.' She held him close. 'Mammy's here, Emmet, everything is OK.' She made a decision then and carried him downstairs, entering the kitchen with her son in her arms.

In the long silence, Malachy's eyes travelled over Emmet from head to toe, taking in the dark-red hair and green eyes. The baby gazed at him for a moment and then buried his face in Lena's neck.

'Lena, he's...he's... Is he...' Malachy's voice was choked.

There was the sound of a key in the door, and moments later, Eli appeared in the kitchen doorway, taking in the sight of Malachy Berger standing in his kitchen and his wife holding Emmet.

'Dada!' cried Emmet joyfully, holding out his chubby toddler arms. Eli dropped his doctor's bag and took the boy, who wrapped his arms around his father's neck and snuggled his face up to Eli's stubbled cheeks. 'Dada!'

'Eli, I was just introducing Emmet to Malachy,' said Lena, trying to sound calm, although butterflies churned in her stomach.

Malachy looked her in the eye, and then stepped towards Emmet and Eli, touching the boy's red curls and stroking his chubby cheek. Emmet frowned and flinched away, burying his face in Eli's shoulder.

'I'm sorry, he's going through a stage of being afraid of strangers,' said Lena.

'Is he?' asked Malachy, with a break in his voice. 'Then I suppose I'd better go and not worry him any longer.'

'I'm sorry for your loss, Malachy,' said Eli, putting out his hand.

'My loss?' Malachy looked perplexed.

'Your father.'

'Ah, that loss. Yeah...em...I'm not, though, so...' With a crooked little smile, he shook Eli's hand, and with a nod at Lena, Malachy stepped out into the hall, unbolted the door and left.

Lena took Emmet from Eli's arms and went upstairs to tuck him in again. When she came back down, Eli was sitting at the kitchen table. He looked up as she entered.

'Malachy came straight here,' he said stiffly. 'To you.'

She sat down to face him. 'Eli, listen. I know you've always wondered if part of me was still in love with Malachy, and to be honest, I wondered too. But I was at the lowest point of my life today –'

'What happened up there?'

'I'll tell you everything, I promise. But for now, I just want to tell you this. When someone knocked at our door this evening, once I'd come home, I assumed it was you, but when I opened the door and found it was Malachy, well, my heart sank like a stone. In that moment, I knew that the only person I wanted to see, talk to, feel their arms around me, be comforted by...that was you, Eli. Only you.'

His eyes flickered with hope. 'Are you sure, Lena? I don't know the details, but I assume it was some kind of misunderstanding that made Malachy leave you? I don't want to stand in your way. I thought I could bear it, being, well, not your first choice, but each day I love you and Emmet more, and I realise now I couldn't stand it if you'd preferred...'

She pulled a horrified expression. 'Eli, my darling husband, don't ever say anything so terrifying again. I love you, and I've never been more sure of anything in my life.'

CHAPTER 31

KILTEEGAN HOUSE, SEPTEMBER 1962

*L*ena found the silver box of tablets in a drawer of the writing bureau. She was emptying it out as her mother measured for new drapes and wallpaper for the drawing room of Kilteegan House, something lighter and more airy than the heavy brocades and velvets from before. She handed them to Eli, who was chasing Emmet and Sarah around the huge room.

Their father distracted, the children turned their attention to their grandmother.

Emmet piped up. 'Nana Maria, Molly and May said you brought iced buns.'

'I did.' She beamed, offering them a hand each. 'Will we go to the kitchen and get them, and maybe we'll make a cup of tea, will we?'

'Can we have the flower drink?' Emmet asked. 'Skipper maked it.'

Maria glanced at Lena, who gave an incline of her head. Skipper could produce the most incredible things. He'd made cordial with elderflowers, and Emmet loved it.

'Well, your mammy says you can, so let's go.'

Sarah, who at a year old was just walking, was dark like Lena, and she followed her brother Emmet with his mop of red curls everywhere. They both went with their beloved Nana happily.

Eli examined the tablets. 'These are just painkillers, fairly powerful ones. But I'll dispose of them anyway, just in case. We don't want Emmet swallowing them. Or little Sarah. Or this new one...' He hugged her suddenly, taking care not to crush her swelling abdomen, and she wound her arms around his neck and kissed him fervently.

'I love you, Lena, and I'm going to confess to you that as much as I despise that idiot you were once in love with, I really adore this house, so thank you for making me swallow my pride, and sorry for taking so long about it.'

'Ah, it's a lot, I know. And this is not a complaint. Doc was exactly the same way, refusing payments from people who didn't have it, supplying medicines out of his own pocket. But if we're waiting for you to make a fortune and buy a big house, we'll be waiting a long time. As I say, I'm not against it as a model – I love it about you, and we have more than enough – but we could never afford a place like this, and it is amazing.'

'I know.' He smiled sheepishly. 'Sometimes you must wish you married one of those consultant chaps with the expensive cologne and well-cut suits.'

'Who care nothing for the patients except to squeeze what last few shillings they have out of them when they are at their lowest with a sick child or parent? No, I would never want that. So maybe we can see this house as a reward for all the good work you do, all the kindness and compassion you show to people?'

'Well, whatever it is, I'm sorry I was so bullheaded.'

'I accept your apology.' She grinned. He was right. They were going to be happy there. 'Wait till Mam gets all the horrible dark, heavy fabrics out of here, and Jack and Skipper say they'll paint for us – apparently they love painting. It will be gorgeous.'

Six months after Malachy had once again walked out of her life, Lena had received a visit from the Kilteegan lawyer, Kieran Devlin, who told her that her son, Emmet Kogan, was now the owner of Kilteegan House, and his parents were required to hold it in trust for him until he was of an age to sell it or raise his own family there, whichever he preferred. There was no accompanying letter and no further instructions. Malachy Berger had instructed the solicitor that if, for whatever reason, Lena did not accept the house on Emmet's behalf, it was to be held in trust for him by the solicitors until he was eighteen and he could then do with it what he wished. Either way, Mr Berger wished no further contact on that or any subject.

Eli resisted the move to Kilteegan House for some time, but once Sarah got older it became increasingly ridiculous trying to cram their growing family into Doc's house, as well as accommodate all the other medical professionals that held clinics there, and in exasperation, Lena put her foot down.

She sat her husband down one night and forced him to see sense. Kilteegan House was beautiful and a wonderful place to grow up. Her father had tended the grounds there, so their children would climb trees their grandad had planted. Yes, Auguste Berger and Phillippe Decker had lived there, but so had Hannah and her family, lovely people by all accounts. And anyway, it was just a building.

'But it's a reminder that Emmet isn't my son, and won't everyone want to know how we got it?'

'I spoke to Kieran. He said nobody need know the details – it's entirely private between him and us. People will assume old Berger died, Malachy emigrated, so he sold the house and we bought it. Why not? The story of his mother and my father and all of that never was public knowledge. Anyone who knew about it, apart from you, me and Malachy, is dead. My mother hated him, but she knows it's a beautiful house. She was a bit reticent at first, but when I brought her up and showed her around, she fell in love with it too. And anyway, that new medication you are giving her is doing a much better job of keeping her level, so that hatred of the Bergers stuff was only when she was low.'

'And when Emmet is eighteen? We tell him the truth then?' Eli asked.

Lena sighed. 'He'll have a right to know the

truth either way, Eli, and he will also know, as anyone with eyes in their head can see, that you are his adoring father. Nothing will ever change that. I don't think we should wait until he's eighteen either. Let's be honest with him as soon as he's old enough to grasp it. There's been enough secrets in this family. And Doc was right about them, as he was about everything. They only lead to trouble in the end.'

'And what if he wants Malachy in his life?'

Lena's heart broke for her darling husband. She covered his big hand with her little one, giving it a squeeze. 'Auguste Berger may have murdered Emmet's grandfather and he certainly tried to ruin my life, but whatever you might think, Malachy is not like him. He wouldn't have abandoned me had he known the truth, had his father not lied to him. He was foolish, or at least very naïve to believe it, and I hope he's learned a lesson, but he's not a bad person, Eli. I wouldn't allow Emmet within a donkey's roar of Auguste Berger, an awful creature, but Malachy is different. I'm not holding any torch for him, I hope you know it, but if he wants to do this by way of apology, or trying to give something to Emmet, I'm not going to turn up my nose. And if he wants to meet Emmet at some point, or Emmet wants to meet him, it will change nothing for us.'

'You're sure about that? Supposing he turns up and sees us living in his house as some kind of hankering on your part for him and what might have been? I know he still loves you, Lena.'

'Whether he does or he doesn't is nothing to do with me – can't you get that into your thick skull?' She smiled to take the sting out of her words. 'For a clever man, you can be as thick as the road sometimes. I love you, only you, forever you. Nobody else. And Malachy Berger, or anyone else for that matter, can dance a jig on the front lawn or climb the trees, serenading me with love songs, and I'd take no notice. You have to believe that.'

He chuckled at the image, and she knew she'd won him over.

EPILOGUE

$\mathcal{H}$e spread the newspaper out on the table as the hot sun streamed in through the window. Nobody would disturb him here. The ads around the photograph were of no interest to him, nor was the story about the preservation of an old blacksmith's yard for archaeological reasons, or the article about how to detect greenfly early. He focused on the only thing that mattered. The christening photograph, posed on the steps of Kilteegan House and a headline screaming that the local doctor and father of three had recently been appointed the Irish Department of Health's Chief Medical Officer for the Munster Region. It went on about how he was so inspirational and how everyone was delighted with the appointment in recognition for his setting up of a medical centre in West Cork, saving sick people costly and uncomfortable journeys to Cork for treatment. The railway was the only way for people to get to the city, and with the increase in the number of private cars in recent years, the service was much less frequent. Having access to specialists in Kilteegan Bridge was a godsend, according to the article.

Lena was radiant, petite and beaming at her baby. As always, he scanned the other faces. There were the O'Sullivans: Maria, the mother, looking well, Lena's brother, Jack, and beside him that friend of his, wearing a wide-brimmed hat, then the twins. Emily and Blackie Crean and their children of course. The others were strangers to him – a couple with four children, another older couple and a young serious-looking woman. And of course, there was Eli Kogan, beaming and holding the hands of two other children, a little toddler girl and an older boy.

He took out his magnifying glass and bowed his head to the photo. He couldn't stop looking at him. The photo was black and white, but he knew the child had red hair and green eyes.

The picture was creased now, almost worn where it had been folded so often. The West Cork

Chronicle was printed on flimsy paper. He should leave it alone, but something compelled him to look at it often.

It was wrong. That should be his. A web of lies had wound around him, and he was trapped. Maybe not forever, but for now at least. That was the trouble with secrets – they always come out in the end.

The End.

ABOUT THE AUTHOR

Jean Grainger is a USA Today bestselling Irish author. She writes historical and contemporary Irish fiction and her work has very flatteringly been compared to the late, great Maeve Binchy.

She lives in a two hundred year old stone cottage in county Cork, Ireland with her husband Diarmuid and the youngest two of her four children. The older two have flown the nest, and are learning the harsh realities of buying their own toothpaste. There are a variety of animals there too, all led by two cute but clueless micro-dogs called Scrappy and Scoobi.

ALSO BY JEAN GRAINGER

To get a free novel and to join my readers club (100% free and always will be)

Go to www.jeangrainger.com

The Tour Series

The Tour

Safe at the Edge of the World

The Story of Grenville King

The Homecoming of Bubbles O'Leary

Finding Billie Romano

Kayla's Trick

The Carmel Sheehan Story

Letters of Freedom

The Future's Not Ours To See

What Will Be

The Robinswood Story

What Once Was True

Return To Robinswood

Trials and Tribulations

The Star and the Shamrock Series
The Star and the Shamrock
The Emerald Horizon
The Hard Way Home
The World Starts Anew

The Queenstown Series
Last Port of Call
The West's Awake
The Harp and the Rose
Roaring Liberty

The Mags Munroe Series
The Existential Worries of Mags Munroe
Growing Wild in the Shade

Standalone Books
So Much Owed
Shadow of a Century
Under Heaven's Shining Stars
Catriona's War
Sisters of the Southern Cross

If you would like to read another of my series, here are the first few chapters of *The Star and the Shamrock*, a series set in Ireland during WW2 for you to enjoy.

The Star and the Shamrock

Belfast, 1938

The gloomy interior of the bar, with its dark wood booths and frosted glass, suited the meeting perfectly. Though there were a handful of other customers, it was impossible to see them clearly. Outside on Donegal Square, people went about their business, oblivious to the tall man who entered the pub just after lunchtime. Luckily, the barman was distracted with a drunk female customer and served him absentmindedly. He got a drink, sat at the back in a booth as arranged and waited. His contact was late. He checked his watch once more, deciding to give the person ten more minutes. After that, he'd have to assume something had gone wrong.

He had no idea who he was meeting; it was safer that way, everything on a need-to-know basis. He felt a frisson of excitement – it felt good to actually be doing something, and he was ideally placed to make this work. The idea was his and he was proud of it. That should make those in control sit up and take notice.

War was surely now inevitable, no matter what bit of paper old Chamberlain brought back from Munich. If the Brits believed that the peace in our time that he promised was on the cards, they'd believe anything. He smiled.

He tried to focus on the newspaper he'd carried in with him, but his mind wandered into the realm of conjecture once more, as it had ever since he'd gotten the call. If Germany could be given whatever assistance they needed to subjugate Great Britain – and his position meant they could offer that and more – then the Germans would have to make good on their promise. A United Ireland at last. It was all he wanted.

He checked his watch again. Five minutes more, that was all he would stay. It was too dangerous otherwise.

His eyes scanned the racing pages, unseeing. Then a ping as the pub door opened. Someone entered, got a drink and approached his seat. He didn't look up until he heard the agreed-upon code phrase. He raised his eyes, and their gazes met.

He did a double take. Whatever or whomever he was expecting, it wasn't this.

CHAPTER 1

Liverpool, England, 1939

Elizabeth put the envelope down and took off her glasses. The thin paper and the Irish stamps irritated her. Probably that estate agent wanting to sell her mother's house again. She'd told him twice she wasn't selling, though she had no idea why. It wasn't as if she were ever going back to Ireland, her father was long dead, her mother gone last year – she was probably up in heaven tormenting the poor saints with her extensive religious knowledge. The letter drew her back to the little Northern Irish village she'd called home…that big old lonely house…her mother.

Margaret Bannon was a pillar of the community back in Ballycregggan, County Down, a devout Catholic in a deeply divided place, but she had a heart of stone.

Elizabeth sighed. She tried not to think about her mother, as it only upset her. Not a word had passed between them in twenty-one years, and then Margaret died alone. She popped the letter behind the clock; she needed to get to school. She'd open it later, or next week…or never.

Rudi smiled down at her from the dresser. 'Don't get bitter, don't be like her.' She imagined she heard him admonish her, his boyish face frozen in an old sepia photograph, in his King's Regiment uniform, so proud, so full of excitement, so bloody young. What did he know of the horrors that awaited him out there in Flanders? What did any of them know?

She mentally shook herself. This line of thought wasn't helping. Rudi was dead, and she wasn't her mother. She was her own person. Hadn't she proved that by defying her mother and marrying Rudi? It all seemed so long ago now, but the intensity of the emotions lingered. She'd met, loved and married young Rudi Klein as a girl of eighteen. Margaret Bannon was horrified at the thought of her Catholic daughter marrying a Jew, but Elizabeth could still remember that heady feeling of being young and in love. Rudi could have been a Martian for all she cared. He was young and handsome and funny, and he made her feel loved.

She wondered, if he were to somehow come back from the dead and just walk up the street and into the kitchen of their little terraced house, would he recognise the woman who stood there? Her chestnut hair that used to fall over her shoulders was always now pulled back in a bun, and the girl who loved dresses was now a woman whose clothes were functional and modest. She was thirty-nine, but she knew she could pass for older. She had been pretty once, or at least not too horrifically ugly anyway. Rudi had said he loved her; he'd told her she was beautiful.

She snapped on the wireless, but the talk was of the goings-on in Europe again. She unplugged it; it was too hard to hear first thing in the morning. Surely they wouldn't let it all happen again, not after the last time?

All anyone talked about was the threat of war, what Hitler was going to do. Would there really be peace as Mr Chamberlain promised? It was going to get worse before it got better if the papers were to be believed.

Though she was almost late, she took the photo from the shelf. A smudge of soot obscured his smooth forehead, and she wiped it with the sleeve of her cardigan. She looked into his eyes.

'Goodbye, Rudi darling. See you later.' She kissed the glass, as she did every day.

How different her life could have been…a husband, a family. Instead, she had received a generic telegram just like so many others in that war that was supposed to end all wars. She carried in her heart for twenty years that feeling of despair. She'd taken the telegram from the boy who refused to meet her eyes. He was only a few years younger than she. She opened it there, on the doorstep of that very house, the words expressing regret swimming before her eyes. She remembered the lurch in her abdomen, the baby's reaction mirroring her own. 'My daddy is dead.'

She must have been led inside, comforted – the neighbours were good that way. They knew when the telegram lad turned his bike down their street that someone would need holding up. That day it was her… tomorrow, someone else. She remembered the blood, the sense of dragging downwards, that ended up in a miscarriage at five months. All these years later, the pain had dulled to an ever-present ache.

She placed the photo lovingly on the shelf once more. It was the only one she had. In lots of ways, it wasn't really representative of Rudi; he was not that sleek and well presented. 'The British Army smartened me up,' he used to say. But out of uniform is how she remembered him. Her most powerful memory was of them sitting in that very kitchen the day they got the key. His uncle Saul had lent them the money to buy the house, and they were going to pay him back.

They'd gotten married in the registry office in the summer of 1918, when he was home on brief leave because of a broken arm. She could almost hear her mother's wails all the way across the Irish Sea, but she didn't care. It didn't matter that her mother was horrified at her marrying a *Jewman*, as she insisted on calling him, or that she was cut off from all she ever knew – none of it mattered. She loved Rudi and he loved her. That was all there was to it.

She'd worn her only good dress and cardigan – the miniscule pay of a teaching assistant didn't allow for new clothes, but she didn't care. Rudi had picked a bunch of flowers on the way to the registry office, and his cousin Benjamin and Benjamin's wife, Nina, were the witnesses. Ben was killed at the Somme, and Nina went to London, back to her family. They'd lost touch.

Elizabeth swallowed. The lump of grief never left her throat. It was a part of her now. A lump of loss and pain and anger. The grief had given way to fury, if she were honest. Rudi was killed on the morning of the 11th of November, 1918, in Belgium. The armistice had been signed, but the order to end hostilities would not come into effect until eleven p.m. The eleventh hour of the eleventh month. She imagined the generals saw some glorious symmetry in that. But there wasn't. Just more people left in mourning than there had to be. She lost him, her Rudi, because someone wanted the culmination of four long years of slaughter to look nice on a piece of paper.

She shivered. It was cold these mornings, though spring was supposed to be in the air. The children in her class were constantly sniffling and coughing. She remembered the big old fireplace in the national school in Ballycregggan, where each child was expected to bring a sod of turf or a block of timber as fuel for the fire. Master O'Reilly's wife would put the big jug of milk beside the hearth in the mornings so the children could have a warm drink by lunchtime. Elizabeth would have loved to have a fire in her classroom, but the British education system would never countenance such luxuries.

She glanced at the clock. Seven thirty. She should go. Fetching her coat and hat, and her heavy bag of exercise books that she'd marked last night, she let herself out.

The street was quiet. Apart from the postman, doing deliveries on the other side of the street, she was the only person out. She liked it, the sense of solitude, the calm before the storm.

The mile-long walk to Bridge End Primary was her exercise and thinking time. Usually, she mulled over what she would teach that day or how to deal with a problem child – or more frequently, a problem parent. She had been a primary schoolteacher for so long, there was little she had not seen. Coming over to England as a bright sixteen-year-old to a position as a teacher's assistant in a Catholic school was the beginning of a trajectory that had taken her far from Ballycregggan, from her mother, from everything she knew.

She had very little recollection of the studies that transformed her from a lowly teaching assistant to a fully qualified teacher. After Rudi was killed and she'd lost the baby, a kind nun at her school suggested she do the exams to become a teacher, not just an assistant, and because it gave her something to do with her troubled mind, she agreed. She got top marks, so she must have thrown herself into her studies, but she couldn't remember much about those years. They were shrouded in a fog of grief and pain.

CHAPTER 2

Berlin, Germany, 1939

Ariella Bannon waited behind the door, her heart thumping. She'd covered her hair with a headscarf and wore her only remaining coat, a grey one that had been smart once. Though she didn't look at all Jewish with her green eyes and curly red hair – and being married to Peter Bannon, a Catholic, meant she was in a slightly more privileged position than other Jews – people knew what she was. She took her children to temple, kept a kosher house. She never in her wildest nightmares imagined that the quiet following of her faith would have led to this.

One of the postmen, Herr Krupp, had joined the Brownshirts. She didn't trust him to deliver the post properly, so she had to hope it was Frau Braun that day. She wasn't friendly exactly, but at least she gave you your letters. She was surprised at Krupp; he'd been nice before, but since Kristallnacht, it seemed that everyone was different. She even remembered Peter talking to him a few times about the weather or fishing or something. It was hard to believe that underneath all that, there was such hatred. Neighbours, people on the street, children even, seemed to have turned against all Jews. Liesl and Erich were scared all the time. Liesl tried to put a brave face on it – she was such a wonderful child – but she was only ten. Erich looked up to her so much. At seven, he thought his big sister could fix everything.

It was her daughter's birthday next month but there was no way to celebrate. Ariella thought back to birthdays of the past, cakes and friends and presents, but that was all gone. Everything was gone.

She tried to swallow the by-now-familiar lump of panic. Peter had been picked up because he and his colleague, a Christian, tried to defend an old Jewish lady the Nazi thugs were abusing in the street. Ariella had been told that the uniformed guards beat up the two men and threw them in a truck. That was five months ago. She hoped every day her husband would turn up, but so far, nothing. She considered going to visit his colleague's wife to see if she had heard anything, but nowadays, it was not a good idea for a Jew to approach an Aryan for any reason.

At least she'd spoken to the children in English since they were born. At least that. She did it because she could; she'd had an English governess as a child, a terrifying woman called Mrs Beech who insisted Ariella speak not only German but English, French and Italian as well. Peter smiled to hear his children jabbering away in other languages, and he always said they got that flair for languages from her. He spoke German only, even though his father was Irish. She remembered fondly her father-in-law, Paddy. He'd died when Erich was a baby. Though he spoke fluent German, it was always with a lovely lilting accent. He would tell her tales of growing up in Ireland. He came to Germany to study when he was a young man, and saw and fell instantly in love with Christiana Berger, a beauty from Bavaria. And so in Germany he remained. Peter was their only child because Christiana was killed in a horse-riding accident when Peter was only five years old. How simple those days were, seven short years ago, when she had her daughter toddling about, her newborn son in her arms, a loving husband and a doting father-in-law. Now, she felt so alone.

Relief. It was Frau Braun. But she walked past the building.

Ariella fought the wave of despair. She should have gotten the letter Ariella had posted by now, surely. It was sent three weeks ago. Ariella tried not to dwell on the many possibilities. What if she wasn't at the address? Maybe the family had moved on. Peter had no contact with his only first cousin as far as she knew.

Nathaniel, Peter's best friend, told her he might be able to get Liesl and Erich on the Kindertransport out of Berlin – he had some connections apparently – but she couldn't bear the idea of them going to strangers. If only Elizabeth would say yes. It was the only way she could put her babies on that train. And even then… She dismissed that thought and refused to let her mind go there. She had to get them away until all this madness died down.

She'd tried everything to get them all out. But there was no way. She'd contacted every single embassy – the United States, Venezuela, Paraguay, places she'd barely heard of – but there was no hope. The lines outside the embassies grew longer every day, and without someone to vouch for you, it was impossible. Ireland was her only chance. Peter's father, the children's grandfather, was an Irish citizen. If she could only get Elizabeth Bannon to agree to take the children, then at least they would be safe.

Sometimes she woke in the night, thinking this must all

be a nightmare. Surely this wasn't happening in Germany, a country known for learning and literature, music and art? And yet it was.

Peter and Ariella would have said they were German, their children were German, just the same as everyone else, but not so. Because of her, her darling children were considered *Untermensch*, subhuman, because of the Jewish blood in their veins.

To continue this novel click this link

https://geni.us/TheStarandtheShamrocAL

Made in United States
Orlando, FL
16 November 2022

24610483R00276